Michael Lynch put a hand toward her so that she clo. lips on hers, kissing her, and time seemed to slow and stop altogether, so that when he took his lips away and she opened her eyes, it might have been seconds, or a minute, or thirty years.

"Julia," he said, his face inches from hers, his warm hand still upon her cheek.

Susanna said nothing, and then, her heart wanting it to be true, she said, "Yes," so softly that she wondered if he heard at all.

A STEP ACROSS

BY LAURIE & CHET WILLIAMSON

To our sisters: Mary, JO, and Joan

And when we dance, we'll dance together
When we cry we'll hold each other
And when we love we'll love forever...

–Tommy Sands, "Down By the Lagan Side"

2002

CHAPTER 1

"I want to tell you about the love of my life."

After Julia spoke, she slowly closed her eyes. Susanna Cassidy thought that her sister had fallen asleep, as she often did from the medication, but in a few seconds Julia spoke again. Her voice, once strong and hearty, was so soft that Susanna had to lean closer to the bed to hear.

"I want you to get a book for me," Julia said, her tired eyes opening to a slit and looking toward a small bookcase on the other side of the sunroom. "Yeats," she said. "Yeats's poems."

Julia's tastes had always seemed to be exclusively popular fiction, so the choice of early twentieth century Irish poetry surprised Susanna. She crossed the room, walking over the lush carpet that David Oliver, Julia's husband, had put in to make the room softer, and to muffle the footfalls of the nurses who tended Julia constantly. When Julia had returned from the hospital to die at home, she had chosen the sunroom in which to make what she smilingly called her last stand. What might have become a mausoleum had been transformed instead into a celebration of her life. All of Julia's favorite possessions were there, framed family photographs and the artistically designed scrapbooks she had created, the porcelains she had collected, a home theatre system with DVDs of the films she loved best, and a vast assortment of plants.

Even though the Pennsylvania winter had been harsh so far, the sunroom was an island of green in the snowy whiteness of the landscape. Potted plants stood about the large room, and four large crystal vases of cut flowers sat on the tops of tables, blazing with color in the afternoon sun that splashed through the brilliantly clear glass panels that walled the room. At first, Susanna had wondered how Julia could stand such brightness, but the malignancies had attacked even the optic nerves, and her vision was fading as quickly as her life.

Susanna knelt by the bookcase. It took her some time to find the small volume bound in dark green leather with the words *Poems of W. B. Yeats* in faded gold on the spine, but when she did, she took it back to Julia and held it close to her eyes.

Julia nodded and smiled. "Open it," she said. "Right at the beginning."

Susanna opened the book to the front endpapers, where there was an inscription in ink:

I saw her by the riverside, down where the Corrib runs,
Was nearly blinded by her, for she fair outshone the sun.

M.L.
1-2-72

"Read it aloud," Julia said, and Susanna did. When she was finished, she saw tears creeping from Julia's eyes. "I'm glad he can't see me now," she said. "Oh God, look at me..."

Susanna grasped Julia's hand and squeezed it. It was true. Her sister's countenance was ravaged. For the past twenty years Julia had weighed 140 pounds, but the disease had wasted her to less than a hundred, *low in flesh and high in bone,* as the old song put it. The therapy itself had been nearly as cruel. Julia's hair was all but gone, and in the endgame comfort had trumped vanity, so that she no longer wore any of the wigs she had sported earlier.

Julia put on her brave smile once more. "I don't think he'd recognize me now," she said with a weak laugh.

"Who was he?" Susanna asked. "M. L.?"

"His name," Julia said, closing her eyes again, "his sweet name was Michael Lynch, and he was the handsomest, tallest, and most darlin' man ye've ever laid eyes on." The attempt at a brogue made Susanna smile. "But don't worry, little sister," Julia went on. "It was before I was married. I've always been faithful to David..." The words trailed off into a heavy silence in which they shared what both had known for years, that David had not returned Julia's fidelity with his own.

Susanna looked again at the inscription in the book. "1972," she said. "January second."

"February first," Julia corrected her. "They switch month and day in Ireland."

"It was in Ireland then?"

"Yes. In Galway. Ever been there?"

"Mmm-hmm." Susanna nodded.

"Oh, you...you've been *everywhere*, haven't you?" Julia gave a little laugh.

"Not everywhere, but a lot of places in Ireland, through the college." Her Chair in Peace Studies at Conestoga University had taken her to several conferences in both Northern Ireland and the Irish Republic, which always provided a pleasant relief from the pressures and tensions of Derry and Belfast. "1972..." she mused. "Was that when you went with Kathy and Liz to Europe? Over a long semester break or something?"

"My senior year. We were on trimester, and the three of us didn't take anything in the January term so we could do the 'Grand Tour.'"

"But you came home early," Susanna said. "You were sick or something."

"*Love* sick," Julia said, and gestured toward the glass of 7Up on the bedside table. Susanna held it for her while she took a sip through the straw. "That's better," Julia said after she swallowed. "It's a long story...and it ends with a favor."

"From me?"

Julia nodded almost imperceptibly. "A last request from a dying woman. How can you refuse?"

Susanna smiled. "We'll see. What is it?"

"First, the story. Sit back and relax."

Susanna did, and Julia told her, with many pauses.

"I was twenty-one, old enough to know better, but young enough to still be stupid. That Grand Tour thing I mentioned? I'd been reading Henry James for a lit course, and I liked the idea of how the young American ladies went off to Europe for a year or so and saw the sights and got involved with aristocrats before they came home and got married to boring men. Kathy and Liz were already practically engaged, and it was getting more and more likely that David was going to bring up marriage before too long. So, it seemed like the perfect time.

"I talked Daddy into paying for three weeks in Europe, and Kathy and Liz did the same with their folks. Liz's dad said that she *had* to stop in Galway and see her great-aunt and uncle while she was over there, so we decided we'd do that first and get it out of the way, just maybe a day or two, then head for London, and then Paris.

"We arrived in Galway on January 23rd, a Sunday, and got checked in at a nice hotel. It was only around noon, and we were all pretty jet-lagged, but we decided not to take a nap. Liz figured her relatives would be home from Mass by then, so we had lunch and Liz and Kathy got a cab to the house, on the outskirts of the town."

"You didn't go with them?" Susanna asked.

"No. They were always tighter together than with me. Liz tried to talk me into it, but I just didn't want to go. I mean, there I was in Ireland, another *country*, for heaven's sake, and the last thing I wanted to do was sit in some stuffy parlor and make small talk with old people. So, I let them go and then bundled up—it was a little chilly, though not as cold as it would have been in the states—and walked out to see Galway.

"The city was magic. The wind was blowing, and I walked down by the docks and gulls were flying all around, and the water was choppy and the sun was flashing on it. There was this row of houses, all painted different colors, and the smell of burning peat in the air. I didn't like the smell at first, but I love it now, because it helps me remember what it was all like.

"I walked back toward the river then, the Corrib River it's called, and I went on this little path right by it. I'll tell you exactly where it was—right across what they call the Wolfe Tone Bridge. He was this Irish rebel or something..."

Susanna nodded. "The 1798 Rebellion. The British were going to hang him, but he killed himself in prison."

"You know everything, don't you?" Julia said with a small

laugh. "Anyway, that's where it was, just off the bridge on the side toward the town. On the path there was this old stone wall, and little balconies that you could step into overlooking the water. I was in the *second* one—remember that—leaning on the rail, just looking down at the water rushing by, and I felt somebody standing behind me. I didn't *hear* anything, but I sensed it. So, I turned around and there was this guy...

"God, but he was beautiful. Really tall, maybe six foot three or four, and he was wearing a pea coat, you know, one of those dark blue wool coats. It was open, and he had on a white cable knit sweater underneath. His hair was kind of longish, but not sloppy, a little curly, sort of a red-brown shade that just gleamed in the sunshine. And Susanna, his *eyes*... I don't think I've ever seen eyes quite that blue. Maybe Peter O'Toole in his prime..."

"Another Irishman," Susanna said.

"Was he? Oh sure, of course he was. Anyway, there he stood, just smiling at me."

"He sounds perfect."

"Well, not completely. His nose was a little crooked. I found out later it had been broken. But it just made him look even better, like he would have been too pretty without it." Julia paused, looking up at the ceiling.

"Then what?" Susanna asked. "Did you just look at each other forever?"

"Sometimes it feels like it," Julia said. "If I could have frozen that moment in time, spent the rest of my life like that, just the two of us seeing each other for the first time, I think I would have. So many times in the past few months I've gone there in my mind and remembered us looking at each other, like we'd just discovered the meaning of our lives, and how from that point on everything would be perfect." She closed her eyes, and Susanna saw tears slowly roll from them.

"But it wasn't?" Susanna prompted.

"No. No, it wasn't perfect, though it was *then*. For a whole week. It was probably the happiest week I ever spent." She took a deep breath. "Finally, he said something. 'I believe your face is brighter than the river.' He said it in an Irish accent that sounded like water rolling over stones. At that moment I would

have followed him anywhere, done anything he told me to do."
Julia smiled. "Easy, wasn't I?"

Susanna smiled back but said nothing.

"But if you'd have seen him, you'd have done the same thing.
I smiled, I couldn't help it. There was just something so *honest*
about him. It was like he was saying, oh, what a pretty bird, or
how beautiful the sun was on the river. It wasn't a pick-up line,
it was…an *observation*. And it touched me so, hit me so hard that
I couldn't help but *beam* at this boy.

"So, we talked. His name was Michael Lynch, and he was
from Galway, going to the university there, studying history.
He pegged me as an American right away. I told him I was on a
trip with some friends, and he said in that case that he wanted
to invite all of us to a pub that night where he and some friends
of his were playing music. He told me where it was and made
me promise I'd be there, and I said I would. He wound up walking me to my hotel, and made me promise again that I'd come.

"The problem was that I didn't want to share him with
Kathy and Liz. But when I went inside the hotel, there was a
phone message from Liz. Her relatives had invited them to stay
for dinner, and she'd left directions for me to join them, with
the address and phone number. That meant—hooray—they
wouldn't be back, so I just had to pretend I hadn't gotten the
message. I could tell them I hadn't come back to the hotel at all.

"At seven o'clock I went to the pub, and there was Michael
sitting in a big booth at the front with three other guys. He was
playing guitar and singing, and the others were playing tin
whistle, fiddle, and one of those little squeezebox accordions.
He grinned when he saw me, and when the song was over, he
sat me next to him. When I told him the other girls wouldn't be
there, he seemed glad, though he didn't come out and say so.

"The four of them played a lot of tunes, but did songs, too.
They sang a lot that Grandpa Cassidy used to sing to us when
we were kids, like 'Cockles and Mussels' and 'I'll Tell Me Ma,'
so I could sing along. Michael bought me pints of Guinness,
but I drank them slow. I didn't want to get drunk—I wanted to
enjoy myself, and hear and see everything crystal clear.

"They took a lot of breaks, and Michael introduced me to his friends—some of them students, some working guys, but all of them nice. We all talked, but after a while he and I just talked together quietly. It was pretty late when the pub closed, and I knew the girls would be back by then and probably worried sick about me. But I just didn't care, you know? All that mattered was being with Michael.

"There was no place to go. It was late on a Sunday night and all the pubs were closed, so we just walked. It was cold, but he put his arm around me and that was all I needed. There was this sweet Guinness smell on his breath and a hint of aftershave, something fresh and clean, and I huddled against his chest like I'd been born there. He told me he was studying history because he wanted to teach kids what had happened in Ireland, how it had been made free and then torn apart again by the English, and his voice got hard when he talked about it. He said he was originally from the North, and that when he was little, he saw things that little kids shouldn't see, and because of that he wanted to help to change things.

"I didn't know much about what was going on in Ireland, but what he said sounded wonderfully romantic. I didn't tell him much about myself because my life was so dull in comparison. So, we walked and I listened to him talk, and finally we stopped down by the river where we met. He turned to me and didn't say any more, but just looked at me and touched my cheek. Then he kissed me.

"His lips were so cool, but then they got warmer, and I kissed him back, and before I knew it, I was kissing him hard and our arms were around each other, and all I could think about was how much I loved him. I know that sounds ridiculous. I'd only just met him. But I loved him, more than I loved David back home, more than anything. And when he asked me to come back to his place, I didn't say a word, I just went." Julia closed her eyes again. "Do you think I was awful?"

Susanna leaned over and placed her hand on her sister's emaciated fingers. "No, I don't think you were awful. I think you were just in love."

Julia winced. "And I never fell out of it again."

There was a knock at the door, which opened a crack.

Rachel, Julia's daughter, looked into the room. "Hey," she said softly. "Anybody awake?"

"Hi, honey," Julia said. "Nice to see you. But could you give me just a few more minutes with your aunt Susanna?"

The tentative smile on Rachel's thin face wavered, then returned. "Sure. I'll be right out here."

Susanna smiled and gave the girl a little wave, but felt a small sting at the disappointment on her face. Rachel had crossed many bridges to come home to her mother's dying. Despite her armored exterior, she was fragile, and Susanna hated to see her receive any more rejection than she already had.

"So, you went home with him," Susanna said.

"Yes. He lived above a grocery store in this little one-room apartment—he called it a 'bed-sit'—with a tiny bathroom, but it looked like heaven to me. You know, I'd only slept with one boy at that point."

"David."

"Yes, David. It was nice, but it wasn't, well, what everybody said it was supposed to be. But with Michael…it was. I spent the night with him."

"Weren't you worried about your friends wondering what happened to you?"

"That was the farthest thing from my mind. It didn't matter. I was totally irrational, I admit it. All that mattered was that I was with Michael. In the morning he had to go to classes, but we arranged to meet afterwards, and I went back to the hotel. Kathy and Liz were crazy with worry. Liz wanted to call the police, but Kathy talked her into waiting till morning."

"What did you tell them?" Susanna asked.

"The truth, that I'd met someone and that I wanted to spend as much time as I could with him. They told me I was nuts, but I already knew that. What about David, they said, and I said it didn't matter, that I didn't know what I was going to do about David or about going back home or *anything*. They were leaving for London the next day, and I just said leave, I'm staying. And they asked what they were supposed to tell their parents, and I said just tell them I'm too sick to travel and staying in Ireland till I feel better."

"They must have been very upset."

"God, they were insane. But it didn't matter. I calmed them down as best I could and then went to meet Michael. I told him I was staying with him, and he looked surprised but said all right. We went back to the hotel and got my bags and took them to his place, but snuck up the back stairs since he wasn't supposed to have women in his flat. It was all…a great *adventure*, you know? We had a wonderful week. It was just—oh, what's that word when everything is perfect?"

"Idyllic?"

"Yes. Idyllic. In the evenings we went to pubs and listened to music, or he played, and then we went back to his place. In the morning, I made us a little breakfast and he went to his classes, and when they were over he showed me the town, and then we went back and made love before we went out in the evening. We talked tons. I told him about my family, about you, about America, and what I knew about Vietnam and the civil rights problems, which wasn't really much, but it didn't seem to matter.

"I called home on Wednesday and told Mother I was having really bad travel sickness, and that I'd stayed on in Galway at the hotel, and I'd probably meet the girls in Paris in a few days. She was worried sick and wanted to fly over and take care of me, but I talked her out of it, and told her not to call David and tell him, because I didn't want him to worry. Then I went back… to my life of sin."

Julia chuckled, and it turned into a cough. Susanna helped her to sip some 7Up until it stopped. Julia put her head back on the pillow and closed her eyes. So much time passed that Susanna thought she had fallen asleep, but then Julia spoke again, her words far away.

"Sunday came. Everything was so good. Then Sunday came." Again, tears slipped from Julia's eyes.

"What happened on Sunday?" Susanna asked into the silence.

"You should know," Julia said, opening her eyes and looking at her sister. "You know all about Ireland's problems. Sunday, January 30th…"

"...1972," Susanna said. "My God. Bloody Sunday."

The day was the most iconic in the history of Ireland except for Easter, 1916. It was the day British soldiers had killed thirteen unarmed civil rights demonstrators and wounded fourteen more in the Northern Ireland town of Derry. After that ill-conceived massacre, nothing had ever been the same again in the politics of the North, and in the delicate balance between Loyalists and Republicans.

Julia nodded gingerly, as though it caused her pain. "Bloody Sunday," she echoed. "And that Sunday had been beautiful. We'd gone to Mass at the big cathedral, then had lunch and went to Eyre Square. Michael had his guitar, and he surprised me with a song he wrote for me. It was called 'Julia By the River,' about where he'd first seen me, and I cried when I heard it, and he kissed my tears away and said he hoped I wasn't crying because I didn't like it, and I told him that I loved it, and I'd remember it forever.

"That evening there was a telegram waiting for him from his cousin up North. He and Michael's uncle had been at the march, and the uncle had been shot and killed. His cousin wanted him to come to Derry right away, so Michael said that he had to go. I thought he just meant for the funeral, so I asked him if I could stay there until he came back or even go up with him. He said that he might not come back at all, that he'd probably stay in the North and help. He didn't want to tell me specifically what he was talking about, I guess to keep me safe if anyone ever questioned me, but it was all too clear. He was going up there to join the IRA.

"I begged him not to. I cried, I told him to come to America with me, I was so afraid for him. But he said this was something he had to do. I didn't understand, I still don't. He said it would take a day or two to get his affairs in order and we could stay together until then.

"The next day he went off to tie up whatever loose ends there were, I guess, and came back late. I helped him pack. We didn't eat dinner—I know *I* wasn't hungry—and went to bed early. I didn't sleep well. I kept waking up and putting my arms around him to make sure he was there, because I knew that he wouldn't be tomorrow. In the morning, we both woke up early. We lay there with our arms around each other, and he told me that he couldn't say where I could contact him because it would probably be impossible to reach him. I gave him my family's address and phone number, but he wouldn't write it down, he just memorized it.

"Finally, he told me that it could be a very long time before he was able to contact me again. 'Julia,' he said, 'I might not ever see you again, not because I don't want to, but because I won't be able to.' I cried when he told me that, but then after a while I made a suggestion. It was the kind of thing a romantic young girl in love would do. It was silly and stupid, but I said it anyway."

Julia lay there silently, and finally Susanna asked, "What was it?"

"I asked him to meet me again. Thirty years later."

"...Thirty years..."

"*Yes,*" Julia said with a touch of pique. "I *told* you it was silly. It just came into my head, and I said something like, whatever happens to us, if we don't see each other again, if I'm not able to get in touch with you, if our paths part and don't reconnect, let's meet here in Galway years from now and say hello, and tell each other what became of our lives."

"What did he...what did Michael say?" Susanna asked.

"He laughed. He thought it was silly, too, I guess. He asked me how long and I just pulled thirty years out of my head. You see, it didn't matter to me if it was thirty or twenty or ten or five—I *knew* I was going to see him before then, so it was just a romantic game. He said, 'That's such a short time—why don't we make it thirty-*one?*' Joking, you know? And I said all right, thirty-one it is, and we decided to meet on the thirty-first anniversary of the day we first met, *where* we first met.

"He gave me that book of Yeats and he inscribed it with a line from the song he wrote for me, and he kissed me goodbye and got on a bus. I never saw him again."

"What did you do?" Susanna asked.

"I went home. I didn't want to meet Liz and Kathy, I didn't want to see Europe. I was miserable and alone and I just wanted to go home and see my mother. So that's what I did. When I got home, I just pretended to be sick, and it didn't take a lot of pretending. David came down and was all concerned. I let him comfort me, hell, I *needed* comforting." Julia paused, then smiled. "I comforted him a little too. *Too* much, I guess. In March I found out I was pregnant. You know the rest."

Susanna did, up to a point. Julia had finished her semester and been graduated, and a week later she and David had been married. Rachel had arrived in November. "But what about Michael Lynch?" Susanna asked. "Did you try to get in touch with him?"

"David and my little unexpected surprise put the kibosh to that. Besides, I didn't know how to reach him. When the Internet came along, I searched, but do you know how many Michael Lynches there are in the world? Even typing in just his name and Galway gave me over ten thousand hits. It was impossible."

"And he never tried to contact you?" As soon as the words left her mouth, Susanna was sorry she had asked.

"No." Julia's voice was pinched more than usual. "Every time an airmail letter arrived, my heart would beat a little faster, but I never heard anything from him. Still, part of me always kept loving him. I guess it was only natural—after all, he never got any older, never lost any hair or put on weight. In my memory he was always young, always my romantic Irish rebel lad. And I guess I was always young in his memory too. Never to get old or sick...never to die..."

She gave her head a little shake. "But every time I thought about him, I remembered the arrangement we had made, and I knew—I *knew*, Susanna—that someday I'd see him again."

"Did you ever try to find him when you went to Ireland?" Susanna asked. Julia and David had vacationed in Ireland every few years, and Susanna had always been aware of her sister's love for the country.

"No. We never went to Galway. I never wanted to. I could just imagine walking down the street with David and running into Michael, or even worse, Michael and his wife. And how could I try to find him when David was there? But I kept going back to Ireland, kept talking David into it, just because when I was there, I could think about him, and remember.

"And now, my dear sister, comes the request. A few months from now it's going to be Thursday, January 23rd, thirty-one years to the day I met Michael by the River Corrib. That's the day we agreed to meet. Only I don't think I'm going to be able to make it..." The sentence trailed off into nearly silent sobbing, and Julia's head shook on her stalk-like neck. The hand that Susanna put on Julia's forehead to comfort her trembled, for she knew what was coming.

"It's all right, honey," Susanna whispered. "It's all right." But it wasn't all right. Julia would be dead by January 23rd and they both knew it.

When her crying subsided, Julia wiped her eyes and looked at Susanna. "I want you to go in my place. I want you to meet Michael for me."

"But do you think...?"

"I don't know. I don't know if he's still alive, I don't know if he's forgotten me. All I know is that if he comes there on that day at that time and I'm not there...if that happens, no matter where I am, my heart will break for him all over again."

Susanna nodded and smiled gently. "All right. If that's what you want me to do, I'll be happy to do it."

"I want you to tell him what happened to me. I want you to show him pictures of me and David and Rachel and our house and the boat. I want you to tell him that I had a happy life, a *good* life, but that I never stopped thinking about him. I never stopped loving him. Tell him that. Will you do that for me?"

"Yes. Of course, I will."

"And I want you to take that book and tell him I kept it all these years, and that I read it often. I know most of the poems by heart. You know the one I've been thinking of most? It starts, 'When you are old and grey and full of sleep...'"

"'And nodding by the fire,'" Susanna continued, for she knew the poem, and they recited the first verse together.

...take down this book,
And slowly read, and dream of the soft look
Your eyes had once, and of their shadows deep...

"I used to know it all," Julia said. "I can't remember the rest." She looked at Susanna pleadingly, and her sister went on to the second verse:

> *How many loved your moments of glad grace,*
> *And loved your beauty with love false or true,*
> *But one man loved the pilgrim soul in you,*
> *And loved the sorrows of your changing face...*

Julia smiled, her face alight, and Susanna could not bring herself to go on to the final and, she had always thought, tragic verse about *how Love fled...And hid his face amid a crowd of stars.* Poor Julia's lot with David had been for the most part *love false,* and Susanna thought it better to leave her with the image of a man whose love never grew old.

"That's so beautiful," Julia said, and closed her eyes. "Susanna?"

"Yes?"

"I don't want you to tell David about this. Or Rachel. I don't want to hurt David. And I don't want Rachel to...to be confused. All right?"

"Mum's the word," she said, using the phrase they had used when they were girls, keeping secrets from the world.

Julia laughed. Her thin fingers sought Susanna's, who took them and squeezed gently. "Thank you. Thank you so much. There's...something else, too." The effort that she put into returning Susanna's affectionate touch brought tears to her sister's eyes. "I want to apologize."

"For what?" Susanna asked when Julia said nothing more.

"For long ago. Even longer than Michael. I want to apologize for what I did to you with David."

It was something they had never spoken of, but which had remained between them for years, until David's behavior as a husband had shown Susanna that she had gotten the best of the bargain. When Susanna had been a freshman at Duke, she had met sophomore David Oliver, and had found him to be the boy of her young and rather non-selective dreams. He, too, lived in the Philadelphia area, and when he visited the Cassidy house

over the Christmas vacation, older sister Julia had taken a shine
to him immediately.

It was only natural that she should have, Susanna had rationalized later. David was everything Julia had gone to college to
find. He was handsome, came from a family with money, and
his future in his father's business seemed assured. He was a
lock, and Julia had zeroed in on him. David was flattered that
an "older" woman was interested in him, and it wasn't long
before he had delicately broken off with Susanna by simply not
calling her anymore. A year and a half later Julia and David
were married.

"I am so sorry," Julia said. "I never told you that before. But
I've felt bad about it all my life."

"Don't," Susanna said, and she meant it. "It was the best
thing. David and I weren't right for each other. If we would have
been, we'd have stayed together."

"But I—"

"No. That was all long ago. I don't want you to even think
about it anymore. You understand me, honey girl?"

Julia nodded her head and closed her eyes. "Yes. Thank
you."

"Now," Susanna said with mock officiousness, "where
and when exactly am I supposed to meet this Irish gentleman,
should he make an appearance?"

"Three o'clock in the afternoon, Thursday, January 23rd.
Where I said—the second little balcony over the river. Carry the
book of Yeats so he'll know who you are. Oh, Susanna, do you
think you'll have any trouble getting away from campus?"

"No, I've got my sabbatical next semester, and part of the
time I'll be in Galway anyway, at the university there."

"Oh God, thank you—I love you, Sue."

"I know, honey, and I love you, too." Susanna leaned over
and kissed the dry skin of Julia's forehead. "You ought to get
some rest now, okay?"

"I want to see Rachel first. Send her in?"

"Sure."

Susanna put the volume of Yeats in her purse and walked
to the door. Rachel was reading a magazine in the next room,

her legs thrown over the arms of a chair. She hopped up when she saw Susanna, and the two hugged each other. Even at thirty, Rachel reminded Susanna of a little girl, thin and wiry, dressed in tight jeans and a baggy sweater, her hair cut boyishly, her makeup minimal.

"Go on in," Susanna told her, then warned, "She's pretty tired."

A determined look came over Rachel's delicate features. She nodded, then walked into the sunroom as though entering a lion's den, and closed the door behind her.

Susanna made her way through the house to the front door, but as she placed her hand on the knob, she heard David behind her. "Leaving?"

She turned around. "Yes. She's ready for a nap after she talks to Rachel." David crossed his arms over his chest and rolled his head back as if to stretch the muscles of his neck and shoulders. At fifty-one he was still in good shape, with no trace of a belly. His hair had remained dark except for stately gray wings at his temples, and his face was still recognizable as that of the college boy for whom Susanna had fallen so hard years before, the sharp lines of the nose and jaw in marked contrast to the softness of his brown eyes.

Susanna had never felt comfortable with David after he and Julia had been married. It wasn't so much the fact that they had once been romantically involved, as it was her sense that David still wished they were. Now, with Julia dying, that thought seemed more appalling than ever.

"How are you holding up?" she asked him.

"Dealing with it like we all do—one day at a time. God, it's hard though. To see her fade like this." He sighed. "When it comes it'll be a relief...for her, I mean."

"Be honest, for all of us," Susanna said as kindly as she could. "It'll be a blessing."

"I suppose so. How've *you* been, classes and all?"

"Fine. It's no problem. I have fairly small class sizes this semester, though I've been getting ready for my sabbatical next year."

"Oh yeah, that's right. Going to Ireland again?"

"Yes. In January."

"You Cassidy girls love your Ireland, don't you? Julia asks for that fiddle music over and over. You still playing at those, what do you call them..."

"Sessions. Yes, once a month."

"You play a lot."

"Just that and the symphony. Something to do." Susanna had played first violin in the local Conestoga Symphony Orchestra for over a decade, but had been playing in Irish sessions in a Harrisburg pub for barely a year. She had learned to love the traditional music on her many trips to Ireland, and found she liked playing the reels, jigs, and airs with other local musicians for several hours in a smoky bar even more than she did playing Beethoven and Mozart.

"Just so you're keeping busy," David said. "Helps get your mind off things. I've been trying, but..." He shook his head in frustration. "Fifty-two is too young to die like this."

"Any age is too young to die like this," Susanna said.

"Well, at least we're there for each other. That's what's good about family. You've been such a help the past few months, and not just getting Rachel and us back together but with everything, just being there. Look, Susanna, if *you* ever need to talk, I'm always here, and I hope that would work both ways?"

"Of course, David. I'm here for you."

"Thanks. You've always been wonderful."

He moved toward her as though to give her a hug, but she turned from him quickly and opened the door. "I'll drop by tomorrow," she said, then flashed a smile and walked out. He said goodbye and closed the door behind her.

CHAPTER 2

Through the window, David watched Susanna Cassidy walk to her little red Geo, climb in, and drive away. He felt sad, guilty, and hopeful at the same time. The thought that nagged at him for thirty years was that he had married the wrong sister. Miraculously, Susanna, the younger one, that woman of depth and peace and quiet beauty, had somehow remained unmarried all these years, and soon David Oliver would be single again.

He knew that there was little more repugnant than a man thinking about a possible second wife while his first lay on her deathbed, but he couldn't help it, despite his guilt. And he did feel guilt. Julia, for all her faults, had been a good wife. She had asked for little and accepted much. Though she must have known about his infidelities, she had never confronted him over them. On the contrary, her refusal to even acknowledge his bouts of unfaithfulness had established her complicity in his crimes of the heart.

Occasionally David admitted to himself that his relationships with other women were merely attempts to recapture Susanna Cassidy. They had all been imperfect clones of her, tall and willowy with facial features slightly sharp, as if holding the hint of danger, the color of hair somewhere between ash blonde and red, and blue-gray eyes. But none had been Susanna, none had captivated him enough to leave the secure comforts of the marriage he had made with Julia and trudge through the exhausting and debilitating marshes of divorce.

He had only once made an overture to Susanna herself, several months after Rachel had been born. It had been in the dying moments of a party, he had been half-drunk, and though he thought at the time that his suggestion had been subtle and safely open to multiple levels of meaning, he had realized in sober retrospect that it had been clumsy. Susanna's response was skillful, but so cold and cutting that he never made the attempt again. It had taken several years before she treated him civilly when they found themselves alone with each other.

His biggest mistake was in giving her up in the first place, but Julia's bubbly flirtatiousness had swept him away. Along with the flattering aspect of an upperclassman being attracted to him, Julia had been far more glamorous and flamboyant than Susanna. Though both girls at the time had been slim, Julia's figure was more womanly and her manner more overtly sexual than the shyer Susanna.

David had tried to push Susanna too far too fast, and she had always rebuffed him. Julia was prepared to go further, especially at the beginning of their relationship when she was trying to shift his affections from Susanna to herself. Once that was accomplished, however, she had become nearly as reticent as her sister. It wasn't until she had come back from her aborted trip to Europe that she had been willing to give herself to him fully.

Unfortunately, the gift had been *too* full. She told him of her pregnancy at the beginning of April. Though he had not formally asked her, their understanding had been that they would marry when they had both been graduated, she from the Bryn Mawr class of '72, and he the following year from Penn, to which he had transferred in order to be closer to Julia. This little accident, she said, would only speed up the process. David thought it would do far more.

He had never liked being forced into anything, and he deeply resented being forced into a marriage, despite the fact that it would have been his own choice in another year. When he mentioned the option of abortion, Julia had bridled, and though he told her it might be more reasonable to wait until they were more secure in their careers to have children, she had replied that there was no way she could give up *their* baby, and besides, a career really didn't matter that much to her, and the only career she needed was to be his wife and the mother of their child. David had bitten the bullet, smiled, and agreed to marry Julia the week after she received her diploma in May.

David had been concerned with how the two sets of parents would react to the news, but all four seemed understanding and forgiving enough. Both mothers panicked more at the short time in which to put together a wedding, but David's father's money did wonders, and the ceremony was satisfyingly grand. When the baby arrived in November, the unofficial announcement was that Rachel was premature, and the circles in which Julia's and his own parents moved were too polite to count weeks, at least publicly.

The decline began shortly after Rachel's birth. He began to resent both mother and daughter for ruining his senior year of college. Money was not a problem, since his father was paying for the rent of a spacious apartment where both David and Julia's mother frequently visited their new granddaughter, keeping Julia company while David was at classes or studying. With Julia breastfeeding, their social life was minimal.

Still, David was occasionally able to slip away to a party, and it was at one of these, two months after his daughter was born, that he had his first of many extramarital affairs, a one-night stand with a graduate student whose first name was Jill but whose last he never learned. He had had several drinks, and she reminded him of Susanna. When he went home, very early that morning, he cried on the way, thinking that his life would never be what he had wanted it to be.

It was, however, in many ways what he expected. He had always planned to follow his father Robert into the real estate business, and so he did. His father was happy to have his son join the firm, despite his disappointment in David's having to get married, and upon his graduation made David a vice-president with a commensurate salary that allowed him to buy a new home.

David had always hated disappointing his father, who showed his disapproval never overtly, but by subtle changes in his attitude, a silent treatment that had devastated David ever since he was little. In order to expiate his sexual transgression, David threw himself into his work and quickly surpassed his father's expectations.

As a family man, however, he remained deficient. While he always made sure that Julia and the baby lacked for nothing corporal, their needs of the heart often suffered. With Julia, David quickly settled into a mode of benign neglect, treating her kindly but seldom warmly.

Rachel felt his emotional distance as well. David faithfully went to her school and social events, and praised her when praise was called for, but he left the nurturing to Julia, who grew ever more protective of her daughter, as if determined to single-handedly give her the love of two parents.

That strategy had failed miserably. Julia's protectiveness of Rachel morphed into a clinging possessiveness that smothered the child, and her response to it was withdrawal from her mother and a constantly growing desire for independence. By the time David finally stepped in, Rachel's path of rebelliousness was set.

David heard a door opening, and he turned away from the window, not knowing how long he had been standing there thinking about his life and about how Susanna might fit into it again. Rachel was coming out of the sunroom. She closed the door behind her and lowered her head. "How is she?" David asked.

"Sleeping. She fell asleep while I was there. We talked for a while and then she just dozed off."

"Your coming means a lot to her."

Rachel nodded but said nothing. Then she straightened up and headed for the door. "I have to go to work."

David stepped into her path and smiled. "Have you thought any more about my suggestion?"

"I told you, Dad, I thought about it enough. I don't want to work for you. I'd be shitty selling houses."

David winced at his daughter's language. She had started swearing in her early teens and had never stopped, at least in front of her parents. Sometimes he suspected she did it for the effect she knew it had on them. "You wouldn't have to actually sell—there are plenty of office jobs that would pay a lot better than what you make now."

"I'm not an office job kind of girl. I *like* working at the music store." She sighed. "Look, I appreciate the offer, but it's really not my thing, okay?"

He bit back his initial response, that *her thing* had so far gotten her only a dead-end career and an abusive husband, now mercifully *ex*-husband. "Okay," he said instead. "If you ever change your mind, there's always a place for you."

"Thanks, Dad," she said with a thin smile. "Not very likely, though." She hugged him perfunctorily and he kissed her cheek. "See you tomorrow."

After Rachel left, David went to the door of the sunroom and opened it carefully. Julia appeared to be sleeping. He walked inside, closed the door, and sat in the chair next to her bed. A shudder went through him as he gazed again upon the havoc the illness had visited on her body. Despite the way he had treated her, she was always waiting for him when he came home, with a smile on her face that had grown rounder with the years. Now it was nothing but pouches of flesh hanging onto the bones beneath, and he felt tears come into his eyes.

She truly *loved* him, he thought. No matter what he had done, she had always been there, never making a scene, never accusing him, just quietly accepting whatever he did, and he knew that he could never love anyone like that. He never had, and knew that it was not in him to do so.

He sat by her side and cried, the first time he had done so since he had cried for the loss of his future back in early 1973. He cried for Julia and he cried for himself, at the thought of being alone, with no one loving him.

His sobbing woke her up. She turned painfully and looked at her husband, and reached out her hand. "Oh, my poor boy," she said through her dry, crusted lips. "My poor sweet boy..."

He took her hand and kissed it and held it against his cheek and pressed his eyes shut to seal in the tears, and tried hard not to think about Susanna's hand, Susanna's face.

CHAPTER 3

Julia became comatose on December 21st and died on the 27th, two days after a Christmas that was barely acknowledged by her family. The last person to see her alive was her night nurse. David had told the nurse to wake him should anything happen, but by the time she did, Julia had passed. David had hoped there would be a look of peace on her skeletal face, but instead he saw only the expression of mild discomfort that she had borne for the past few months.

Julia had requested cremation and David put her wishes into action immediately, calling the funeral home, confirming the arrangements, and making the travel plans for Julia's widowed mother to fly from Phoenix to Philadelphia. Susanna and Rachel were both frequently at the house in the days preceding the memorial service, and Susanna made it a point to be with David only in Rachel's company. The situation became easier when Susanna's mother arrived and moved into David's house during the week of the service.

Helen Cassidy had visited the Olivers in October, shortly after Julia had come home from the hospital to die. Helen and Susanna had spent a great deal of time in Julia's sickroom trying to encompass her life in images and memories, going through photo albums, looking at videos of when Rachel was little, recalling the past with laughter and tears. The experience, necessary as it had been, had exhausted Helen, who had a heart condition. When she flew back to Phoenix, she knew she would not see her older daughter alive again.

Before she left, however, she had shared with Susanna something that Julia told her. "To this day," Helen had said, when she and Susanna were sitting together in a café after doing some recuperative shopping, "she still feels guilty about taking David from you."

"She needn't," Susanna said. "That never would have worked."

"Do you think she and David *did* work?"

"They stayed married."

"But at such a cost." Helen gave a *tsk tsk*, shook her head, and sipped her coffee. When she set down her cup, she looked at Susanna over the rim of her bifocals. "*I* should be the one to feel guilty. I could have stopped it, you know—when she went after David. I knew what she was going to do."

Susanna felt a small shock of surprise and betrayal. She had never before realized her mother's prescience. "So why didn't you, Mother?"

"Because, sweetheart, I knew that you'd land on your feet, and I wasn't so sure about Julia. If she didn't get a good husband, she wouldn't have had anything to fall back on. We both know she went to college for an MRS. Degree. But you were different. You were bright, talented...and also, I didn't think David was a good match for you. He was shallow. I thought you'd find someone more, what, up to speed?"

"But I never did."

Helen sighed. "No, you never did."

"Better that, though, than life with David. You did me a favor, Mother, you and Julia."

"He did turn out to be...less than perfect, didn't he? And that's another reason for me to feel guilty."

"For letting Julia marry him?"

"For that, but also in a way for not letting him marry *you*. You say it wouldn't have worked and maybe you're right. But I can't help but feel that if David had married you, he might have become a different person. Better."

"What makes you say that?"

"Because men tend to live up to the expectations set on them by women they love. Julia's were very low—money, a nice place to live, the outward semblance of affection. Yours would have been much higher." Helen smiled sadly. "And you would have been smart enough not to get pregnant." Helen picked up her teacup again and sipped delicately. "Just be ready when Julia... seeks penance from you."

"It's funny," Susanna said, "but I think I always wanted her to *feel* guilty, though I got over it a long time ago." She laughed. "Decades, really. Still, I never did find anyone, did I?"

"After David, I think your standards increased. Mister Right became Mister Perfect. And you didn't want to be hurt again. That combination makes things very difficult. But I have no doubt, darling, that you will find him someday."

"No, Mother, I've pretty much given up. Once my childrearing years were over—and they are, believe me—marriage didn't seem as important. It never did, really, once my career got going."

"Well, you got a taste of childrearing with Rachel. I always think she preferred her aunt Susanna to her mom and dad."

"That's because she didn't have to *live* with Aunt Susanna."

"But she did for a while," Helen reminded her. "You know, after she finally got smart and left that guitar player."

"She needed someone and I was there."

"So were her parents, but all she got from them was 'We *told* you so.' I don't know why my progeny didn't inherit my good taste in picking men."

"I don't either, Mother. I certainly didn't."

"You never know. You may still find your man."

"And we'll both totter down the aisle on our walkers."

"Oh, *stop* it," Helen said. "You are forty-nine years old, and you look as if you're in your mid-thirties. You stay in great shape, you've got legs to die for, there's not a touch of gray in that beautiful hair, and you're still as pretty as when you were twenty. With that bone structure and the way you take care of yourself, you'll never need a facelift or Botox, believe me. So, stop pretending you're Grandma Moses. Besides, if *you're* ancient, what does that make *me*? I'm your *mother*, for God's sake."

"All right, fine, I'm *gawgeous*, okay?"

"Was that supposed to be Barbra Streisand?" Helen asked. "Darling, you never could do impressions."

"I thought mothers were supposed to be unquestioningly

supportive of *all* their children's endeavors."

"There's a codicil regarding bad Barbra Streisand impressions."

"You still make me laugh, Mom."

"That's how I kept your father interested all those years." Her face lost its smile. "I'm glad he isn't here to see this happen to Julia. I don't think he could have handled it. Men can be lousy at this kind of thing."

"Daddy was good with his own passing." Susanna's father had shown her how to die—calmly, stoically, but not without humor.

"I think he was relieved he was going first. Dying's not as hard as being left behind, sweetie. That's the tough part. Waiting to be with that dear man again."

"You believe you will, don't you?"

"Oh, sometimes I have my doubts. Death seems so final, doesn't it? But most of the time I just know it'll all be all right in the end. And if it isn't, well, I'll never know, will I? It's always sweeter to believe and have faith." She smiled. "And I have faith that you'll find your man someday. Now I don't know about you, but I could do with another scone…"

After Julia's memorial service at the church, and after the many visitors to the Oliver house had left, the immediate family milled about as if uncertain of what to do next. Helen sat talking quietly to Robert, David's father, while various cousins, aunts, and uncles chatted in low tones.

David's eyes were dry, as were Rachel's, but Susanna thought that he looked slightly lost. Though he and his daughter had sat together at the service in the same row with Susanna and Helen, they seemed to now be in two different orbits. David stood at the window. He was talking to his younger sister Grace and her husband, but mostly looking out onto the vast expanse of lawn at the rear of the house. Rachel sat on the bench of the Steinway grand on the other side of the large room, softly picking out a tune with her right hand.

Susanna strolled over and sat next to her. "That's pretty. What is it?"

"Just a tune my mom used to hum to me when I was little."
Susanna nodded. "Does it have any words?"

"I don't know, she never sang any." Rachel stopped playing, and put her right hand on her leg as if holding herself in place. "It's so weird. I couldn't stand her for years and years, and now I miss her."

"It's good that you got to know her again…to know her better," Susanna said.

"Yeah, I guess so. But you know, if I hadn't, I wouldn't care as much." Her words wavered, and her lower lip trembled as soft little sobs shook her body. Susanna put an arm around her.

"It's okay. You know, having you come and see her as often as you did—getting to know you again, too—I think it meant more to her than anything these past months."

Rachel sniffed and straightened her shoulders. "I was surprised by how much she talked." She gave a small laugh. "Sometimes she'd just talk until she fell asleep."

"What about?"

"Oh, all sorts of things. Like when I was little, and things I did. Sometimes she told me about stuff that she did when she was young. And about places she liked and said she'd like to see again, but she knew she wouldn't. Like the Bahamas—you know, she and Dad used to go down there every winter. They took me when I was little. She talked a lot about Ireland, too."

"Ireland?"

"Yeah, she loved that place. They never took me there, though. You're going back there again, huh?"

"Yes. In a couple of weeks."

"Is this for the college?"

Susanna nodded. "A sabbatical. I'm doing a study on the violence in Northern Ireland, and how the attitudes of former political prisoners in both the North and South affect the peace process."

"I just never got it about that place. I mean, why should religion make people so ready to kill other people?"

"Well, the violence there really isn't so much religious as it is political. Though sometimes the political issues disguise themselves as religious..." She stopped. "I'm turning into a yammering academic, aren't I?"

Rachel smiled at her. "That's okay. I don't really know what you mean, though."

"Well, let's just say that things have improved but still aren't great, and I'm just trying to learn about reconciliation, what people can do to understand each other's fears and concerns."

"And that's how you get to peace."

"Hopefully."

"And you get to go to Ireland, too. Nice trick. I'd like to go there myself and see what Mom thought was so great about it. Need a research assistant?"

"It would be nice, but I don't think that the grants committee who fund my airfare and my tiny per diem would swing for an assistant."

"Ah well. Maybe I'll just go over on my own sometime."

"You should. If you ever want to take a little vacation, I'd be happy to go with you—if you don't mind an old lady tagging along."

"Ha. More guys would probably hit on you than me." Rachel's expression grew thoughtful. "But I *am* getting some money from Mom's insurance." Her eyes grew teary again. "That'd be a great way to spend it."

Susanna gave Rachel a hug. "Sounds like a plan. I think she'd like knowing that you used some of it to go over there and see the places she loved. Just in case you decide to do it in the next few months, I'll let you know where I'm staying, so you can get in touch with me."

"Great. Thanks, Aunt Sue."

"And if you need me for anything—to talk to or whatever— just give me a call. I'm not leaving until the 18th of next month."

"Leaving?" came David's voice from behind her. "Oh, your Ireland holiday."

"A *working* holiday," she said, standing to face him. "I'll be doing interviews and some lecturing in Limerick, Galway, and Derry."

It seemed to Susanna that David was trying to look

impressed, but, since Susanna's Irish trip did not involve vast amounts of money, failed in the attempt. "Oh. Well, that's great," he said.

Rachel got up. "Excuse me, I need another drink," she said, and walked to the bar set up at the far end of the room.

"She still doesn't like me," David said so only Susanna could hear. "I thought maybe patching over things with her mother would extend to me, but I guess not."

"Old wounds can be slow to heal." As soon as the words passed Susanna's lips, she wished she could take them back again. She had meant to imply only the difficulties between Rachel and her parents, but David's expression told her that he read more into it than that.

"I know," he said. "Believe me, I know." His voice grew even more confidential. "Listen, Susanna, now that Julia's... gone, I hope we don't become strangers. We're still family, after all. I know you'll stay in touch with Rachel and I'm grateful. She needs someone like you to give her advice and help her out, and I'm going to try and do that myself if she'll let me. But please, do call me and come visit. Maybe we could have dinner now and then to catch up on things. I'd be interested in hearing about your trip to Ireland. Julia loved the place, but you know that..."

He was starting to talk more quickly, as though to work himself up to something that Susanna didn't want to hear, so she interrupted him. "Of course, David. We'll stay in touch. After all, there's e-mail too," which was impersonal and could be ignored when necessary. "I'll be busy the next couple of weeks getting ready for the trip and finishing things up at the college, but maybe when I get back, we can touch base...oh, it looks like Uncle Frank's about to leave, and I barely spoke to him. Excuse me..."

Susanna knew her brother-in-law all too well. Though his approach had been subtle, she had seen him in action for years, flirting at cocktail parties Susanna had attended at Julia's request, insinuating himself into conversations in which his only interest was an attractive woman, regardless of her age or marital status.

And now he was interested in Susanna again. She would never reciprocate that interest, though the day of her sister's memorial service was not the proper time to make that clear. If she had to be rude she would be, but at a less sensitive moment.

To Susanna's relief, David didn't call her in the few weeks before she went to Ireland. She did talk to Rachel on the phone every couple of days, and met her niece once for lunch. The Saturday before Susanna left, Rachel came to stay overnight at Susanna's townhouse.

They cooked dinner together, watched the DVD of *All About Eve*, which Rachel had never seen, and chatted long into the night. They talked about Julia, and of Rachel's difficulty in dealing with her parents, her failed marriage, and her hopes for the future.

"I just don't need any romantic entanglements right now," Rachel said. "Maybe not ever, I don't know. I mean, *you've* done all right."

"I'm content. I have my work..." She rubbed the ears of the tiger-striped cat purring in her lap. "And I have Gandhi here."

"That is *such* a weird name for a cat," Rachel said, and Susanna laughed. She always thought of her niece as thirty going on twelve. "But then she's a weird cat."

"I'll miss this weird cat," Susanna said, nuzzling its head with her chin.

"I'll take good care of her, promise." Rachel had never cat-sat Gandhi before. She had always been afraid of what Ty might do to him when he was drunk, but that was no longer a problem.

"Just one piece of advice, Rachel," Susanna said. "Don't shut yourself out."

"From Gandhi?"

"You know what I mean. From other people."

"Oh, from *luh-uh-uv*," Rachel nearly sang.

"Yes, from love. You're still young. Don't let one bad experience with men close you off."

"I'm not closed off. But you can bet that the next guy isn't going to be some..." She shook her head, not able to find words vituperative enough. "Isn't going to be Tyler Madden. So, like how's *your* love life?"

Susanna did what she always did when someone was rude enough to ask that question. She smiled and said nothing.

"Well," said Rachel, stretching and yawning, "maybe you'll find a nice guy in Ireland."

2003

Chapter 4

Susanna Cassidy's flight left Newark Airport on a Friday evening and was over Irish airspace by the next morning. Susanna felt more than the usual thrill upon looking down and seeing the patchwork of fields, now brown rather than green, bordered by stone walls that made the countryside one vast chessboard. Though she was there on academic business, there was a more intriguing dimension to this trip.

She was also there because she had promised Julia that she would meet her lost love. The odds were long that Michael Lynch would even show up at a liaison planned thirty-one years earlier, but Susanna would be there nonetheless. And if the man, probably bald and fat by now, appeared, then she would tell him all about Julia and her affection for him through the years, show the pictures of the family and the house and the boat and the things with which Julia had filled the gap that Michael's departure had left in her life.

Susanna felt nervous about even the slim prospect of confronting this man who had had such an effect on her sister. What would it mean if he *did* show up—that he had felt the same way about Julia as she had about him? Or might he just come out of curiosity? That was doubtful. If he came, it would be because Julia had meant something to him, even all those years later.

The whole thing was stupid. No one would be there. Susanna knew that she would just stand by the river for an hour holding that volume of Yeats, and then sadly walk away, hoping that Julia wouldn't somehow see that she was alone and know that the love of her life had forgotten her, or was dead, or just didn't care. Why, Susanna wondered, did it always have to be so hard to love someone?

The plane landed at Shannon Airport at 8:30. The day was bright and chilly and the sun was shining as Susanna stepped outside the terminal building, dragging her two wheeled suitcases like huge and reluctant leashed dogs. Once she had stowed her luggage in the small trunk of the little red Ford subcompact, she climbed into the driver's seat thinking *left, left, left*. It had always taken her a few days to get comfortable driving on the opposite side of the road.

Susanna found a radio station that played Irish traditional music, drove out of the airport, and headed north on E20. There wasn't much traffic, and she quickly grew accustomed once more to the roundabouts, the circular intersections that kept the traffic moving without stop signs.

She had decided to take her own sweet time getting to Galway. Since she didn't have to be there until Thursday, she planned to spend a day or two in Doolin, a tiny town that had been recommended as having several pubs where one could hear some of the finest traditional music in Ireland.

At Ennis she headed west on 85, planning to stop at the spectacular Cliffs of Moher, which she had seen only once. She was tired from the plane ride, but had learned that the best thing was to just keep going that first day, let your internal clock get acclimated to the time change, and sleep like a log that night. She expected that the *craic*, that unique Irish spirit of fun and fellowship, would be fine enough at the Doolin pubs to keep her awake until midnight. Then up at eight for the Irish breakfast that her B&B would provide, and she'd be right on schedule.

Unfortunately, as she drove through the small seaside village of Lahinch, it began to rain. She stopped for lunch, thinking that it might blow over, but after her light meal the rain was coming harder than before, and a cold wind lashed the water into her face as she dashed for the car. She could easily visit the cliffs on a brighter day. With Galway as her base in the South, the whole western part of the island was readily accessible.

She arrived in Doolin at three in the afternoon, and was amused to find that the rain stopped abruptly as she pulled into the drive of a bed and breakfast which one of her fellow musicians in the states had recommended. Susanna introduced herself to Mrs. Moloney, who showed her to a spacious room at the rear of the house overlooking a back yard that Susanna was delighted to see contained a respectable two-story castle ruin. Once settled in, Susanna walked down the hill and over a tiny bridge that led to the gently curving row of shops and pubs that constituted "downtown" Doolin. Susanna smiled broadly when she saw the buildings painted in pastel shades of yellow and red, as well as the more subdued whitewash.

Even off-season, Doolin was a popular pilgrimage for lovers of Irish music, and Susanna's first stop was the tiny but well-stocked Traditional Music Shop. There she browsed for a half hour, looking for Irish and Scots fiddle CDs unavailable in the states.

Susanna thought of herself as a "closet fiddler." She had learned classical violin as a child, had studied through college, and now played in her university's faculty/student orchestra. When she first heard Irish music in a pub setting in Dublin, however, it touched her in a way that the meticulously rehearsed and prepared symphonic music never had. Despite the emotional heights to which a classical performance could take her, there was a freedom and spontaneity in these few players, sitting around a table in a smoky pub, that she had not experienced before. It was the sheer joy of music-making at its purest.

When she got home, she searched for more of the same, and found that there was an entire subculture of Irish music in her area. Sessions were held every week at one pub or another within the triangle made up of Lancaster, Harrisburg, and York, and if you went as far afield as Philadelphia and Baltimore you could hear and play the music somewhere every night.

It hadn't taken her long to find a convivial and welcoming group of musicians who met at a pub near Harrisburg, only a half hour drive from Conestoga. She simply sat and listened the first few times, nursing pints of Guinness and clapping with other listeners when the musicians finished a tune. It wasn't long before some of them started chatting with her, and when they learned she played violin and read music they invited her to bring along her instrument next time and buy a copy of *The Fiddler's Fakebook*, which had many of the tunes they played. It was, she learned with relief, permissible for new players to read music.

Susanna studied the tunes, and before too long when someone called out a title, she could play it by memory like the others. There was a steady core of about six musicians and others who came to the pubs nearest them, so that most sessions had from eight to twelve players at any one time. There were fiddles, guitars, and tin whistles at every session, as well as occasional button accordions, mandolins, and bodhrans, the Irish hand-held drum made of goatskin.

Susanna loved the sessions and went to them as often as possible. What made it even more relaxing was that there was no sexual tension in the air. The men, ranging in age from twenty-five to seventy, were happily married, gay, or otherwise spoken for, a situation that more than suited her.

She had not, however, been in Ireland since she had begun to play Irish music, and the legendary lure of Doolin had been too great to dismiss. Her shopping finished, she stepped out onto the narrow sidewalk, and a short stroll took her to Gus O'Connor's Pub. The same musician who had recommended her B&B had told her, "O'Connor's is the one. You'll see two more if you come into town from the north, but keep going. You get the *real* thing at O'Connor's."

There she learned that the music would start that night at about ten. That was three in the morning on her biological clock, but she resolved not to think about it. She returned to her B&B, where she sat in the common room and read a new Maeve Binchy novel that had not yet been released in the states. She nearly dozed off once or twice, but came to with a jerk.

At six o'clock, Susanna took a quick shower and drove to the pubs at the northeast end of town. She had dinner at McDermott's, where some music had already started. Unfortunately, it consisted of songs by Elvis and Donovan sung by a man with a battered and out-of-tune guitar. After dinner, she walked across a picturesque stone bridge to McGann's. There she found that the music didn't start until ten-thirty, so she drove back to O'Connor's.

There was already a decent crowd, but she snagged a seat against the far wall from the area reserved for the musicians and started a series of long-nursed half-pint glasses. The Guinness in Ireland was a different creature from the import, smoother yet richer than the version found in the states.

To her relief, three women tourists from America joined her, giving her a defense against the possibility of unwanted attention. That happened seldom in Irish pubs, however, which retained more of a sense of community than bars in America. A woman alone in an Irish pub was not considered as meat on the hoof. Here pubs were a traditional gathering place for everyone, safe and warm and comfortable.

So, Susanna nursed two glasses of Guinness and had a pleasant if shallow conversation about Irish music, since the women were unfamiliar with much beyond the Chieftains and Riverdance. She was adding to their education when the band came in, two young guitarists and an older electric bass player. It was hardly the ideal traditional band, and Susanna prepared for disappointment.

Despite the instrumentation they were a delight. One guitarist strummed strong rhythm while the other played melody lines as liltingly as on a whistle, and the bass player provided a steady bottom. He had a fine voice, too, and did a number of familiar songs with which everyone sang along. Susanna left the pub just after midnight and was asleep by twelve-thirty.

She awoke at eight, was treated to a traditional Irish breakfast of eggs, sausage, bacon which was more like ham, two puddings, tomatoes, mushrooms, and coarse, delicious wheat bread. It was more than enough to keep her going until dinner in Galway, and she hopped in the car and headed northeast through the vast expanse of limestone, tufted here and there with brown grass and other vegetation, that made up the area known as the Burren.

Susanna had been in Galway before, but never for more than a day. Despite the overcast sky and the desolate landscape, she looked forward to making the acquaintance of a town she had always found so charming.

Her only stop was at the partially restored sixteenth-century

Dunguaire Castle just outside of the town of Kinvarra, but she was saddened to find it closed for the winter. The grounds were open, however, and she was able to at least walk around it on a precarious path.

That was a nice thing about Ireland. There was such a strong sense of community, as though these sites, both modern and ancient, were shared by everyone, and no one thought twice about hopping over the fence of an attraction closed for the season. She had first become aware of this generosity of spirit when she had gone to see Grianán of Aileach, a prehistoric round stone fort in County Donegal. The visitor's center was officially closed, but a few people were working there, and the woman in charge not only told her to drive right up, but even opened the exhibit for her without charge and seemed almost embarrassed by Susanna's profuse thanks.

That generosity toward others seemed to be lacking more and more in her own country, with its sense of outright aggression. America, she feared, was turning into a nation of bullies, where those with the most power and the loudest voices were making new rules for everyone to obey, not just in their own country, but around the world.

She tried to shake away such gloomy thoughts by thinking about what lay ahead. Her work wouldn't really start until the beginning of February, when she gave her first lecture at a university peace center in Limerick. There would be several more speeches and seminars at universities in both the North and South, along with visits to a number of community leaders in both countries, and a series of interviews that would form the core of her studies.

She wanted to speak to ex-prisoners living in the Republic and the North, and learn how their attitudes affected those of the communities in which they lived and worked, and how the attempts at reconciliation had affected them and changed their attitudes. Hopefully, it would result in yet another book to add to the small pile of university press imprints with her byline. It would be a busy few months, all the more reason to enjoy this week or two of freedom until the work began in earnest.

The clouds cleared as she approached Galway, and though

she knew she should have been appreciating the way the city, with its brightly colored buildings and its splashes of trees, revealed itself to her, she was more concerned with following the directions to the guest house in which she'd be staying the next few weeks. Leaving the N6, she took a smaller road down through the city center until she arrived in Lower Salthill, an area that had changed from a seaside resort into another suburb of the ever-growing town.

She found the Bayside Guest House on a quiet residential street, met the landlady, Mrs. McCarthy, and was pleased to find that the room was nicely furnished with a desk big enough to easily contain her laptop and notes, unlike many B&Bs' small decorative desks that could scarcely hold a writing pad. There was a kitchenette, as she had requested, so she could do some of her own cooking and save the college money and herself several additional pounds around her hips. She was also happy to see that the small suite had an outside exit reached by a wooden staircase, an amenity that Susanna, who valued her privacy, found a great plus.

Mrs. McCarthy, a short, rotund woman, helped Susanna haul her bags up the stairs, then invited her to the kitchen for tea. Susanna guessed her to be in her mid to late-fifties, but when she remarked on a wedding photo hanging in the hall, Mrs. McCarthy said, "Oh yes, Bob and I will have our thirtieth next year. We were both only eighteen when we got married, barely kids ourselves. And now we have four of our own, all grown and with their *own* kids."

Susanna realized with a shock that the woman was actually younger than she was, even though she seemed matronly, almost grandmotherly.

"And are *you* married then?" Mrs. McCarthy asked, her gaze slipping to Susanna's left hand. "Or is it *Miss* Cassidy?"

"Oh, just Susanna will do. No, I'm not married."

"Ah well, there's plenty of time for that, a young woman like yourself." Susanna didn't correct her. It would have been too embarrassing.

Susanna liked the Bayside Guest House. During the next three days there were only two other tenants, and she didn't even see them, eschewing the calorie-laden Irish breakfasts and preparing her own of yogurt, toast, and fruit. The city center was within walking distance of the guest house, as she learned Monday morning. It was a lovely stroll along the Grattan Road, which hugged the shore of Galway Bay. All along that shore was a bar of huge gray stones which discouraged descending to the water.

The road led to the former site of the Claddagh, an old fishing village at the mouth of the Corrib River, and then turned north, up past the Ballyknow Quay to the Wolfe Tone Bridge, the same bridge that Julia had described to Susanna as the site of her fateful meeting with Michael Lynch. The first thing that Susanna did upon crossing it was to find the spot that Julia had told her about.

A walkway led to the left above and along the river. Susanna rested her elbows on the top of the chest-high stone wall and looked down at the water. It was rushing rapidly, pouring under the three low arches of the Wolfe Tone Bridge on its way to the bay. The walkway curved gently to the right, and she saw the two small balconies, concrete semi-circles that jutted out over the water. She walked past the first and stepped into the second, placing her hands on the black iron railing.

In spite of herself, she felt a little tingle. So, this was where her sister had stood when she met the man she had called the love of her life. Susanna had to admit that it was a romantic spot with the river roaring beneath, the old bridge named after an Irish martyr to her left, the weathered stone buildings on the other side, covered with ivy, some of them seemingly deserted, their broken windows like tearful eyes. To her right the dome of Galway Cathedral lifted itself above the other buildings, and all around the small trees were shaken by a chilly wind.

Susanna gripped the iron rail and closed her eyes, hearing the water and smelling the scent of the sea from the bay. It was a perfect place to fall in love for the first time.

Then voices interrupted her reverie, and she opened her eyes and turned to see two young couples coming briskly down the walkway, talking and laughing and holding hands. They smiled at her and she smiled back, then followed them toward the bridge and into the town center where she passed her time until the end of the day. She went back to the guest house after dinner and was in bed by ten, resolving to find some good music in the next day or two.

The first thing on Tuesday, Susanna rented a cell phone and set up an account, but spent most of the day at the Galway campus of the National University of Ireland, where she gave her letters of introduction to the librarian and received a temporary academic staff card, as well as permission to use the library's data links on her laptop. The librarian invited her to lunch in the cafeteria, and they shared a pleasant chat. Then Susanna spent the rest of the day in the library and online.

She caught up on her professional contacts, but also e-mailed her mother and Rachel, telling them she was settled in and giving them her phone number. By the end of the day, she realized that her jet lag was finally catching up with her, so she went back to her rooms after dinner and was in bed by ten, vowing to make the next night a musical pub-crawl.

In the morning, she shifted back into tourist mode and visited the cathedral. Despite the fact that her family no longer practiced Catholicism, Susanna was deeply moved by cathedrals. It was not so much for the massive buildings themselves as for the amount of faith and devotion that had gone into their construction.

The experience was darkened only by her encounter with an old woman in a worn winter coat. She begged Susanna for some money, claiming that she needed enough to buy some food. Susanna gave her a two-Euro coin, and the woman whispered, "God bless you, dear," and made her way down a side aisle to her next prospective donor. Susanna's soul felt invaded by this juxtaposition of dire poverty with ecclesiastical plenty. At least, she rationalized, the woman could come into the cathedral to stay out of the cold, and those in charge were willing to let her try and raise money in perhaps the only way she knew how.

After a light lunch, Susanna wandered by the docks. The sun had come out, and she walked under the old Spanish Arch, named to commemorate Galway's early connection with

Spanish traders, and down "The Long Walk." To her right were the waters of the quay, to her left a charming row of town houses, painted in subtle shades of pink, yellow, and green, as well as the traditional white. She sat on the concrete barrier and watched the gulls wheel overhead. Across the river near Nimmo's Pier, the swans congregated around people who were tossing them food.

She walked back, then across the bridge and down to the pier to better see the swans. There were dozens of them in earnest competition to grab the next bit of food from a bag of crackers an elderly man was tossing to them. A large flock of gray pigeons dogged his heels for the dropped crumbs. Susanna thought the swans looked less graceful than frenzied in their attempts to peck at the next bite as it hit the water, and she laughed at their clumsy greediness.

The old man looked up and smiled at her. "More like pigs than swans they be," he said, continuing to dole out the crackers. At last he was finished and called to them, "That's all, now be off with yez!" The show over, Susanna nodded a farewell to him and walked back toward the town.

After dinner she decided to stay for some music. She visited two pubs, both of which had been recommended by her friends in the states. However, she gave up after waiting nearly a half hour at The Quays.

Taaffes Pub was next, where she managed to get a seat at the bar and a glass of Smithwick's beer in only five minutes. The band played well, and if Susanna could not agree that the "craic was ninety," the highest praise for a pub, it was at least eighty-five. So, she was surprised when she overheard two older men who were making their way through the crowd to the door.

"Craic, me arse," said one to the other. "Had enough of the watered down."

"Aye," said the other, "let's get over to the Banshee then…" As he passed Susanna, he noticed the look of mild surprise on her face, and paused and grinned. "Join us, miss? Best music in town."

"No, thanks," she said.

"From the states?" he asked, divining her country from the

accent in two words, and she nodded. "Well, mebbe this'll be more your style then, but if you're lookin' for the real try the Banshee..." He nodded and joined his friend outside.

Susanna felt a slight flush suffuse her cheeks. The old rascal had been *flirting* with her. But what was this Banshee they were talking about? When the barman passed by, she said, "Excuse me, but is there a pub called the Banshee?"

"Yeh, if it's the *Lilting* Banshee you mean—just down the way on Guard Street. Wee place, though. You havin' another then?"

Susanna did have another. It was already too late to seek out another pub, and if the place was *wee*, as the barman said, it was probably packed this time of night. So, she had another glass and stayed until shortly after midnight. Then she walked back unafraid along the bayside to the guest house.

Susanna had trouble sleeping that night. She kept thinking about the next day, wondering if Michael Lynch would actually show up. It had been in the back of her mind ever since she landed at Shannon. Oddly enough, she felt like a girl on a blind date, and in the even more unenviable position of not knowing if the date was going to be there or not. But after all, it wasn't really her date to begin with. It was Julia's, long deferred.

She finally got to sleep by thinking that there were only two possible scenarios. The first was that Michael Lynch would not be there, in which case there would be no stress on her at all. She could simply walk away and forget about the whole thing, and Julia's secret would be safe. In the second scenario, Michael Lynch *would* come and, though it might be a bit uncomfortable at first, they could have a cup of tea together and she could explain what had happened to Julia, show Lynch the photographs that Julia had sent, give them to him if he wanted to keep them, and then walk away, having done what her sister had asked her to do.

Susanna awoke in the morning with butterflies in her stomach that her light breakfast did little to still. She tried to read a novel in the guest house's common room but couldn't concentrate, so at ten o'clock she put the small volume of Yeats into her handbag and set out on foot for town.

It seemed like forever until three o'clock, the hour when her sister and this legend named Michael Lynch had agreed to meet at the river, and Susanna tried to make the time pass quickly by walking into every shop she passed and browsing whether she was interested or not. Carefully examining every storefront, she made her way up one side of High Street and Shop Street and then turned and worked her way back down, guiltily aware of the book in her purse, as though it was something she had shoplifted, and was now growing larger in size, refusing to be ignored.

She finally came to the southwest end of Shop Street, where three other lanes split off from it. The center one was Guard Street, and she remembered the barman from the night before telling her that The Lilting Banshee was located there. Curious, she walked down the narrow street which, like the others in the shopping area, was closed to traffic, and quickly saw the pub on her right.

The ornate woodwork was painted a bright red with black trim, and seven partly frosted windowpanes, decorated with Celtic designs, spanned the center of the storefront. *The Lilting Banshee* was painted in a flowing script above the windows, with the name in smaller script in Gaelic on either side. Hanging above was a traditional sign with the pub's name beneath a humorously formal painting of a beautiful banshee playing a fiddle, her flowing white hair intertwined with musical notes flying upward from her bow. A smaller sign by the door stated:

Traditional Music Sessions
Bar Food Daily

Susanna went to the door and looked inside. It was far smaller than the pubs she had visited the night before, but that was part of its charm. It looked cozy and hospitable, and she decided to go inside and have a coffee and a toastie, one of those simple toasted sandwiches made of ham, cheese, tomato, and onion, or any combination thereof. Every pub in Ireland seemed to offer them.

She stepped through the door. A stairway ahead led down,

probably to the rest rooms, and she turned to the left into the pub. A bar seating ten was on her right, and assorted chairs, stools, and tables were to the left. A long, padded bench that could accommodate a half dozen people ran partway down the wall, and right against the window was a shorter bench. There were more small tables there with stools around them, and Susanna thought it a perfect place for the session players to set up shop. At the rear of the pub she could see more padded benches and spacious, polished wood tables.

On the walls were dozens of framed photographs of musicians, none of whom Susanna recognized. Along with the photos hung, for decorative reasons, she assumed, a bodhran and a fiddle and bow in a wood and glass case. Ornamental shelves in the corners held books, jugs, and knickknacks.

The pub was nearly full, but Susanna saw a little table in a corner and situated herself there, then went to the bar and ordered a coffee and a cheese toastie. A smiling young man behind the bar in a *Lilting Banshee* sweatshirt drew a cup of coffee from a Bewley machine and told her he'd bring her toastie when it was ready. She took the cup and saucer back to her corner, sipped it, and watched the people.

It wasn't the usual pub crowd, at least not the usual *tourist* pub. These folks were Irish through and through. In one corner were what looked like several university students, their heads bobbing up now and then from their textbooks for another sip from their black pints of Guinness. A thickly bearded, middle-aged man and his wife sat at the bar, chatting with an older man dressed in a crisp, clean suit and tie that had been out of fashion for years.

Near Susanna, at a narrow counter built against the wall, two men sat drinking, one in a hooded sweatshirt with holes at the elbows. His red beard touched with gray was neatly trimmed, but his equally fiery hair was as tousled as if he'd been through a gale. His slightly older companion had one of those lumpy, rough-hewn faces that looked as though it was made of pine knots.

The place had atmosphere galore, and Susanna had to wipe the grin off her face when the barman brought her toastie, lest he think she was laughing at the clientele. She was, but from joy, not from any sense of superiority or mockery. This was the best, the most *real* place she had been in since coming to Ireland, and she nearly forgot her nervousness about the forthcoming liaison with Michael Lynch. On top of everything else, the toastie was delicious, far from the edible afterthought it was considered in most pubs.

By the time she finished the sandwich and her second cup of coffee, it was two o'clock. Punctuality, particularly in social matters, did not seem to be of great concern in Ireland, and Susanna found it a great relief from the American insistence upon strict adherence to schedules, even in less than critical situations.

Still, the meeting near the bridge, if indeed there was to be a meeting and not merely a woman standing alone looking for a middle-aged Irishman, was something that she felt she should be early for. Considering the intervening thirty-one years, it would not be a surprise if Michael Lynch got the time wrong by an hour or so.

So, Susanna placed the money for the bill on the bar, along with a generous tip, and the barman smiled and nodded his thanks as she headed for the door. There she paused, for it had started to rain heavily, and reached into her deep handbag for the retractable umbrella she had brought just in case.

Suddenly she was jostled by someone rushing in from the pelting rain, and dropped the still closed umbrella and would have fallen herself had not a strong arm grabbed her beneath the elbow. "Sorry," said a deep voice, and she looked up into the sober, concerned face of a tall and lanky Irishman. "Are you okay?" he asked.

"Yes, fine, thanks."

He released her arm and handed her the fallen umbrella. "Might want to wait a bit...pretty wet out there."

"Oh..." She smiled. "I have to be going."

"Aye. Well." He nodded as if to signal an end to the conversation, then stood back to let her by. Susanna stepped into the doorway, opened the umbrella, and walked outside. She glanced back once to see the man standing watching her, his craggily handsome face made indistinct by the falling raindrops.

She knew it was foolish to wait in such weather for an hour—longer, really, as she planned to stay until after three just in case Michael Lynch was delayed. Still, she didn't want to chance missing him, and standing in the rain for a time seemed little enough that she could do for Julia.

Susanna walked to the corner and then down High Street until it changed to Quay, then turned right onto the walkway at the bridge. She passed few people in the streets. Rain meant little to the Irish, but this was a strong, cold, pelting downpour that pounded on her fragile umbrella like a soldier on a drum as she made her way to the second balcony overlooking the river. Below her the waters of the Corrib leapt frantically as the rain poured into it, rushing it along even faster.

Susanna huddled under her umbrella, the collar of her coat pulled up against the wind, as fat raindrops slapped down onto the flat top of the stone wall on either side of her. Michael Lynch, she thought, would have to be one of the great romantics of all time to come out in such weather for a three-decade old assignation. Either that or a duck.

She tried not to think about the time, but when she slipped back her sleeve, she saw that her watch read only two-twenty. Forty minutes more of standing in this monsoon, and then how much longer before she gave up? She would wait until four o'clock, she decided, and not a minute more. Surely the rain's ferocity couldn't continue for much longer. She sighed, wiped the water from her handbag before she opened it, and drew out the volume of Yeats, trying to keep it under the umbrella and safe from the rain, but still visible to any passersby, particularly gentlemen in their early fifties.

Twenty more minutes passed, and the rain fell less furiously, but by then everything below Susanna's shoulders was wet, thanks to the blowing wind. She found herself constantly turning away from it to keep the book dry, which she had succeeded so far in doing. As the time dragged closer to three, her sense of anticipation increased, though she could not imagine Michael Lynch actually showing up. Had it been a bright and sunny day, she could have believed more readily in the power of romance and the possibility that he would come, but on this altogether dreadful, cold, and soggy afternoon, she knew she was on nothing more than a fool's errand. At least it would soon be over, her obligation to Julia would be paid, and she could go back to the guest house and get a hot shower to restore the warmth to her flesh and muscles.

Then, along the path from the north, she heard some shouting, and turned to see four boys in parkas and jackets chasing another down the walkway. Twenty yards from her, one of them caught up with the fleeing boy, grabbed him by the arm, and flung him onto the wet and muddy grass. The other boys were soon on him as well, and Susanna was shocked to see one of them strike the boy on the ground across the face with a half-fist.

She looked quickly up and down the walkway but saw no one who could be of help, then jammed the book under her arm and trotted up the path to the boys. As she neared them, she saw to her dismay that they were older than she had hoped, perhaps in their late teens, and far too big for her to handle physically, though that was hardly her intention. Still, she walked right up to them and said, "Stop that and let him up, please."

The boy who had caught the other and was now straddling him looked up with hooded eyes, but when he saw only a woman standing alone, he sneered. "Go away, missus. Not your affair."

"It is," she said. "Very much so."

"You know him?" one of the others asked.

"No."

"Then what's your business?" asked the first boy.

"This," Susanna said, indicating all of them. "What did he do to you that you want to treat him this way?"

"Stole his girl," said one of the boys, indicating the one who had struck the boy on the ground.

"Stole her?" Susanna said. "How? Did he take her by force? Did he throw her into a car while your back was turned?"

The attacker straightened up slowly, like a cobra uncoiling and spreading its hood, and took a few steps toward Susanna. He glanced back at the boy on the muddy ground, as if ordering him not to move, and the boy looked up at Susanna hopefully.

Susanna braced herself in case the angry boy moved closer to her. "Like I said, what's your business?"

"You've made it my business by choosing to beat this boy in front of me. So, if I'm supposed to stand by and watch, I'd like to know what he's done to deserve it."

"You know. He took my girl."

"And I asked you if she went with him against her will. If it was her choice, then he didn't take her. And beating him won't make her want to come back to you. It does nothing—for you, for your friends here, for anyone."

"It makes me—"

"Feel better," she said, completing his sentence. "You may think that, but it won't. You'll feel worse, a *lot* worse, and so will your friends."

"You going to the Gardai then?" he asked, as though he had no fear of the police.

"No. And that's not what I meant. The Gardai won't have anything to do with the way you'll feel if you harm him further."

"That's just too damned bad then, because he's gettin' what's comin' to him." The angry boy's face shimmered with rainwater and the force of his emotions.

Susanna lowered her umbrella and walked past him. Her intention was merely to stand between victim and attacker, but the quick movement made her slip on the wet surface. Umbrella, purse, and book all flew from her hands, and she fell right over the recumbent boy, her arms on one side of him and her knees on the other, so that she bridged his body with her own. She heard a sharp "*Oof*" from him as she landed.

Oh shit…. It was a word she seldom used but often thought. As if the situation wasn't bad enough, now her legs and skirt were sodden with rain and mud. Her rescue had turned into slapstick, and she would look even *more* bedraggled should Michael Lynch actually appear.

But when she turned her head to look up at the boys, they weren't grinning. On the contrary, they seemed taken aback, and she realized that they thought she had thrown herself down on purpose, to protect the boy. Ah well, she quickly thought as the rain pattered onto her face, since she was already a shambles, she might as well try and save something out of it.

"All right then," she said to the angry boy. "If he gets what's coming to him, then it has to come to me, too."

"Christ almighty, missus!" said the boy standing above her, his fists clenched. "You don't even *know* him!"

"I don't know you either," Susanna said, "but I'd do the same for you."

The angry boy's body trembled, but she could see his resolve start to weaken. Two of his friends were looking sheepish, and the third, the tallest of them all, wore a more resolute look. "C'mon then," he said after a moment. "Too damn wet for this anyway." He put his hand on his friend's shoulder, but the angry boy shook it off and stalked off the way they had come. Two of the others followed him, not looking at Susanna, but the one who had spoken held out a hand and helped her to her feet.

"He's got a temper, missus," the tall boy said. "He'll get over it." He looked at the other boy and his face grew hard. "But *you* better stay the hell out of his way for a while." Then he leaned down, picked up Susanna's purse and the volume of Yeats, and handed them to her. "Your book got wet, missus," he said, then walked off in the direction of his friends.

The damp and frazzled victim pushed himself to his feet. "Thanks," he said. "You a friend of me ma or somethin'?"

Susanna smiled despite the rain and the way her legs were soaked to the skin. "You'd better do what he said," she suggested, "and stay out of their way for a while. When you can, make your peace with them, all right?"

"Yeh," he said, trying to brush the mud from his clothes. "I can't help she likes me more'n him. Thank you, missus. Sorry for all the trouble." He bowed his head quickly at her, and went hurrying off in the opposite direction from the other boys.

Susanna was still trembling, and not only from the cold rain. She had been afraid. The boy and his friends might very well have attacked both her and the other lad. There had been no secret indication that only she was able to read that they would back down, but it hadn't mattered. She had to do what she did. Thank God the *shoot if you must this old gray head* bit had worked. It was a fortuitous accident.

Susanna gave a shuddering sigh, picked up her umbrella and held it over her, though it seemed too little too late. She was soaked. She could feel her hair hanging in damp strands on her neck, and knew that its naturally glossy red had transformed into a dull rust. Her makeup too must have been nearly flooded away, and she suddenly remembered the reason she was there in the first place. In near panic, she looked at her watch and saw that the big hand was only a minute away from three o'clock.

"Hello," she heard a soft voice say, and whirled around, feeling like a drowning cat about to be pushed under for the last time. But instead of some stranger, she saw the man she had bumped into at The Lilting Banshee. He was holding a tweed cap in his hands and smiling at her strangely.

She was about to return his greeting with a self-conscious laugh acknowledging her appearance, but the man reached out and gently took the sodden volume of Yeats from her hand. A deeper, intense look replaced his smile. He handed back the book without opening it, looked into her eyes, and said, "*Was nearly blinded by her, for she fair outshone the sun.*"

Then he put a hand on her cheek and leaned toward her so that she closed her eyes and felt his rain-wet lips on hers, kissing her, and time seemed to slow and stop altogether, so that when he took his lips away and she opened her eyes, it might have been seconds, or a minute, or thirty years.

"Julia," he said, his face inches from hers, his warm hand still upon her cheek.

She said nothing, and then, her heart wanting it to be true, she said, "Yes," so softly that she wondered if he heard at all.

CHAPTER 5

Several weeks before Michael Lynch kissed Susanna Cassidy on the walk by the Wolfe Tone Bridge, he was having his first Christmas dinner at his mother's table without his wife Siobhan. Though those dinners had seldom been merry, this one was sadder than most.

The dinner was held in his mother Molly's dining room in her flat above the pub, and there were six at table instead of seven. Michael sat at one end with his grown son Gerald on his left. Siobhan had always sat on his right, but this year everyone had been moved down a seat so that his cousin Malachy now sat there, Malachy's mother Brigid beside him. Danny Clarke, their oldest barman and an orphan who had no family, sat next to Gerry, and Molly sat at the other end nearest the kitchen so that she could pop up and dart in and out, bringing the various dishes, having an occasional bite while seeing that all the platters remained filled and that the food on them was piping hot.

Siobhan had been dead for nearly a year, but her absence was still sorely felt. There is nothing, Michael thought, like annual family gatherings to truly mark the passing of its members. There had been the same feeling when Michael's stepfather, Tim Sullivan, had passed in the autumn of 1986. That was when Michael had ascended to the head of the table, and though all tried to be jolly, remembering that fine old man with humorous and affectionate stories, Michael had been deeply sad beneath his smiles.

The same sadness seemed to claim Gerry, who sat stiffly by his father's side, picking at his goose and stuffing. He had loved his mother deeply, far more than he had loved Michael, but that was only natural since Michael had not lived with the boy until he was ten. It had been Siobhan who been his sole parent.

"So, Malachy," Molly said, finally sitting down to a plateful of food, "how goes your work then? People still buying books, are they?"

"They are, Aunt Molly. Even with computers and the telly and everything else, folks still like to read, God be praised."

Michael thought the *God be praised* was a little much. He was familiar with Malachy's real work, and thought that his constant harping on books and things bookish while he was around his Aunt Molly was overdone, though she didn't seem to mind. He suspected as he always did that his mother knew far more than she let on.

"God knows," Malachy went on, "if it hadn't been for those books you sent Michael when the two of us were away, what would've become of me."

"Pretty exciting times those musta been," Danny interjected, but neither Michael nor Malachy rose to the bait. Malachy never talked of those years in front of Molly and hardly ever in front of others. Michael never spoke of them at all.

Aunt Brigid, however, was not as circumspect. "Those times were shite," she said, her mouth so full of food that her words were mercifully muffled.

"Brigid," Molly said quietly but pointedly.

"They were and it's the truth. Both lost our men to it, nearly lost our sons, too. Took an eye and crippled mine."

"Over and done," Molly said, her gaze on her plate.

"Not where *I* live -- *never* be done," Aunt Brigid said as she chewed.

"It's done in *this* house," Molly replied, in a tone that allowed no contradiction.

Aunt Brigid shook her head like a dog shaking a rat, but made no further reply. Though she saw her sister-in-law only twice a year, she knew better than to push Molly. Michael liked to think that he took after his mother in that way—quiet and gentle, but best not to be riled. Malachy took after his Ma as well, quick to flare up, quick to settle down again, but with Malachy and Aunt Brigid there was always the sense that they were holding back, that there was more they'd like to say or do.

Michael also sensed that Aunt Brigid had never forgiven his mother for remarrying, for not remaining Mrs. Patrick Lynch until her dying day, the way Aunt Brigid had remained Mrs. John Lynch. But only two years after her husband's killing in 1958, Molly had become Mrs. Timothy Sullivan. Aunt Brigid and Uncle John had not come to the small wedding, but a month later Tim, Molly, and Michael had visited them in Derry. Though they'd been standoffish at first, Tim's kind and self-deprecating manner brought Brigid around at last, though John had always kept his distance from the man who had crept into his brother Patrick's bed.

Still, they had stayed in touch like family does, and gathered together on the holy days of Easter and Christmas. Michael had continued to go to Derry for a few weeks every summer to spend time with Malachy, who was as close to a brother as he'd ever had, and Malachy had come down to Galway as well. All was fine until the Troubles began in earnest.

Still, there they were all those years later, gathered around the table as families did, not being very happy nor pretending to be, as families often did, too. "How's the teaching going then?" Michael asked Gerry, trying to change the focus from Aunt Brigid's audible and angry chewing. Gerry taught writing and English and Irish literature at St. Eunan's Boys' School in Galway.

Gerry shrugged. "Pretty well, I suppose."

"Boys behaving for ya?" Malachy asked.

"Best as they can," Gerry said.

"I don't know about these kids today," Malachy said. "When you and I were lads, Michael, we respected our teachers, our das and mas."

"Aye," Michael said, "'cause the Christian brothers would smack our arses if we didn't." Everyone laughed, and even Gerry smiled, and for a moment, Michael could almost pretend his family was a happy one.

After dinner was over, the plates were cleared away, and Molly and Aunt Brigid washed up in the kitchen. Gerry was having a chat with Danny, and Michael went out onto the small balcony built flush with the front of the three-story building that housed the pub and the two floors of apartments above. Malachy limped onto the balcony behind Michael, shut the door behind them and lit a cigarette. He exhaled thankfully, and the smoke mingled with the condensation of his breath in the cold air, becoming a single great cloud.

"Had to be hard," he said to Michael, who knew what he meant.

"Like having Banquo's ghost at the table," Michael said quietly.

Malachy nodded. "There's no need to feel guilty though, y'know."

"Aye, that's what Ma tells me all the time. But Gerry's never said it."

Malachy looked thoughtful for a moment. "Well, he loved his Ma."

"Implying that I didn't?"

"Didn't say that. *Never* said that, Michael, never will. Man's own business what he holds in his heart, nobody else's. We both know that better than most."

"Aye, we do."

"You didn't make her get in the car, y'know."

"No. But I could've stopped her and I didn't."

"Other people coulda stopped her, too, and they didn't."

"It wasn't their business—it was mine." Michael's mouth had started to taste of metal. He had to change the subject. "So how goes the book business?" he asked with a soft smile.

Malachy snorted. "How's it *ever* go? Hard. Always hard and gettin' harder."

"What's the problem?"

"Ah, y'know, the way things are now. People forget what it's really like. Like me ma said, never be done, nothing's changed. But people think it is, so they're not so generous as they were. Hard to make ends meet, keep things going." He cocked his head and eyed Michael. "Haven't gotten much help from a certain someone of late."

"Aye, make me feel guilty, it's not hard." Michael took a small envelope from his front pants pockets and held it open so

Malachy could see five hundred-Euro notes within, then closed it and handed it to his cousin. "My contribution. Wish it could be more, but I'm paying rent now."

"Aye, don't blame you—it'd be hard living here now, being that she was here and all. Nonetheless," Malachy said, smoothly pocketing the envelope, "any amount's appreciated. If y'ever want to contribute more than money, you'd be of great use to us all."

"Those days are over for me, I've told you before."

"Aye, but I thought maybe since you've no woman holdin' you here…"

"I've got me ma, and her apron strings are tight, boyo. Besides, I'm too old for all that."

"Hell, I'm older than you."

"Yeh, well, maybe I mean in my soul or somethin'."

"Goin' all poetical on me, Michael? Why the hell should your soul, such as it is, be any older than mine? You've had a family and good work runnin' a pub, a job any man'd give his *own* soul for, and what've I had?"

Michael grinned. "More women than any other ten men in Letterkenny, for one thing."

Malachy smiled back broadly. "Aye, 'tis a wonder the way they all come cooin' like pigeons when they see the old guerrilla hero with his war wounds, eh?"

"No denying you cut a fine figure with that limp and the eye patch," said Michael, "once the lasses know how you got them."

"Aye, like Parnell, or Michael Collins even."

"I don't think Parnell or Collins limped as such. Or had an eye patch."

"Well then, like *some* damned hero with a limp and an eye patch," Malachy laughed. "Ah, God knows I've shared myself with the women. But you, you great fool, you've ten times my looks—well, all right, five maybe—you coulda been a monster with the ladies and you never did."

Michael's smile faded to a thin line. "I was married, Malachy."

"Married, oh my yes," said Malachy, dropping his voice. "To

a girl with whom ye'd broken up, who you had the misfortune to get with child, and who you couldn't sleep with on your wedding night nor for ten years after."

"Still, she was my wife, she had my child, and she waited for me all that time."

"Hell, what else was she to do? Mess with somebody else while you're inside?"

"She could've easily enough. Galway wasn't Derry."

Malachy gave an exasperated snort, ground out his cigarette butt on a brick, and tossed it down into the street. "Did y'ever have a happy day with that woman? One single happy day?"

"Yes, I did," Michael lied. "Quite a few, in fact."

"Well, now you can have some other happy days with other women. Got your own fine place down on the quay with no Aunt Molly to hear the headboard bangin' against the wall."

"We'll see," said Michael, shaking his head.

"Ah, don't be so damned modest. I seen the way the ladies look at you. That pretty one with the long black hair playing the fiddle in the pub, what's 'er name? Caitlin?"

"Kate. Kate Quinn."

"Aye, that's the one. She spoken for?"

"Widow."

"Ho ho, there you go, lad, practically handed to you on a platter. Pretty widow sets her cap for you, hell, ask her over to see your etchings, y'know? She got kids?"

"Three, all grown up and gone."

"Hardly looks old enough for to have three grown kids."

"She's about forty-five or six."

"So much the better. You're not robbin' the cradle and people won't be lookin' at you sayin', 'Lookit that young woman with that old geezer—he must have it by the fistfuls.'"

"You bastard," Michael laughed, and hit Malachy gently on the arm.

That evening, after everyone else had gone home, Michael remained to have a quiet cup of tea with his mother. Even though Molly had been on the go the entire day, getting up before six to start the goose, she seemed happy and contented with the success of the dinner and the gathering. "T'was good to see Brigid and Malachy again," she said, easing herself into her chair on the one side of the lamp table, "even though she's sour as an old lemon."

"She wouldn't be Aunt Brigid if she wasn't," said Michael, who was sitting in his stepfather's old chair. Molly never sat in it, even though Tim had been gone for seventeen years, and she never minded others using it. Once Michael had asked her about it, and she had said that she just felt more comfortable in her own chair.

"It was different without Siobhan here, wasn't it?" Molly asked.

"Aye."

Neither spoke for nearly a minute, and Molly said, "Have you thought more about her things then?"

Michael nodded. "I'll go through them this week."

"I know it'll be hard for you, but it has to be done. And it's been nearly a year now. It's a shame to have all those clothes and things going to waste when they could be used. The St. Vincent's would be glad for them."

"What about the church?" Michael asked. "The jumble sale's in March."

Molly shook her head firmly. "I'll not be seeing her things sold to those that knew her. Besides, it'd make folks uneasy to buy them, remembering her wearing them and all."

"Aye, that's true, I suppose. All right, I'll do it this weekend. Clear everything out but the furniture." Michael smiled slyly. "So's you can let the rooms."

"Oh, you go along then!" Molly said, waving a hand at him. "You know I won't rent them. If I let them at all, it'd be to Danny or our Gerry, and I wouldn't charge them. After all, you might want to move back in someday, you get tired of your fancy town house."

Michael's rental of the house on The Long Walk had been a bone of contention between his mother and him. The row of pastel-painted houses on the quay were shown on nearly every tourist publication, were much in demand, and never for rent. But the previous July Michael had learned that one of the pub's patrons with whom he was friendly was leaving the country for two years and was willing to let his house for that period. Michael, tired of living in the rooms that were so redolent of his late wife's stolid spirit, made arrangements with his patron and moved in shortly after.

Molly had thought it foolish and spendthrift of him to take on extra expenses when he already had a fine flat above the pub (and directly above her own), but money was not the issue. Michael had a good deal banked, seldom having spent on his own pleasures. His stepfather, Tim, had been a saver, and had imbued Michael with the habit. Though his rent was steep, it made little more than a dent in the nest egg he had built over the years.

"D'you want any help?" Molly asked. "Goin' over her things, I mean, not paying your fancy rent."

"No, I can do it fine. But you watch now, you're starting to sound like Aunt Brigid."

"Then I'd best put on my sunny smile and ask my wee boy if he wants some cakes with his tea."

The next Saturday, Michael spent much of the morning helping Danny wash the pub's outer woodwork and sweep up the cigarette ends and other outside rubbish. Then the big blue Guinness truck came, and they brought the empty kegs up from the cellar and took the full ones down below through the metal trap that opened onto the sidewalk.

By ten-thirty the pub was ready to open. Danny was behind the bar and Finn was setting clean ashtrays on the tables. On the half hour, as she always did, Molly popped in to make sure all was well. "I thought you were going upstairs today," she said quietly to Michael.

He nodded, knowing there was no further reason to keep him in the pub.

"There are some paper boxes and plastic bags on the landing," his mother said. "You can put the things in there." She smiled at her son and patted his cheek, then turned quickly away to begin her usual procedure of running a finger over every area of the bar for dust or the remnants of dried spills that hadn't been properly cleaned up, and God help Danny and Finn if she found any.

Michael went through the door marked *Private*, and climbed the two flights of stairs, picking up the boxes and bags on his way. He had not been in the apartment for months, but when he opened the door it didn't smell stale or musty, and he assumed that his mother must have regularly aired it.

He thought he caught a trace of Siobhan's perfume, an overly sweet scent of which he had never been fond. One year for her birthday he had bought her a bottle of another, more subtle brand. Though she had thanked him, she never used it. Her rejection of his gift hadn't made him feel as bad as the thought that he might have insulted her by giving it to her in the first place. After a year, the still full bottle had disappeared from her dressing table. He had never found out what she had done with it.

Michael went to her bedroom first. The apartment had three of them. When he came back to Galway in 1983, he and Siobhan used the big one at the end of the hall, but when Gerry moved out to go to school, and there was no further need to pretend, Michael made the guest bedroom his own, leaving the double bed to Siobhan. The decision was made amicably, a natural result of her increasing comments about being awakened by his snoring. Michael knew the complaints were only an excuse. He had slept in the same cell as Malachy for ten years, and Malachy had always said that Michael slept quiet as a cat.

It was with relief that he had finally quit Siobhan's bed. Nothing physical had existed between them for years, and he doubted if anything had ever bound them emotionally beyond youthful lust in the guise of romance. Try as he would, he could recall nothing deeper. God and sad circumstance had thrown them together, given them a child, made them man and wife, and they had accepted it and lived by the rules.

That bedroom had always been devoid of love, and now it was devoid of life. Its four walls seemed to confine a barren desert, and Michael wished to spend as little time inside it as possible.

He started with the closet, taking the dresses, skirts, and blouses and placing them into the boxes, hangers and all. He filled two boxes and took them down a flight, bringing back more boxes when he returned. The shoes he dumped into the large plastic garbage bags, knotting them closed when they were full.

When the closet was empty, he went to work on the chest of drawers, putting blouses, t-shirts, jeans, and slacks into the boxes. The lingerie and stockings he put in a garbage bag to be discarded. As he continued almost automatically to place the used clothing into the boxes and bags, he became aware that he was crying. He didn't know why. It wasn't because he missed Siobhan. He had never missed her. Even during the ten years in Long Kesh, he had missed his freedom and a thousand things connected with it, but Siobhan had never been one of them.

He thought that it might be because of guilt, and he still did feel guilty, not only because of her death but her life as well, and he dropped the clothing he was holding and sat heavily on the floor, his back against their loveless bed. As he continued to cry, he realized that he was crying for both of them, for the way he had wasted Siobhan's life and for the way she had wasted his.

At last he stopped and sat for a while longer in silence, listening to the quietness inside the room and to the sounds of the world outside coming through the shaded window. Then he pressed the heels of his hands against his eyes, pushed away the tears, and continued to put the things that Siobhan had worn into the boxes and bags.

He went to the dressing table next, and put the bottles of perfume, lotions, and powder into the bag with the lingerie. The framed photos of Siobhan, both with him and with Gerry, he let sit on the glass surface. He would let his mother deal with those.

Michael opened the jewelry box and sighed when he saw the gold Claddagh ring that his mother had bought for him to give to Siobhan on their wedding day, since he could do no shopping of his own. Siobhan had glowed when he put it on her finger, the crowned heart, supported by a pair of hands, pointing toward her knuckles to indicate that her own heart was spoken for. She had never taken it off her finger and had been wearing it when she died. They removed it before she was buried, and Molly, he supposed, had put it into the jewelry box.

Michael shut the lid. This was something else that his mother could deal with.

The last repository was her bed table. There were a few dog-eared paperbacks and a Bible. The paperbacks he put in a bag with the recyclable clothes, the Bible he set beside the jewelry box. Then he opened the drawer. Inside it were a few embroidered linen handkerchiefs, a pair of reading glasses, and some tubes of prescription ointments. At the back was another book. He pulled it out, and memories came rushing back to him of the day he had given it to her, just after they had dated a few times, but before he had slept with her.

It was a small volume of poems by William Butler Yeats, and he smiled when he saw it. He had loved Yeats's poetry when he was going to college, had committed much of it to memory, and still read it occasionally. Siobhan had not been exposed to much poetry or literature, and he thought the gift might make her more appreciative of Ireland's cultural heritage.

Michael opened the book and saw the inscription he had written years before: *To Siobhan, with the hope that she will find magic here, Michael.* It was not particularly romantic, but he had never felt romantic toward Siobhan. He supposed he thought he had loved her at the beginning, but had quickly found it not to be true.

Then he remembered the other girl, the American, to whom he had given a copy of the book as well, a few months after he and Siobhan had broken up. Her name had been Julia Cassidy, she had been pretty and vivacious, and Michael thought that she had been in love with him. It had been a treat to have such an intense affair with an attractive American girl, and Michael still thought of her now and again.

He had started talking to her as a lark, nothing more, but the flirtatious way she had responded to him led him to invite her to a pub that night, and from then on things had just happened. Before he even realized it, a lover far more passionate than Siobhan had ever been had moved in with him.

Still, for all her education she didn't seem much brighter than Siobhan. Her knowledge of history was skeletal, and she seemed naïve about life in general. One thing she *had* seemed certain of was the way she felt about him. Julia had been so possessive that it almost scared him. When he left the flat for classes, she had clung to him, begging him not to go. It had been playful, but he sensed a more serious undercurrent beneath, and when he had to go North it had been a relief.

She would not be able to get in touch with him where he was going, and it could be a long time before he could contact anyone. So she had come up with that silly and desperate little idea of their meeting again in thirty years—no, it was thirty-*one*, wasn't it?—on the anniversary of the day they had first met.

Then Michael realized with a shock, Jesus, it *had* been thirty years, hadn't it? He'd left university and gone North in 1972, and 2003 was only a few days away. It was hard to believe all those years had passed. It certainly didn't seem that long ago, but by God it was. It would be thirty-one years in January since he'd met Julia Cassidy by the Corrib River.

Michael sat wearily on the bed, the years pulling him down. It seemed unfathomable that so much time had passed. He'd occasionally thought about that proposed meeting with his old lover, but always as something far in the future. Now here it was, right around the corner. And no mistake, it *was* around the corner, just down the street.

When he had thought about that meeting with Julia, he always dismissed it, never imagining that she would show up. And if she did, there would be nothing romantic about it. He was married and had a grown son, and had run a pub for the past seventeen years, and she would tell him that *she* was married and had a raft of kids, and wasn't it funny that they both showed up, even though nothing could come of it? And they'd maybe have a cup of tea, or maybe she'd introduce him to her husband, if he came along on her cute little romantic odyssey, and Michael would be uncomfortable, and say goodbye when tea was over, and never see the silly woman again.

But with Siobhan's death, things were different. Julia might see a widower as a suitor with designs on breaking up her marriage, when nothing was further from the truth. The last thing he wanted, now that he was single again, was to reestablish an old romance that had wisely ended long before.

God, what the hell was he even imagining all this for? Surely, she'd forgotten that foolish promise by now. If he went to the river at the time they had said, he would be the only one to keep the appointment.

Still, he could not help but be curious. She had felt deeply toward him, and the idea of her returning to the riverside tugged at his ego. Maybe, just maybe he would go down on that day and watch from the bridge to see if a middle-aged woman showed up. If she did, well, he could decide what to do about it when—and if—he saw her. But what would be the time and the day?

Thirty-one years from the day they had met, at the *time* they had met. He remembered that much anyway. If he went backward from Bloody Sunday, he ought to be able to figure it out. Bloody Sunday had been January 30th, a date he would never forget, and he had met her the Sunday before, mid to late afternoon, as he recalled. That would be January 23rd then.

There was no calendar in the room. He decided to finish his work, so he put the little volume of Yeats on top of the Bible and left it there, then carried all the bags and boxes down to his mother's flat. She had offered to wash and fold all the clothing before he took them to St. Vincent de Paul. The items for discard he put in the cellar near the other trash.

When he checked a calendar, he saw that the 23rd of January fell on a Thursday. That would be no problem, since he could adjust his hours at the pub to suit his schedule. All right then, he would go, say at two-thirty or three o'clock, station himself across the bridge and stay there for an hour or so just to make sure. He felt like a daft eejit thinking about it, but he knew he would do it, out of curiosity if nothing else.

The new year came, and the following week he took Siobhan's washed and pressed clothes and other possessions to the Society of St. Vincent de Paul. The volunteers there were happy for them, and he left with assorted blessings on his head. Despite the workers' good wishes, he felt as though he had betrayed Siobhan by discarding her things.

Michael saw Gerry twice during the weeks after Christmas. On New Year's Day, they went to Molly's for dinner, and a week later he met Gerry at their old flat and offered him any of his mother's jewelry that he cared to claim, "maybe for your wife someday. I'm sure she'd want her...her daughter-in-law to have something that was hers."

Gerry picked up the Claddagh ring. "Would this be okay, then?" he asked his father.

"Of course," Michael said. "That's only right."

"What'll you do with the rest?" Gerry asked, looking at the assortment of inexpensive costume jewelry accented by a few better pieces that Molly had handed down to Siobhan over the years.

"Why don't you take them all?" Michael said. "That way, you get married someday, your wife can have what she likes."

Gerry nodded. "Right, thanks," he said, and closed the lid. Michael thought he saw tears forming in his son's eyes, and looked away. "That's it then," he said, and stood up. "I'd best get back downstairs."

As the 23rd drew nearer, he started to think more and more about Julia Cassidy, and was surprised to find himself wondering what she would look like. Years changed people, that was certain. Michael had put on a few pounds in thirty years, but little of it around his belly, since he had never been much of an imbiber of what he sold. A pint a night was enough for him, with tea before, and maybe a diet soda afterwards.

He thought he would recognize Julia. Her features had been slightly sharp, but in a way he had found attractive. Her cheeks, however, had been round, with the promise of weight gain should she be immoderate in her diet. He'd seen plenty rosy-cheeked girls of his youth grow in girth as years advanced and their children came.

But so what if she had gotten round? It wasn't like they were going to resume where they had left off. If she showed up at all, their reunion would be brief and friendly, nothing more.

Still, when the morning of the 23rd arrived, he was nervous enough to keep telling himself that she wouldn't be there at all, and afterwards he could tuck her once more in the back of his mind where she had resided before. Though he went to the pub in the morning, he took the afternoon off, and went back to his house to wash up, shave, and grab a spot of lunch. He decided not to add a slice of onion to his sandwich.

He dressed neatly, in a shirt, sweater, dark wool pants, and short brown leather jacket, topping it off with a tweed cap and an umbrella to keep off the rain. Then he walked down the quay and over to the pub, just to check on things before he went to the bridge. His mind was a thousand miles away when he went through the door, and he clumsily bumped into a woman who was leaving, knocking over her umbrella. She looked slightly familiar, and in their brief exchange he could tell by her accent that she was American.

For a moment, as he watched her walk away through the rain, he wondered if she could be Julia Cassidy. She had had the same kind of features, and when he wished he'd thought to look and see if she was wearing a wedding ring, he realized how foolish he was. There were hundreds of American tourists in Galway at any one time. Besides, this one looked a bit young. Still, if it *had* been her, he would not have been disappointed.

"Michael!" He heard his name called from inside the bar and looked around to see Kevin, a young barman who had been working for him only a few weeks. There was panic on his face, and impatience on the faces of those at the bar.

"What's wrong?" Michael asked.

"No Guinness, that's what," Liam Ivers, one of the regulars, replied. "The well's run dry and the pump don't work."

Kevin demonstrated by pulling the Guinness tap, and Michael saw to his dismay that nothing was happening. "So, what's wrong with the other one?" he asked.

"Empty," Kevin said. "There was only a wee bit left and that ran out a while back. Couldn't put the new keg in on me own."

"Aw Jesus, well, let's put it in then and I'll look at that tap."

"And make it fast," Liam said. "I'm expirin' of the thirst."

"And would it kill you to drink Smithwick's for once?" Michael asked with a smile. "Or help a barman change a keg, if you're so damned thirsty?"

"God, man," Liam replied. "I'm looking to patronize the brewing trade, not seek out a career in it."

Michael and Kevin got the old keg out and the new one in

place, and then Michael took off the tap and found the problem. By the time he fixed it and got it reattached, to much applause from those at the bar, it was 2:45.

"All right then, Kev," he said, putting on his coat, "see if you can't keep these good people well lubricated until I return."

Michael left the pub, tugged on his cap, put up his umbrella, and walked to the Wolfe Tone Bridge and across it to the other side. He went a bit further down the street and stopped. From where he stood, he had a view of the walkway on the other side of the river, but anyone looking in his direction would see only an umbrella, as though someone was waiting for a bus.

He looked across the river to the walkway and saw a woman standing under an umbrella, the same woman, he was surprised to see, who he had bumped into in the pub. Could it, he wondered, be Julia after all? She was holding something tight against her, and he struggled to make out what the small object might be.

When he realized what it was, he felt a mixture of relief, shock and apprehension. He had forgotten until now that Julia had said she would be carrying the volume of Yeats he had given her. Although he could not see the title, the book was the same size and color as the one he had found in Siobhan's night table drawer a few weeks before. There was no doubt in his mind. It was Julia. That was why she had seemed so familiar when he had first seen her at the pub.

For the past few weeks, he had been living with the possibility of her showing up, but now that she was there, he didn't know what to do. Julia had been as shallow in her way as Siobhan, living out a romantic dream, but knowing nothing about the reality of relationships, what it meant to be truly attached to another person. Maybe the years had changed her, but—

Michael's thoughts were interrupted by the sight of a gang of boys coming down the walkway. He couldn't hear what they were saying, but could see what they were up to. He had expected the woman he thought was Julia to walk away from the trouble, but she surprised him by walking into it. Michael knew how boys could be, so he started slowly back across the bridge, keeping an eye on the situation. He was big enough to handle them all if he had to, though if they were good fighters it might be dodgy.

The woman talked to them, and one of the boys seemed very angry, and then to Michael's amazement she dropped her things and got down on the ground as if to protect the boy lying there. Michael, nearly across the bridge by now, stopped walking and watched as the boy wavered, then backed down and walked away, his mates joining him, and the woman and the other boy got to their feet and parted. Though he hadn't heard a word, Michael could guess what had transpired, and thought he had seldom seen such a brave and selfless act. If this was Julia Cassidy, she had by God changed, and for the better.

This was a woman that he would be proud to meet again, a woman that a man could love with little effort.

As he walked toward her, old words came to him from long before, the words of the song that he had written for her, and he heard himself speaking those words aloud. Then, before he was even aware of it, he was kissing her, and the reality was far better than memory, or any dreamt-of expectation. For the first time in many years, Michael Lynch felt young.

CHAPTER 6

As she looked up at Michael Lynch, the rain now dropping onto both their faces, Susanna Cassidy laughed a little, in joy and embarrassment, and Michael lifted his umbrella and held it over both of them. "Sorry for that," he said, his cheeks reddening. "Guess I got, uh, carried away by the moment."

Susanna hardly knew what to say. *Carried away* scarcely described the feeling she had. It was as though she had been *swept* away by a torrent, or whisked into the air so that solid ground was no longer beneath her feet. And this man, this Michael Lynch, looked as though he had been equally stricken. His eyes were filled with wonder and delight, and the same confusion that she now felt that such a thing could be.

"It's been...a long time," Michael said.

"Oh, not that long," she said, laughing again. "Just about an hour ago—when we bumped into each other!"

To her relief he laughed, too. She didn't know what else to say. She knew that she should tell him immediately who she was, but she couldn't. She *wanted* to be Julia, *wanted* to have been this man's lover and be meeting him again after years of separation. Susanna had become part of an illusion she could not bear to break. If she told him the truth now, it would put an immediate gap between them that might never be bridged. It would ruin the moment.

For her entire life, Susanna had thought about the future, considering how what she did in the present would impact upon it. But now, for the first time, she wanted the *moment*. The moment was enough, and if her unspoken impersonation of Julia had consequences down the road, well, she would deal with them later.

"So," she said, brushing a hand through her wet hair, "what have *you* been up to?"

Michael laughed again. "A fair amount in thirty-odd years. But look at you, you're soaked through. We ought to get you dried out."

Susanna realized that she must look a fright. Her hair was sodden, her clothes were damp, and she was glad that she never wore heavy makeup, or her eyes would have looked like a raccoon's.

"The price you pay for being a good Samaritan, eh?" Michael said.

"You saw that?"

"I did. A brave thing it was you did. Thought I might have to come wading into those lads, but from what I saw you handled them better than their mas would've."

Susanna felt embarrassed. "At the expense of my appearance, I'm afraid." She shivered involuntarily, and Michael juggled the umbrella and took off his jacket.

"Here," he said, clumsily slipping it around her shoulders with one hand. "You must be freezing, wet as you are."

"Thanks. You know, maybe I should go back to my rooms and dry off and change, and we can meet later."

"Do you have plans for dinner?"

"No."

"Well then, let me take you out for a good Irish meal, and we can have a fine long talk. Would that be all right?"

"Why...yes, sure."

"So where are you staying?"

"Over in Salthill."

"Did you drive from there?"

"No, I walked."

"Well, you'll not be walking back in that state, you'll catch your death. My car's just a couple blocks away, I'll drive you over. And that way I can see where to pick you up tonight. All right?"

Of course, it was all right. Anything he had suggested would have been all right. He had what struck Susanna as a dark velvet and whiskey voice, deep and mellow. With the soft, broad Irish accent on top of it, it was irresistible.

They walked southeast along the quay, huddled under his large umbrella, her arm through his. She was holding the damp book and her own umbrella in her free hand, her purse over her shoulder. His car was parked in front of the row of townhouses on The Long Walk, a tiny English Ford that was such a pleasant contrast, she thought, to the huge SUVs that filled the roads of her own country.

"How do you get such a good parking place?" she asked him when they were both inside the car.

He tapped a sticker on his windshield. "Resident."

"Of the town?"

"No, that's my house," he said, pointing ahead. "The yellow one."

She gave a breathy laugh of disbelief. "My God, you live in a tourist brochure!"

"Just for another year and a half. Renting it from a mate who owns it."

He started the car and pulled away. He hadn't invited her inside to dry out there, and Susanna didn't know if she was relieved or disappointed. She thought about the romantic cliché of a woman wrapped up all snug and warm in the man's thick bathrobe while her damp clothes dried by the fire, and felt a tinge of regret.

"So how long since you've been in Galway?"

"A few years," she said. They made small talk on the way to Salthill, and Michael pointed out several changes en route that might have occurred since Susanna had last been there. At the guest house, he got out of the car and opened her door for her, and asked if seven o'clock would be all right for dinner. She said it would, they said goodbye, he got back in his car, and she walked toward the stairway to her rooms.

Halfway up the stairs, she turned and looked back down to see him still sitting in the car, looking up after her. He smiled and waved with a little embarrassment, Susanna thought, at having been caught watching her. She waved back and he drove off. She watched his car vanish around a corner and stood on the stairs a bit longer, as though she could still hear the soft hum of his car engine.

"I am an *idiot*," she said aloud, and then grinned.

It was not until she was under the hot water of the shower that she started having misgivings. She hadn't been honest with Michael Lynch. He had thought she was Julia, and she hadn't corrected his misapprehension.

It was an easy mistake to make. The sisters had resembled each other when they were young, though the years had changed Julia more, rounding her features. Still, if Michael Lynch had been ready to see a thirty-years-older version of Julia, thinking Susanna was she would not have been too far a stretch. Apparently, it hadn't been.

But what to do now was the question. She knew that when she saw him again, she should tell him the truth right away, despite the risk to whatever relationship was developing, or *re*developing, from his point of view. The problem was that she didn't want to. She *wanted* to be who he thought she was. She wanted to have had that intimacy with him, to already be past that point in a relationship, to be able to meet with him and touch his hand and have it seem as though the years had simply rolled back, that the emotions were the same, if now subdued and mellowed.

Besides, the odds were that no harm would be done, and that he would never find out she was not Julia Cassidy. They would have dinner together, at which point she'd probably learn about his happy marriage and his seven children, even though she'd seen no wedding ring on his hand. Ah well, there were many men who didn't like wearing them, and maybe he had taken it off before meeting his old flame.

As she toweled herself dry, however, an unpleasant thought came to her. Was she betraying Julia? She had promised to meet Michael, should he come, and to show him the pictures of Julia and her home and family. That was all. She had not promised not to be attracted to him.

In a way, she couldn't help but think that Julia might approve of what she was doing. To carry out the charade, to have Michael Lynch think her still attractive and desirable, to have him go back to his portly wife and noisy children knowing that Julia Cassidy was still out there, footloose and fancy-free—wasn't there a certain poetic justice in all that?

Or, she thought sourly, was she just trying to rationalize her attempt to steal Julia's old boyfriend the way Julia had stolen David years before?

She shook the thought from her head. She had forgiven Julia for that long ago. No, Susanna felt that Julia would have told her to go for it, or at least to enjoy herself playing a part for an evening.

Though she was scarcely able to admit it, Susanna knew that she felt more toward Michael Lynch than merely mild interest and curiosity. She knew all too well that she was falling, falling into a webwork of falsehood, and into something possibly much deeper.

As he drove back to his house, Michael Lynch couldn't stop smiling. It was, he thought, a combination of miracles that had brought Julia and him back together after all these years. First was the miracle that she showed up at all, next was the miracle of his finding Siobhan's copy of Yeats in time to remind *him* to be there, and finally was the miracle of Julia herself. The lovely but bubble-headed schoolgirl had become an amazing woman, capable of facing up to and backing down a gang of young toughs that he himself might have thought twice about confronting.

There was also the fact that she was a damned handsome woman. The years had improved her looks if anything. She had, Michael recalled, been very pretty, but now she was beautiful. A perfectionist might have found her features less than ideal, but her face seemed to reflect a radiant soul within. Even with her hair pressed flat to her head and the artificialities of makeup washed away by the rain, Michael still could have kissed her over and over.

He reminded himself to keep his emotions in check. After all, he knew next to nothing about her, and it was easy to get carried away by a moment, and by the sheer romance of meeting her again after a lifetime. Two lifetimes, really. He had lived thirty-one years without her, and she had done the same without him. That length of time meant histories, paths chosen and discarded, ways that had become set, opinions and preferences formed, choices made, for good or ill, that might not easily be unmade to please another.

After all, except for the little he had learned that afternoon, he knew nothing of who she truly was, and she knew no more of him. It was best not to even think about…what, falling in love?

He pushed back his heart and made himself laugh at the thought, then considered where he might take Julia Cassidy for dinner. He said her name aloud, and the sound of it made him realize that he didn't even know if she *was* Julia Cassidy any more. She might be Julia Smith or Jones or something else. True, he hadn't seen a wedding ring on her left hand when he was able to look without her noticing, but she might have removed it for his benefit, or she might be divorced. Americans were so much more casual about marriage than Irish Catholics.

Well, he would learn what he could. The past couldn't be changed, he knew that all too well. *His* past was a living part of him. What had happened to his father in Derry when Michael was a child, and what happened to Michael as a result, had formed him, made him the man he was. His past and the past of his country had created in him the hatreds and the duties he felt now and would feel to the grave. No woman would change that.

Though choosing what to wear had taken Susanna some time, she was dressed when she started looking out the window at a quarter of seven. Michael Lynch would not catch her off guard again. Looking like a drowned rat once was quite enough.

She had decided on a plum-colored knit cotton dress that hugged her figure nicely while not making her look too hippy. As she peered into the full-length mirror on the back of the closet door, she wished her hips were just a little bit smaller and her chest a tad bigger, but all in all she liked what she saw. The dress fit snugly, and the short length showed off her legs to full advantage, but the neckline was high enough to balance out any perceived immodesty elsewhere. A pair of simple gold earrings and a thin gold chain finished the ensemble.

Michael's car pulled up at two minutes before seven. Though it seemed to have stopped raining at last, Susanna slipped on her raincoat and went down the stairs to meet him.

He looked good to her. His full head of reddish-brown hair, gone gray at the temples, was styled casually but neatly, and the glow of his cheeks showed that he was freshly-shaven. Beneath his leather jacket he was wearing a blue button-down shirt and a subtly figured necktie for a touch of formality. In the car she caught a hint of aftershave, something clean and slightly woody.

They drove back toward the city center, and Michael parked the car on a side street. "Have to walk a few blocks," he said. "Galway's a grand town for walkers, but not so good for motorists."

They strolled to the restaurant through the Galway streets, old buildings rising on either side. Buskers began to appear. A young man sang and played Bob Dylan songs on his guitar, and nodded when Michael smiled at him. Further along, an older man played traditional tunes on an accordion and called, "Thank ye, Mr. Lynch," when Michael tossed a Euro coin into his open case.

"You know him," Susanna observed.

"Aye, that's Gordon. Just about everybody who plays music in this town knows everybody else."

"You play?"

"Guitar. And sing a bit. Nothing to make Bono jealous."

They both laughed. "Lynch is a pretty famous name in this town, though, isn't it?" Susanna asked. "In fact, your castle's just up the street."

Michael grinned. Lynch's Castle, which now housed a bank, was a city tower-house possibly five hundred years old. "So it seems. The Lynches were mayors of Galway for a long time. Do you know that tragic tale of James Lynch Fitzstephen?"

"Wasn't he the one who hanged his own son?" Susanna asked.

"That's him. Story goes that his boy Walter killed a Spaniard Lynch had sworn to protect, and as mayor Lynch then had to condemn his own son. Thing is, nobody knows if there's a drop of truth to it. Seems to have all been made up by a writer who wanted to stick a good story in his history. Then it became a leg-end, and now people take it for granted." Michael smiled wryly and shook his head. "Awful silly, when you think of all the *real* history we've got in Ireland, much better stories than that one. Ah, here we are then..."

The restaurant was on a corner, and its high windows gleamed in the night. They climbed a few steps and went inside. "Good evening, Mr. Lynch," said an elderly woman behind the counter. "Your regular table?" She nodded at Susanna and gave her an appraising smile.

"Maybe by a window tonight, Mary. Miss Cassidy might want to gaze upon our lovely town."

"Window it is then," said the woman, leading them to a cozy table that looked out onto the street.

"Do they know you everywhere?" Susanna asked when they were seated and Mary had left them with the menus.

"No, I just eat here often. You don't think I'd take you to dinner at some place I didn't know, do you? To take a risk like that..." Michael clucked and shook his head, and Susanna gig-gled, delighted at his dry sense of humor. She felt comfortable with him, in spite of her masquerade.

They ordered drinks, a Jameson's on the rocks for him, an Irish Mist for her ("Have to keep it local, after all," Michael said), and then looked over the menu, both deciding on a fish chowder to start. Susanna chose smoked salmon for an entrée, and Michael ordered lamb cutlets.

When their drinks arrived, they clicked them together in a toast. "To old friends," Michael said.

"To old friends," she echoed.

"So, first things first then. What have *you* been up to for the past thirty-odd?" Michael asked. "Husband? Family? I saw you weren't wearing a ring, so I called you Miss Cassidy just now with Mary, but wasn't sure. I figured she'd be less shocked than if I introduced you as *Mrs.* Somebody-or-other."

"No, I'm Miss Cassidy all right. Never got married."

"No? That surprises me. You seemed, I don't know, ready to settle down when we were together. I thought you'd forget me quick enough and find somebody else back in America. I actually didn't worry too much about you."

"You didn't think that..." Susanna hesitated, not quite daring to cross the line and say that she was Julia. "...that young Miss Cassidy had lost her heart to a handsome young Irishman?"

"Truth to tell, no. I thought that maybe you *imagined* you'd lost your heart, but that once I was out of sight, I'd be out of mind, too. You seemed a bit...well, as though you were living a romance story and were caught up in it. But I figured you'd just as quick say to yourself, well now, that's over, back to real life—hmm, *there's* a good-looking lad..."

"Then you must have been very surprised when you saw someone holding a copy of Yeats on the walkway this afternoon."

"That I was, for sure. I was even more surprised by what I saw that someone do. You were very brave to rescue that lad the way you did."

Susanna closed her eyes and waved her hand, as though brushing away the compliment, but kept the secret of her accidental fall to herself. "Oh no, it's...that's what I *do*, kind of."

"What, you're a boxing referee then?"

They both laughed. "No, I teach peace studies at an American university."

"Ah, peace studies. That explains then why you didn't punch those lads, eh?"

"Exactly. I use my super-human powers only when all diplomatic methods break down."

Michael laughed again. My God, but it felt good to be sitting with a woman and feeling happy. He hadn't done it in ever so long. There had seldom been anything remotely funny about Siobhan. They hadn't laughed together since before they were married. Kate Quinn had been the only woman he'd been slightly close to since Siobhan's death, and though she had a wicked wit, Michael always felt on the defensive, as though she was trying to get him to say or do something he didn't want to, and catch him out on it.

With this dear woman, however, this lovely Julia Cassidy, there was no effort required. He joked with her as he joked with his few mates or his cousin Malachy. And this was even more fun, for he didn't get the feeling that she was trying to do him one better. She seemed so happy to be with him that she'd laugh at anything he said the least bit witty and mean it, and her reply would also show that humor and...what else? Affection?

Yes. He felt affection for her, and sensed the same *from* her.

"So then," Michael said, "what is it that you teach exactly? I mean, what subjects are in peace studies? Besides beating swords into ploughshares, of course."

"And advanced ploughshare maintenance," Susanna said. "Most of the courses I teach are in sociology. For example..." She leaned toward him. "Last semester I taught a course on mediation and two others on ethnic conflict—one for under-grads and a graduate seminar on Northern Ireland. That's the area that really sparks my interest, and it's why I get over here as much as I do. In fact, I'm on a sabbatical now. I'll be here for a few more months doing some interviews, and giving some university lectures..."

Susanna trailed off when she saw Michael's face. His expression of good humor had suddenly turned grave, and she wondered if it was because she said she would be in Ireland indefinitely. Did the prospect make him uncomfortable? Had he expected this dinner to be their sole meeting? She had thought she recognized more than mere interest in his demeanor, but perhaps she had been wrong.

The silence sat heavily between them for a moment, and then he said, "The North. The Troubles. That's your...field of study?"

"Yes, it is," she replied slowly, realizing that it was not her, but the mention of the North that had sobered him. She said no more, knowing that he would have to lead the conversation, and, after another uncomfortable pause, he did.

"What is it that you find so...*interesting* about it then?"

Julia had told Susanna that Michael had gone to the North after Bloody Sunday, so she knew he had strong opinions on the subject of Northern Ireland. She also knew that she had to choose her words carefully.

"The whole process of the search for peace there, I suppose," she said. "You've got an historical rift that's hundreds of years old, between Catholic and Protestant, Republican and Loyalist. There's a history of violence that continues to the present day, but still you have people on both sides who believe that peace can be reached. And slowly the situation's improved."

"It has, eh?"

"Yes, I believe it has. The signing of the Good Friday Agreement in 1998 was a huge step forward. I realize there've been difficulties since, as well as violence, but major change doesn't occur overnight."

"And you think the violence will eventually stop?"

"I hope it will. But there are bound to be extremists who resort to violence for a long time to come. Every country has them. Europe, certainly the Middle East..."

"And America."

"Yes." Her lips tightened. "And our extremists have easier access to guns, unfortunately."

The arrival of the soup interrupted the conversation. When the waiter walked away, Michael gave a small chuckle. "Well, we've gotten a wee bit serious, haven't we?"

She smiled apologetically. "It's a serious subject."

"Aye," he said, "and a little close to home. I was a lad in the North. Spent my first eight years there."

"I know you had relatives there. Wasn't that why you...left Galway?" He nodded, but said no more, only sipped his chowder, so she decided to change the subject. "So, what is it you do now?"

"I run a pub. Been there for almost twenty years."

"The one I saw you in?"

"Aye, The Lilting Banshee. That's mine."

"Oh, that's a *charming* pub. I loved just being there."

Michael beamed at the compliment. "Well, it's the real thing. Much the same as it was when I started there. I own it with my mother. It was my stepfather's and his da's before him, and his before him. So old that the people of the Claddagh would come in for a pint when they could afford it, after a good haul of fish. The town's changed a good deal, but the Banshee's stayed the same."

"Where did the name come from?" Susanna asked.

"'The Lilting Banshee' is a tune. Tim's grandfather—Timothy Sullivan, that's my late stepda—named his pub after it. Almost changed it a few times when the more superstitious wouldn't come in a pub named after the banshee, but he stuck to his guns, and it's worked out fine."

"So, your stepfather's passed on?"

"Back in 1986. He was older than my ma. He left her the pub, and she and I managed the place. Wasn't long before she made me a co-owner."

"So, she helps to run it?"

Michael smiled and shook his head in mock frustration. "Does she ever. Old enough to be retired twice over, but she's there every morning and evening. Lives over the place, does a lot of the bar cooking, though we don't offer much. We're a pub, not a restaurant."

"Well, I thought my toastie at lunch was delicious."

He laughed. "I'll pass along the compliment. But then why don't you tell her yourself? Maybe tomorrow night?"

"I'd like that. Do you have any brothers or sisters?"

"An only child, alas, a great rarity in a Roman Catholic country. How about yourself? Any more at home like you, as the saying goes?"

The moment of truth, Susanna thought, had come round at last. Or was it the moment of falsehood? "A sister," she said, and reached into her purse for Julia's pictures. "She passed away just a short time ago. Here are some pictures. The first one's her with her husband and her daughter."

Michael took the photos and looked at the top one. "God, you could have been twins. You weren't, were you?"

"No. She was a few years...younger than I."

"What was her name?"

Susanna paused. She couldn't see down the road, but she didn't care. She'd come this far without incident, and was still very much in the moment. If she had to pay later, she would. But for now, it was too wonderful being Julia Cassidy to change a thing.

"Susanna," she said. "Her married name was Oliver."

Michael continued to look through the photos of the Oliver family, their house, their boat, their pool and greenhouse and SUV. "She looks very happy," he said. "What happened to her?"

"Cancer."

He shook his head. "Sorry," he said, handing back the photos. "It's always hard losing family."

"It is. She was a kind and friendly woman."

"What did she do, she and her husband? They looked fairly well off."

"David is in real estate, and…and my sister did a lot of volunteer work. But what about your family? A mother and no siblings, but what about…"

"A wife?" he finished for her. "Yes." Her heart stopped, and she hoped it didn't show on her face. "She died about a year ago. Traffic accident."

For a split second the news made her feel relieved, until guilt immediately took its place. "I'm so sorry," she said.

He nodded his thanks. "We had…*have* a son. Gerry. He's a teacher at St. Eunan's. That's a boy's school here. Teaches writing and does some on his own. Had a few things published."

"You must be proud of him."

"I suppose. He's a good lad. Ah, but here's our dinner then…"

The meal was delicious, the smoked salmon pink and tender, served with an artfully prepared assortment of greens. Through the end of the meal, Susanna steered the conversation away from family matters, and Michael seemed anxious to follow her lead. Over coffee, they talked about films and books, and the difference between Irish and American television. She was surprised to find that Michael was extremely well-read, more in non-fiction than fiction.

She was also surprised to find that it was nearly ten o'clock by the time they were ready to leave. Michael asked her if she'd like to go anywhere else, but sustaining the illusion of being Julia had been psychologically wearing, especially the overt lie she had told when she had given her late sister's name. "I think I'm still a little jet-lagged," she told Michael, and he nodded understandingly.

"So, do you have plans for tomorrow?" he asked her, and she felt a simultaneous pang of fear and thrill of delight shoot through her.

"Not really. I wasn't planning to actually start my work for another week or so."

"Well then, how about letting me show you some more of Galway?"

"Oh, well, what about the pub?"

"Sure, we can go there if you like."

"No, I meant...don't you have to work?"

She saw his expression droop. "Not really, but if you'd rather not..."

"No, no!" she said quickly and smiled. "I'd *love* to have a tour guide! I just didn't want to mess up your schedule."

"No fear of that. What's the point of being the boss if you can't come and go as you like?"

When he picked up the check, Susanna opened her purse and asked him to please let her pay, but Michael shook his head. "I invited you. You're my guest."

"Well then, you'll have to let me reciprocate."

"Perhaps tomorrow for dinner then, after our day of touring."

As they started back to the car, he offered his arm, and she slipped her own through his, walking together so that their bodies touched. The night was cold, and she huddled into his warmth, loving the scent of him, the way he felt against her. The side street where the car was parked was empty of people, and when they went around to the passenger side, he paused before he opened her door, and turned her gently toward him.

He touched her face with his hand, then leaned down and kissed her. She did not pull away, but closed her eyes and let the kiss happen. His slightly parted lips were warm and soft and dry, and moved gently against her own. Susanna could scarcely breathe, and felt her heart starting to race, purely from the contact of their lips.

Michael slowly withdrew his face from hers, keeping his hand on her cheek, and as she opened her eyes, she saw his opening, too. He smiled at her. "I didn't get carried away by the moment that time," he said. "I did that because I wanted to."

Her lips trembled, partly from the memory of the kiss but also because she didn't quite know what to say, until she decided to speak a simple truth. "So did I," she said, and returned his smile.

He took his hand away from her face then, and the loss of contact saddened her, made her feel just the least bit diminished, as though a small but necessary part of her had been stolen. She wanted to hold this good, strong, kind man and not let him go. It had taken so long to find him.

"We'd best be getting you home," Michael said, and opened the door for her.

On the way to the guest house, they decided that Michael would pick her up the next day at ten o'clock. When they said goodbye, they kissed again, and this time they embraced as well. His arms were around her and hers around him, and she thought that nothing had ever felt so perfectly right to her before.

Still holding her, he looked down into her face and said, "I am so glad that you came back today. I am so glad to see you, and be with you again."

She said nothing in reply, only held him more tightly, pressing her face against his chest, hating herself for being a liar, and for not having the courage to destroy the illusion that she had created and he had accepted. Then she said, "Goodnight," and gave him another fleeting kiss before she made herself leave his embrace.

"I'll see you tomorrow!" he called after her.

She glanced back and smiled and nodded, then continued up the stairs. Inside, she sat on the bed, torn between laughing and weeping. What in God's name was she *doing*, she asked herself, and the answer came clear.

She was lying, not only to Michael but to herself. She could tell him the truth, in fact she knew she *must*. But if what seemed to be his infatuation with her was born out of romance, of the idea that a woman from his past had thought enough about him over the years to never marry, and to return to the place they had first met and loved, then destroying that illusion could destroy whatever relationship was building between them. She couldn't bear that. She *loved* it, even though it had developed in less than a day.

Or had it? From Michael's point of view, it might have developed and lasted over decades. The memory of Julia and their time together might have been a romantic spark that had been aglow all those years, and now, with one flat admission, Susanna would not only blow it out but also destroy whatever was beginning to exist between her and Michael.

But what kind of relationship could develop from something that started in a lie?

Susanna fell back onto the bed, wearied by her own duplicity and by her unwillingness to change her current status by telling the truth. She was a liar, but she could not risk the truth, not yet. If this all ended in a few days, then let it end as it began. Michael would know no differently, and the only one hurt by her lies would be herself.

And if it didn't end, if their relationship deepened, then hopefully it would strengthen, too, strengthen to the point where she could confess what she had done, and hope that Michael would forgive her.

Too many ifs, she thought as she prepared for bed. Best to just stay in the moment and enjoy what fate had given her. Still, as she drifted off to sleep, she remembered that what fate generously bestows, it can all too capriciously take away.

CHAPTER 7

The next day, when Susanna saw Michael step out of his car, she felt a tightness in her chest. She hadn't felt that sensation since she was in college, and David Oliver had stepped into her view, bright and clean and handsome. Michael Lynch had turned back time for her, and although the many lines in his face told her he was no college boy, she also saw the way his eyes brightened and his face broadened in a smile at the sight of her.

"It's a lovely day," Michael said, and it was, crisp and clear, the rain clouds having given way to bright blue skies. "Would you like to walk along the bay to the town?"

"Of course," she said, and they strolled down to the sidewalk that paralleled the Grattan Road and headed toward the city center. Sunlight danced like diamonds on the wide bay to their right. Michael didn't attempt to take her hand, nor she his, but he seemed friendly and conversational, telling her about the bay and the town, about the changes in the fishing industry, and about the boats—pucans and hookers—drifting on the gentle waters.

They had a wonderful day together. Michael related anecdotes and tales about certain buildings and sites that only a long-term resident would know, and he told them with deft expression and an immediacy that brought the long dead to vivid life. On the grounds of The Collegiate Church of St. Nicholas, he enlightened her on everything from the design of the gargoyles that spat down the water from the roof to the various coats-of-arms inlaid into the outer walls. Back on the street, he told her the history of the mosaic of the pig on the wall of a butcher shop, and she laughed.

"Were you ever a tour guide? You'd make a fortune!" she said.

He chuckled and shook his head. "No, this stuff just seems to stick to me once I hear it. And believe me, working in a pub for years, you hear more than your share." His face grew more serious. "History's important, y'know. People *should* know these stories and pass them on."

"It's true," Susanna said. "If people knew more history, they'd be less likely to repeat the mistakes of the past."

"Aye, but not always. Some things don't change. Especially here in Ireland."

His tone had gotten prickly, and Susanna saw that it was a sore subject. She shifted the conversation, asking if the Joyce coat-of-arms they had seen was the same family as that of the author of *Ulysses*, and the storm cloud passed.

After a light lunch at a small café, they went back out onto the street and walked toward the bay. When Susanna remarked on how many pubs and restaurants had signboards outside advertising music sessions, Michael became more enthusiastic. "D'you like Irish music then?" he asked.

"Love it. I play a little back home in the states."

"Do you really? What do you play?"

She told him about playing classical violin, and then getting interested in Celtic music. When he heard about their sessions, his eyes widened.

"A dozen or more players at a time?" he said in near disbelief. "How can you hear the music?"

She smiled. "It can get pretty wild, but we manage to keep it together. I know sessions over here are a lot smaller."

"Aye, five's a grand number, but I've often heard just two make beautiful music—a guitar and fiddle, say. I play guitar myself. None of that fine finger-style you hear so many of the lads do. Just chording really, but I keep the rhythm going when there's no bodhran."

"So how do your sessions work at The Lilting Banshee? I suspect an awful lot of the session bands are really paid, aren't they?"

"They are," Michael said. "Many of the players play two or three nights a week and trade off so there's always a wee band playing in the different pubs. They sound like they're getting paid, too—not much spirit to it. They just go play for the tourists. But at the Banshee, they play for themselves and for each other." He cocked his head at her. "Which is a high and mighty way of saying they don't get a penny." She laughed at his mock-seriousness.

They had arrived at the quay side and were slowly strolling along The Long Walk, watching the gulls sail on the wind and the boats drift in and out of Nimmo's Pier. "You'll hear a lot of the old tunes at the pub. Friday nights my ma sings some of her *Sean-Nos* songs. That's tonight, in fact. Would you like to come over for the music?"

Susanna thought it sounded wonderful. Not only would it give her an opportunity to be with Michael, it would also let her hear a good session. That she would also meet his mother and be introduced as Julia Cassidy was daunting, but she had already decided to play out the hand, for better or worse. "I'd love to," she said.

"You might even play, if you've a mind to," Michael said.

"Ooo…" She shook her head. "I don't think so."

"Everyone's welcome," Michael said. "We had a woman and her boyfriend from New York a week or so ago, dropped in without knowing a soul. By the end of the evening we were all great friends. She played like an angel, and her boyfriend was marvelous on the guitar."

"Did they know all the tunes?"

"Surely not, but they knew some, and they played some of their own for us. Made for a fine night. Really, you walk in with an instrument, you're welcome."

"Well, it's a good thing then that I didn't bring my instrument."

"We do provide loaners to our very *special* guests."

"That's nice," Susanna said, "but I'll be happy to just sit and listen."

"Your choice, but you might get carried away by the desire to make some music."

"That's a risk I'm willing to take."

They walked past Michael's town house, but he made no move to invite her inside, and once more she was relieved. She wasn't quite ready for that, and whatever it might bring. At the end of the dock they sat and watched the bay. "It's such a beautiful place," Susanna said. "Of all the larger towns I've seen in Ireland, I think it's the prettiest."

"It is indeed," Michael said. "But there are times...oh, I don't know..." He left the thought unfinished, and she didn't push him. "So," he said, "what plans did you have for dinner tonight?"

"That depends on when the music starts at the Banshee, and how long it lasts."

"Nine o'clock Irish time, which could be anywhere from nine-fifteen to nine-thirty. Part of the *down* side of not paying musicians is that they get there when they damn well please. As for how long it goes, that depends. We often play till after midnight."

"In that case," said Susanna, "I'd better get some rest first. Besides, I'm going to be in Galway for some time, and I don't want you getting in the habit of buying me dinner every night."

"We could go Dutch," Michael said, smiling.

"On my college's budget, I can't afford to eat out every night. I'll just make something in my rooms tonight."

"Well, as you like. As long as you let me treat you to a complementary bag of nuts at the pub." He bowed his head in a courtly manner and she laughed. Then he sat back and looked out at the bay again. The next time he spoke, his voice was softer. "Remember how we used to sit here, the two of us all those years ago, holding hands against the chill and watching the boats?"

Susanna only smiled serenely, not wanting to lie.

"My God, but we put a whole lot of life into just a week, didn't we?"

Susanna kept smiling, hoping that her appearance was closer to the enigmatic Mona Lisa than to the simple, grinning idiot she really was.

"And here we are, sitting side by side once again, looking at

Galway Bay. Amazing the things that life does, isn't it?"

Now *that* one she could answer. "Yes, Michael. It certainly is."

That evening Susanna arrived at the pub shortly before nine. Michael had offered to pick her up, but she told him she didn't like keeping him from his work, and that she would meet him there. Besides, she added, she needed more practice driving in Galway.

She knew the pub would be smoky, so she wore a heavy cotton dress she could wash afterward, as she did whenever she played a session in the states. Smoke was in the nature of the beast, and it did no good to complain about it. At least Ireland's government required strong ventilation systems that partly cleared the air, and threats were in the wind of banning tobacco altogether in pubs and restaurants.

When she walked in the front door of The Lilting Banshee, the place was nearly full. The room was rich with mingled conversations, and she caught the occasional convivial word or two as she made her way through the crowd. All the stools at the bar and most of the tables were filled. The only unoccupied area was at the very front of the pub, due no doubt to the hand-lettered sign, *RESERVED FOR MUSICIANS*, that sat on one of the tables. It demarcated the area perfectly, and no one dared cross the line.

Several people nodded and smiled at her in typical Irish friendliness, but she didn't see Michael anywhere. Behind the bar was an older, gray-haired woman Susanna guessed might be Michael's mother. She was tall and not a bit stooped. Her features were stern, almost gaunt, but she let a smile fly from time to time at the patrons who spoke to her.

There was a young man behind the bar as well, with a broad face seamed in a constant grin. While the woman worked with stately efficiency, the young man seemed everywhere at once as he served draught beer and stout. Pouring the Guinness required special care, and Susanna watched as he pulled the tap and filled a tulip glass three-quarters full, then set it on the metal drainer while he darted off to some other task. The

Guinness settled, turning from muddy brown to black, and the man reappeared and put it under the nozzle again, this time pushing the tap backwards until the head rose just over the edge of the glass, forming what Susanna had heard called The Bishop's Collar. It was, she thought, as fine a work of gustatory art as sushi.

The area in the back held several booths, but they were all full, so Susanna found an empty stool near the rear of the bar against the wall, where a chest-high rail provided a secure haven for pints and ash trays. One of the two barmaids flitting through the room asked her what she'd like, and she ordered a pint of Guinness. When the girl brought it, Susanna asked if Michael Lynch was in, and she said, "Oh him, he comes and goes...he'll be about..." and dashed off again.

"And is it Michael you're looking for, then?" said the thin man on the stool beside her. He had gray tousled hair, and a scrawny moustache sprouted from beneath his straight, patrician nose. "Friend o' his, are ye?"

He seemed friendly rather than intrusive, and Susanna smiled and nodded, and stiffened herself for the lies she knew she would have to tell. "From years ago."

"Ah, from the old days, is it? When he was, ah..." The man shook his head as though he'd forgotten something, then stuck out his free hand to Susanna. "Dermot Rooney," he said.

Susanna took the hand and returned the pressure. "Julia Cassidy. Nice to meet you."

"Ah, there's the lad now," Rooney said, nodding toward the front of the pub. Michael was walking in, easily hefting a case of club soda he had apparently brought up from the basement. He stowed it under the bar, and saw her when he straightened up. His face lit up with surprise and he smiled, gave her a short wave, and headed through the throng toward her.

"Uh-oh, I see Dermot's gotten ahold of you," he said as he came up to her.

"Aye," Rooney said. "Miss Cassidy and I have made each other's acquaintance, and spending but a few minutes with me, any other man now becomes second-best in her eyes. Isn't that so?" he asked Susanna.

Taken aback, she gave a little laugh, but Michael jumped right in. "In the dictionary next to the word, 'blarney,' you'll find this old man's picture."

"Not so old I can't steal this young lady away from you," Rooney said, daintily brushing his sparse moustache.

"There's to be no stealing in this pub," Michael said in mock seriousness. "Come on, Julia, I've got a better seat for you up front. You don't want to be hanging around with the likes of this one."

Rooney laughed as Michael picked up Susanna's pint and led her toward the front where he seated her on a stool against the wall on the edge of the musicians' circle. "Who waited on you?" he asked her, handing her the pint. Susanna pointed out the girl who had served her, and when she passed Michael told her, "The lady's drinks are on me tonight."

The girl grinned at Susanna. "Gonna be playin', then?"

Susanna's jaw dropped at the prospect of playing fiddle for these aficionados who knew their Irish music inside-out, but before she could reply, Michael said, "She just might..." and added in an easily heard stage whisper, "...if you keep the Guinness flowin'!"

The girl laughed and vanished into the crowd, and Michael turned to Susanna. "I'm only joking. You don't have to play if you don't wish to. But I'm about to, so I'd best get my guitar."

As Michael turned to go, a man and a woman carrying instrument cases entered the pub, and he gave a quick wave to them and headed toward the rear of the bar. The pair came into the circle, sat down on the bench along the front wall, and put their cases on their laps.

The woman shrugged off her coat. She looked a few years younger than Susanna, and was tall and wide-shouldered with full breasts that her red v-neck sweater accentuated. Her brown hair was shoulder length and seemed naturally wavy, like the women's hair (or wigs, Susanna thought cattily) in *Riverdance*. But this was no wig. The woman appeared to be all natural, like some Irish earth mother, or a reincarnation of Queen Maeve herself. Her face was broad but attractive, and she smiled at Susanna with a closed mouth.

By the time the woman opened her fiddle case and took out a nearly blonde violin with a high gloss, Michael returned holding his guitar, a Taylor with gold hardware. Susanna thought that he must take his playing seriously to have such a good instrument. "Evening, Kate. Hello, Aengus," he said in a subdued tone to the woman and the middle-aged man who had just taken out a small accordion and was sliding its case under the bench.

"Evening yourself, Michael," the woman called Kate replied, in a much higher voice than Susanna expected. The edge in it didn't make it any more mellifluous. The man with the accordion said hello as well, more jovially than the woman had.

"Let me make some introductions," Michael said as he walked between Susanna and the two musicians. "Kate, Aengus, this is Julia Cassidy, a friend from long ago. Julia, Kate Quinn and Aengus Cleary."

From the sharp look that Kate Quinn gave her, Susanna had the feeling that any female friend of Michael's was not a friend of hers. "Hello," Susanna said, and stood to shake Aengus's proffered hand. Kate offered hers as well, but did not stand, and the shake was abrupt and over quickly.

"So, Guinness for you both?" Michael asked, and, handing his guitar to Susanna, went to the bar to fetch them.

Kate started to tune her fiddle. "You're a Yank, then?" she asked Susanna.

Susanna smiled. "You got that from one word?"

"Oh, it's easy to figure out people from one word," Kate said, flashing a smile that vanished as quickly as it had come.

Oh-kay, Susanna thought, there was definitely something going on here. Fortunately, she was prevented from having to talk to Kate further by the entrance of a short, slim, spiky-haired girl in her twenties who carried a small pouch a foot and a half long. "Where the hell's the music then?" she called in a loud, gravelly voice, and a dozen shouts of greeting hailed her. She sat on the bench, jostling Kate so that the older woman gave her the same look she had hurled at Susanna. The girl ignored it. "Evenin', Kate, Aengus," she said, shrugging off her coat to reveal a wine-colored *Galway United* football jersey. "Where's the big man?"

"Here I am, Fiona love," Michael said, returning with a tray loaded with four dark pints. "Heard you come in—who didn't?—so I brought you a pint as well."

"Only the first, I hope," the girl said with a grin.

"Ah, don't fret," Aengus chuckled. "Your whistles'll be spoutin' stout by the time the night's over."

When the girl unzipped her case, Susanna understood. Inside was an assortment of Irish whistles finished in nickel and brass, as well as a larger one in black. Fiona took out one of the smallest and blew a startlingly quick run from low to high and back again. The sound cut through the pub and silenced everyone for a moment before the roar of conversation swelled up again.

Michael took his guitar from Susanna and introduced her to Fiona Bailey. The girl's friendly greeting was in marked contrast to Kate Quinn's veiled hostility. Then Michael sat on a stool near Susanna, and Aengus moved from the bench to a stool so that they all faced each other. Michael tuned his guitar and they all warmed up. Then he said, "'Humours of Tulla,'" and they launched into a tune Susanna had never heard.

It was a lively reel in the key of D, and Susanna couldn't help but grin as the music filled the room. The drinkers turned toward the band. Some shouted encouragement while others clapped in rhythm, but all seemed caught up in the joyous sound. Fiona's whistle sang in unison melody with Kate's fiddle, while Aengus provided both melody and harmony with his chords. The bright, clear guitar also contributed the chords, but with a rhythm that drove the tune onward while providing a strong underlying bass pattern. Susanna instantly saw that, though not fancy, Michael was a fine rhythm guitarist.

She wanted to dislike Kate's fiddle playing, but could not. The woman played well, though it was obvious she had been trained in the Irish tradition rather than classically. While her playing was powerful and melodic, Susanna heard little nuance or purity of tone. Still, the sound fit The Lilting Banshee as snugly as the fiddle fit beneath Kate's chin.

Kate smiled frequently at Michael as she played, and Susanna wondered what exactly was going on between the two of them beside music. Then she told herself that her own relationship with Michael had not reached the point where jealousy was excusable, and decided to put it away and concentrate on the tunes. She was sure there was much she could learn by listening closely, not just to Kate, but to how the players interacted with one another.

As in all good sessions, the musicians seemed tuned in to each other almost preternaturally. Though each contributed an individual and unique sound, they functioned most strongly as a unit, as did the symphony in which Susanna played. These four players needed no music, however. The tune seemed more than memorized, it seemed ingrained, as much a part of them as their breathing.

It ended as cleanly as it had begun, and the crowd applauded and cheered tipsily. "'Smash the Mud!'" Aengus called next, and started playing. The others joined in quickly. Michael seemed transformed. His face was aglow as he played, and while he often seemed lost in the music, at times he smiled toothily at Susanna and at others in the room, his right hand moving up and down like a piston, but his wrist loose and supple, the left hand switching gracefully from chord to chord on the frets. He seldom looked at Kate Quinn, and Susanna wasn't sure if that made her glad or apprehensive.

After the tune ended, they all sat back and relaxed for a few minutes, sipping their pints. "What do you think?" Michael asked Susanna softly. Kate set down her pint and tuned her fiddle. She seemed petulant, and Susanna wondered if it was because Michael was talking to her.

"It's wonderful," she told him. "You all play so well."

"You ready to try a tune with us?"

Susanna gave a long exhale and shook her head. "I hardly think so. Besides, I don't have a violin."

"Ah ah—they're *fiddles* here. And I think we could find you a loaner."

"Um..." Susanna dropped her voice even further. "I really wouldn't want to ask Kate to loan me hers."

"You don't have to."

"Especially if I don't play."

Just then Fiona started a tune on one of her whistles, and the call was inescapable for the others. Their pints went back on the table and their instruments came up. It was one that Susanna knew, "Munster Buttermilk," and she smiled in recognition. The musicians played it through several times, and when it and the applause afterward ended, she said, "That's *such* a great tune, so lively..."

"You know it?" Fiona asked. "Do you play then?"

"Julia's a fiddler," Michael announced, "but a very shy one."

"Aw," said Aengus, "one of those we have to beg to play, are ye?"

'Oh no, really, I can't," Susanna said. "I'm...I'm really not in your league."

"Oh," said Kate with a little smile. "Are you more like Itzhak Perlman then? Or Heifetz? A little too good for our simple tunes?"

Susanna was nearly shocked speechless by Kate's rudeness. "Oh no," she said, "that's not what I meant at all...I meant..."

"Ah, Kate knows what you meant," said Fiona, nudging the fiddle player with her elbow. "She's just playin' games with your attempt at self-deprecation. I'll explain that word to you later, Katie."

"I know what it means, thank you, Fiona," Kate said dryly. "Just joking with you, dear," she told Susanna. "Now let's play something, all right? Let's burn things up a bit..."

She set a sprightly pace to a reel Susanna knew, "The Wind That Shakes the Barley," and the others joined in. Susanna noticed that Fiona and Aengus gave each other a weary look, and that Michael's expression was somewhat disgusted, but she didn't know why. The woman was playing the tune expertly, using many double stops, in which the bow played two notes at once. Her fingers darted along the neck and the bow flashed back and forth, while the others played brilliantly in support, Michael's chords and strong bass supplying the bottom, the accordion filling the middle, and the high sound of Fiona's whistle arching over all.

Then, as they went into the second time through the tune, Kate picked up the pace considerably, and those in the crowd who had been talking turned to pay closer attention. It was a speed at which Susanna might have been able to play, but she would have been hard pressed to keep the notes clean and distinct. Kate's notes were fairly crisp, although she relied on an occasional slur, but Susanna still envied the woman's proficiency.

The third time through, however, Susanna knew what Kate meant when she suggested that they *burn things up*. She increased the tempo to the point where Michael could no longer play two strums to each beat so that the bass notes rang out individually. Instead he had time for only one downstroke, like a bass drum. Aengus, too, had been shut out of his proper accompaniment, but made the most of it by squeezing his chords on the off-beat, filling in where Michael was now absent. As for Fiona, she kept up nearly perfectly with the melody, missing a note or two only to grab a quick breath, a necessity to which Kate was not subject.

This time around, however, Susanna saw that Kate was making some sacrifices for her feverish speed. The beginning of each phrase was powerful, but the strings of sixteenth-notes that ended them were no longer distinct. At best they were slurred, and often notes dropped out completely, or the wrong one was heard. Still, the dissonance lasted only a moment, until Kate attacked a new phrase. Her furious energy saved her, and it was having its effect on the crowd, who by now had given up clapping in time and was egging her on with whoops of encouragement.

Susanna had to give her credit. The speed had made the tune less musical but more exciting, especially to those who were willing to overlook musicianship for flair. Only trained musicians—or those trying to accompany her, Susanna wryly thought as she observed the other players' determined but not happy expressions—would hear the flaws, and she doubted there were many in the throng. Irish music could be wild and woolly as well as tender and delicate, and she was hearing that side of it now.

The tune surged breathlessly to its end, with Aengus and Michael desperately whaling away on their instruments, reduced now to nothing more than rhythm, and even Fiona was left behind as Kate ripped into the last run like a sprinter's final burst of speed crossing the wire. As Kate ended with a three-beat tremolo, Fiona blew an ascending figure that seemed more like a note of surrender than any sympathetic finale.

The place erupted in cheers and applause, while Kate glanced at Susanna with a look in her eyes that unmistakably said *Top that*. The ovation went on for some time, and Kate merely sat there with a smug smile.

The other musicians picked up their drinks, and Aengus shook his hand as though playing at such speed had pained him. "Only one of those a night, all right?"

"Just a wee bit o' fun," Kate said. "Don't be such a baby."

"Yeah, well, you just have to wiggle your bow. I've got to squeeze that damned thing."

"And what happened to picking a tempo and sticking to it?" Fiona asked.

"They liked it, didn't they?" Kate said, nodding to the still boisterous crowd. "Got to give 'em a crowd pleaser now and then. Speaking of which, I think our new friend from the states should honor us with a tune."

Susanna realized what Kate had done. She had set her up with a fiery showcase of speed and skill. No matter how brightly Susanna played the next jig or reel, she would come out second best, unable to equal Kate's velocity. To even attempt to do so would be a fiasco.

"Now that's up to Julia," Michael said. "We don't want to make her uncomfortable if she'd rather not play."

"Aye," said Aengus, and Fiona nodded her agreement, her look almost begging Susanna not to rise to the bait.

"Well, if she'd rather not..." Kate said. "But we're all missing a grand opportunity to hear how they do it in *Amerikay*." She said the last word almost mockingly.

"I wouldn't mind playing something," Susanna heard herself say quietly. "Only I don't have a fiddle."

"You can borrow mine, dear," Kate said, holding out her instrument to Susanna. "After what I put it through, I hardly think you'll harm it." Susanna looked at the fiddle, but didn't take it. "Of course, if you'd rather not..."

Michael leaned toward her. "Do you really *want* to play? Don't feel pressured if you don't."

Susanna shrugged and smiled. "I'm willing."

Michael gave her a tight smile. "Just you wait then." He handed her his guitar and made his way through the crowd, then reached up to the glass and wood frame that protected the fiddle and the bow high on the wall. He turned a key in the lock, swung open what Susanna now saw was the glass door, and removed the fiddle and the bow from their hangers and started to bring them back to Susanna.

Then the older woman Susanna had assumed was Michael's mother stepped in front of him. Susanna couldn't hear what they were saying, but her face was unsmiling. Michael said a few words, then brushed past her. Her gaze followed her son back to Susanna's side, and she looked at Susanna for a moment, her face still expressionless, before she turned back to her work.

"This was my stepda's," he said, handing the fiddle to her. It looked as burnished and smoke-stained as the pubs in which it had been played, and smelled of old wood and tobacco. There was another scent, too, and she inhaled deeply and looked questioningly at Michael.

"Peat," he said. "Years and years of it. It won't need dusting—we treat it like a relic—but it'll need tuning." He gave her an A on the guitar, and she started to tune the fiddle carefully, surprised to find that it was already close to pitch. She took the bow and tightened it, rosining it with the cake of rosin Kate Quinn too graciously offered. Then she played a few practice scales and intervals. The fiddle had a deep, rich sound, smoky and velvety, not brash and bright like Kate's, and it was the sound that told her what she should play.

"Now what are you going to honor us with?" Kate said. "I trust it'll be something that your fellow musicians'll know? *I* don't have to—I'll let you play all on your own so I can appreciate it." Susanna would get no help from Kate. She'd be out in the open, for better or worse.

"If it's not heresy," Susanna said, "I'd like to play a Scottish tune."

"Not at all," Aengus said. "We play lots of Scots tunes."

"Would you mind a slow air?" Susanna asked. "As a change of pace?" They nodded agreement, and she said, "It's called 'Niel Gow's Lament for the Death of His Second Wife.'"

Aengus shook his head sympathetically. "Heard of it, but don't know it," he said, and Fiona shook her head as well.

"I've played that one, but not for some time," Michael said a trifle uncertainly. "In D, with a lot of minor chords and such?" Susanna nodded. "Well, you start it, and I'll try and come in when I get my bearings."

"Listen, everyone!" Kate called. "Our guest from the states is going to play for us now—some fella's lament for his dead second wife."

A number of people turned toward them, among them Dermot Rooney, and, at the bar, Michael's mother. Kate Quinn settled her own fiddle on her lap, crossed her arms, and cocked her head at Susanna, as if waiting to hear just what she could do.

The pub was noisy, but she started, softly at first. The tune was plaintive and tender, and Susanna put all her skill into its playing. She kept her vibrato at a minimum, just enough to make each long note tremble a bit as it rang. Her rhythm was free, with long pauses on certain notes, and she put in trills where they seemed natural, like little breaths of sorrow and love.

Slowly Susanna began to be aware that the pub had grown quieter, and now she heard voices saying *Whist,* and shushing others until the only sound was that of the fiddle, as she finished the tune the first time through. She started it again, a bit more forcefully but with no less emotion, gaining in confidence, though she dared not look up from her hands upon the neck for fear that her concentration would be broken.

Then she heard the first gentle chord from Michael's guitar, feeling its way into her soft soliloquy, and she nearly smiled. The chords, strummed a string at time like an arpeggio, added immeasurably to the tune, and she felt, as she played on, as though she and Michael were drifting together high over green hills, their fingers interwoven in the tapestry of music they were making together.

They soared on, on a long-dead Scots fiddler's notes of regret and passion and loss and love, and made him and his dear wife live again in that smoky room, until at last Susanna rose to the penultimate phrase, holding the high note until it faded away, then coming back down, as though descending from the joys of heaven to the sadness of earth once more, letting the final low notes drift away like mist.

When Susanna lowered the fiddle and bow, there was no applause. There was no sound at all. She looked up and saw everyone in the pub gazing at her. Some of the eyes were teary, and some of them were men's. Then Dermot Rooney spoke. "Jaysus, Mary and Joseph, that man musta had a *powerful* love."

Several people laughed softly in agreement at the comment, and then the clapping began. It was not the raucous acclaim that had greeted Kate Quinn's reckless speed, but a deeper applause in which shoulders spread wide and palms were slammed together as though the patrons were smashing walnuts in their hands. It was the sound of approval and respect.

Susanna glanced at Michael, and he was beaming and nodding his head. He looked over at the bar, and when she followed his gaze, she saw his mother with a smile finally on her face, and a glint of a tear at the corner of her eye. She looked at Susanna and brought up her hands in a genteel flutter of applause.

When the ovation at last died down, a mass of people moved in to congratulate Susanna. Aengus said, "Ah, that's the real thing, that."

"Well done," Kate added. She was smiling, but her attitude told Susanna she was less than pleased with her success.

"Well, I'm off downstairs to make room for more Guinness," said Aengus.

Kate rose and put her fiddle and bow on the bench. "I'll go with you," she said.

"Not the whole way, I hope," Aengus said with a laugh, and the pair headed in the direction of the stairs. Michael gave Susanna an approving pat on the shoulder and went to fetch more pints.

"Brilliant," Fiona said to Susanna when the crowd went back to their places. "Just like Hawk and Prez."

"I'm sorry?" Susanna said.

Fiona laughed. "Hawk—Coleman Hawkins—and Prez—Lester Young—were the two top tenor sax players of their time. I play jazz, too, see? And they had a cutting session late one night in a club to see which of them could crush the other playing. Well, Hawkins had this great, fat agro tone, and he played up a storm, loud, powerful, fast. Lester? He just played a ballad, played it pretty as you like, and everybody who was there says *he* won." Fiona winked. "All I'm sayin' is there's a bit of a parallel here, if you catch my drift."

"Well, thanks...it *is* a pretty tune."

"Pretty tune, hell—you kicked her arse and she deserved it."

"Is she always this, well..."

"Hostile? Nasty? Bitchy? Nah, Kate's a grand woman when she wants to be. Jealousy brings out the worst in her."

"Jealousy..." Susanna repeated, not wanting to follow the implications.

"Katie's a widow five years now, her kids are grown, one in Dublin, two in England. She set her cap for Michael soon as the last one got out of the house, so she hears you and Michael are old friends, she reads something into it." Fiona smiled. "Or maybe she sees what's already there. Any road, she's not too happy about it. And showin' her up like that isn't goin' to endear you to her either."

"I didn't mean to...show her up. I just knew that I couldn't play as fast as she could, so..."

"Aha—so you *did* see it as a cutting contest then. Don't blame you, as Katie threw down the gauntlet plain enough. God, you play well, though. Classically trained?"

"Yes."

"Thought so. Can always tell. Me, too, on flute. Trinity College Dublin. I teach music for a living."

"Really, I teach, too..." They chatted about their work until the others returned, and then started playing again. They asked Susanna for the name of tunes she knew, and played many of them. When they called one with which she wasn't familiar, she was happy to sit and listen. She and Kate played well in unison, and Susanna was relieved that Kate didn't try to speed up any of the tunes, though the cold edge was still present.

When they took another lengthy break, Michael said to Susanna, "My mother'd like to meet you." He took the fiddle and bow from her and, holding them, led her down to the end of the bar. "Mother," he said to the woman, who was now smiling, "this is Julia Cassidy. Julia, my mother, Molly Sullivan."

"I'm very glad to meet you, Mrs. Sullivan," Susanna said.

"And I you. You play beautifully. Tim's old fiddle never sounded so good."

"It's a wonderful instrument. It has such a deep, rich sound, almost like a viola."

"Aye, but like he always said, it's the player and not the instrument that makes the music, and you make it well." Susanna nodded her thanks.

"So, Ma, are you going to sing tonight?" Michael asked.

"Aye. Gerry just came in a few minutes ago." Molly Sullivan nodded toward the rear of the pub. Just inside the back door was a narrow waist-high counter on which a pint might be precariously perched, with a single stool next to it. There sat a man in his late twenties, with dark blond hair over the collar of his corduroy coat. He wore a pair of thin-rimmed glasses, and was straining in the dim light to read a thick paperback book, ignoring the talk at the tables around him.

Michael nodded toward him. "My son, Gerald," he told Susanna. "He comes the nights Ma sings *Sean-Nos*."

"Heard it from the cradle," Molly said. "And nobody does it anymore except for old ladies like meself, so the lad has to come here to hear it. Well, I suppose I'd better take the stage, as they say."

"Fine," said Michael. "We'll come and listen."

Susanna thought it curious that Michael had not introduced her to his son, but she didn't mention it to him. By the time they reached the front of the pub, Molly was settled in the corner on a stool, her hands on her lap, and the patrons were shushing each other again, as they had when Susanna had played.

Molly Sullivan started to sing then, her eyes closed, and Susanna felt something lock in her throat. The singing was eerie and unworldly. Though Susanna couldn't understand a word of the Irish language in which Molly sang, the sheer emotional breadth of the sound stunned her.

There was no accompaniment, nothing but the steady droning of the old woman's voice. She used neither vibrato nor dynamics, but the rhythm was free and the ornamentation seemed to spring from her spirit rather than her throat. The melody changed slightly from one verse to the next, making the performance creative as well as interpretive.

It was the sound, Susanna thought, of old Ireland, of the rain in the hills and the sun on the sea, and it pierced her like a spear.

When Molly Sullivan finished her song, there was a soft expulsion of breath from the listeners. Murmurs of approval served as applause, and words of thanks spoken gently were Molly's ovation. She sang two more songs, both as moving as the first, then stood up, took a little bow, and went back behind the bar.

Susanna saw Gerry Lynch standing in the back. The young man pushed his glasses up onto his nose and went over to his grandmother. He kissed her cheek, they exchanged a few words, and then he turned up his coat collar and headed for the back door, not having spoken at all to his father. It seemed odd, but Susanna had no time to think about it, for she felt Michael's hand on her shoulder. "Ready to go then?" he asked.

She nodded. There was a half hour for "drinking up," when patrons could finish pints they'd already purchased, but she knew that everyone would be out the door by one. Aengus came over to her, shook her hand, and said he hoped she'd play with them again, and Fiona echoed the sentiment. Seeing the others, Kate came over and told Susanna that she played well, and gave her a smile that had less menace in it than before.

"I'll walk you to your car," Michael said when the three had gone. He put the fiddle and bow back in the frame and locked it, and they said goodbye to Molly. As they headed for the door, Dermot Rooney called to Susanna, "You come back and play again—you two were made for each other!" He let a beat go by, then added, "Not *you*, Michael, you great goof—the lass and the *fiddle!*" Laughter followed them onto the street, where Susanna took Michael's arm as they walked.

There was still music coming from the doors and windows of pubs they passed, and she smiled at the sound. "That was wonderful. Thank you so much for a lovely evening."

"You helped make it so. You play very well."

"It wasn't hard with such a good instrument." She considered her question for a moment, then asked it. "Your mother... was she hesitant about my playing it?"

"Aye, but that's only natural."

"I guess so. It having been her husband's and all."

"And nobody having played it since old Tim passed."

She slowed and stopped. "What?"

He turned and smiled down at her. "No one's drawn music from it since he died, over fifteen years now. Ma always said it was waiting for someone, and that we'd know when that fiddler came. I thought you might be the one. I was right." He looked back toward the pub, as if remembering. "Reason I knew that tune is he used to play it. It was one of his favorites. But nobody remembers now except me and Ma. Well."

They started to walk again, not talking, the night growing quieter as they left the lighted streets for the dark side lanes. At the car, Michael opened the door for her, but before she got in, he kissed her, and they held each other for a moment. Then he stepped back and smiled. "And that's the extent of demonstrations of affection tonight. For as you so well proved this evening...*faster* isn't necessarily *better*."

He winked and she laughed, then said goodnight and climbed into the car. As she drove back to her rooms, she heard the sound of the *Sean-Nos* in her head, and it even slipped into her dreams.

CHAPTER 8

Ireland sure wasn't the Emerald Isle this time of the year, Rachel Oliver thought as she drove north from Shannon Airport. Everything looked kind of brown and gray. She sighed, thinking how stupid she had been to fly to Ireland at the end of January, for God's sake, instead of waiting a few months for spring when everything would be the green it was supposed to be, and lambs would probably be frolicking or gamboling or whatever they did all over the place.

And there was another reason she should have waited— money. Though she had put her air ticket and the rental car on her Visa, she wasn't sure that her mother's insurance money would come in time to pay it off in full. Well, if it didn't, she could always pay the minimum. That had been standard operating procedure when she was married to Ty. Run up a bill, pay the minimum every month, and watch their balance get higher and higher, until Ty did one of his "deals," disappearing for a day or two and coming back with enough cash to pay off the total so they could start over.

Rachel tried to concentrate on the bleak landscape and get her mind off Tyler Madden and the years she had spent as his wife, co-dependent, and punching bag. She wasn't in Ireland to relive her own past, but to try and imagine her mother's.

The past month she had missed her mom terribly, and regretted the way they had grown apart. Rachel had cut her mother off until she had needed her help, both emotional and financial, when she finally decided to leave Ty for good. Julia's dying had brought them back together even more, but it hadn't been enough. Now that her mother was gone beyond recall,

Rachel wanted to know her better.

But she couldn't learn more about her at home. The house had too many unpleasant associations, from Rachel's unhappy youth there to her mother's dying. It also had her father, who seemed to have learned nothing from his wife's death.

David had treated Julia with the same disdain with which Ty had treated Rachel, although her father had never struck her mother. His infidelities were the sole topic with which Rachel had never baited Julia. That would have been too cruel, and too close to home.

She and her mother had had more in common than she had realized, and now Rachel wanted to meet her somewhere where there was no extra emotional baggage packed by either of them, somewhere neutral, a place her mother had loved and one that Rachel might learn to love. Ireland was perfect.

Besides, Rachel needed a change of scenery. The cold Pennsylvania landscapes brought her mother's death too much to mind. Here in Ireland Rachel hoped it would bring her *life* to mind instead.

She had considered calling Aunt Sue and telling her that she was coming, but once Rachel had made up her mind to go, she didn't want her aunt or anyone else talking her out of it. *Oh honey*, she could almost hear Susanna saying, *why don't you wait a few months until the weather's better?* Rachel knew she would have no answer other than, *But I want to come now.*

She hadn't told her father either. She knew he would disapprove, and she didn't need the hassle. Just before Rachel had walked out the door to go to the airport, she had sent her father an e-mail telling him where she was going, and that if there was an emergency he could get in touch with her through Aunt Sue, who she'd be contacting when she hit Galway.

The only people who knew where she was headed was Pete, the owner of the music store where she worked, and Lisa Tran, her co-worker there who had taken Susanna's cat Gandhi to her apartment while Rachel was away. Rachel felt guilty about entrusting Aunt Sue's fuzzy pride and joy to a third party, but fortunately she didn't have to feel guilty about leaving the store for a few weeks. Sales were always down after Christmas, and

Pete seemed relieved at the prospect of not having to pay her for a while.

At any rate, everything had worked out, and here she was in Ireland, only a little over a week from the time her Aunt Sue had flown over. Rachel had arrived at seven in the morning, had gotten her car quickly, and was now coming into Galway at just past ten. She stopped at a gas station on the outskirts and asked an attendant how to get to the address of the guest house where her aunt was staying. The attendant, who had a *great* accent, told her it was "a wee bit tricky," but wrote everything down for her.

It was *damned* tricky, but she finally found the street and saw the sign for the guest house. Rachel pulled into a place several spaces away, and was about to open the car door when she saw a big man get out of a car parked closer to the house and walk toward it. He waved, and Aunt Sue appeared coming down a flight of stairs.

Rachel grinned when she saw her aunt. Susanna's face was beaming. She was wearing a waist-length jacket, and her knee-length skirt showed off her slim legs. Rachel thought she looked fifteen years younger than she really was. But the grin left her face when she saw Aunt Sue step into the arms of the big man, embrace him, and kiss him, quickly but firmly.

At last the big man turned so that Rachel could see him. Even in her state of bemused shock, Rachel thought that Aunt Sue had done pretty well for herself. Although the man's face was a little craggy for her tastes, he was ruggedly handsome and well-built, and he looked as delighted to be in Aunt Sue's company as she did to be in his.

Before Rachel could consider what to do next, the man had whisked her aunt into his car, and they were pulling out onto the street. It didn't even occur to Rachel to follow.

She sat there, thinking that still waters did indeed run deep. The kiss and embrace they had shared had most definitely not been platonic. Rachel sighed. She had told Aunt Sue that maybe she would find a guy in Ireland, but she hadn't really expected it to happen. Her aunt had been her role model of independent womanhood for years, and here she was apparently swept off her feet by a tall, rangy Irish Spring model, maybe a little old, but still damned sexy.

Well, Rachel decided, if Aunt Sue was having a little Irish fling, she wasn't going to mess it up. There was nothing that could chill hot emotions more than an adult niece popping up asking about the tourist attractions. Maybe she'd touch base with Susanna in a few days, but for now she'd be an independent woman and do some exploring on her own.

Rachel had no idea where to find a place to stay, but there seemed to be bed and breakfasts all over. She decided to look around the town first, and if she got a conversation going with some of the locals, maybe they'd give her a tip about lodgings.

She drove back toward the center of the town, and after a great deal of trial and error finally found a parking place not too far from the area that seemed the busiest. She had no map or guidebook, but she had always preferred to let her feet take her where they would.

This time she hoped they would take her somewhere she could get some lunch. She'd had no breakfast other than the sad offering on the Continental flight, and she was starving. As she walked up what she saw was Quay Street, she noticed a number of pubs that served food, and chose one at random. Inside a waitress told her to sit anywhere she liked.

There were a number of tables in the front room by the bar, but most of them were occupied with older people talking amongst themselves, none of whom looked up as she passed, let alone nodded a welcome. Rachel kept moving back through another room that was equally full, and still further back into a smaller room in which the only available seats were three chairs at a table for four.

The other chair was occupied by a tall, thin young man with hair that fell down over his collar. He was wearing his coat, and in front of him on the table was a yellow legal pad next to a pint of something dark and an empty plate. He was peering through his glasses at the paper as though expecting it to obey a command he had just given it, and he tapped it with a pen he was holding as though to spur it to life.

"Um...anybody sitting here?" Rachel asked.

The man looked up, and his expression softened as he saw Rachel. "No, no," he said in a low but gentle voice. "Please, make yourself comfortable." He smiled at her and then looked back at the paper. The lines were in rows, as though he was working on poetry or lyrics. His left arm, the one not holding the pen, was leaning on a thick paperback book, and despite the shadows in the dark pub, Rachel recognized the spine.

A waitress came over surprisingly fast for the pub being so crowded, and handed Rachel a one-page laminated menu. "I'll have a...pint of Guinness," Rachel said, "and, let's see...a fish sandwich."

There was a sudden intake of breath from across the table, and when Rachel looked at the man, he was peering at her from over the top edge of his glasses and giving his head a quick shake.

"Um, tell you what, hold that sandwich," Rachel said to the waitress. "Let me think about this a sec, okay?"

"Right," the waitress said. "Bring your drink then."

When she had vanished into the next room, the man gave an apologetic smile. "Sorry," he said, "but the fish here's about the worst you've tasted. Fried frozen stuff. Wouldn't want you to get the wrong idea about our Galway seafood."

"Thanks," Rachel said smiling. "So, what do you recommend?"

"Well, their oysters are passable." Rachel made a face. "But if you're not keen on oysters, the soups are good, and the coddle's decent."

"Cuddle? What's that?"

"*Cod*dle. It's sausage and bacon cooked with potatoes and onions. Sort of like a stew. Fill you up, it will."

"How are their hamburgers?"

"They're hamburgers, no more, no less. I've eaten plenty of them here and I'm still standing."

She laughed. "Maybe a burger and soup then."

"Sounds safe enough." He gave a little smile and nodded, then looked back down at his paper as though the conversation was at an end. Rachel had thought he might have been trying to pick her up, but his seeming dismissal of her put the lie to that.

In truth, she was disappointed. He was cute in an ascetic sort of way. Hunched over his paper, he reminded her of one of those young Irish monks devoted to the study of the scriptures. She could almost see him in a cassock with a tonsure shaven on the crown of his head, if Irish monks wore tonsures. For a few moments she imagined herself as the local village girl delivering milk and cheese to the monastery and giving him a wink when he looked up shyly, then watching his face turn red.

Her fantasy was interrupted by the arrival of her pint of Guinness. She ordered a cheeseburger and a bowl of mushroom soup, and sipped her stout. It tasted good, though different from the way it did in America. The man across the table from her had said nothing since his return to his paper, and it piqued her. They had been having a nice little conversation, and now nothing. Maybe he was just shy. If so, she'd give him another chance.

"So," she said, waiting until he looked up for the question. "Are you a 'Skunk Hour' person or a 'Quaker Graveyard in Nantucket' person?"

He looked at her oddly, then chuckled and patted the book on the table. "Being a Galway man," he said, "how could I resist a poem dedicated to 'Warren Winslow, dead at sea?'"

She recited the phrase along with him, blessing the course in American poetry that had introduced her to Robert Lowell's work. She had liked some of it enough to memorize certain lines.

"How about yourself?" he asked her.

"I used to be 'Skunk Hour,'" she said, "introspective and morose and all. But now I like his earlier work better, all that texture and muscle. Sort of like good hard rock." She nodded at the legal pad. "Poetry?"

"Lyrics," he said, and she sensed some embarrassment. "Song lyrics."

"You a musician?"

"Not really. I teach literature." Which explains the volume of Lowell's collected poems, Rachel thought. "And I write poetry. Had some published, but there's hardly any paying markets for the stuff. Songs, on the other hand..." He shrugged. "You never know."

"You don't like teaching?"

"Oh, I like it fine. I'd just like to do...a bit more."

"Know what you mean. I've written some songs myself."

"Yeah? You should give me lessons. I can come up with lyrics, but I can't write tunes."

"I'm the other way around—no good with words, but I can always pull a tune out of the air." Rachel smiled. "Maybe we ought to collaborate."

"Maybe we should," he said seriously, to Rachel's surprise not flirting at all.

By the time Rachel's meal came and she finished it, she knew quite a bit about Gerry Lynch, and he knew quite a bit about her. Shortly after one o'clock, he said that he had to return to his school for teachers' meetings, as the boys had the afternoon off that day. First, however, he walked with Rachel to her car, where they got her luggage, and then led her to a hostel near Eyre Square, where she could get a single room for twenty-eight Euros a night. They agreed to meet for dinner that evening, and Gerry promised to bring some of his lyrics for Rachel to look at.

Alone in her room, she sank back on the narrow bed and smiled. Even without the assistance of Aunt Sue, things were going well. She had a cheap place to stay, she'd met a friend, and even had a date for dinner. All in all, it was a propitious start to her two weeks in Ireland. She decided to continue to play things by ear and see what happened. She would contact Aunt Sue later. Why cramp her aunt's style with her Irishman when, with a little bit of luck, Rachel might have an Irishman of her own before too long?

Gerry Lynch was a cutie, no doubt about it. He was shyer than shy, though, the kind of guy who didn't realize what a catch he was. Maybe he wasn't the handsomest man around— his face, along with the rest of him, was awfully thin—but there was a sweetness and a gentleness about him that she hadn't come across in American boys.

She had expected Irishmen to be all bluff and hearty, calling everybody *boyo*, but Gerry wasn't like that at all. Even the dark beverage he'd been drinking from a pint glass had been Coke, since his school frowned upon their teachers drinking during the day.

Oh yes, Gerry Lynch was a sweetheart all right. But there was no point in daydreaming. After all, she thought realistically, he could very well be gay.

That evening, he met her at the hostel at seven, and they walked a few blocks to a restaurant. On the way, Rachel sniffed the air and wrinkled her nose. "What *is* that?" she asked Gerry.

"That's turf," he said. "Somebody's burning turf."

"That's what turf smells like?" Rachel said, scarcely believing it.

"That's it. I'm happy to see that reaction for a change. All the Yanks think it smells so...*quaint*. I think it smells like what it is—somebody burning dirt." They both laughed.

At the restaurant they were seated in a basement room with old dark wooden walls. Their table was in a corner, and Rachel was happy that they could talk without being overheard. "This is great," she said. "Like eating in a dungeon."

"Let's hope the food isn't torture," Gerry replied. When she laughed, he looked embarrassed, as though the joke didn't deserve a chuckle. There was a self-effacement about him that she liked.

She let him order for both of them, with her approval, and was more than pleased with the results. Over coffee he opened a small portfolio and took out several printed sheets, which he apologetically handed over to her. They were his lyrics, and when she looked over the first sheet, she saw that it was very good stuff indeed, though rhythmically complex.

"How do you hear this scanning?" she asked him. "'There isn't a moment when I haven't thought about all of the songs that we sang,'" She read it aloud as triplets with a stop after *thought*.

"That's it exactly," Gerry said. "But on the next line I thought it might be cool to have two beats after 'But now they're locked'—two, three—'within the rocks'—two, three, y'see? And then the last line..."

"'Of my frozen heart,'" Rachel completed. "Yeah, I get it."

"So, you think you could come up with a tune to it then?" He was leaning across the table toward her, as though expecting her to burst into song at any second.

"Well, not while you're sitting there *waiting*," she said with a grin. She hefted the small stack of papers. "These aren't your only copies, are they?"

"No, they're for you—mark them up if you like."

"I'll need some music paper."

"Ah…" Gerry pulled a new tablet of notation paper from his portfolio and passed it over. "Picked some up this afternoon."

She cocked her head at him and gave a wry smile. "You seem to have been pretty confident that I'd be willing to take a crack at this."

Gerry shrugged. "I figure you've probably read *worse* lyrics."

"Yeah, and I've written music for a lot worse, too." She dropped her smile. "But how do you know that I'll write the kind of music you want to go with your words? You've never heard a thing I've done."

"I don't know," he said, just as serious as she. "But there are some people you meet and you just know there's music in them. It didn't take me long to hear it when I was talking to you."

She hadn't expected it, but just like that he had said something so dear, so sweet, so *loving* that it took nearly all her will just to keep from dropping her jaw and staring at him. As it was, she could feel her mouth start to open. She regained her self-control and snapped it shut, then said, "Now *that* you ought to put into lyrics."

He smiled and nodded at the papers she held. "I did. About the fourth one down." She laughed in surprise. "I'm joking. But it wouldn't be bad, would it?"

Damn, but she liked this guy, someone who could move her one minute and make her laugh the next. "No, it wouldn't be bad. Why don't you work on that, and I'll work on this."

"How long are you in Ireland?" he asked suddenly.

"Two weeks, why?"

"Do you think we can form…a solid professional relationship during such a short time?"

She looked at him with what she hoped was a touch of seductiveness in her violet eyes. "I think so. At the very least, we ought to be able to hear each other's music."

Then he surprised her again, reaching across the table and taking her hand, giving it a gentle squeeze. "I hope so. I surely do hope so," he said.

He paid when the bill came, stilling her protests with a raised hand and a shake of his head, and they walked out onto the streets of Galway.

"Now where?" she asked.

"Wherever you like. The whole world's before us."

"That's a good way to look at things."

"It's the only way. So, what do you feel like—music, drink, dancing, all three?"

"What time do you have to teach tomorrow?" she asked with a sidelong glance.

"Why, are you my nurse?" he asked playfully.

"No, and I'm not your mother either," she returned in kind, and was surprised to see Gerry's smile vanish. "What is it?"

He took a deep breath and smiled again. "My ma passed away a while back."

"I'm sorry."

"Sometimes it's like I forget, and then somebody says something and it just hits me all over fierce."

"I can relate," Rachel said. "My mother died, too. A little over a month ago."

"God, I'm sorry to hear it. What happened?"

"Cancer," Rachel said. "How about yours?"

"A motor accident. Been about a year now. She was right young, only about fifty."

"My mom was fifty-two. She's why I'm here, actually. She loved Ireland. She and my dad used to come over, but they never brought me along. So, I thought I'd see what was so great about it."

"And what do you think so far?"

"So far I like it just fine. Everybody I've met has been really nice."

"So, who have you met besides me?"

"Nobody." She stretched up to kiss him, and he leaned down to make it easier. His kiss was as gentle as she thought it would be. "You know," she said, "maybe we could do that music, drink, and dancing stuff at your place."

"I don't see why not."

CHAPTER 9

By Wednesday, five days after she played "Niel Gow's Lament" in the Lilting Banshee, Susanna Cassidy still hadn't told Michael Lynch who she really was. Other than that slight omission, Susanna thought everything was going swimmingly. Her secret, however, was like the Ancient Mariner's dead albatross around her neck, getting heavier and heavier with every passing day, and, like a dead albatross, she was almost certain she was starting to smell it. She just hoped that Michael didn't.

She told herself over and over that she *must* tell him the truth, but the opportunity hadn't yet presented itself. There were always other people about, or, if they were alone, she was just too happy to take the chance of ruining everything.

Susanna and Michael had been almost inseparable since that Friday evening in the Banshee. Over the weekend he had shown her the town, and they had spent the evenings drifting to various pubs so that she could hear the full spectrum of traditional music to be found in Galway. Sunday morning he invited her to attend Mass with him and his mother, but she declined.

"It's not because I'm uncomfortable with the Mass," she told him. "It's just that…well, it's a very *family* thing to do, and I don't know that we're ready for that…do you know what I mean?"

"I think so," Michael said, nodding.

"Does it bother you that I'm not Catholic?" she asked him, bracing for the answer.

"Oh…" He put on an expression of mock seriousness. "It's always a concern as to how the wee ones will be raised." He broke into laughter on the final word, and she joined him, both of them howling.

Susanna spent her Sunday morning with a thick *Irish Independent* and the afternoon with Michael, then drove sixty-five miles southeast to Limerick and found the B&B Michael had recommended. The next day she met with several professors at the university, and returned to Galway that evening.

On Tuesday morning, Michael picked her up and they drove out to the Cliffs of Moher. As they pulled into the car park she said, "I probably haven't been out here for ten years or so."

"Good," Michael said. "Then you can show me the sights. I haven't been here since I was a lad."

"You've got to be joking."

"Why? Do you think New Yorkers constantly visit the Statue of Liberty? It gets so you take things for granted. What's in your own back yard isn't very exciting..." He stopped the car and pulled the brake. "Unless you have someone to share it with. Then it can be like seeing it for the first time." He reached for her hand and gave it a squeeze. "Shall we?" he asked, nodding toward the sea.

They walked the short distance to where the paths split and chose the one on the right that led up toward an old stone observation tower. The path was bordered on the ocean side by waist-high slabs of gray stone spotted with white lichen, and the view everywhere was awe-inspiring.

To the left was the most dramatic vista, five cleanly hewn cubes of rock towering seven hundred feet high, jutting nearly as far into the sea. They looked, Susanna thought, like a fanned hand of cards played by gods. Seabirds bobbed and spun in the wind, and below white froth curled around the base of the cliffs. Moss dotted much of the rock, speckled white in many places with the nesting birds.

Sitting on a stool by the path, a bearded man with hair that billowed around his shoulders like waves was playing an Irish flute, oblivious to the chilly wind blowing in from the sea. The tune was in a minor key and melancholy, suitable for the cloudy day, but not for Susanna's bright spirit. She held Michael's hand tightly as they continued on the rolling path.

"Looks like O'Brien's Tower is closed for the season," Michael said as they reached it and found a locked door. "Probably be open in May when most of the tourists start coming. Funny, though," he said, looking about, "it's hardly changed since I was a boy."

"That's the beauty of this country," Susanna said, feeling the sea wind tug at her hair. "In the states, this place would be commercialized to the hilt. The only view you'd have would be straight ahead. But here you can look all around, and there's nothing but...well, but Ireland."

"Then you haven't read about Bewley's Tea having paid the country half a million Euros to paint ads on the cliffs next summer," Michael said so wistfully that for a moment she almost believed him. Her face fell for a fraction of a second, long enough for him to grin a *Gotcha* at her before she laughed.

Hand in hand, they walked back the way they had come. There weren't many other people at the cliffs that day. A few couples, several families, and some solitary strollers were admiring the views and taking photos, but the area was so large and spread out that Susanna felt as though she and Michael had the place to themselves. It was a grand feeling.

A low stone wall separated the official walkway from the cliffs themselves, and many people had stepped over the wall and were heading up the steep walk to the top of the nearest cliff. There was also easy access to several wide and not-so-wide ledges that dropped straight down to the sea and the rocks below. "Come on," Michael said, climbing over the wall and holding out his hand to her. "Let's get up close and personal with these rocks."

Susanna took a breath and climbed over the low wall. She didn't mind heights if there was something to hold on to, a rail of some sort between her and the drop, but here there was nothing. You could go as close as you liked to the sheer edge, could even stand with your toes on the brink and look hundreds of feet straight down if you'd a mind to.

"This is something else you'd never be able to do in the states," she said. "There would be park rangers and who knows what else to grab you."

"Don't worry—*I'll* grab you...should you start to fall, I mean." He smiled, and they walked hand in hand on the rock.

It wasn't too bad. Here the ledge was a good thirty feet wide and perfectly flat. It was like taking a stroll on a hotel veranda.

Then Michael started to move out to where the rock narrowed to form a point, and Susanna held back. "It's all right," he said. "I just want to look." She held on to his hand, leaning backward as he placed his front foot on the very point of the rock and craned his head forward to look down. She wondered what she would do if she felt him start to fall, if her weight and strength would be enough to keep him from toppling over the edge. But in another second, he was by her side, moving away from the sharp edge of rock.

"It's amazing," he said. "It just plunges straight down."

"Doesn't it make you dizzy?" she asked.

"Not really. Besides, I had you to hold onto. Come on, let's go over there…" He led her toward another ledge, this one a bit narrower, and she hugged the ridge of gray rock that rose on their right. Six feet to the left was the edge and open sky.

They stopped just before a place where the ledge narrowed sharply, angling until there was less than a foot of walking space, then widening again onto a ten-foot square on which Susanna could have stood with some ease. The problem was that in order to get there she would have to step across the gap.

"The view down is breathtaking from over there," Michael said.

"That's what I'm afraid of."

"You don't have to be afraid. You can just step right across it."

"I don't think I can."

"Of course you can."

"I don't mean physically. I know I'm capable of it. It's only a few inches. It's just the thought that stops me, of stepping across…an *abyss* like that." The fact that she was trembling annoyed her. She didn't want to seem a coward in Michael's eyes.

"Watch," he said, and, making sure that she was standing safely against the rising rock on the right, he released her hand, walked a few paces to the gap, and stepped right across it, then turned back to her, his feet inches from the brink, and reached out across the space between them. "Now, you come, too. Just take my hand and step across to me. Don't look down. Don't think about what's there. Just look at me. Think of me. Take my hand. Step across."

There was a heaviness in her throat that she could not swallow away. It was absurd, she thought. It wasn't as though he was asking her to leap across several feet of empty space. It was just a gap, a small gap that widened once you were on the other side. She would be safe all the time.

"Do you remember the lines in your song?" she heard him say. "The one I wrote for you?"

Susanna swallowed hard. "Why don't you...why don't you sing them for me?"

"All right." And he sang softly, "'I'd step across the river, I'd step across the sea...'"

She edged closer toward Michael, her right hand on the rock face, her left outstretched toward him. At last their fingers joined above the gap, and she tried to keep looking at him, but something that she couldn't help pulled away her gaze so that, just for a moment, she glanced down.

Only inches from her left foot she saw the cliff edge, and the sea swirling below. Her breath locked within her.

And Michael sang, "'If that would bring my lover back to me...'"

Then something stronger than fear possessed her, and she stepped toward Michael with her left foot, and her right followed, and then she was with him, and they were both on the other side, moving back from the edge, back to safety. She burrowed into his arms.

"There, that's my brave girl," he said. "Not so bad now, was it?"

"Actually, it was. But I made it." She gave a nervous laugh. "The only thing keeping me from celebrating is knowing that I have to go back again."

"You looked down, didn't you?" he said.

"Yes. I think that was why I had to step across. It seemed that if I didn't move...the sea was going to pull me down."

"Not while I'm here."

"Whenever I'm on high places like this, I always think about that story by Poe, 'The Imp of the Perverse.' Did you ever read it?"

"I recall the title, but not the story."

"I read it when I was a kid," Susanna went on, "but what I remember is something Poe says about when you're standing on the edge of an abyss, there's…*something* that draws you toward it, the horror of your own death from falling, and you become fascinated with the idea, and unless you can drive that thought from your mind, you might actually go over the edge."

"So, did he mean, say, if a person was suicidal?"

"No. It had nothing to do with your will. It was just some self-destructive tendency that took over, something primitive. The easiest, the most natural thing to do is just go with the feeling and fall rather than struggle against it."

"Even if falling means your death."

"Yes."

They both stood silently watching the sky and the sea. "I don't think I believe that," Michael finally said. "Unless you really want to die for some reason, I can't imagine that anyone would just let himself go like that. I mean, I can understand dizziness, vertigo, what have you, but you'd never willingly fall into the deep if you could fall *away* from it."

"Maybe you're right," Susanna said. "At any rate, it gives me the creeps. I don't like thinking about it, especially knowing that I've got to cross back over." She gave a mock shudder so that he held her more tightly.

"Would you feel better on the other side?"

"Yes. It's beautiful here, but the apprehension over the return trip is dulling my enjoyment."

"Spoken like a true academic. Then might I invite you to take a return stroll with me? We might stop at yon souvenir shop where weak tea can be had in paper cups."

"It sounds so inviting, how could any woman decline?"

Arm in arm they moved toward the gap. "After you?" Michael asked.

"I think I'd prefer that we handle it the way we did before."

"Leaving you alone on this precipice? What about the wolves

that swoop down and drag away stray lambs and American ladies?"

"I'll take my chances for the three seconds it takes to gather my courage and join you." She held the rock with one hand and gestured with the other. "Fly, fly..."

Michael grinned and stepped across, then turned back and held out his hand. Susanna smiled with tight lips and grasped it, then stepped across the gap once more. She didn't look down, and it was easier.

"Let's get that cup of tea now," Michael said. "I'd say you even earned a scone."

The tea was indeed served in paper cups, but it was strong enough and hot enough to drive out the chill, and the huge scone they shared was fresh. "So," Michael asked as they perched on high chairs at a small round table and sipped their tea, "what does the rest of your week look like?"

"Aren't you bored showing me the sights?"

"Hardly. Remember, I'm seeing a lot of them for the first time in years."

"Well, tomorrow's free, but Thursday I'm going up to Letterkenny. Two of the students from my school are at the Institute of Technology there on an exchange program, so I'm going to visit them, talk to some faculty, make sure everything's okay."

"Were you thinking of doing the trip in a day?"

"I was hoping I could. I mean it's not like Limerick, where I had to be there for a morning meeting, but it *is* about a hundred and seventy miles."

"Aye, and you're not going on motorways here. Give yourself a good four hours one way."

"That long?"

"You can do it in a day—leave early, get up there by noon, have your meeting, and come back."

She frowned. "I hate to drive that much in a day."

Michael paused for a moment and ate a morsel of scone. "Listen, I have to work at the Banshee tomorrow, but Thursday I'm free. I'd be happy to drive you up and back."

"Oh, I couldn't ask you to—"

"You didn't have to ask, I offered."

"Well..." Susanna paused in thought. It would be wonderful to have Michael's company on the trip, but she was suddenly concerned that her false identity as Julia Cassidy might be revealed. The faculty members at the institute would know Susanna's full name, and if Michael called her Julia in front of them it could be awkward at the least.

The answer was to tell him the truth immediately, but the problem was that she was afraid to. She had thought that, as she got to know Michael better, it would be easier to be honest with him. What she had not reckoned on was that, as their relationship deepened, it had become all the more precious to her, so that she was now even more fearful of losing it.

"In fact," Michael said, as though just thinking of it, "I could drop you at the institute and pick you up whenever you like. My cousin Malachy's up in Letterkenny, and I could visit him while you're doing your work."

The prospect, she thought, was a godsend. That way Michael would never meet the faculty members. "All right...but only on the condition that we take my car. After all, the university's paying for the gas and rental. But you're sure you don't mind?"

"Not at all. Having you all to myself for four hours up and four back? Couldn't spend a better day than that. Besides, Malachy will be happy to see me, and I him. It'll be a grand day all around."

CHAPTER 10

They were all grand days so far, Susanna thought that Thursday as she drove her little rental car through the early morning streets to pick up Michael. Though she had worked at the university's Centre for Human Rights the day before, she had spent the evening with him, making it her treat for dinner for a change. She had even chosen the restaurant, the bright and airy one to which he had taken her on their first evening together. Mary, the hostess, had smiled at her in a way that told her the older woman was surprised to see her back with Michael, but not displeased by the sight.

After dinner, he had driven her back to her room early, since they planned to leave for Letterkenny at seven the next morning. They had sat in the car for a long time, kissing deeply, and she thought that, perhaps, had they not had the early morning ahead of them, she might have yielded to her impulses and invited him up, or even returned with him to his place to spend the night.

They had not yet slept together, indeed had not even gotten much beyond deep and tender kisses, but she reminded herself that it had been scarcely a week since they had met. Emotionally, if not sexually, things were going blazingly fast, particularly for Susanna.

She could count on both hands the number of affairs she had had since her twenties. In not quite fifty unmarried years she had slept with only half a dozen men, the last of whom, to her chagrin, had been married. His name was Kyle Martin, and he was a professor of literature at the university at which Susanna taught.

Their affair began five years earlier, when the college sent the two of them to a conference in California. Kyle had come to the faculty from Gettysburg just a year before, and Susanna had felt immediately drawn to him. He wasn't the most handsome man she had ever met, but he was intelligent and had a splendid sense of humor. When they were alone, he had acted lightly flirtatious toward her, and she had returned the banter. At the conference, they had gone to his room for a comradely drink at the end of the day, and almost before she realized it, they were in bed together.

She had been to blame even more than he. She knew he was married, but it had been years since she had been with a man, and Kyle had treated her tenderly and thoughtfully. Even though it was like something out of one of those trashy novels she occasionally read, she found herself falling in love with him.

When they returned to the campus, they continued the affair for several weeks, always meeting at her town house, usually on weekdays between classes. Then one evening at a reception for a visiting speaker, Susanna met Nikki Martin, Kyle's wife, and immediately the affair was over. Nikki was an extremely bright and attractive woman who also happened to walk with two metal crutches as the result of multiple sclerosis, which she had had for six years.

The prospect of cheating with a healthy woman's husband was bad enough, but the fact that the woman Susanna was cuckolding had a chronic disease was too much for her. Though she talked brightly with Nikki, *too* brightly, she realized later, her stomach churned with sick guilt. The next day she told Kyle that she couldn't see him again, that whatever they had had was now over. Whether Kyle loved her or Nikki was beside the point. Susanna had engaged in a relationship that had been dishonorable, and it wasn't until she had seen Nikki that she had realized it fully. Even if the woman had been of sound body, Susanna thought she might have ended it anyway after she met her and put a face to what had been only an abstraction.

Now, as she drove toward The Long Walk and Michael, she tried to put away the past and think about the present. He was sitting on one of the low stone curbs on the dockside, and she stopped the car and got out. When she kissed him he smelled of aftershave and toothpaste. It was a smell she liked. They had agreed to eat a quick breakfast before meeting to save time, but he held up a large metal travel mug and a green thermos bottle. "Coffee," he said. "Thought we might need it. Hope you don't mind sharing a mug. Only have one."

"Not at all," she said, and kissed him once more. Then they got into the car, Michael behind the wheel.

They took Route 17 all the way to Sligo, passing through dozens of small towns like Tuam and Knock. Susanna could never quite get over how picturesque Ireland was. Its roads weren't thronged with billboards and roadside stops the way they were in America. Instead there were fields and hills and lakes and mountains, unsullied by signs of commerce. In many places there were no signs of civilization at all but for the road on which they drove, and in most others the only traces were stone or wire fences to mark the land and contain the sheep, which were far more populous than people.

"God, it's so gorgeous," she said as they passed a small stone cottage with a green roof and door but no windows. It lay at the foot of a stony mountain and was surrounded by gorse, boulders, and recumbent sheep, their heavy wool marked with a red dye that rain had washed to a weak pink. "Beautiful desolation."

"And a desperate poor way to make a living," Michael said.

Susanna made no reply. He was right, of course. She couldn't understand how people were able to scratch enough out of this harsh and unyielding land to get by. Elsewhere on the island the soil was richer, but in vast parts of the west it seemed impossible to eke out a minimal existence. The stark beauty of the landscape was, she was certain, more of a curse than a boon to those who tried.

The silence between them lasted only a minute, and they began to talk again. Though she knew of the economic difficulties that Ireland had experienced, Michael told her how it had affected the people involved, and the tales his stepfather Tim Sullivan had told him of relatives who stayed on the farms when Tim's family came to the towns to work. Most of them were sad stories.

They arrived in Sligo mid-morning and paused to get tea

and a muffin in a shop, then continued on. Here the rocks gave way to more vegetation, and as they headed north on N15, the massive plateau of Ben Bulben, in whose shadow Yeats had written, kept pace with them for a long time.

Michael and Susanna began talking about Yeats then, and traded their favorite lines back and forth as they motored along. From his gift of Yeats to Julia years before, Susanna had known that Michael had an affinity for the poet, but she was amazed at the number of works he had committed to memory. While Susanna could recite a few in their entirety, and a number of individual lines and couplets, Michael could reel off whole poems as soon as she came up with a title.

Anyone reciting Yeats, she thought, should have an Irish accent. Michael made music out of "An Irish Airman Foresees His Death," "The Wild Swans at Coole," and "The Song of Wandering Aengus," which nearly put a tear in her eye.

"Many criticize him," Michael said, "because they say he didn't do much for the political struggle, that he spent too much of his time thinking and writing about fairies and not about a free Ireland." He chuckled. "Some of that spiritual stuff makes him sound off his nut. Did you ever read *A Vision*? Pretty odd, that. But I say so what if he didn't give Ireland his arms? He gave it his words, and that was enough."

"'Easter 1916,'" Susanna said, coming up with the title of one of Yeats's poems about the Republican rising.

"Oh, that's a grand one:

'MacDonagh and MacBride
And Connolly and Pearse
Now and in time to be,
Wherever green is worn,
Are changed, changed utterly:
A terrible beauty is born.'

"That's just the end of it, but it was the first Yeats I learned by heart. My father taught it to me."

"When you lived in the North," Susanna said.

"Yes." Michael's face lost its smile.

"Was that hard for your family?"

He nodded. "Yes. It was. Wicked hard." His face grew firm, his eyes stared flatly at the road ahead.

"There's another line from that poem," she said gently. "It's one I've used at peace conferences...even during one-on-one reconciliations. It says, 'Too long a sacrifice/Can make a stone of the heart.'"

Michael glanced at her, gave a quick smile, then a nod. "I'm sure that's true. I've seen it happen." The smile returned as he concentrated on the road. "There's another Irish poem about that very thing—not by Yeats—by Patrick...*Padraig* Pearse."

Susanna knew that Pearse was one of the martyrs of 1916 the British had executed in reprisal for the Easter rising. "He was a poet?"

"Oh yes. They were all poets in their way, but he wrote his poetry down as well as lived it. The one I love is 'Renunciation.'" Michael recited it then, like a man in a dream.

"Naked I saw thee,
O Beauty of Beauty
And I blinded my eyes,
For fear I should fail.

I heard thy music
O melody of melody,
And I closed my ears,
For fear I should falter.

I tasted thy mouth,
O sweetness of sweetness,
And I hardened my heart,
For fear of my slaying.

I blinded my eyes,
And I closed my ears,
I hardened my heart
And I smothered my desire.

I turned my back,
On the vision I had shaped,
And to this road before me,
I turned my face.

I have turned my face,
To this road before me,
To the deed that I see,
And the death I shall die."

"It's beautiful." Susanna said after a long moment. "And tragic. As though he knew he was going to die, but accepted it and gave up everything he loved for Ireland."

"Here's the irony," Michael said. "Pearse wrote that poem in 1910, when he wasn't involved politically at all. It was just…a poem to him at the time."

"I think it was more than a poem. There's certainly a sense of deep grief in it. I wonder what—or who—he gave up, and what he hardened his heart for, what that something was that was more important than love…"

The sad words of the poem echoed in her ears as they drove, but eventually they found a new subject. The mood in the car lightened until, shortly after noon, the road took them over a crest of a hill, and they saw the city of Letterkenny below.

Even from a distance it seemed a lively, sprawling town. It had grown out rather than up, and its low skyline was pierced only by the spire of St. Eunan's Cathedral. The sunlight that had accompanied Susanna and Michael since morning had been replaced by gray clouds that hung low over the town.

"We may have gotten here just in time," Michael said. "Looks as though it might bucket before too long. Do you want to get a spot of lunch before you go to the institute?"

Susanna thought that something in her stomach might help settle it after the long ride, so they drove toward town in search of a café. "Pearse Road," Susanna read from a street post. "Named for Patrick, of course."

"Of course. Go far enough and it runs into De Valera Road.

We Irish know how to honor our heroes. Letterkenny streets are a primer in our history. See there?" He pointed at a street post reading *Oliver Plunkett Road*. "Know him?"

Susanna nodded. "An Irish Catholic martyr, teacher. Seventeenth century. A saint, too, as I recall."

"Correct. Gold star. He had the audacity to perform the services of a priest when the English wanted them all out of Ireland. In a typical display of English mercy and understanding, he was taken to England, hung, burned, and quartered. Now..." He nodded to the right of the car at another post. "Who was Neil T. Blaney, who has *that* lovely road named for him?"

"More recent," Susanna answered. "He was a Fianna Fail politician who supported the Republicans in Northern Ireland. They accused him of smuggling arms into the North."

"*Importing*, not smuggling. And he was acquitted."

"That's true, he was."

"I have to hand it to you, girl, you know your history. One might almost guess you were a teacher." They both laughed and then Michael nodded ahead. "My cousin's bookshop is right up that road a ways. *But...*" He pulled the car over and parked. "There's a nice little restaurant here."

They took only fifteen minutes to have sandwiches, and Michael dropped off Susanna just minutes before her one o'clock meeting with the two students. "I should be finished by three or three-thirty," she said as she opened the door of the car.

"No trouble," Michael said. "Malachy and I will have plenty to ramble on about for a few hours." He leaned over and kissed her. "Have fun."

The visit took far less time than Susanna had anticipated. She talked to the two students for only twenty minutes, long enough for them to answer her questions and assure her that everything was fine. They had even acquired a trace of Irish dialect, and she had to bite back a grin when one of them described their faculty advisor as *bleedin' deadly*, which she assumed from the context was a compliment.

She spent another half hour with Peter Connaghan, the advisor, who showed her some of the newer facilities, but by the time she was ready to take her leave, it was just after two, and a soft rain had started to fall. She didn't fancy the idea of standing outside waiting for Michael to return at three, so she told Connaghan that she wanted to meet a friend at a bookshop nearby, run by a Malachy Lynch, and asked if he knew where it was.

He looked at her a bit oddly, then gave her directions. It was within walking distance, but if she wished to avoid the rain there was a bus due any minute.

As she walked out, she saw the bus rounding the corner and trotted down to meet it. She told the driver what she was looking for, and, after several minutes of stop-and-go driving, he nodded for her to get off.

The area she found herself in was a residential one elevated above the main street of the town. A hanging sign simply stated *BOOKS*, with an arrow pointing down a short stone driveway to a large cottage. Her rental car was parked near the house, and a door on the side of the house read *Shop*. The rain began to fall harder, and she hurried toward the promise of shelter.

As she walked closer, she saw that the bookshop had been built from an attached garage to the right of the cottage, and an extension added on to that so that the whole structure rambled toward the right. A display window was in the center of the shop, but because of the books in the window she was unable to see any further inside.

Susanna opened her car door and tossed her small portfolio onto the back seat, then continued toward the bookstore. As she reached the door, it suddenly swung open, startling her. In the doorway stood a man with a fist for a face, punctuated by a black eye patch. Though only an inch taller than Susanna, he seemed to loom over her. "You've business in that car?" he asked in a harsh, high voice.

For a second she couldn't speak, then said, "Well, yes…it's mine." The man looked surprised, and she went on. "Is Michael Lynch here?"

His face cleared, and the knuckles of it relaxed into what he might have thought a welcoming smile. "Ah, and are you the lady then, Miss…"

"Cassidy. Yes."

"Well, come in, come in," he said, stepping back awkwardly. "Don't be standin' in the rain. My apologies, didn't mean to gobsmack you. Heard the car door, and didn't know what was transpirin'..."

As he moved into the shop, she saw that his awkwardness was due to a pronounced limp. She followed him and saw Michael, who hopped off a stool next to the counter and smiled quizzically at her. "Finished early then?" he asked.

She nodded. "Didn't take as long as I thought, so I took the bus over here. I can't resist a used bookshop."

"Now there's a woman after me own heart," the man said. "Too bad you've got her already, Michael."

"Introductions then," Michael said. "Julia, this is my cousin, Malachy Lynch."

"Your *big* cousin," Malachy said, playfully bumping against Michael and looking up at him. "Got a few years on you, boyo."

"Aye, and you always will," Michael replied with a straight face, then grinned. "And this is Julia Cassidy."

"Pleased I am to make your acquaintance," Malachy said, giving a little bow. Despite Susanna's first impression, he now seemed pleasant and boyish, and she wondered if he was portraying a stage Irishman for the lady tourist's benefit, or if he really was such a sprite. "It's a soft auld day out there, isn't it?" he went on with a fatuous smile. "Good thing you didn't have to walk over here in this weather. Michael and I were just having a nice catch-up. If you'd like to look around my humble shop, feel free. Should you find anything you like, it's thirty per cent discount to friends of the family."

"Thank you."

"Michael tells me you're one of those, what do you call them in the states, peaceniks?"

She smiled tightly. "That's a pretty ancient term. My field is peace studies and conflict resolution."

"Ah. And you're interested in Ireland in particular? The Troubles and all?" She nodded. "Well, then you'll find a lot of books here to suit your fancy. Most of them in that room through there..." He pointed to the doorway that led to the addition, and waggled his fingers as though to urge her through.

Susanna nodded and went into the other room. Malachy Lynch was right. All about the room were floor to ceiling shelves, most of which were filled with books about the history of Ireland since 1916. On the wall space that remained hung faded, framed portraits, some of which came from old newspapers, of the heroes of Ireland from the Easter Sunday martyrs to Bobby Sands, who starved himself to death in Long Kesh Prison in 1981.

There were many titles that Susanna had never seen, and as she browsed she realized that while there were a few books on the peace process itself, the vast majority were biographies of Irish rebels, histories of the Republican movement and the IRA, pro-Republican political fiction and volumes of poetry, and hundreds of pamphlets costing between fifty cents and a Euro each.

She picked one up and saw the title: *Report of the Committee of Inquiry into Police Interrogation Procedures in Northern Ireland.* As she looked through more of them, she saw that they were all anti-English and Northern Irish tracts. There was no mistaking where Malachy Lynch's sympathies lay.

Susanna continued to browse as the soft voices of the men in the next room came to her through the doorway. Though she couldn't make out their words, Malachy's high, piping voice sounded more animated than Michael's deep and calm one.

She found a paperback edition of *To Take Arms: A Year in the Provisional IRA*, for which she'd been looking for years, and headed back toward the doorway. When she passed through, both Michael and Malachy quickly looked up. She felt as though she'd walked in on two boys planning how best to filch cookies.

The angry look on Malachy's face immediately shifted to a fawning smile. "Find something?" Susanna held up the book and Malachy's smile weakened. "Ah, the old informer McGuire's book, eh?" he said, referring to the author. "Glad to see that one go. And why is it you're wanting it then?"

"I like to hear all sides of a situation," she replied. "And the early seventies were a particularly violent time. I'd like to know how people back then thought, what were the...conditions they faced that allowed them to rationalize violence." Malachy's expression grew more sour, and Susanna frustratingly felt as though she had to rationalize herself. "It's not morbid curiosity, really."

"Aye," Michael said with a smile at her. "The lass is an *academic*, Malachy, so wipe the hump off."

Malachy grinned again. Changing his face as circumstances dictated came too easily to him. "Well, let me see the cost…" He took the book from her and opened it. "Ah, just three Euros—well, take it and call it a gift. I'd feel guilty sellin' such a piece of propaganda. Girl barely met Mac Stiofain, and lets on he was her mate." He held the book with two fingers as though it smelled, and Susanna took it back and thanked him.

In the silence, a sudden sharp noise came from beneath their feet. It was a sound like metal striking concrete, and it made her jump. Michael shot a hot, angry glance at his cousin, but Malachy's expression was the more surprising.

His whole face clenched as though someone had just scraped fingernails on a chalkboard. His eyes narrowed and his body tensed, but, when there were no other sounds, he quickly relaxed, and the overweening smile returned. "Cats!" he laughed. "I've three bloody cats in this house, and they're always up to something." He laughed again and stamped on the floor. "Quiet down there, you miserable bastards! Right pain in the hole y'are, knocking things over." Malachy looked at Michael and shrugged. "Damned animals—what can you do?"

"They don't come in the shop?" Susanna asked.

"Shy," Malachy whispered. "Used to be feral, they did."

"Maybe you should have them fixed," Michael said, but Malachy made no reply. "Well, we'd best be getting on. Have a bit of a drive ahead of us."

"Right. Well, it was good to make your acquaintance, Miss Cassidy," Malachy said, nodding like a B-movie merchant as the rich folk left his shop. "Hope we'll see you again."

"Good meeting you, too, and thanks so much for the book."

The rain was falling heavily when they stepped outside, and it had grown considerably colder. They ran for the car, Susanna bending over the book to keep it dry. Michael opened the door for her and then ran to the other side. "Quite a day," he said as he settled behind the wheel. "Not looking forward to driving back through all this." It was as though he didn't wish to speak of his cousin at all.

"Maybe it'll ease off," she said.

"Maybe." Michael started the car. As they backed out the drive, Malachy appeared at the doorway and waved goodbye. His presence gave Susanna the opportunity to speak of him again.

"Your cousin has a nice shop. There's a surprising amount of material in there, but it's so...specialized. Does he have a large clientele?"

"That I can't tell you. He's able to keep it going, so I guess so."

"Does he sell through the internet at all?"

"Don't know—don't really think so."

"He seems to be a strong Republican."

"Now that he is. As was his father. Malachy believes all Ireland should be free, as do many of us." Michael looked at the sky through the windshield, which was scarcely kept clear by the rapidly twitching wipers. The raindrops were thickening and becoming heavier. "Devil of a day."

"You two grew up together?" Susanna asked. In spite of the tension between Michael and Malachy, Susanna had sensed a strong bond as well.

"We did. Malachy was a few years ahead of me. He was like my older brother when we were boys." Michael gave a short laugh. "He tormented me fierce back then—still does to this day. But he's a good man. A bit hard to get to know. Shy, in his way."

"He has trouble with his leg?"

Michael nodded. "An accident. Years ago."

"Is that when he lost the eye too?"

"No, that was...something else." He glanced at her. "So how was your meeting?"

He seemed to want to change the subject, so she told him about the students and how their speech was becoming more Irish. They had a good laugh over it, and the atmosphere in the cramped quarters of the car grew more relaxed. Susanna was careful not to mention Malachy again, and they both grew cheerier as the miles passed.

Over the next hour, the rain fell more slowly but with greater solidity, and Susanna was surprised to see that it had actually changed to snow, big heavy flakes that were easily swept away to the sides of the windshield, but which were collecting there in clumps.

"I've never seen snow in Ireland before," she said.

"We get it now and again. Awful mess when it happens. We're never ready for it, so it ties things up pretty bad."

"The way it does in our American South, I guess. Is it slippery?"

"A bit." Susanna was glad that Michael kept their speed down. He was a careful driver, even more so than she might have been, and seemed reluctant to overdrive his visibility, which was rapidly diminishing.

By seven that evening they were only a few miles north of Sligo. Susanna guessed that an inch of snow had fallen. Several times Michael opened the window to brush the excess snow off the side of the windshield as he drove, and once the car went into a slow skid from which he skillfully righted it.

"Would you like to stop soon—for dinner?" she asked him. "You must be ready for a break."

"Aye, this white-knuckle driving's wearisome. Yeats Tavern's along here soon. Good place to eat." They passed the Drumcliff churchyard, where Yeats was buried. Susanna thought the site would look beautiful under a blanket of white, but she could barely glimpse the high square tower of the small church through the darkness and the heavily falling snow.

Soon she saw the lights of the tavern, and Michael pulled gingerly into the car park, turned off the ignition, and sat back with a sigh. "Well, that put the heart crossways in me. Not used to driving in this mess." Despite his exhaustion, he smiled brightly at her. "So, I think what's called for is a good hot meal and several cups of coffee."

"No pints?"

"I'd no sooner drive on these roads with a pint in me than I'd jig on the edge of the Cliffs of Moher."

"You seemed pretty comfortable there."

"Just a pose to impress the pretty ladies."

They walked arm in arm across the car park, holding on to each other for support on the slippery surface. Inside, the restaurant was nearly empty, the snow having kept all but the most dedicated travelers off the roads. The coffee, which arrived ahead of the food, warmed them nicely.

"I can't think of anyone I'd rather be stuck in the snow with," Michael said, taking her hand across the table.

"Do you think we're really stuck?"

"No. Just wishful thinking." When the waiter brought their soup, Michael asked him, "Heard a weather report?"

"Aye. Snow's stoppin' but a freeze is comin' on. Roads'll soon be ice. Where you headed?"

"Galway."

"Think again," the young man said. "I'd not drive there tonight, and I'm a mentaller on the road." He nodded at the bowls. "Enjoy your soup."

"A *mentaller*?" Susanna asked when the man had gone.

"A crazy man." Michael sighed. "Doesn't sound good, does it?"

The prospect for travel might have been bad, but the food was good. They even had dessert over still more coffee. Michael set down his fork after finishing his last bite of porter cake and sighed. "Shall we try and find a place to stay?" he said. "I don't want to risk banging up your car, let alone getting *you* into an accident."

She nodded. "It's silly to take a chance. I don't have to be anywhere tomorrow. But since it's my fault we're here, I insist that you let me pay for the rooms." She used the plural on purpose, though she wouldn't have declined a change to singular.

"Let's cross that bridge when we reach it," Michael said. "I suspect there'll be a lot of stranded travelers on the roads tonight. We may be lucky to find a place at all."

After they paid the bill, Michael asked the cashier if she knew of any B&B's that might have rooms. She gave him a list of several, and they sat in the warmth of the entry and started calling.

The first two were full up, but the third try was successful. "That'll be grand. Thank you," Michael said, and rang off.
"Ben Bulben Farm," he told Susanna. "Big house back a lane.
There are two dormer rooms on the third floor that share a bath
with each other, no one else." He smiled. "I wonder if they have
complementary toothbrushes for snowbound wayfarers."

"We'll make do," she said.

Outside the snow was not falling as heavily as before, but
it felt colder. They brushed the snow off the windshield and
windows, and started off. The road was slick and treacherous,
and Michael drove cautiously, the defroster on full to melt the
ice from the quickly freezing windshield.

They were going so slowly that they were easily able to see
the sign for the farm, and pulled off the road onto the long drive,
nearly invisible under the snow. Fortunately, stone walls were
on either side, and Michael kept to the middle. After a hundred
yards, Susanna saw the lights of the house ahead, which they
used as a guide.

The host, a Mr. Healy, was friendly and welcoming. Michael
explained that they had no luggage, since they had expected to
return to Galway that night, and Healy gave them each a plastic
bag with a toothbrush and a small tube of toothpaste. "There
are towels, soap, and shampoo upstairs," he told them, "and tea
and coffee makings in both rooms. The door between, at the top
of the steps, opens onto a wee widow's walk. You'll no doubt
want to leave that closed tonight," he added with a chuckle as
he led them up the stairs.

The rooms were paneled with a dark wood, and the inward
angles of the encroaching ceiling made them seem even cozier.
The larger of the two rooms had a king-sized bed and a pair of
easy chairs, while the smaller had two recessed single berths that
could be closed off with curtains. "I'll leave you then," Healy said.
"Breakfast's from eight to nine. They say it should be warmer by
morning, so the roads should be melted. Have a pleasant night."

They watched Healy descend the stairs and close the door at
the bottom, and found themselves truly alone for the first time,
with the long night before them. "Well," Susanna said, "which
room do you prefer?"

"It doesn't really matter," Michael said. He suddenly seemed as shy as she felt.

"You can take the big bed then. I'll fit fine into one of the berths." She laughed. "It'll be like being at sea, but without the swaying."

Michael turned to her and looked straight into her eyes, and the intensity of his gaze made her tremble. "You don't have to sleep in the small bed," he said. He took two steps and covered the distance between them until his face was inches from hers. He started to say something, but then shook his head, and frustration appeared on his lean face.

"I don't know...how to say what I want to say," he whispered. "It's been too long. It's been..." He shook his head and looked away.

"I know," she said. "I know. Too long."

She didn't want him to have to say it. She wanted the decision to be hers, so that he could not blame himself afterwards. And she wanted him, too, like she had wanted no other man, not even when she was young.

Susanna pressed the palm of her hand against his cheek and turned his head so that he was looking at her again. Then she raised her mouth to his and closed her eyes and kissed him with all the love and passion she felt for him. His arms went around her, his lips returned her warmth and her need.

In spite of her pleasure, she felt as though she was drowning, and she pulled her face away to breathe. When she did, one of his big hands caressed the side of her face as though holding her heart, and she heard him say, "Oh Jesus, but I love you..."

Then they were on the big bed, and their clothes were falling away from them, and they were falling into each other, eyes and mouths and arms and legs and hands and hearts all one.

Not once did he call her by a name, neither false nor true.

CHAPTER 11

"'Naked I saw thee…'"

Susanna heard the whispered words, but did not open her eyes.

"'I heard thy music…'"

She felt a smile tug at her lips, and a featherlike fingertip traced their line.

"'I tasted thy mouth…'"

She opened her eyes and saw Michael Lynch's face on the pillow next to hers. She didn't know how long they'd been sleeping, but it was still dark outside, and the room was lit only by a small table lamp near the door.

"But I have no intention," he continued, "of blinding my eyes and closing my ears and hardening my heart." He leaned toward her and kissed her lips gently. "I meant what I said. I do love you."

"You've only known me for a week," she said. Try as she might, she could not put the smile from her face.

"A *day* and a week," Michael corrected her, and kissed her again. "It's long after midnight. And let's not forget long ago. You've changed in that time."

"I know," she said, feeling uneasy at his mention of the past of which she'd not been a part.

"Changed for the better. You're different in every way."

Susanna didn't want to hear about the non-existent changes, so she put her finger to his lips and kissed him again, harder and deeper. Their two bodies pressed together beneath the duvet, and the feel of his flesh on hers raised the heat within her so that she clung to him. She felt him respond, and they made love again, not with the hungry desperation of before, but with an exploratory sweetness, a sense of physical and emotional wandering over the landscapes of each other's bodies.

Afterward she lay in the crook of his arm, her head against his cheek, her hand upon the light hair of his chest, as he stroked the smooth whiteness of her arm. "I think," he said, "there are a few things I should tell you."

"Like what?" she asked lazily. She would have preferred to drift into sleep again by his side.

"Some things you should know. Some things that are...a bit hard to talk about."

Susanna was suddenly awake. The tone of Michael's voice put a chill into her. "You don't have to tell me anything you don't want to," she said. Honesty on his part would require reciprocation on hers, and she wasn't ready.

"But I do want to tell you," he said. "There are some things you have to know about me. And the first is that I'm an ex-convict."

"You..."

"I spent ten years in Long Kesh. But I want to tell you why. I want to tell you how I got there. It's a long story. Goes back to when I was a boy. But to know me, you have to hear it. And after you do, well, then it's your choice as to where we go from here." He craned his head and looked down at her. "Would you like a cup of tea before we start?"

She wrapped herself in a blanket and he slipped on his trousers, and they made tea together. Then they sat in the two easy chairs with the small table and their teacups between them, and Michael told Susanna his story.

I was born and raised in the North. In Derry. Spent my first eight years there. My ma and da were Catholic, and my da's family—Patrick was his name—were County Derry men as far back as anyone could tell, so they'd stayed when it became Londonderry. Stayed and starved. My da couldn't get a decent job, never could. You probably know this already, but if you were Catholic in Derry or Belfast or anywhere in the North, it was ten times as hard for you to find any work at all. The Orangemen, the Protestants, ran the government at Stormont and the industries, said who got hired and who didn't, and there was no way to stop them, so Catholics did whatever they could.

Some men were willing to do anything to keep their families from starving and going cold, so they took the worst jobs you can imagine, filthy and demeaning work that made them sick and old before their time. But that wasn't the worst of it.

For some men, the worst part was when their pride was taken away, when the Protestant Unionists would see them working or going to their jobs, and they knew from what they were doing that they were Catholics. To many of those cruel men, if you were Catholic, you were dirt.

When I was a little boy, I saw men spit at my father in the street, I heard men, and women, too, call my mother a Fenian bitch and me her wee bastard as we walked hand to hand on Sundays to what passed for a park. I didn't know what it meant. I just knew it wasn't good, and it made me feel sick for myself and for her, too. When things like that happened, they always outnumbered us. There were always three men or more before one would spit at my father, always three or four fine *ladies* calling us names.

My da was one of those who were too proud to do the work that Catholic men could get, so he went on the dole, which they had in the North. My ma worked where and when she could, in the linen mills until the bottom fell out when I was about four, and then she mostly did laundry and cleaning when she could get it. Da'd bring home some coin now and then, I think from petty theft or something else illegal, though I was never sure. Maybe he got odd jobs now and again, but I never heard it spoken of, or saw him do a day's work anywhere.

There was nobody to stand up for the Catholics back then. They were discriminated against in every way—jobs, housing, you name it. There were a few IRA men in Derry, but nothing well organized. Mostly just sour men. A great many tried to ignore it all, but others were so angry at the Unionists that their anger spilled over onto their families, their friends...themselves. To them, self-hatred was the order of the day, and many drank to ease their pain. But then the money spent on drink was money that couldn't be spent on the family, and that would make the men hate themselves even more.

My father, God save him, was a hater. His family was strong Republican, and he used to hang around men in Derry who were supposed to be linked to the IRA. I remember going with him once to see a Mr. Timmoney and a Mr. Ramsaigh. They talked freely in front of me, since I was just a boy. Year after I was born, there was a raid on a barracks in Derry where a lot of guns and ammunition were stolen. I recall they always talked about that a lot, as though it had been a great thing in their lives, but I never knew if my da had anything to do with it. He'd sit there, his eyes bright as buttons, and listen to them go on and on about it.

My da was bitter for another reason, one I didn't know about till I was older. Because everyone knew he was strongly Republican and because of the men he hung about with, the B-Specials kept a close eye on him. They were a Protestant state militia formed after the split in 1920, supposedly to help the police fight any paramilitary Republicans. But their main job was to keep Catholics in their place.

They were a bunch of sadists and bullies, nearly all of them members of the Orange Order, and it didn't take much for a Catholic to anger them. So, my da, who wore his contempt for them like they wore their sashes on their Orange Day parades, was a clear target. There's a nasty old Irish tradition called pruning that you don't hear much about. It's when a bunch of lads holds another man down and one of them squeezes his privates. It's sometimes done as a joke, but not a funny one for him who's taking it.

It wasn't meant as a joke when some B-Specials did it to my da just after I was born. They maimed him for life, caused him permanent damage, "unmanned" him, as my mother put it when she finally told me years later. That's why I was an only child, one of the few in a Derry Catholic family. And that's why my da hated them even more than before, and why he taught me to do the same. So I hated them, too, and I hated them even more after they killed him.

I was eight when it happened. I think my da was active in

the Border Campaign that began in 1956. The IRA went to work in earnest then, blowing up BBC radio transmitters, customs huts, and bridges around Derry and all over the North. They played their cards close to the vest. After all, they were spies and saboteurs in their own country, and the local police, the RUC, weren't picky about evidence. If they had enough to arrest somebody, all well and good, since it made fine headlines that they'd caught another Catholic rebel. But if they didn't, if they just suspected somebody of being in on a plot to bomb this, that or the other, well then, they'd just put a bug in the ear of the B-Specials.

I really don't know how involved my da was in it all. I recall that he was always very pleased and proud when the news came that there was another bombing, but he never came out and said that he'd had aught to do with it. My ma was always strong in her disapproval, so he didn't say much around her, but when we were alone, he'd hint to me that he might've had a hand in things.

I found out how true that was one evening in July. It was the height of the Orangemen's marching season, and they were feeling their oats. They'd wear their sashes and march through the streets, not just their own neighborhoods, but our Catholic streets as well, celebrating their victory at the Battle of the Boyne, pounding their lambeg drums and laughing in our faces, putting us in our place, you see. Since the IRA had started their campaign, it was worse than ever.

It was a warm evening, so my da and his mates, some of whom I was fairly sure were IRA men, were sitting on the stoop in front of our house when we heard the drums and knew the Orangies were coming. My da, who was a bit drunk, said he'd not watch those bastards go by their good Republican houses and insult good Republican families, and that he'd go down to the River Foyle until he couldn't hear those goddamned drums anymore.

He staggered off toward the river and the rest of the lads went off to their homes or the pub, and my ma took me inside. We stayed there as the parade passed, but I looked out the window and saw them, great fat men with their big orange sashes, singing "The Sash My Father Wore" at the top of their lungs. The whole point was to intimidate us, to show us who wore the pants in the North, as though we didn't know.

My father didn't come home that night, nor ever again except for the wake. My ma thought he'd slept off his drunkenness down by the Foyle, and that's where someone found him the next morning, with a bullet hole in the back of his head.

The RUC, liars that they were, said it didn't look like there'd been a struggle, and maybe there wasn't. Best we could figure, one of the marchers who knew him by sight saw him and followed him, probably with a few of his Loyalist friends. They found him sleeping, maybe, and did it that way, or could be they just grabbed him and held him while another one did the deed. However it happened, he was beyond coming back.

There were reprisals. Two Orangemen were shot and killed a few days later outside a grocer's store, and a day or so after that a teenage Catholic boy was beaten to death. Then another Orangeman was shot, and shortly after, one of my da's friends. It was at that point my ma had had enough.

I guess I wasn't helping matters. I was like a fury. All I could think about was how I might someday do to them what they'd done to my da. I was a little Republican through and through. Da'd even had me join *Na Fianna*, like the Boy Scouts, but for Republican lads. If you didn't get enough of it at home, *Na Fianna* would pour it deep into you.

Ma saw a miniature version of my father forming, and she figured that the faster she could get me out of Derry the better. There were other reasons, too. She was from the South originally, and hated the North, but could never talk Da out of leaving. Now there was nothing to stop her except for my Aunt Brigid, who thought that a Lynch leaving Derry was a venial sin at the least. It didn't stop my mother. What was left of her family was in Galway, so we packed up what little we had, I said goodbye to my cousin Malachy and my aunt and uncle, and we took a train to the South.

It was a grand adventure for me. I'd never been on a train, indeed never been much outside of Derry, so I was all eyes. When we crossed the border into the South, it seemed like the promised land. Everything looked greener somehow, and though economically it was worse off than the North, that didn't mean a thing to me.

And Galway was...well, it was like heaven after Derry. We stayed with my mother's widowed aunt at first, Aunt Colleen, and she was less a colleen than could be imagined. But she was kind enough, and introduced Ma all around as the new widow from the North, and me to the lads.

I never had much trouble making friends, and that served me well. Of course, the fact that I could tell—and make up— adventurous stories about the IRA didn't hurt any. There wasn't much talk about politics or the North at all. It was almost like Northern Ireland was a faraway country, so I became like some exotic beast for a while, before they finally figured out I was just like any other boy.

Ma got a job at a shop in Galway. Even back then there was a constant influx of tourists from all over—America, England, and many from the North. Everybody seemed to get along. I'd never seen anything like it before. I suppose you could say that I mellowed a bit. I still hated the Orangemen, but since there were none around to hate, it took the edge off.

I stayed in touch with Malachy, writing him letters every week or so. He kept me apprised of what was happening in Derry, mostly the bad, things that kept me angry at the way my relatives there were being treated. Ma and I went up to visit Uncle John and Aunt Brigid at Christmas, and the next summer they invited me for a couple of weeks and I talked my mother into letting me go, though she was hesitant.

From then on, I spent two weeks every summer in Derry, and the link between myself and the IRA grew stronger. Uncle John was in it thick, and though he had a decent job, he spent a great deal of time and energy in the movement. I guess you could call him an assistant to the quartermaster. He helped with the weapons and ammunition, as well as the material with which they made bombs, shuffled them around from place to place so that the RUC and the B-Specials couldn't find them on raids.

It wasn't long before Malachy and I became go-betweens

for them. Most of my summer weeks in Derry were spent doing boyish things, but often Malachy and I would be "called upon" to serve the cause, and we did what they asked, carrying messages back and forth, small packages, whatever. I never told my mother a word about it.

Two years after we moved to Galway, she married Tim Sullivan. She'd lost her shop job after a year when the old owner retired and the new one replaced most of the help with family members. Ma went into The Lilting Banshee now and again with the other shop girls, and got to know Tim. When he found out she was out of work, he told her he could use another hand around the pub, so she took the job.

Tim was fifteen years older than Ma. His wife had died some years before, and he had no children. He took a shine to Ma, and in spite of the age difference he started courting her like a true gentleman. In the pub he was business as usual, and he'd kindly ask her to do something and she'd do it. But when he was courting it was something different entirely, like out of a storybook. He'd never come to Aunt Colleen's door without flowers for Ma and a bottle of stout for Aunt Colleen, who took her spirits with discretion, as she always put it.

They'd go for walks or to the cinema or a restaurant, and sometimes Tim would ask me if I wanted to go along and I always did, of course. He was a grand kind man, sweet and caring, and when, after about a year of this, he finally asked Ma to marry him, I was glad. He wasn't much to look at, with a wizened little face like a pixie, but he was strong. He could haul a keg around that cellar like no one I've seen since. Still, for all his strength, his fiddle seemed light as air in his hands, and he could coax such sounds out of it that at one time you'd swear it was an angel playing, and then it would get so hot and fevered you'd think it was a devil.

It was the angelic bits that won my ma. I don't know that she actually loved Tim when she married him, but I think she learned to. Looking back, I suspect she did it more to give me a father than out of anything stronger than friendship for him. Still, they got along grand, and I never heard them fight. They were always kind and respectful of each other, and if that's not a loving marriage it's a good second finisher.

Tim was wonderful to me. He taught me how to play guitar, helped me with my schooling when I needed it, showed me all the jobs involved in running the pub. He really was more of a father to me in that regard than my own da. Still, every summer I went back to Derry, revisiting my past, seeing where my father was killed, experiencing again the indignities, the sullen, petty little hatreds that were visited on my people over and over again, and being around men who were willing to do something about it and did.

When the time came, I scored more than enough on my Leaving Certificate to enter university, and I went here in Galway. That was when I stopped going to Derry in the summers. I had to work to make money for my education. The late sixties and early seventies were wild times for the IRA up North, but I wanted a degree. Then Bloody Sunday came along and everything changed. My Uncle John was killed, not at the march itself, but at a small set-to right afterwards with the Ulster Volunteer Force, Protestant paramilitaries. Malachy told me in his telegram. It read, "Da killed. Please come. We need you."

I had no choice. I knew what he needed me for, and I knew I had to go. All those innocent people shot down by the English, my uncle dead. All I could think about was that we had to drive the bastards out once and for all, and if I could help and didn't, I was betraying my country, my family, and my father.

This may be the hardest part of all to tell, and I have to ask you to remember that I was young and terribly stupid about many things, and I thought that I might be going North to die.

That Monday I left you in my flat and went out to put things in order. I informed the university that I'd be taking an indefinite leave, and I took what money I had from my bank account, but what I didn't do was go tell my ma and Tim I was leaving. I knew she'd never let me, that she'd grab me and hold onto me, and that if she did, I might not be able to leave at all.

I had gone into a café to rest and have a cup, when Siobhan Kelly came in. Siobhan and I had dated steady for about a year, and she knew all too well how I felt about what was going on up in the Six Counties. When she saw the expression on my face,

I was sure that she knew right away what I was planning, and she sat down next to me.

We'd broken up a month or so before, over what I don't even recall. She was quick-tempered then and I was, too, far more than now. She asked me what was wrong, and I told her nothing, but she knew anyway and said we had to talk, but not there, and that I should come up to a friend's flat nearby. I didn't want anyone overhearing her going on about me going to the North and joining the IRA because that kind of thing was illegal in the South as well, so I went with her.

Her friend was out, and the flat was empty but for us. After she pushed me a bit, I told her I was planning to go to the North indefinitely, and she tried to talk me out of it. She said she still cared for me, that she was sorry we'd broken up, and that she wanted me to stay.

"Then...Jesus, but this is hard for me to say..."

"The two of you made love," Susanna said softly, smiling at him.

Michael nodded, unable to look at her. "Yes."

He was silent for a minute, and she kept smiling. It didn't matter. It was a long time ago, and it hadn't even been her that he had cheated on, if you could even call it cheating. In truth, he had owed Julia nothing.

Michael took a deep breath and a sip of tea and went on.

Except for going to the North to fight, it was the worst decision I've ever made, but I wasn't to know that until later. Afterward, I told her that as sweet as it was, it was only a sweet goodbye. She cried when I left, and I felt terrible sad.

I left the next day, but you know all about that. I went to my aunt's house when I got to Derry, and stayed there only until the wake was over and Uncle John was in the ground. Then Malachy and I went in the ground, too—underground, joining the Provos, the Provisional IRA. What I did, and what I was finally arrested for, was making bombs from gelignite. I was told, and I believed at first, that they'd be used only on military targets or in places where they'd cause civic disruption but no loss of life, like bridges late at night, and transmitting towers and waterworks and custom huts—the usual targets.

Things got out of hand fast. In the weeks after Bloody Sunday there were four bombings every day in the Six Counties. We were shown how to build new types of bombs, and I didn't learn until later that they were car bombs. Once they left the storerooms and cellars and warehouses where we worked, I had no idea how they were used, but I know now that the bombers weren't as selective as they pretended. There were a lot of civilians killed, a lot of innocent people. It took me a long time to realize it.

By then it was too late. They knew who we were and they were tracking us down. We went from safe house to safe house, but just before Christmas of 1972 they raided a house Malachy and I were in and we were caught. I'm not going to go into what they did to us. It was inhumane, but no more so than what our bombs did. We were detained in Long Kesh Prison.

When my Ma and Tim found out I'd been arrested, they came to visit. Ma was furious at me. I'd never seen her that angry. I suppose it was her worrying over me combined with what I'd done and the way I'd just disappeared. I tried to make her understand that I hadn't contacted her for her own sake and Tim's, that if they didn't know where I was or what I was doing, they couldn't be held complicit in any way for what I did. She said she didn't give a damn about any of that, that what she cared about was the people I'd hurt and the way I'd ruined my life, and, she said, maybe the life of my son, too.

That brought me up short, I can tell you. Then she told me about Siobhan. She found that she was pregnant a month or so after I left, and she went to my ma and told her I was the father. She was scared to tell her own da. He was a widowed fisherman and a hard man. So, the two women went together and told him. Naturally he demanded I marry Siobhan, and my ma said that I would soon as I could be found.

That was harder than it sounded, and by the time I was captured Gerry was already born. Ma took care of Siobhan through her pregnancy, as her father wouldn't have a bastard born in his house. The boy was about four months old when Siobhan and I were married. They got permission to bring a priest into Long Kesh and he married us in one of the visitation rooms there. It was a ceremony without joy. When I kissed her, I felt nothing but guilt, and I think she felt trapped herself. A convict wasn't the husband she'd been wishing for. A month later I was sentenced to ten years in prison.

Siobhan and Gerry went to live with her father, who was willing to take her now she was wed. Ma wanted her and Gerry to stay with them, but Siobhan said she needed to be with her da. What *he* needed was a maid. Tim gave Siobhan a job at the pub, but when she was through, she and Gerry went home and she did her father's work until she dropped. He gave no love or care to either her or the boy, so thank God my ma and Tim did.

They all visited me faithfully once a month—Siobhan, Ma, Tim, and Gerry. That was as often as we were allowed to have visitors. But what meant as much to me were the books Ma sent. Every week she mailed me two books. Most were used, but that didn't matter. Sometimes they were paperbacks, sometimes hardcover, and it was always something different. Novels, biographies, history, science, poetry, everything but politics, but there were plenty of political books in the prison library. Malachy and I shared the same Nissen hut and the same books. We'd each start one, and when we finished we'd switch, then pass them on to other inmates. It helped the bonk, which is what we called that awful depression you could get from being inside.

The years passed and the books kept coming. We read well over a hundred a year, which gave us a grand education in the things that mattered. It got worse in 1976. That was when they took away our Special Category Status. We were in the H-blocks by then, and the name had been officially changed to Maze Prison.

From then on, we were no longer considered political prisoners, and were expected to wear prison uniforms, but many of us wouldn't do it. When they took our own clothes away, we made clothing out of bed sheets and blankets. The screws— the guards—treated us worse than ever then. There were times when they'd urinate on the books before they gave them to me, but I read them and so did Malachy. We needed those books, and when we read them anyway it said something to the guards, and after a while they stopped doing it.

I was even part of the Dirty Protest, but I'd as soon not talk about that. Frankly, I'd as soon not talk about Long Kesh at all, but it took ten years of my life. It did worse to Malachy.

The screws broke his leg in a beating shortly after we got in. The medical care was less than excellent, and it never set right, so he walks with a limp. That you noticed, I'm sure. As for his left eye, that happened during the Dirty Protest. The guards used to throw an ammonia liquid under our cell doors, then turn hoses on it to dilute it. They often threw it against the doors as well, right through the cracks.

We had open peepholes in the doors, and one time, Malachy looked through it when they were tossing in the disinfectant. It hit him right in the eye, blinded him in seconds. They let him scream and cry in there for an hour before they finally came back. I tried to clean out the eye with the water they sprayed under the door, but it was no use.

The day I left Long Kesh, I swore to myself I'd never go back inside again. I hated the Ulstermen worse than I ever had for what they'd done to me and to my mates, but I felt that my first responsibility was to my family. I had a son I didn't know at all, and a wife I barely knew. It was time to change that. I would go and live in the South, and though I would do what I could to make all Ireland free, I would never take up arms again.

They were all there to meet me when I was released, and we drove back to Galway. It took all day, with me in the back seat with Siobhan and Gerry. She and I talked some, about things that didn't matter, that were unimportant, inconsequential. We said nothing about what was in our hearts. It was like that until the day she died.

CHAPTER 12

Susanna didn't know what to say. Michael seemed to have come to a stopping place in his story, and sat looking down at the intricate patterns of the carpet as though the emotions had drained out of him. While most of his narrative had been straightforward and matter-of-fact, it was now as though he had become lost in a dream, or had once again realized that he had only left one prison for another.

At last he took a sharp breath, then looked at Susanna again. "I'm sorry. This is a lot to take in, isn't it?"

"It's all right," she said. "I want to know...about everything that made you what you are. Because I think that what you are now is fine. More than fine."

He smiled crookedly. "Wish I could believe that. I wish I could be what I see in your eyes. Anyway...back in Galway I worked at the pub. There was no point in finishing my degree. I'd had my education. So, I tried to be a good worker and a good husband and a good father. I only stuck one out of three.

"Tim died in 1986, a stroke that felled him in the street. I don't think he felt a thing. I started running the pub then, with my ma and Siobhan's help. That was the year they finally released Malachy. He'd had to serve extra time for a number of reasons. I invited him to come to Galway and work with us at the pub, but he said he didn't want to go that far from his ma, and she wouldn't leave Derry. He compromised and moved to Letterkenny, just over the border, so that he could stay near her."

"Is that when he opened the bookshop?" Susanna asked.

"Yes. He got some help from the IRA, sort of a payoff for the time he'd spent inside. He told me he paid it back a long time ago, but I don't know."

"All those books must have had an effect on him."

"He loved to read and that's a fact. Still does." Michael took a sip of the tea, which had grown cold, and he made a face.

"I'll make some more," Susanna said, but he shook his head.

"The story's almost done, and then we'll get a bit more sleep. I was telling you about my marriage." He sighed. "Not much to tell. I don't think we ever really...felt much for each other. There were no more children, and I didn't do such a good job with Gerry. Oh, he was a good boy, but he and I...well, it was hard being without a father for his first ten years, and we were like strangers when I came back. Never got much beyond that. I tried to do for him what Tim had done for me, and taught him some music. That was an area where we always got along fine.

"He was always much closer to his mother, and to my ma. They were who he went to with his troubles, not me. He got away from Galway when it came time for college, went to Dublin, then came back and taught here. I think he missed the place and his ma and grandmother. He's never married. I suppose Siobhan and I weren't much of an example of what to expect.

"She died over a year ago. Shortly after Christmas. A friend of mine owns a pub in Moycullen, a bit northwest of Galway, and was having a party for other pub owners—a bunch of us do it every year, taking turns being the host. Siobhan and I went and she had too much to drink, as she did now and again. She wasn't an alcoholic, but I think that sometimes she just liked to get a bit drunk to help her forget...whatever it was she wanted to forget. Or be something other than she was.

"Anyway, I was talking to the wife of a colleague, an older woman nearing retirement age, the last person Siobhan should've been jealous of, but for some reason she was. I'd never given her cause. Whatever my other shortcomings might have been, I was always faithful to her. But she said that she'd had enough of my flirting and she was ready to leave. I told her that I wasn't ready and she could just wait. Then she said that she wasn't going to wait and I could find my own way home.

"I knew that'd be no problem, as there were a lot of pubmen

from Galway there, but I should have stopped her, or I should have gone out with her and driven her home. I didn't. I let her walk out the door. I watched as she did, and she seemed steady on her feet so I thought she'd be all right driving back. But honestly, I didn't care. I was tired. I was just tired of everything. So I let her go.

"She crashed the car just outside of Moycullen. Killed instantly." Michael's voice sounded far away again. "It's a miracle it doesn't happen more often, what with the narrow roads, stone walls, and too many people driving with too many pints in them. It's the combination of things, you see, that makes motor accidents such an *Irish* way to die." He shook his head. "I blamed myself. And Gerry blamed me, too." Michael leaned his elbow on the arm of the chair and chewed at the flesh of his knuckle.

"Some friends were taking me back, and the rescue squad was cleaning up the scene of the accident when we got there. The ambulance was gone by then, but I recognized the car. The garda told us that the woman in the car had been killed, and I was shocked at first, but then, God help me, I felt...relieved. Relieved and exhausted, like a great weight had come off my back."

He looked up at Susanna, and she could see tears in his eyes. His knuckle was red and ridged from the indentation of his teeth. "I never told anyone that before. But that was how I felt."

She stood up and then knelt by his side and put her arm around him. "It's all right," she said. "You did what you could."

Michael shook his head roughly and sniffed. "No. You're a dear woman and I love you. But you know that I didn't do everything I could."

"There are some things that, no matter how much you think you should, you just can't do. And you can't make yourself love someone you don't love." She kissed him on the cheek and rubbed his hand, caressing the place where he had chewed at himself. It was the perfect time. He had shared his truths with her, and she would do the same and tell him who she really was.

She was about to say, *as long as we're being honest*, when he spoke. "Christ, I *hate* liars and I hate lies, but I lived in one for thirty years, then pretended to grieve when I...wasn't sad at all. Christ forgive me."

I hate liars and I hate lies. His bitter words locked Susanna's confession within her. There had been enough truth for one night. "It's all right," she said. "Let's get some sleep. It's still dark."

He smiled. "It'll be brighter soon."

They got back into the bed and held each other until they went to sleep. It took Susanna a long time. The daylight woke them several hours later, and when she looked through the window, she saw that the morning sun was already beginning to melt the snow and ice.

They entered the dining room at eight-thirty and a friendly woman who introduced herself as Mrs. Healy served them a banquet of an Irish breakfast that they both finished. By nine-thirty they were on the road, and found that the ice and snow had turned to slush through which they moved easily.

As they drove, they talked freely and laughed often, and Susanna felt more at ease with Michael than before. The sexual tension that had lain between them was gone, and now when they touched each other, she laying a hand on his shoulder or he patting her knee, it was done almost without thought. They had no further discussion of his tenure in the prisons of both Long Kesh and his marriage, and Susanna hoped that her attitude showed that his past made no difference to her. He might tell her more about Siobhan and Long Kesh someday, but she would not press him. She knew it had taken a great deal for him to tell her what he had.

She only wished she had had as much courage to tell him the truth about herself, but his tirade against lies and liars had frightened her. Her truth would have to wait a bit longer.

They pulled up in front of Michael's house in the late afternoon and made arrangements to meet at the session that evening at The Lilting Banshee. When Michael kissed her goodbye, it was, she was delighted to realize, with the comfort of old lovers, not the shyness of new ones.

"I've never felt this happiness with a woman before," Michael said, smiling down at her. "Thank you."

"My pleasure," she said, speaking the truth.

As she drove away, she reaffirmed to herself that Michael's imprisonment made no difference in the way she felt about him. When Julia had told her of his departure for the North, she had assumed that he had been involved with the IRA or some other Republican paramilitary group, and that assumption had become a certainty. Michael had paid the price for his involvement, and it had been a heavy price indeed.

Susanna knew from her previous reading and from talking to a number of ex-prisoners that Long Kesh had been a hell on earth for those prisoners the British and Ulstermen considered terrorists. Their treatment made what U.S. authorities did to captured Taliban fighters look avuncular in comparison. It got even worse for those who refused to relinquish their Special Prisoner Status.

But Michael had been a free man now for twenty years. He seemed to have weathered well both his imprisonment and his loveless marriage, since the Michael Lynch that Susanna knew was a kind and gentle man.

His admission of his past proved him honest, too. Soon, she told herself, she would reveal her secret as well, and then, as he had put it, it would be *his* choice as to where they went from there.

"So...do you think you're ready to meet the family?"

Rachel Oliver looked up in surprise. She and Gerry Lynch were taking a stroll through South Park along the bay, pausing now and then to make a snowball from what was left of the nearly melted snow and throw it at a tree, or, occasionally, at each other. "What?" she asked in disbelief.

They had known each other for only four days, and though they had become lovers that first night, it was nevertheless an abrupt question. "Not as serious as it sounds," Gerry said. "My grandmother's singing *Sean-Nos* songs at the family pub tonight, and I thought you might like to hear her. They usually have a good session, too."

"Your family has a *pub*?" Rachel asked. "Here in Galway?"

"They do. The Lilting Banshee."

"Oh, I've seen that—kind of a small place with a red front?"

"That's it. I only go once a week, on Friday nights when my grandmother sings. My dad runs it with her help, and since I don't get along all that well with him, I don't hang out there much. Seems he's got a new girlfriend now as well. Sometimes I think he was just waiting for my mother to die so he could start womanizing."

"You were lucky in one way—my father wasn't that patient."

"Well, when I finally tie the knot, the lucky lady won't have to worry about that." He grinned and Rachel grabbed his arm, knowing he was teasing.

That was what she liked most about him. He never took anything too seriously, not even himself. She knew that his writing meant a lot to him, but he was always humorously self-deprecating about it.

Something else she liked was his openness. From the first night they spent together they'd been honest with each other. Rachel made sure that he knew she had been married and was now divorced, and when he asked her what the problems had been, she had told him, sparing neither Ty's flaws nor her own.

He in turn had told her about his family and how his early life, with his father in prison, had made a hash of his psyche for a long time. "My dad was a mad bomber," he had said, "and my mother the poor soul who waited for him ten years to find that he didn't give a damn about her. So, is it any wonder I'm off my nut? And a poet on top of it?"

Rachel liked him, off his nut or not, and wondered if she might be feeling more. She'd dated a few guys since her divorce, but hadn't liked any of them even well enough to sleep with, let alone consider falling in love with. Yet she'd slept with Gerry the first night they were together. So far, he had exhibited none of the territoriality that a lot of men did, needing to do things at their own convenience, in their own time. He thought of *her*, and seemed to do the things that he thought would make her happy, and that made him happy, too.

Still, she couldn't help but wonder if what she was

getting was his *modus operandi*, if he made a habit of seducing American women by playing the thoughtful and sensitive Irish poet, appealing to some as yet undocumented Yeats Groupie Syndrome.

He put his arm around her and the feel of their bodies together brushed the thought away. No, what you saw with Gerry was what you got. They were two of a kind, both artsy, both wearing everything right on their sleeves, both a little off their nuts, and she liked the hell out of him and thought he felt the same about her.

Rachel didn't know, however, if the joining of such similar souls would eventually prove heaven-sent or hell-bound. Best for now, she thought, to tread the earthly path between the two and see where they were headed. She could always hop off if she didn't like the direction.

Before she drove back to her flat, Susanna went over to the university library, where she planned to email her own university and assure the necessary parties that the students in Letterkenny were doing fine and had become neither drug addicts nor alcoholics. When she logged on, she found a few messages from the college, and several from David Oliver.

The first had been sent Wednesday afternoon, and the others had followed every few hours. The tone of all the previous ones echoed the first:

Dear Susanna—

Have you heard from Rachel? I just checked my email and there's one from her saying she's going to Ireland, and was leaving yesterday morning! She didn't say a thing to me before, and said she doesn't even know where she's staying, but I'll be able to contact her through you. So, have you heard from her? Tell her to call me right away collect. I can't believe she went off without letting me know. Thanks. Hope your vacation is good.
Love,
David

Susanna didn't know which hit her harder—the surprise that her niece was in the country, or David's referral to her working sabbatical as a vacation. The latter was annoying, while the former could be delightful or disastrous, depending upon how Rachel made her presence felt.

Susanna read the rest of David's emails, which increased in both irritation that she had not responded to him and the seriousness of his threat to come over there if he didn't hear of his daughter's whereabouts, and find out what the hell had happened to her himself.

That was an option that Susanna hated to contemplate. David Oliver had to stay in America where he belonged, so she wrote, thinking to herself as she did:

Dear (*only in the familial sense*) David:

I haven't heard from Rachel, but I'm certain she'll contact me shortly. (*So, don't panic and haul your unwanted self over here.*) This really comes as no great surprise to me, since before I left she expressed a desire to see Ireland, since her mother loved it so (*and oh God, you don't want to know why*), and of course it's been such a vital part of my own work and research. (*So, you know what you can do with that "vacation" crack.*) I didn't get your emails earlier because I was very busy up in Letterkenny and didn't have Internet access there. (*See? Busy! No "vacation!" Even though I have had the leisure time to fall in love with a man as unlike you as Guinness from a wine cooler.*) I'll let you know as soon as Rachel contacts me, and I'll give her your message (*rather your command, your majesty*) to call her. Your coming over here would serve no purpose (except to severely annoy your daughter and sister-in-law). Ireland's a big enough country that you won't stumble across her, and she's a big girl. I'm sure she can take care of herself. I'll be in touch soon.
Best, (*Love? I don't think so.*)
Susanna

She felt a great deal of satisfaction as she hit *Send*.

Susanna would have felt far less gleeful had she known that hours before David Oliver's computer musically announced her email's arrival in his Inbox, he had already made a business class reservation on a USAir flight that would arrive in Shannon the following Sunday morning. An hour later his secretary had confirmed a reservation for a week's stay at Galway's Great Southern Hotel, at three hundred Euros a night. It was a little pricey, but David wanted to make an impression on Susanna.

He had decided, since Julia's death, that he eventually needed to remarry, and the only person he wanted to marry was Susanna Cassidy. For the past thirty years he had told himself he'd been an idiot to marry Julia when it was Susanna he loved, and now that he was free, that fact mocked him more than ever.

David, with an ego born of wealth, good looks, and a high success rate with women, had come to the conclusion that Susanna, despite her stand-offish manner, was in love with him all these years as well. That she never married lent credence to his theory, and her inability to admit her love to him, and perhaps not even to herself, was because of loyalty to her sister. David had to admit that Susanna had chosen the proper path. For him to have divorced Julia to marry her sister would have been sordid and ugly, a scandal from which neither of them would have emerged unblemished.

But now there was no reason not to obey the instincts that first brought them together as teenagers. David had planned to wait until Susanna returned from her sabbatical in Ireland, but the more he thought about it, the more he looked for a valid reason to join her there and break the question that he hoped she would answer the way he wished. Now Rachel's unexpected trip gave him the excuse he needed.

He would join Susanna in Galway. If she heard from Rachel by then, fine. They could relax and he could get down to the romantic business that really brought him there. If not, they could join forces and try to find his daughter, a mission that he imagined would bond them even more closely.

He was enough of a realist, however, to know that she was

bound to have some initial objections and wouldn't immediately leap into his arms and pledge undying love. She couldn't help but be aware of some of his marital indiscretions, and that would undoubtedly be the primary obstacle he'd have to overcome. The truth, he hoped, would do just that.

He would simply and honestly tell her that his infidelities had come about as a result of his trying to find a replacement for *her*, that those sad and unfulfilling relationships had been an attempt to recreate what he had foolishly thrown away. If he came hat in hand, begging for forgiveness for having ruined both their lives with his youthful mistake, her contempt might turn to pity.

And then, his confession behind them, they could correct the mistakes of the past. Things could be the way they always *should* have been. The wrongs could be made right, and they could live happily ever after.

David turned his attention to what he might wear, and told his secretary to get a weather report for the Galway area for the next week.

That evening Rachel Oliver made up her mind. She was indeed falling in love with Gerry Lynch. Before they had dinner, they went back to Gerry's flat and she played his guitar and sang the musical setting she had written for one of his poems. When she finished, he shook his head in awe, kissed her, and said, "That was exactly the music I heard in my mind, but I couldn't bring it out. Rachel, you're more than a muse. I think you're the other half of my soul."

"Oh my," she said, half mocking. "Now you need to work *that* into a song."

Gerry laughed as well, but Rachel felt that he meant what he said, and that his sweet comment was neither teasing nor hyperbole. It touched her in a way no other remark from lovers or friends ever had, and she thought, and found herself hoping, that it might be true.

Now they headed for The Lilting Banshee, walking arm in arm through the narrow streets of Galway as the sky darkened and the lights of the town brightened in response. Gerry led her down Churchyard Street, with the gray bulk of St. Nicholas's Church on their left. "I always go in the back," he explained. "Farther from the music, but it's less rowdy. And when Grandmother sings, the place gets quiet as a grave."

He opened the door for her and they walked inside. The pub was small but charming, and very crowded. People occupied nearly every seat, and others stood in small groups, chatting and drinking from their pints. She and Gerry paused, taking in the mass of humanity, and Gerry looked about for a pair of seats.

Rachel stretched her neck to look over the heads and see the musicians in the front. As the crowd moved back and forth, she got an occasional glimpse, catching sight of one woman holding a fiddle and a man with a guitar who looked vaguely familiar. "My dad, with the guitar there," Gerry said in her ear over the din. "And there's his girlfriend."

A big man moved into Rachel's view, and she shifted to look around him. In the gap framed by bodies she saw the man with the guitar reach out an arm to a woman she instantly recognized as her Aunt Susanna, and realized that she had seen the man before at her aunt's guest house. For a moment Rachel was startled by the coincidence, then gathered her senses enough to open her mouth to cry out *Aunt Sue!* But just before she said the words, she saw a spike-haired girl pop up in front of her aunt, and heard her loud, piercing voice cry "*Julia!*" as she gave Susanna a quick hug.

"Her name's Julia Cassidy," Gerry said in her ear. "From the states like yourself."

Rachel's mouth was still hanging open, the cry to her aunt hanging on her lips. She closed it slowly, not understanding, feeling a disconnect from everything around her. "Could we…" she said softly, then louder when she realized Gerry couldn't hear her. "Could we just sit back here for a while?"

To her relief he didn't argue or ask why. He only looked at her oddly, then, as if knowing that something was upsetting her, nodded. "Sure. How about over there?"

He gestured toward a small corner booth that had just opened up, and they slipped into it. It was relatively dark and

slightly elevated so that Rachel could occasionally see the musicians between the standing bodies.

"Want a pint?" Gerry asked, and she nodded.

By the time he got back from the bar with the two glasses,
the music had started. It was as vigorous and aggressive as rock,
but Rachel was too confused to enjoy it, though she smiled at
Gerry and pretended nothing was the matter.

"Are you sure you're okay?" he asked her during a break
between tunes.

"I'm fine," she said. "Just a little tired. Too many late nights,
I guess." She heard the guitar playing then, and the crowd
hushed. She maneuvered her head so that she could see Gerry's
father, playing and starting to sing a song in a full, deep baritone:

"On a sunny afternoon, all in the winter time,
I went out a-walking, by the river running fine..."

Rachel recognized the melody. It was the one her mother
used to hum wordlessly to her when she was a little girl, on
nights when she was sick or couldn't get to sleep. "I know that
song," she told Gerry.

"You couldn't, not if you've never been here before."

"Why not?"

"My dad wrote it. Years ago. Been singing it for ages, on and
off."

Rachel looked back toward the man playing the guitar and
listened more closely. She couldn't make out every line, due to
the low buzz of voices and the clatter of glasses, but she heard
the lyrics, "...and said her name was Julia, as clear as rain in
spring..."

Julia. Her mother's name. The name that the girl had called
Aunt Sue.

"Always wondered who that 'Julia' was," Gerry said. "Guess
I know now. Nothing like an old flame to reignite the fire in an
old man."

Then came a sudden lull in the talk and the din, and she
heard clearly the words of the chorus:

"I saw her by the riverside, down where the Corrib runs,
Was nearly blinded by her, for she fair outshone the sun..."

Now Rachel recognized the words as well as the tune. At first, she couldn't recall where she had heard them before, and then she remembered that she had never heard them. She had *read* them, written in one of her mother's books, read them when she was young, and forgotten about them until tonight.

Her mind whirled as though she'd just downed several pints of stout and then spun around. Desperately she tried to fit the pieces into place. As best she could figure, her mother had been here before, years ago, and met the man who was now playing and singing, Gerry's father, and he had fallen in love with her, at least enough to write her a song and write in a book...

And that was why her mother had loved Ireland so much, wasn't it? Because of that young love years before, that love she was never able to forget.

What Rachel didn't understand, however, was why they were calling her aunt Susanna Julia, why she was pretending to be her sister.

It would be too awkward to confront Aunt Sue there in the pub with all the people around. Rachel decided to go back to Susanna's guest house and wait for her there, tell her what she had seen, and ask for an explanation. Aunt Sue had always been straight with her, far more so than her parents, so she was sure that whatever masquerade she was engaging in, there must be a good reason.

Now was the time to leave. The longer Rachel remained in the pub, the more likely she was to be introduced to "Julia Cassidy." She leaned across the table and took Gerry's hand. "I don't feel so great," she told him, and it wasn't far from the truth. "I have to get some air."

The look of concern on his face told her everything she needed to know about Gerry Lynch's sincerity. There wasn't a hint of irritation in his manner as he helped her to her feet and guided her out the door, only concern for her well-being.

She kept her head down so that there wouldn't be a chance of Susanna glimpsing her as they left.

Once outside on the chilly street, Rachel actually felt better, but continued the charade. "I'm sorry," she said, "I know you wanted me to hear your grandmother, but do you mind if we put it off till next week? I feel really weird. I don't know if it was something I ate, but I'm kinda woozy."

"Sure, no problem. You want to go back to my flat? Just to sleep?"

That wouldn't work. Rachel had to see Susanna. "If it's okay with you, I'd rather crash at my place tonight, get a good night's sleep. I don't know *what* might happen if I find myself alone with *you*."

"I'd be a perfect gentleman, really."

"I know you would, but..." She smiled and ran a finger across his lips. "I'm not sure if I could be a perfect lady. Best not to take the risk."

His smile told her it was all right, and he walked her to the hostel where she kissed him goodnight and went into her room. She waited until she was sure he was gone, then left the hostel and headed toward the bay. It was a long walk, so she had plenty of time to think, but couldn't come up with any theory that explained Susanna's impersonation of her mother.

When she reached the guest house, she wasn't surprised to find the upper story dark. Susanna would probably be playing for several more hours. It was chilly on the street, but Rachel decided she wouldn't freeze. She began to wait for her Aunt Sue to return.

CHAPTER 13

For Susanna, Friday night's session was a combination of musical fun and psychological unease. Her night with Michael had changed the chemistry between them. Though they tried to pretend around the others that nothing had happened, she knew Michael's mother suspected, and so probably did everyone else who knew they had been stranded by the storm. That constituted, she imagined, all the regulars of The Lilting Banshee.

It started when she walked in. None of the musicians had arrived, but Dermot Rooney was holding down his usual stool, and when he saw her his tremulous smile made his moustache look like a skinny gray caterpillar wriggling under his long nose. "Well, and it's Miss Cassidy, and how is she this fine evenin'? None the worse for wear after your recent ordeal amid the ice and snows of our ferocious land?" It was the wink, blended as it was with the clenching of his jaw as though he'd just snapped a bug out of the air, that lent a touch of the salacious to Rooney's query.

"Your Irish weather can be hazardous, Mr. Rooney," she said with a smile.

"More hazards than the weather, and here comes one of the most pernicious right now," Rooney said as Michael came around the bar to join Susanna. "You better watch this one—probably ordered up that snowstorm special just to get alone with you."

"Enough out of you, Rooney," Michael said, and smiled as though merely pretending to be annoyed, when Susanna suspected he truly was. He swept her away from the old man, freed

Tim Sullivan's fiddle from its case, and handed it and the bow to Susanna. Now that she knew its history, she handled it gingerly.

"It won't break from playing," Michael said with a grin. "You should have seen old Tim saw away at it when he played fierce. You'd have trembled in fear for it. But I never saw him break even a string."

Susanna looked up from the precious instrument and over to the bar where Molly Sullivan was setting out clean glasses. Molly looked up at Susanna, so Susanna smiled and gave a little wave, and Molly raised a hand in greeting, cracking her own smile and nodding. There was an intelligence in her deep gray eyes that made Susanna feel uncomfortable, as though Molly had looked directly into her soul and unerringly read that this woman had slept with her son. If so, her smile suggested no angry disapproval.

That was the province of Kate Quinn, who came in the front door like a gale sweeping into a quiet bay. The cold air that entered with her remained as she glared at Susanna, who decided to show neither chagrin nor guilt. She smiled and nodded to Kate, whose mouth twisted in a half-smile as she took her perceived rival's measure and sat down in the spot that had been Susanna's the week before.

It was a childish gesture, Susanna thought, but the look that Kate had given Susanna was nothing compared to the sharp glare she hurled at Michael when he came into the circle with his guitar. As soon as he turned toward Kate, however, her look melted into a fatuous and worshipful simper, and Michael's hearty "Good evening, Kate" was returned with a smile and nod of what struck Susanna as diabetes-inducing sweetness.

Aengus Cleary and Fiona Bailey came in only seconds later, and Fiona's squeal of *"Julia!"* caught the attention of everyone in the pub. For an instant Susanna was certain that everyone had heard an unspoken congratulatory cry, an implied *Julia, you lucky thing, heard you spent the night with Michael, you GO, girlfriend!*

Once the session began, Susanna grew more comfortable, but the cool spot within a yard of Kate Quinn remained all too formidable. It became far chillier when, after several fiddle tunes, someone called for a song and Dermot Rooney shouted out, "Aye, a *love* song!"

Michael sat hunched over his guitar for a while, looking at the floor. Then he straightened up, a determined, the-hell-with-it look on his face, and started to pick out some chords. Fiona smiled as though she recognized it, and Susanna noticed her sidelong glance at Kate, as if to gauge her reaction. The other woman's face was like stone.

Then Michael started singing a soft, slow ballad, and Susanna realized that it was the song he had written for young Julia Cassidy all those years before. The lines about the River Corrib were there, and even Julia's name was mentioned.

As the song went on, Susanna felt flattered and embarrassed that Michael was making such a public statement for those who knew how to listen. Then, as the name *Julia* was sung again, she felt embarrassed for another reason, and ashamed that she had stolen her sister's name and her sister's love, that she was listening and responding to a song not her own.

When she looked at Kate Quinn again, the woman was glaring at her with contempt, and she hoped that Kate wouldn't read her incertitude as a response to that evil eye. Susanna looked back at Michael and kept watching him until the song was over. The touch of red in his cheeks told her that he was as embarrassed in his way as she was in hers, and that his singing of that song had cost him much emotionally.

As if to banish the sound of it, he called for a jig that Susanna knew, kicking it off as the others joined in. The rest of the evening passed more smoothly. Molly Sullivan sang several unaccompanied *Sean-Nos* songs, after which the musicians played again.

The session broke up around midnight, though Kate Quinn had left at eleven, claiming weariness. While Michael secured old Tim's fiddle back in its place, Molly made her way to where Susanna was sitting with Fiona, who was having one last pint for the road.

"You play very well, dear," Molly said in her deep, almost manly voice as she sat on the padded bench next to Susanna. She gave a quick glance at Fiona, who picked up on it right away.

"I'd best be getting along," she said, draining the bottom third of her pint in one long swallow. "Brilliant, that," she said as she wiped her lips with a forefinger. "Grand playing with you, Julia, grand seeing you, Mrs. Sullivan." And with that, she was off.

"So how long are you in Ireland, then?" Molly asked Susanna.

"Through the summer," she replied, wondering if this was the first in a series of questions. As if to anticipate them, she gave Molly a rundown on what she was doing in both the South and the North, and told her as well about the errand that had taken her and Michael to Letterkenny.

"Ah, I see," Molly said at length. "I didn't quite understand what you were doing up there...or here, for that matter." She smiled. "It sounds like rewarding work."

"It is. At least I like it. Maybe you wouldn't mind talking about it with me sometime. How your experiences living in the North have affected your views now."

"I'd be glad to tell you what I can," Molly said. "Maybe we could talk over tea sometime. Perhaps some Sunday after Mass? Do you go to Mass?"

There it was. Best to be honest about something at least. "Well, no, I'm not Catholic."

"Ah, I see. Well, perhaps you'd like to join us sometime anyway."

"That would be lovely," Susanna said. "I'll look forward to it."

"To what?" Michael said, coming up to them.

"Miss Cassidy is going to join us for Mass one of these Sundays."

"Oh, Ma," he said, "you're not pressuring her to come with us, are you?"

"There was no pressure necessary. Miss Cassidy said she'd be happy to come along."

Susanna nodded. "I did. Really."

"See there?" Molly said to Michael as she stood up. "I'd best get back to the bar." She smiled and nodded and walked away.

"She likes you," Michael said.

"Even though I'm not a Catholic?"

"Well, I'm sure she's grieved over your soul spending eternity in hell, but it's nothing she can't live with." He grinned down at her. "So, what do you say? Ready to call it a night?"

She nodded. "It's been a long day, and a longer one before that."

"I take it then," he said, lowering his voice, "you'd rather hie yourself home to your wee bed than come over to my place for a nightcap."

She tried to look rueful. "If I did, I'm sure I'd get a lot more sleep."

"I'm sure you would too. Let's plan on tomorrow night then. Give me a good reason to go to Confession. 'Forgive me, Father, for I've lost me heart to an American Protestant.'"

She laughed. "Escort me to my car?"

"Absolutely."

As they walked through the cold night, Susanna pressed more closely to Michael. "I think people are starting to suspect," she said.

"No," he said in mock surprise. "What makes you think that, Rooney's teasing or my ma's invitation to Mass? When I was a lad, a couple would've had to get married if they were stranded together in a snowstorm. Folks around here believe that if a man and a woman are given the opportunity, they're certain to take advantage of it. Of course, in this particular case they're dead right."

"Aren't they just?" Susanna said. "And your song certainly put any doubts to rest."

"I just wanted to put the nosey parkers in their place. At least now they'll stop guessing."

Susanna hesitated for a moment. "Kate Quinn didn't seem any too pleased by the affirmation, such as it was."

"I don't answer to Kate Quinn," Michael said, and Susanna could feel him pull away.

"I'm sorry. I didn't mean anything."

"It's all right," he said, and she saw him smile in the dim light. "A lot of people thought that Kate and I would end up together...her included. But it's not to be."

They arrived at Susanna's car, and Michael kissed her tenderly. "Goodnight then. Tomorrow's Saturday. Good day for touring, yes?"

She grinned. "What does my guide have in mind?"

"Have you ever seen Thoor Ballylee?" She shook her head. "It was Yeats's summer home, not very far south of here. A big tower house with a cottage attached. How about if I pick you up at noon and we'll have plenty of time to get back for the evening session."

"That would be wonderful. But a full session tomorrow?"

Michael nodded. "The first of February is when we celebrate the opening of the pub. Well over a hundred years now. There'll be a full session, some special food...there's always great fun."

"It's a date. See you at noon," Susanna said, and kissed him once more before climbing into her car.

She turned on the heater full blast as she headed out of the town center and south over the Wolfe Tone Bridge. Several minutes later, when the car had finally warmed up, she pulled along the curb near her guest house and turned off the ignition.

The lights were off in the guest house, as they normally were at this late hour, but when she looked through the windshield toward the stairs that led to her rooms, she saw a figure in the shadows. Susanna felt a rush of fear go through her as she tried to imagine what legitimate purpose anyone would have for sitting on her steps. Maybe it was just a drunk gathering his strength for the final lurch homeward.

When the person moved, however, there was no sign of staggering. The figure rose swiftly and straight and started walking toward her car. Susanna's hand sought the horn pad, ready to press it down and hold it, but there was something familiar about the figure that stayed her hand. When it walked into the light cast by the street lamp, she was both shocked and relieved to see that it was Rachel, her niece.

"Oh my God," Susanna said, getting out of the car and hurrying to meet the girl, "you scared the hell out of me."

Rachel returned her hug, but Susanna felt something stiff and reserved in her embrace. "Could we go in?" Rachel asked. "I've been freezing my ass off out here."

They climbed the stairs and went inside, where Susanna turned on the lights and started to boil some water. "Unfortunately, I don't have anything stronger than tea," she said, and gestured to Rachel to sit down on the couch.

They made small talk as Susanna prepared the tea and got out a bag of cookies. Rachel told her when she had arrived and where she was staying, and Susanna told Rachel about her father's concern for her whereabouts. Finally, she set the tea and cookies on the little table in front of the couch and sat next to Rachel.

"Are you all right?" she asked her niece. "You seem a little upset."

Rachel took a sip of tea, then set down the cup carefully. "I was at the pub tonight. The Lilting Banshee. I saw you there. I was going to come up and say hi, then I heard somebody call you *Julia*."

"Oh honey..." Susanna said, but Rachel cut her off.

"I just watched for a while, and I heard that guy sing that song, the song that Mom used to hum to me, and I started putting things together, and I remembered what was written in that old book she had, and the only thing I could figure out was that the guy knew my mom years ago, and that for some reason you were pretending to be her.

"Now I know this sounds crazy and I might be full of crap, but Aunt Sue, would you please tell me what the hell is going on here? I mean, I've gotten kind of tangled up right now with this guy, and that's complex enough, and to add this to the mix is really messing with my head more than I like it messed with."

Susanna took a deep breath and blew it out, then tried to let the tension go as she leaned against the back of the couch. "Honey," she said, "have another sip of tea. This is going to be a long story, and after you've heard it, well, you might feel very differently about your dear Aunt Sue."

Susanna told the story then. First, she told Rachel everything that Julia had told her about what happened back in 1972, except for the fact that Michael Lynch and Julia had become lovers. She told her about Julia's request to Susanna to return to Galway in case Michael should show up at the reunion, and how circumstances had thrown her into the role of Julia.

"I knew it was wrong from the start," Susanna said, "but sometimes things just...oh, I don't know. I never thought it would come to this. I thought he'd get tired of the novelty of the old 'lost love' routine, and that would be it, that I could keep the illusion going until the end, but now neither one of us want there to *be* an end. I have to tell him, that's all there is to it."

"Yeah," said Rachel. "And there's *another* reason you have to tell him." The girl's mouth twisted. "At this point I've pretty much fallen in love with your new boyfriend's son."

Susanna felt her mouth drop open. "Gerry?"

Rachel nodded. "*Quelle coincidence*, huh? Of course, in his case he *knows* who I really am. I ran into him in a pub, we got talking, he had lyrics, I had music, and...we had a thing. Correction, are *having* a thing. And I like it better than any *thing* I've had since, oh, I don't know, since birth, maybe. He's an incredible guy—maybe he takes after his daddy." She chuckled, then her smile faded. "Of course, it's a little weird that I'm hot for the son of the guy my mom was hot for thirty years ago... and who my aunt's hot for *now*. The whole thing's got kind of a Kentucky backwoods feel to it, Hatfields and the McCoys and all."

"Nobody's feuding," Susanna said, trying to laugh it away. The backwoods comment had struck home, making her think of something that had been nesting uncomfortably in the back of her mind ever since Julia had first told her the tale of her Irish lover. It was possible that Rachel could have been Michael Lynch's child rather than David Oliver's, in which case Gerry would be...

Susanna drove back the conclusion. There was enough on her plate right now. Besides, if she knew Rachel, her definition of *thing* extended to sexual intimacy, so the deed was already done. Best to take care of problems one at a time, and she had a huge one to deal with. The truth would have to come out if Michael and she and Gerry and Rachel could ever be in the same room together.

"I'll tell Michael tomorrow," Susanna said. "I'll tell him who I really am. I've been afraid to, afraid that I'll lose him because of it. But if I do, then I'll know it just wasn't meant to be."

"Look, it'll work out," said Rachel. "I mean, it always works in the movies, like that *Roman Holiday* you showed me, when Audrey Hepburn pretends to be a commoner and not the princess she really is, and she and Gregory Peck, um…" She paused as though confused.

"They don't wind up together at the end," Susanna said.

"Okay, bad example. What about, what about….*Vertigo!* You remember, that was *so* romantic—Kim Novak pretends to be that other woman, and Jimmy Stewart falls in love with her, and…" She paused again.

"And she falls off the tower to her death," Susanna said.

"Okay, okay, another bad example. But there have got to be *some* that work out all right. What about *An Affair to Remember?*"

"Nobody pretended to be somebody else in *An Affair to Remember.*"

"Okay, then I got it mixed up with that other one with Cary Grant."

"Rachel, I think it's late and we're both mentally exhausted," Susanna said. "Do you want to sleep here tonight?"

"No, I'll head back to the hostel." She saw an expression in Susanna's eyes that made her add, "Yes, Gerry and I are, but not tonight, Aunt Nosey."

Susanna shrugged. "Your private life is private, dear."

"Not tonight it ain't, and neither is yours." She laughed and gave her aunt a big hug. "I'm sorry I was so tense when you got here. I just didn't know *what* was happening." She wrinkled up her face. "And I'm not so sure that knowing makes things any easier."

"It'll be easier when the truth comes out. And it will tomorrow. Oh, by the way, give your dad a call ASAP. He actually threatened to come over here."

"Dear God, anything but that," Rachel said. They exchanged phone numbers, and Rachel left after another hug.

Left alone, Susanna let herself flop back onto the bed. This was it then, that moment of truth she had so feared. Susanna was optimistic about most things, but she had always been pessimistic about personal relationships, since life itself had taught her to feel that way.

In her professional life and in her friendships, she felt totally at ease, as she did among her family, with the exception of David. Yet when it came to matters of the heart, she began every flirtation expecting to hear the gong of doom announcing the end before the beginning was even underway. She had come further and in a shorter time with Michael Lynch than she ever had with anyone, and the irony that it might come crashing down on her head due to her little omission of truth at the surprising and unpredictable start was more than she could bear. Had she known it would come this far, she would have blurted out the truth instantly. The same thing would have happened, wouldn't it?

Or wasn't it Susanna that Michael had fallen in love with, but Julia? Had his heart opened to a memory of his youth? It was a time that all middle-aged men yearn for, an age when they were so far from the abyss of mortality that they couldn't even see the edge. But when they hit their fifties, they felt their toes curling over it. And there was always that sense of curiosity as to what might have happened had they chosen that different road, married that other woman.

Reflection on their youth and the choices they made then seemed a constant with men, but not with women. Though there were exceptions, most of Susanna's female friends, married, divorced, or single, seemed more contented than did the men in their lives. Many of them had told her that they liked their age, and that they would never want to go back to being younger. Oh yes, it would be nice to get rid of the tummy, or see the spider veins disappear, or no longer need the goddamned estrogen, but they were only too happy to accept those outward signs of age as tradeoffs for the inward treasures the years had brought—wisdom, experience, peace.

Of course, the fact that so many of them were grandmothers helped. Susanna didn't have that luxury of experiencing many of the joys of parenthood without the attendant responsibilities. Then again, she'd never even had the joys and responsibilities of actual parenthood. There were times when she thought she missed it, but on the whole, she was happy with her life. The idea of sharing marriage and children with a man she didn't really love was inconceivable to her. No, better to have lived alone and happy than to have led one of Thoreau's lives of quiet desperation in a loveless marriage.

But now she had finally met a man she really loved. Michael Lynch seemed to be everything she'd always looked for. He was strong yet tender. He was sensitive and artistic, with the soul of a poet and musician, yet he was all too familiar with the harsh realities of life. He knew when to be serious and when to laugh at himself. And, most important of all, he loved her.

How much, would depend on how he reacted to what she would tell him the next day.

CHAPTER 14

The sun woke Susanna the next morning. She had fallen asleep on the bed with her clothes on, and when she sat up, she felt stiff and uncomfortable. After she showered and washed the smell of tobacco smoke from her hair, she felt nearly civilized again. A small pot of coffee and a container of yogurt aided in the transformation, and also helped to restrain the fluttering wings of the butterflies in her stomach.

By the time she finished breakfast, it was 9:30. There was no way she was going to be able to stay in her room until Michael arrived at noon, so she walked down to Grattan Road and watched the birds flying over the bay. They proved no distraction. As she sat on one of the large, cold stones that covered the quay like huge grains of sand, she tried to decide exactly what she would say to Michael.

Everything she came up with seemed totally inadequate. How could she express the ineffable in words, or give names to emotions she couldn't even identify? How could she tell him that she had been swept away by their meeting, that the question of what was right or wrong had altogether evaded her in the light of...what? His smile? His eyes? His kiss? It all seemed so feeble when you tried to verbalize it, like some Motown song lyric that sounded great with a beat behind it, but which standing alone made the sappiest greeting card sentiment seem eloquent.

Slowly she made her way back to the guest house. She thought she would wait until she and Michael were at Thoor Ballylee to tell him the truth. If the setting were romantic, he might be more forgiving of the trick played upon him. Also, since they would have driven a distance together, he couldn't walk away if he grew angry. On the ride back she might be able to partly repair the romantic illusion her admission had shattered.

What she was most afraid of was that he would feel she had made a fool of him. That could be the hardest thing for a man to forgive.

She told herself to stop thinking about it. Worrying over all these different scenarios would do her no good. It would only make her crazier, like a few years earlier when they found a suspicious shadow on her mammogram. Between the time she received the news that she had to go back in and when the doctor declared it a benign cyst, she suffered a thousand deaths, all for nothing. Susanna wasn't a hypochondriac, but it had been her first medical scare and she had overreacted, as her doctor put it. Though she didn't say it, she thought there could be no *over*reaction in matters of life and death. And though her relationship with Michael didn't extend that far, it certainly felt as though it did.

She heard his footsteps on the wooden stairs and took a deep breath. He was ten minutes early and she was glad, since it meant ten fewer minutes of apprehension. When she opened the door, he grinned and said in a dreadfully broad brogue, "Ah, and top o' the mornin' to ye, miss. And is it mair of the Emerald Isle ye're ready to be seein' this foine day then?"

"Don't look now, but you forgot your Lucky Charms," she said. He kissed her. He smelled fresh and clean, and his lips were soft and warm. "Mmm, magically delicious."

"Well," he said, reverting to his normal tone, "I thought I'd better give you what tourists expect of their guides."

"Kisses before lunch?"

"Any toime of the day or night, miss. Ready to go visit Mr. Yeats?"

The day was perfect for a drive, and they opened their windows a bit to let in the cool air. They stopped along the way for a light lunch, and Michael remarked on how Susanna hardly touched her sandwich. She felt barely able to participate in the conversation, but made herself nod and respond and smile, though she suspected Michael thought something was wrong.

The back roads were nearly empty, and the snow that had fallen two nights before had vanished so that not even puddles remained. It felt like a day in spring.

The narrow road finally ended at a small, empty car park. "The tower's closed for the season," Michael said, "but we can go right up to it, if not inside."

Susanna saw Thoor Ballylee as soon as they stepped onto the roughly paved private road that led to it. It was a massive square tower of gray stone, twice as high as it was wide, with patches of ivy creeping over the edge of the roof. Small windows looked out from each of the four floors, and she thought it must be terribly dark inside. At its base ran a wide but shallow river, and as they walked across the stone bridge that led to the tower they paused and looked down into the water.

"The River Cloon. It's low," Michael observed. "Last time I was here it was much fuller."

"What does it mean? Thoor Ballylee?"

"*Thoor* means tower, and Ballylee is just the name of the castle. It's in the Norman style, from the sixteenth century. Yeats bought it from Lady Gregory, had it renovated, and lived here for about ten summers. Wrote a lot here, too. Come on."

He took her hand and they walked the few yards to the tower, where Susanna pressed her hands on the cold gray stone as if to affirm the solidity of it. A stone plaque was laid into the wall, and on it she read:

I, the poet William Yeats,/With old millboards and sea-green slates/And smithy work from the Gort forge,/ Restored this tower for my wife George./And may these characters remain/When all is ruin once again.

Hand in hand they walked on past the attached cottage, its roof green with moss. "There's a museum and a tea shop inside," Michael said.

"I'd like to come back and go in sometime."

"We will. There's just a big room on each floor, and a spiral staircase. Not really a very friendly place to live, as far as

I'm concerned, but Yeats liked the romance of it, I'm sure. Don't know what old George thought about it."

They walked down the lane until it left the surrounding trees and came to an open field, then walked back again. As they were crossing the bridge, Michael turned toward her with a sly smile. "Would you like me to recite some Yeats to you?"

"I'd love it." Anything, she thought, to keep from telling him what she had to tell him.

"All right then. How about 'Aengus' again?" He lifted her as lightly as if she'd been an empty Guinness keg and set her so that she was sitting on the low stone wall. "My audience." Then he stepped back, took a quick bow, and started reciting "The Song of Wandering Aengus," about a man who catches a little silver trout with a berry. But when he takes it home and blows the fire into flame...

"'It had become a glimmering girl,'" Michael intoned, his face aglow with the sense of the near mystical words, "'With apple blossom in her hair/Who called me by my name and ran/ And faded through the brightening air.'"

She raised her hand to stop him then. She didn't want to hear the final verse which tells how Aengus has wandered for years to find his lost love, and to be with her *till time and times are done*. In those lines was a blending of sorrow and joyous expectation that she could not bear.

"What is it?" asked Michael, and the concern on his face made her realize how near to tears she was. "What is it, love?"

He put a hand on her shoulder, and it only made her feel weaker and more of a liar. She knew that she was going to tell him, but she didn't know how, and she heard herself say, "Oh Michael, "I'm just like that *fish*..."

Had she really said that? Had she come to perhaps the most influential moment of truth in all her life and just told the man she loved that she was like a fish? The confused look on his face only made her own confusion worse.

"I mean...I'm not what you *think* I am. That man caught a fish, but it *wasn't* a fish, it was a *girl*, and that's what I'm trying to say..."

"That you're not a fish, but a girl." He nodded solemnly. "I knew that."

"No, *no!* There's more to it than that." She laughed in spite of the tears forming in her eyes, and tried to get control. This was not going to be one of those Laura Petrie *"Oh Rob!"* moments. "Let me..." She cleared her throat and shook her head. "Let me start over. Because what I have to tell you is really very important, Michael. And I think that because it's so important I find myself getting a little hysterical, because if I tell you and you hate me, I don't know...well, I just don't know..." she finished feebly.

"Will you have to become a fish again?" he asked without the trace of a smile.

"Oh..." She half laughed, and tried to wave away his silliness with her hands. "This isn't *funny*. What I was *trying* to say with the fish/girl analogy was that...I'm not who you think I am." Susanna didn't feel silly or flighty or hysterical anymore. She felt like someone who had a nasty job to do. "You think I'm Julia Cassidy, and I'm not."

Despite Michael's smile, she thought he seemed serious, too. "You're not."

"No, I'm not."

He shrugged. "Who are you then?"

Here it was. The best way was flat out, with no further delays. She looked straight into his face. "I'm *Susanna* Cassidy. I'm Julia's sister."

His smile had retreated until now only a ghost of it was present. He nodded slowly, looking at her, then looking down as his gaze fell. He rested his hands on her knees, and they remained like that, she sitting on the wall, he standing, for what seemed to Susanna like time enough for the ice caps to melt and the River Cloon to overflow its banks and cover both them and Thoor Ballylee. She was actually hoping for such a cataclysm when Michael finally spoke.

"I think," he said slowly, "that Susanna is a lovely name. And I do believe that I prefer it even to Julia."

Michael looked into her eyes again, and she knew that everything was going to be all right. She hopped off the wall and found herself wrapped in his arms, and, though she tried not to and hated herself for doing so, she cried in relief and happiness and rage that she had taken so long to tell the truth to this man she loved so much.

"There, there, now," he said, lightly rubbing her back and nuzzling the top of her head with his chin. "It's all right." He raised her head and kissed the wetness of the tears on her cheeks. "Nothing to cry about. We all pretend sometimes. I was really afraid you were going to tell me you were a fish."

She laughed and sniffed and accepted the tissue that he handed her from his pocket.

"So," Michael said, his face turning more serious, "you said that your sister had died. Is that true?"

Susanna nodded. "Yes. In December. That's what started all this."

"And those pictures you showed me..."

"That was Julia."

He was quiet for a moment, then said, "You know, I think the reason I'm not more surprised is because I knew all along. You seemed to have changed so much. I mean, people do change through their lives, but before, well, the Julia Cassidy I knew was a sweet girl but she was also, how shall I put this, more self-centered than you. She had trouble seeing beyond her own little sphere. When I'd tell her about the history of Ireland, about the reasons I felt the way I did politically, when I tried to explain to her why I had to go to the North, she didn't really understand. She couldn't..."

He paused, and Susanna tried to put his thought into a word. "Empathize."

"That's it. She wasn't cruel or unkind, just...ignorant of certain things, and there didn't seem to be any desire on her part to learn or change. Or grow. And I remember when I thought about her afterwards—and I did—I thought that she'd be the same person ten, twenty, thirty years later that she was when I knew her.

"And then there you were, there was *Julia*, and she was...so *different*. Another person. A better one. Someone who put others before herself, someone who was socially aware, who really cared about the way things were. And I thought, what a miraculous change."

Susanna shook her head. "With all those qualities you're heaping on me, aren't you angry that telling the truth wasn't among them?"

"You know...*Susanna*," he said, and her name sounded glorious to her, "you don't have to be perfect. I assume you had a reason for not telling me right away. And look at it this way, you've only kept your little secret for a bit over a week. Hardly the impersonation of the century. But the first thing of about three that I want to know is, were you telling me the truth about yourself otherwise? Are you a professor, and most importantly are you unmarried?"

"I *am* a professor, and no, I'm not married. I never have been."

He nodded as though the answers met with his approval. "And now for the second thing. How did you come to be standing by that river at that time?"

That part was relatively easy to relate. Susanna told him all about Julia's dying request, how she had given Susanna the volume of Yeats, and how she had kept Michael in her heart for thirty years. "I think she really loved you," Susanna said.

Michael gave a bittersweet smile and shook his head. "No. She didn't love me any more than I did her. She never really knew me. And she wouldn't have been happy with me. She made the right decisions for who she was. From what you've told me, from the pictures I saw, Julia got what she wanted out of life. At the end she loved the *idea* of me, of what might have happened if her life had been different." He took a deep breath and looked up at the branches swaying in the wind. "That's what took me down to the river that day last week. That curiosity, that need to know what might have been." He looked back down at her, then reached out his hand and touched her cheek. "And what can still be."

Then he crossed his arms and tried to look stern. "But now for the third question. Why didn't you tell me who you were that day?"

Suddenly a cry startled them both. "Hey! Hey there—do you want to come in then?"

Saved by the bell, Susanna thought. They looked down the

lane, and in the doorway that led to the cottage a man with white hair was leaning over the gate and looking at them. "Did you want to come in?" he asked again.

"Aren't you closed?" Michael called back.

"Officially, yes, but if you'd just like to come in for a cuppa tea, you'd be welcome. Warm your bones." The man twitched as though he didn't have all day and if they'd be coming in, they'd best be quick about it.

Michael looked at Susanna and she nodded quickly. "All right, thanks!" he called back, and they walked to the cottage.

"Come on inside, then," the man said. "Freeze to death out there." When he turned his back to lead the way, Michael and Susanna eyed each other. The weather was practically balmy for the beginning of February.

"That's more like it," the man said when they were inside. He introduced himself as Aloysius Hardiman, and they introduced themselves to him. Susanna used her real name, and Michael smiled when she did. "Well, I can't let you into the tower, but have a look around. The wee museum's in there. Anything's missing, I'll know who's to blame. I'll put a kettle of tea on the boil. I've no fresh pastries, but I've some tinned biscuits if you're hungry."

"Oh no, the tea will be fine. Thank you so much," Susanna said.

"Ah, I like to hear voices now and then, more than my own," Hardiman said, and set to getting the tea ready. It was amazing, Susanna thought again, how gracious people were here, not only permitting them to enter a site during the closed season, but serving them tea as well.

She and Michael went through the museum, paying close attention to the Yeats first editions on display. Still there was a sense of something left unfinished between her and Michael, a bothersome awareness of how their conversation had been left dangling by Hardiman's invitation. She thought about how she was going to answer Michael's third question, and decided that it was foolish to hold anything back. He knew that she loved him, but what he would learn was that she had done so the moment she'd seen him at the river.

"Tea's ready!" Hardiman called, and they joined him in the tea room. They sat around a table, and the old man poured out the tea and offered milk and sugar. "So," he said when they were all sipping, "do you like Yeats?"

"Very much," Michael said. "Read him since I was a lad."

"That's the time to start. Get him in your blood early." Hardiman leaned in towards them as if confiding a dread secret. "Truth to tell, he was a fool in a lot of ways, but he had the soul of us. How about you, mum," he said to Susanna. "American, are you?" In response to her nod, he went on, "I've relatives there. Visit them now and again. Good country. Slipped off the tracks the past few years, but the little people will bring it round again. Run for the rich right now. Willie would've written about it, to be sure."

"You talk as though you knew him," Susanna said.

"You get to feel that way being here, especially when you're alone. Sometimes I think I hear the children playing by the river, and sometimes I speak his poetry aloud, and I can swear I hear another voice speaking it with me. I did meet him once, though, when I was a babe. In 1932 it was, when he was in Dublin. My mother held me out to him and he kissed my forehead, at least that's what they tell me."

"So, you don't actually remember it?" Michael asked.

"Only sometimes in dreams, and you know how dreams are. I see him, it's outside on the street, and he's old and his hair is white." He smiled. "Like mine. But it's just a dream. And as for ghosts, I've heard things here as I say, but I think it's just echoes or imagination. Or the wanting of it to be true."

Susanna listened in the silence, but heard neither the laughter of children nor a stately voice intoning verse, even though she almost expected to.

"So, tell me," Hardiman went on, "are youse two married?"

"No, we're not," Michael said.

"Well, you should be, you look well together." Both she and Michael laughed self-consciously. "I've been married to my wife now over fifty years. Good years, too. I was lucky, I found her when I was young. Now no offense, but neither of you are children no more, so when you find her...or him..." He nodded to them both. "...don't wait for the heavens to part and a voice to tell you that you've picked well. I never tell my wife this, but I think it a lot: 'Time's bitter flood will rise/Your beauty perish and be lost/For all eyes but these eyes.'"

"Yeats?" Susanna asked.

"Now however could you tell?" Hardiman said. "More tea?"

They each had another cup and talked more, of Yeats and love and growing older. Susanna kept waiting for Hardiman to spoil the effect by saying something stupid or sexist or bigoted, but he didn't, and it was lovely to think that there were still people like this, who were kind, and who had inherent wisdom and the souls of poets. Her cynicism told her that if she spent any longer than an hour or so with the man, his flaws would become all too obvious, but for now he was just what she needed, a stabilizing force outside of herself and Michael, an example of sense and order.

"Well," Michael said at last, "I suppose we should be getting back soon."

"Before you do," Hardiman said, "you owe it to yourself and the lady to take a little walk along the river down to the old mill. They say old Willie used to go down there and write. But then they say he wrote everywhere. Not a spot between Ballyhillin and Skibbereen that didn't inspire him to scribble something down, if you'd be believing what everyone says. Biggest export of this country is shite, if you'll pardon the expression, mum."

Susanna had to grin. So Hardiman was human after all.

"Now it might be too cold for you out there, in which case you can come back and walk it another day." There was another flaw. She wondered if he and his wife of fifty years agreed on the temperature in their bedroom.

"Thank you for your hospitality, Mr. Hardiman," said Michael. "And the next time you're in Galway, please stop by The Lilting Banshee and allow me to return it."

"That I will," said Hardiman as he nodded them out into the sunshine and returned shivering back through the gate, so hunched against the perceived chill that he was barely able to raise an arm to wave farewell.

"Lovely man," Susanna said as they strolled toward the

river and the path to the mill of which Hardiman had told them.

"Indeed he is. A bit cold-blooded, though. Feel like that walk?"

"Yes. And it'll give me time to answer your question. About why I kept the masquerade going?"

"I hadn't forgotten," Michael said as they walked on and he took her hand.

Susanna breathed deeply of the Irish air, and then began. "When you met me that day, when you said those words from your song and you kissed me, it was like...it was like I'd finally come home. It just felt *right*. I don't know how to describe it beyond that. I could use superlatives, but it was so simple. I wanted you to love me, and I thought you could love me more easily if I was Julia." She gave a weak laugh and shook her head. "And I looked a *fright*. I guess I thought the first impression would be stronger if you thought I was an old love. So, I let you think I was."

Michael nodded. "Later on, though, why didn't you tell me sooner?"

"I was afraid."

"Of what? Me?"

"Of losing you. I didn't know you well enough then to know how you'd react. So, I kept digging myself in deeper. And the other night, with what you said about hating lies and liars..." She sighed. "The longer it's gone, the harder it's been to tell the truth. You thought I was someone I wasn't, and I was afraid *that* was the person you...you loved."

He stopped walking and turned her toward him. "I love *you*, whoever you are."

"You know who I am now."

"I've always known. Who you are isn't a name. It's the things you do and the things you say." A crooked smile lit his face and he cocked his head at her. "I think I became even more suspicious Thursday night. When we made love?"

"I believe I remember something like that," Susanna said, thinking how silly she felt to be blushing.

"Not that it's gentlemanly to compare such things, and I trust you'll forgive me for doing so, but you are...an unselfish lover. And before..." He shrugged and left it unfinished but had said enough. "At any rate, I'm glad you are who you are, and I'm even more glad that I finally know."

"It's going to be a little awkward when we get back," Susanna said, anticipating the confusion and odd looks the announcement would bring to those in the pub.

"Well," Michael said, "just a few people think I knew you from years ago, and no one but my mother knows about the scheduled meeting at the river. I can explain it to her, she's a woman, she'll understand. The tricky part is how do we explain why you're now Susanna instead of Julia?"

"Maybe Julia was my stripper name." Michael looked at her curiously, and she quickly shook her head. "*Very* bad joke, I'm sorry."

"Maybe it's not as tricky as it seems," Michael said. "Why don't we just say it was a misapprehension on my part, and I wasn't aware that you preferred being addressed as Susanna."

"Better yet, what if you just introduced me as Susanna? To the people I'd met before."

Michael thought for a moment. "Maybe. Just matter of fact. And if anyone says they thought your name was Julia we just say no, it's Susanna, there was a bit of a mix-up before but now everything's sorted out. People will be curious but they won't ask, and if someone does, well, maybe we'll tell them and maybe we won't."

"There is," Susanna said, "one other person who knows the whole story. My niece, Rachel. She's over here in Galway on a little vacation. I saw her last night."

"Ah, well, that's all right then. And did you tell her you were going to tell me the truth?"

"Yes. She's pretty much what brought me to the crisis point. She was at the pub last night...with Gerry."

Michael was quiet for a moment. "With *my* Gerry?" Susanna nodded, not knowing what to expect. "Ladies in your family seem to have a weakness for Irishmen."

She laughed, and it felt good. "She didn't say hello because she heard someone call me Julia. They left before I saw her and she went to the guest house and waited for me."

"That's interesting. Gerry doesn't usually bring girls round to the pub."

"I had the feeling they're getting serious, at least on Rachel's part."

"Hmm...another story to work itself out then. Time will tell, I suppose." Michael looked around them. "Lovely mill. Or I assume that it once was." He turned toward Susanna and kissed her lightly. Then he kissed her again. Her arms went around him and they stood holding each other for a long time.

"I just have one more question, if I may," Michael said, still holding her.

"Yes?"

"Are you the younger or the older sister?"

"Would it matter?"

"Not at all."

"The younger."

"Ah, thank the Lord..."

CHAPTER 15

When Susanna and Michael arrived back in Galway, they went directly to The Lilting Banshee, where he led the way upstairs to Molly Sullivan's flat. They had decided that it would be best if they told his mother about Susanna's ruse together.

Molly wouldn't hear a word until they all had tea in front of them. Finally, in her sitting room, Michael introduced the topic and Susanna gave Molly the details. When she had finished, she said, "I'm very sorry. I hope that you'll forgive me for deceiving you...and your son. And everyone else," she added weakly, then shook her head. "Oh, I feel like such an *idiot*."

Molly neither smiled nor frowned. She took a sip of tea, then cocked her head to the left. "I can see," she said softly, "how a woman might easily do such a thing, being carried away by the moment, as it were, and then being forced to continue out of fear of losing the man involved. But for the life of me I can't imagine anyone doing it for the likes of this one here."

Michael, apparently relieved, smiled. "Now what kind of thing is that for a mother to be saying of her son?"

"A common thing, when a mother *knows* her son the way I do you, you scamp."

Michael laughed, and Molly let slip a quiet smile. Susanna felt relieved, too, until Molly's next words.

"Now, Michael, you go downstairs for a time and let Susanna and me have a moment alone to talk." Susanna was pleased at least to see that Molly did not put any unusual stress on her name.

Michael looked as Susanna as though he were leaving her

in a nest of vipers, but could do nothing about it. "Go on, lad," Molly repeated. "If I was planning to eat her, I'd have done so already."

"Be careful she doesn't talk your ear off," Michael said as he stood up. "And you, Ma...just...don't...ah, never mind." He sighed and walked out the door.

"Men so often have trouble with words, don't they?" Molly said, and Susanna had to laugh. "Especially when trying to caution their mothers as to this or that." Molly set her cup down on the little table and placed her hands on her knees. It was, Susanna thought, a very schoolmarmly attitude.

"I want you to know, Susanna, that I'm truly not angry with you for what you did, nor even disappointed that you let us think you were someone other than yourself. I must say that I don't believe I ever heard you introduce yourself as your sister, though you may have. I believe you let my son do that for you. So, you didn't so much lie as, let's say, omit the truth. Like your American politicians. And like ours, for that matter. And I understand. The heart can make women do things...well..." Her eyes seemed to look somewhere far away. When she came back, she said, "So it seems you feel warmly toward Michael then?"

"Yes," Susanna replied. "I do."

"He's a good man, and I don't say that just because I'm his mother, though I should, of course. I might not have said as much thirty years ago. He's told you all that, has he?" When Susanna nodded, Molly continued. "Michael's been hit hard through his life, and he *took* things hard. While others might've shrugged and turned their backs, he felt it all. His father's death was what started it. I brought him here to the South, but his heart stayed in the North. Sometimes I think it's still there. Does he talk much about it, the North, I mean?"

"A bit. He doesn't seem fixated on it, but I can tell it's a sensitive topic for him. I think he finds my work—peace studies— rather futile, but he's not argumentative about it."

"Aye, he never says much about it anymore, but I think, in the deep heart's core..."

"Yeats," Susanna said.

"Begging your pardon?" Molly's expression was suspicious as though Susanna had just said *catamaran* or *vestibule* or some other definitive *non sequitur* that suggested Tourette's Syndrome.

"Yeats," Susanna repeated, in a much smaller voice. "'The deep heart's core'—it's from one of his poems. Sorry."

"Yeats is part of our tongue here," Molly said. "We never realize, and we never notice. Now, what was I saying?"

"Um, that Michael feels...down deep...an affinity toward the North."

"Yes. I never approved of his visits to Malachy when he was a lad, and I'm still uncomfortable when he sees him now. Old wounds of the flesh may heal, but not the heart. By the way, that was me, not Yeats, though you could probably tell."

Susanna didn't know if the comment was meant to be funny, but she had no choice but to smile and restrain a laugh that puffed through her nostrils. It made Molly laugh aloud. "Aye, it's fun to laugh at ourselves," she said, "but I still worry about my boy. You never stop worrying about them, and when they've had such a past it makes it worse. He's overcome most of it, but I don't know if he'll ever be able to leave it all behind." She leaned slightly toward Susanna. "You could be a help to him with that."

"I'd be happy to if I can. But I don't want to be too intrusive."

"Men *need* us to be intrusive. Not overly so, but they need us in their lives to make them civilized. They're fools, most of them, and sometimes so are we. But were it not for us and the way we change them, they'd still be living in huts and bashing each other's brains out, and the one with the biggest club wins." She snorted. "Call me a cynic, but that's what they still do when they get off on their own, from gang boys to presidents, still think that fighting's the only way to settle things. We women settled *them* without it, and they don't even realize it.

"Which is all a roundabout way of saying that you can be a strong influence on Michael, because I think he loves you, and men'll do a great deal for women they love...yes, they will." She got the faraway look again. "Well, that's all I wanted to say. I hope you don't think I've been too forward."

"Oh no, not at—"

"I don't know what your intentions toward Michael are, nor his to yourself, and it's not my business to ask. But I did want you to know that your road with Michael might not be the smoothest because of the things he's done and the way he is. He's a fine man, but he wants watching."

"Thank you for telling me. I'm not…really sure where we're going myself from here, but I'm glad to have, um…"

"My approval? Well, you have that, for what it's worth. I fancy myself a good judge of character, though I've been wrong a few times, but I'm not wrong about you. I think you're a finer woman than Michael is a man, but then I know his faults and I don't yet know yours. You do have some?"

"I definitely do, yes."

"If that's true, you hide them well, and that shows a strength of character all on its own. And I do know you've got one hell of a poker face, Miss Julia-Susanna, and there's nothing wrong with that either. I'm rumored to have one myself, I understand."

"I think you're just…circumspect, Mrs. Sullivan."

"And you're a skillful flatterer, Miss Cassidy. I happen to find that a good quality in my friends as well." She rose and started to gather the teacups and saucers, and Susanna followed her out to the kitchen with her own. Susanna was hesitant to bring up the next subject, but thought that Molly Sullivan would be the ideal person to ask.

"The one thing that Michael and I were a little leery of," she said as she set her cup and saucer carefully on the sink next to the others, "was how to break the news of my, well, change in identity to the people in the pub."

Molly waved her hand as though brushing away a gnat. "Leave that to me. Come in a little late, a bit after nine, and don't worry about a thing. Now, stop wasting your time in this old lady's flat and go down and see that boyfriend of yours."

Molly Sullivan was as good as her word. When Susanna arrived at The Lilting Banshee shortly after nine o'clock that evening, several people looked at her strangely, but most seemed to take in stride whatever private announcements Molly had made.

Aengus Cleary was already sitting down, warming up his

fingers on the buttons of his accordion, when Susanna walked in, and he nodded his head and said, "Evenin', Susanna," with just a bit of stress on the name. Still, he was smiling as though happy to see her.

A moment later Fiona made her way through the crowd, holding a pint of stout. While before she had wailed *Julia!* upon seeing her, she now said, "*Susanna!*" with exactly the same schoolgirl inflection. "How are you," Fiona went on. "You've not changed much since yesterday, except for your name, but no more about that then, eh?" She winked. "Wouldn't want to get in bad with old Molly now. Want a pint?"

Susanna was relieved to feel Michael's arm around her. "This one giving you trouble?" he asked.

"Oh, you're the only one giving Susanna any trouble," Fiona said.

Michael drew Susanna away from the others into the entry-way. When they were alone, she asked him, "What on earth did your mother *say* to them?"

"I overheard her telling some of the regulars," Michael said, and Susanna noticed that his cheeks were pink. "She told them the truth flat out, rattled right on—'Oh, Michael knew a girl named Julia years ago, and that's this one's sister, but the sister's dead now, and Michael thought this one was her and she didn't correct him for fear he'd be sad, but now she did, and he's not sad at all, and her name's *Susanna* Cassidy and not Julia Cassidy, and that's all there is to it, so call her by that now.'" Michael took a long pause, shaking his head in disbelief.

"And…what did the person she told this to say?" Susanna asked.

Michael looked stricken as he answered. "Not a thing. Just nodded as though it all made perfect sense. I think she must be a witch, only way I can explain how they just accept what she says."

A rush of cold air engulfed them both as the front door opened and Kate Quinn walked in, her fiddle case hanging from her back by a strap. "Well," she said, "the two people I wanted to see. Hope I'm not disturbin' you." She unwound a long scarf from about her neck and opened the front of her wool coat. "I'm a bit late, but I see the music hasn't started yet. I didn't want to miss the pub's anniversary, seeing as how *I've* been a regular here for many years. But I got a bit involved in some computer doings over at my cousin Frank's, on that Internet he's hooked up to, you know. We did some searching and you'd be amazed at what we came up with, Michael."

Kate looked at Susanna like a cat that already has the canary's head in its mouth and is about to bite down. "And I wouldn't?" Susanna asked. "Be amazed, that is," she added in response to Kate's quizzical look.

"No, I don't believe so. I think you're already privy to the information I found."

"Well then, invite me into the privy too, will you?" Michael said with more than a touch of pique.

"Hey, are we gonna play, or are you gonna stand out here gabbin' all night?" It was Fiona, who followed her interruption with a shrill run on her whistle. Aengus strolled up behind her, obviously wondering what was going on.

"We *were* talkin' privately," Kate said.

"Feel free to continue," Michael said. "No secrets from my bandmates."

Kate looked at him for a moment, and then that furtive expression slunk back onto her face. "All right then. It may interest you all to know that our new friend here isn't Julia Cassidy at all. According to the information on her university's web site—"

"Her name's Susanna Cassidy," Fiona said. "Right? Ho hum, been there, done that, old news. If you'd been here on time, you wouldn't have *had* to prowl around the Internet. Anything else to report, Madam Sherlock? She's still a prof, right?"

"Y...yes..." It was easy to see that Kate had been poleaxed. The bird had been yanked out of her mouth just as she'd been about to swallow. Though it was hard for her not to grin in triumph, Susanna kept her face expressionless.

Just then old Dermot Rooney pushed by toward the stairs on his way to the basement. "Dermot," Kate said, clutching at straws, "what's this woman's name then?" She pointed at Susanna.

Rooney squinted and leaned toward Susanna, looking her

up and down, smiling as his gaze passed over her legs, hips, and torso, finally ending at her face. Then he glanced at Kate. "You know," he said with annoyance.

"But do you?" Kate said. "Come on, out with it!"

"Her name's Cassidy, are you daft?"

"But what's her *first* name?"

"Susanna, of course, what'd you think, Rumpelstiltskin? Now if you're done with your silly games, Old Man Guinness is strugglin' to escape, and I'm not sure I can hold him much longer," he said, and disappeared down the stairs. They all heard his clattering footsteps as they struggled not to laugh. Only Kate's face was pale and empty of humor.

"Come on then, wee Kate," Fiona said, "and old Aunt Fiona will buy you a pint and tell you a story of how this naming misapprehension came to be. I'll make it simple so that even you can understand."

She put a hand on Kate's shoulder, but the woman shook it off roughly. "I don't appreciate being made a fool of," she said in a low voice. "It's happened to me before..." This with a sharp look at Michael. "...but it won't again."

Kate whirled about and pushed the door open, but the fiddle case on her back got caught on the sides of the door as she was halfway through. Aengus tried to help by turning the case, but Kate tried to turn it the other way at the same time, so that now she was held firmly in place, and had no choice but to back up, making her dramatic exit a farce.

She shot everyone a last hard look, turned the fiddle case vertically, and tried to go out the door again. This time the case hit the top of the door frame, and the impact knocked her straight back so that she came down on her rear and might have fallen on the case itself had the others not grabbed her.

With no energy left for defiance, she let herself be helped to her feet and out the door, and it was not until it was fully closed and she could no longer hear them that Susanna, Michael, Aengus, and Fiona finally allowed themselves to laugh at the sheer slapstick of her departure. As they were doing so, Dermot Rooney came back up the stairs.

He paused, looked at them with their faces red from

laughing, observed, "Aye, that Old Man Guinness line always does the trick..." then pushed past them into the bar as they all started to laugh again.

Ten minutes later, when they had calmed down, Michael took Tim Sullivan's fiddle from its place of honor and they started to play. A few people asked where Kate was, and Fiona told them that she hadn't been feeling well and left early.

They had just sat back to relax after a particularly spirited set when Susanna saw Rachel coming through the crowd from the rear of the pub, holding Gerry's hand. She had called her niece earlier that evening and told her that the truth was out, so she and Gerry could feel free to come.

Rachel kissed Susanna on the cheek and said, "Hi, Aunt Sue. This is Gerry."

"Good to meet you, Gerry," she said, offering her hand which he hesitantly shook. "And this is my niece, Rachel, everyone," Susanna said, introducing her to the other musicians. Susanna watched Michael as the introductions were made, but there was nothing odd about his response. He smiled politely and nodded, though the smile faded somewhat when he looked at his son.

Jesus, Michael thought, so this was Julia's daughter. She looked to be Gerry's age, maybe late twenties to early thirties, and the thought crossed Michael's mind that he may have been unlucky twice, the way he was with Siobhan. He could not escape the thought that had arisen when Susanna had told him of Rachel's existence, the idea that this girl could be his daughter.

He looked for a family resemblance, and thought he saw in Rachel's countenance his mother's eyes and perhaps the line of her jaw. As though on cue, Molly Sullivan appeared just behind the girl so that he could make a solid comparison, and was relieved to find no real resemblance. Still, that meant nothing.

Of course, none of it meant a thing. He didn't know when the girl had been born, and told himself that it must have been long after he and Julia had been together. Still, the possibility gnawed at him, pushing down the happiness he had felt when Susanna had told him the truth about herself earlier that day.

He had been certain there was something she'd been keeping back from him, and had hoped that when he told her about his past it might spur her to make her own admission of, if not guilt, then at least the truth. At the end, he had been certain that it was a question of identity. Though the physical appearance was similar, the kind you often find in sisters, this "Julia" didn't seem to be the same woman emotionally.

No, Susanna was another breed entirely. He'd never met another woman like her, though he had met men in prison who were willing to sacrifice themselves for not only their cause but their fellow prisoners as well. They had been willing to risk crippling beatings to get a bit of tobacco or a cigarette paper or a sweet to their comrade in the next cell. When he thought too long about their Christ-like willingness to comfort their brothers at the cost of their own health and sanity, a great shame overtook him that he hadn't been more like them.

Susanna Cassidy was far more like them than he, and had put her strength and convictions on the side of peace. Her sole flaw was that she had loved him too well, denying her own identity for fear of losing him. Still, that was past, as was his own long tenure in prison. It was the future they could think about now, and as he did, he wondered what else she might be willing to deny in order to keep the two of them together. There was, he feared, more to him than she realized, or less, depending on your viewpoint.

He came back to reality when he realized his mother had asked him a question. He looked at her curiously and raised a hand to his ear as though he hadn't heard.

"I say do you want me to sing the *Sean-Nos* now?" Molly said.

"Aye," Michael answered with a nod. "That'd be grand."

They all slid over so that he and Susanna were pressed hip to hip, and his mother sat down. As she did, the pub quieted as if someone had cast a charm upon it, and every head turned toward Molly Sullivan. She started to sing, and Michael's hand found Susanna's and held it, not caring who saw.

There were his good friends, his dear strong mother, and his son, who always seemed stirred beyond words by his grandmother's art. And there was the woman he loved, and he thought that no matter what the days ahead might reveal, he was happy for now.

So was Susanna. The lies were put away and the truth was out, she was with a man she loved and who loved her in return. The only thing that bothered her was the thought that Rachel could be the half-sister of the young man she seemed to love so much.

Rachel and Gerry stood together, his arm around her waist, and from time to time during the song they looked at each other. In those looks Susanna saw Gerry's pride in his grandmother and his joy that Rachel could share the music, and in Rachel's looks Susanna saw his pride reflected, and her love for him.

A sour taste roiled up from her stomach and she swallowed it back down again. Maybe it didn't matter. Maybe things would work out best if everyone just remained ignorant of the logistics and their implications. After all, it wasn't like Rachel and Gerry had announced their engagement. A great many things could happen. People sometimes fell out of love as quickly as they'd fallen into it.

Susanna concentrated on the beauty of the music, trying to let the sweet majesty of *Sean-Nos* wash over her. By the time Molly had finished her recital, Susanna felt at peace again, the bad thoughts ignored if not forgotten. There was always another day to deal with them. Tonight she would belong to the music and to her Irish lover, and if he asked her to go home with him she would, and love him and hold him through the night.

Chapter 16

Susanna went to sleep that night with Michael's arms around her, and awoke in the morning with her arm over him. The sun was already bright through the curtains of the front window that looked out onto the quay. There were two bedrooms on the second floor—rather the *first* floor, she reminded herself—and Michael had picked the smaller of the two in which to sleep since it had a view of the water.

She gently removed her arm from around him, sat up, and padded quietly to the window, where she drew the curtain back just enough to see out. The sun sparkled on the water below, and there were already a few early morning risers strolling the pavement of The Long Walk just beneath her.

"I'm dead for sure."

She turned her head and saw Michael leaning on an elbow and looking at her. "What?"

"I'm dead and gone to my reward. Lying in bed for eternity with a naked angel standing at my window, the light streaming through her auburn hair. Aye, dead and in heaven."

She turned and walked back to the bed and lay down next to him. "You, sir, are a flatterer."

"And you, miss, are a beautiful woman." He kissed her, and soon they were making love again. They lay in each other's arms afterwards, and then Michael spoke. "Back to earth again, alas and alack. What time is it?"

"You have another appointment?"

"It is, as if you didn't know, Sunday morning, upon which time Holy Mass is celebrated…" He picked up his watch from the nightstand. "Holy God," he said, "it's twenty minutes until eleven. Ma'll have my hide if I'm not at St. Augustine's to meet her."

As he leapt naked out of the bed and dashed to the bathroom, Susanna laughed and called after him, "You sound just like a little boy!"

"All Irishmen are little boys when it comes to their mas," he called back. "Would you be a darlin' and get my blue suit out of the closet and a white shirt and tie?"

"Sure." She slipped on a terrycloth bathrobe and opened the closet door. Michael's closet was well organized, and she had no trouble finding what she needed. "Socks and underwear?"

"Second drawer," he said over the sound of the running water in the bathroom. From the drawer she took a pair of neatly folded boxers and a pair of tightly rolled black socks.

In another minute Michael came back into the bedroom, still naked, drying himself with a big white towel. "Sorry for the rush, but I had to make sure all the venial sin was washed off of me." He grinned to show he was joking, and Susanna laughed.

"You mean all that pleasure only qualifies as venial?"

"Well, if we persevere, I'm certain we can bring it up to mortal," he said as he slipped on his boxers and pulled on his socks.

"Oh no," Susanna said, holding his shirt as he put it on, "I don't want to be responsible for you spending eternity in a place you'd rather not."

"Wherever thou goest, darlin' Susanna, and I'm sure Father Pearse could tell you exactly which circle you Episcopalians will inhabit."

"What about *lapsed* Episcopalians?" she asked as he submitted to her buttoning his shirt while he tied his necktie. "I've been attending the peace church associated with my university for a few years now."

"Hmm, don't know where the good father stands on peace. He may be for it if it improves the interests of Rome. Seriously, Susanna, I'm sorry I can't make you coffee and look at you over a plate of eggs and bacon instead of having the host for breakfast. Just relax and make yourself whatever you'd like. *Mi kitchen su kitchen*, as they say."

"I don't think they say that, but thanks anyway."

She helped him on with his suit coat, and he grabbed his wallet, coins, and keys from the top of the dresser. "Listen," he said, "I've got to have lunch with Ma and her friends. I'd invite you but you'd hate it, and they'd have you a Catholic and us married by the time the apple tart came. Why don't you meet me at the pub around one. Finn'll be there to open at noon and I'll get there soon as I can and we'll do something fun. Up for it?"

"Of course," she said, and kissed him. His mouth tasted minty, and she rubbed a stray bit of toothpaste from his lip, then held him for another moment before letting him go. "Later then," he said, and he was gone, down the steps and out the door.

Susanna went to the window, looked out the curtain and smiled as she saw his tall, lean form cross the narrow street and walk on the four-foot-wide stone edge nearest the water. A little boy indeed. He seemed to feel he was being watched, and glanced up at the window, beaming when he knew she was watching him. He gave a happy wave, then walked with increased speed up the little street, toward his church and his mother.

Susanna wished she were walking with him. *They'd have us married by the time the apple tart came.* And what would be so wrong with that?

Okay, girl, she told herself, slow down. Just because you're having an affair doesn't mean you have to get married, and just because you love someone doesn't mean it either. She loved Michael and he loved her, but there were potential problems, like not being the same religion, having totally different national and political backgrounds, and...what else? They were nearly the same age, they got along beautifully, and they were certainly sexually compatible.

Susanna went down to the kitchen and found a drip coffeemaker that she quickly put to use. She was happy to see that, like herself, Michael ground his own coffee beans. There was a loaf of brown bread in a wooden breadbox, and she made herself some toast, upon which she spread some orange marmalade.

When she finished her small but satisfying breakfast, she drove back to the guest house, showered, and changed her clothes. Then she found the address of St. Augustine's Church in the phone book, and headed back to the town center.

There she parked and walked toward The Lilting Banshee, but passed the pub when she reached it. Just further on she turned down a narrow alley with the charming name of Buttermilk Lane. At its end she passed under a glass arch, and there in front of her was the great gray stone bulk of St. Augustine's. The doors were all closed against the February chill and she could hear nothing from within, so she stood and looked at the impressive building, thinking about Michael inside, hearing the Mass and taking communion.

One of the church doors opened, and people started to come out. Susanna turned and trotted back up Buttermilk Lane, not wanting Michael or Molly to see her. She would wait for him in the pub as he suggested, and she bought a newspaper on the way so she had something to read.

Finn greeted her when she walked in and, though she said she didn't need anything, brought her a cup of tea. A grateful Susanna settled in, and Finn brought her several refills as she read her paper.

As it neared one o'clock, she kept glancing toward the windows, waiting to see the familiar forms of Michael and his mother as they returned from their luncheon. Then through the etched and frosted Celtic designs on the glass she saw a familiar movement.

Expecting Michael, she followed the man as he walked briskly toward the pub's front door, then realized with a shock that it was not the long and easy movements of her lover she had recognized, but an aggressive and purposeful tread she had known for years. In another second her brother-in-law, David Oliver, had walked into The Lilting Banshee.

Though David had been to Ireland several times with Julia over the years, they had never been to Galway. That had been fine with him, since he had gone mainly to please his wife and fulfill the unspoken contract between them. As a result, he had never particularly cared what they saw or did as long as there was a good hotel with a decent restaurant. He was indifferent to pubs. The beers were heavy as lead, and that damned Guinness was like drinking thin molasses without sugar. Only in hotels that catered to Americans could you find a drinkable beer like Heineken, his personal preference.

Galway was easy enough to find, straight up 23 and 18 from Shannon. The Mercedes C he had rented was comfortable, but big for the narrow roads, and he was glad he hadn't followed his first impulse to rent the kind of SUV he drove in the states. Hardly anybody had them over here. The Irish drove those tiny little cars that nobody but public radio station listeners had back home. Of course, with the price of gas so high it was no wonder they tried to cut costs where they could.

No, David didn't like driving in Ireland. Between the narrow roads, those goofy roundabouts, and staying on the left, he was surprised he didn't see an accident every mile or so. At least the roads weren't busy this Sunday morning. He figured that most of the Irish were probably at church. All the better for him.

Still, he was relieved when he rolled into the entry of the Great Southern Hotel. They knew how to take care of guests here, and he was graciously swept into the lobby, his car and bags taken care of by unseen and proficient hands. The room had all the amenities, and he showered and shaved. Afterward he toyed with the idea of a quick nap, but was too excited by the prospect of seeing Susanna.

He dressed in a tweed sports jacket, brown wool slacks and a white shirt, and took a long time selecting a tie, finally deciding on a more colorful and abstract design than those he usually wore. It would show Susanna that just because he was in business didn't mean he was stodgy. At first, he couldn't remember ever wearing it, or even where he had bought it, but when he saw the Jerry Garcia label on the back, he recalled that Rachel had given it to him a few Christmases ago.

Rachel. There was another thing to be dealt with, but she'd have to wait until he found Susanna.

David got directions from the concierge to the guest house

where Susanna was staying. It was a pleasant drive through what seemed a pleasant town, and he was surprised that Julia had never dragged him there before. Galway seemed in its quaintness to be more than equal to the others he had slogged through on earlier trips.

Even the area where Susanna was staying on her academic budget seemed livable, with a seaside-suburban feel to it. He turned down the street as directed and parked in front of the Bayside Guest House. He checked his hair and the knot in his tie, and then got out of the car, brushing his top coat to press out the wrinkles. He felt suddenly nervous, like a kid picking up a first date.

As he walked toward the front double doors, another of those sardine-can cars pulled up behind his Mercedes, and a middle-aged man and woman got out. David pressed the button at the door, but the woman called to him, "That's us you'll be wanting then. Were you looking for a room?"

"Uh, no, actually I'm looking for someone who's staying here. Susanna Cassidy?"

The woman came up to David with her husband, he assumed, in her wake. "Oh yes, Miss Cassidy lives up there," she said, pointing to the stairway. "I'm Mary McCarthy, this is Bob."

"Hello. David Oliver," he said, shaking her hand and then Mr. McCarthy's. "Is Susanna in?"

"I don't see her car," Mrs. McCarthy said. "She's out and about a great deal. Stays on the go, she does."

"Do you have any idea when she might be back?" To the woman's negative look David added, "Or even where she might be?"

"Well, she's here and there. Spends some time at the university, of course, being a professor and all."

"The Banshee," her husband interjected.

"Pardon?" David asked.

"The Lilting Banshee," Mrs. McCarthy explained. "It's a pub in the town center. She has some friends there, plays music there now and again. I wouldn't know where else to tell you. Do you want to leave a message here for her, how to get in touch with you?"

"No, no, that's okay, I, uh, kinda wanted to surprise her. If you see her, don't mention I was here, okay?"

"Well, all right," Mrs. McCarthy said, though David thought that she looked at him suspiciously. He was certain that her husband did. Mr. McCarthy's eyebrows dipped in a frown so intense it seemed he tried to peer straight through David.

"Can you tell me how to get to this Laughing Banshee place?"

"*Lilting*," Mr. McCarthy corrected, and remained silent while his wife gave David directions.

As he drove away, he could see them in the rearview mirror, still looking at him. Maybe he shouldn't have told them not to tell Susanna he was there, but he wanted this to be special, damn it. He wanted to be able to appear from nowhere and sweep her away, to make all the wrong things that had happened over the years right again, and to live happily ever after, and there was no reason he shouldn't be able to do it.

He parked where Mrs. McCarthy had suggested and headed toward the pub on foot. He couldn't imagine why Susanna would be sitting in a pub at one o'clock on a Sunday afternoon, but maybe they did things differently in Ireland. If she wasn't there, he'd head back to her rooms and stay put until she showed up. The McCarthys probably had a sitting room where he could stay rather than roost in his car like some stalker, which was probably what they thought he was.

David felt wired, nervous as hell but ready. He'd hardly slept on the flight, and though his body clock told him that he'd gone through a whole night without rest, he felt far from exhausted. On the contrary, he felt energized, as though nothing could stop him. Whatever Susanna said, whatever she did, he wouldn't take no for an answer.

The cool air was fresh in his lungs as he walked up the narrow streets with shops on either side, his brightly shined shoes slapping the bricks with each step. Then he saw The Lilting Banshee just ahead, its woodwork a bright red that glowed in the sunlight. He took a deep breath and whispered, "Here we go," then walked up to the front door and stepped inside.

Susanna was there. Yes, thank you, God, she was there all

right. It was like a scene from a movie. She looked beautiful, the sunbeams through the window making her red hair radiant. Jesus Christ, she looked like the girl he'd been in love with all those years before, and it was as though they'd never passed, as though none of it had happened, and they were starting fresh, a new life before them.

"Susanna…" he said, and walked up to her.

Susanna wondered if she looked as stupid as she felt. She had known it was possible David would make an appearance, but had thought it unlikely, as her brother-in-law hardly ever did anything spontaneously unless, perhaps, women were concerned.

"David," she said, rising. "I can't believe you're here!"

He smiled and embraced her, kissing her on the cheek. He held it longer than necessary, so that she stepped back from him.

"Sit down," she said. "Do you want something to drink?"

"What are you having?" he asked, nodding at her cup.

"Tea."

A quick frown passed over his face. "Maybe coffee."

"Sure…Finn? A coffee please?" She looked back at David. "When did you get to Ireland?"

"Just this morning."

"Is this because of Rachel?"

"Well, I've been worried, naturally, not hearing from either of you." Susanna thought he seemed very much at ease for a man concerned about a missing daughter. "But there were other reasons, too. So, what about Rachel? Have you seen her?"

"Yes, didn't you get my email?"

"Yeah, but there was nothing definite in it."

"I saw her just after I sent it. She's here in Galway, and she's fine, having a great time."

"Nice of her to let me know."

"Well, you know Rachel. She's always been independent. I'm just surprised that you came over because you were worried about her."

He shook his head wearily. "I've always been worried about her," he said. Finn brought a cup of coffee and a small metal pitcher of cream over and set them down. David poured a bit of cream into the coffee and frowned again. "Excuse me," he said to Finn. "Fella? This cream's curdled."

Finn came over and peered down into the cup. "Where?"

"Those streaks. It shouldn't do that."

"Sorry, that's what that cream does."

"You got any non-dairy creamer?"

Finn nodded. "You want that?"

"Yeah, and another cup."

Finn shrugged, took the cup and pitcher and went back behind the bar.

"Anyway," David said, "there's another reason I came over here. To be honest, maybe more because of that than because of Rachel." He paused and looked at her, then down at the table-top, and she thought with a shock that she'd been right about his spontaneity. Only a woman could make him do something as unpredictable as come to Ireland, and she was the woman.

"Jesus Christ," David said, "how do I put this without sounding like a total asshole?" Just then Finn put down a fresh cup of coffee in front of him along with a packet of creamer. David ripped open the packet, stirred it into the coffee and took a short sip.

"Susanna," he said, putting down the cup, "a long, long time ago, I made a really big mistake, and over the years a lot of people suffered for it. Me, Rachel, Julia, and maybe you, too. I think we both know what I'm talking about."

"David, listen, I—"

"No, let me talk, please. You know how we felt about each other. There have been a lot of lies since, but that was no lie. I really loved you, and I don't know why I let Julia come between us, but I did, and I've been sorry ever since. It was wrong, and it was a mistake that a whole lot of other mistakes followed from. But if there's one thing I learned after all my years in business, it's that no matter how many mistakes you make, as long as you're alive, you can always set things right again, and that's what I'd like to try and do with the two of us..."

Susanna let him ramble and watched his face, but she scarcely heard his words. She should have seen this coming, but what would she have done, told her newly-widowed brother-in-law that she never wanted to see him again? There was no way. Like it or not, they were family, and there would be times when they'd have no choice but to be together and be civil to each other.

But now here he was, having flown all the way to Ireland and tracked her down to apparently declare his love for her. What was next? Was he going to ask her to marry him, the way he thought he should have all those years before?

"...and that's why I want to ask you to do what we should have done long ago." She braced herself. "That's why I want to ask you to be my wife."

Oh my God, she thought, this was so totally wrong, even from the aspect of propriety alone. Odd she should think of that, but maybe that argument would make the most sense to David, status-conscious as he was, though she'd never use it. God, what was wrong with her? Her mind was shooting off to a dozen places at once when it had to go to one place only, the place that would tell David no way, forget it, no going back.

Susanna had experience in declining proposals, but never from a member of her family, and no matter what she did she knew it was going to be awkward. "David," she said, "I'm sorry, I'm flattered that you would still feel that way, but I can't accept your proposal."

"I know, I know, Susanna, you've seen for years how I acted in my marriage, but...how can I put this...I did what I did because I always wanted *you*, and since I couldn't have you I was always looking for someone *like* you. It took me years to figure that out, but I finally did. And you...I may be giving myself too much credit, but I can't help but think you might feel the same way about me. You never got married, and I think it was because you never—"

"*David*," she said, stopping him brusquely. "I got over you, believe me. And I've *been* over you for nearly thirty years now. I didn't stay unmarried because you spoiled me for all other men, I just never *found* the man, and the selection pool included you, okay?"

He looked taken aback for a moment, but then his easy smile

returned, and Susanna read into it something that enraged her, a patronizing condescension as though he was explaining something to a child who just didn't get it. "I know," he said calmly, with that infuriating smile still in place. "I know, this must come as a shock, and I know that you're thinking about my past...indiscretions, and I admit them, it's true, but it will never happen again, not with you. So, there's no reason to put up a front. I love you, Susanna, and I really believe you love me, and nothing else matters."

Susanna sighed in exasperation and closed her eyes. She felt David's hand on hers and yanked it away as she opened them again. "David," she said more calmly, "I want you to listen to me. And know that what I'm saying is the truth, all right? Don't talk until I'm finished. Will you do that? Just nod, okay?" He did. The smile, however, was still on his face, and in spite of all Susanna's training in conflict resolution, she kept thinking about how badly she wanted to slap it off.

"David," she said in a very low voice, "you're at a tricky place in your life. You've lost your wife, who you were married to for three decades, and to whom you'd been unfaithful for about that same amount of time, and you feel guilty about that, because you still love Julia. You may think you love me, but I don't think you do. You love the memory of me, or some idealized me with whom you imagine you might have lived a perfect life. But you wouldn't have. We'd have been divorced within a matter of years, because I would not have put up with the *bullshit* that Julia put up with."

The smile started to fade, and he opened his mouth to speak, but Susanna raised a reprimanding finger. "Ah, ah," she said. "Just wait and listen. I wasn't your perfect match, David. Julia was. You had the same tastes, the same wants, the same things you needed out of life. And I think that what you had was as good as you could have gotten, though I'm sorry to say Julia could have done better. She was good to you, David, she was *so* good to you, and you didn't even know what you had until she was gone. Now you're trying to fill the gap, but I'm not the one to do it. I'm sorry, but I'd make you a terrible wife, David. And you'd make me a worse husband."

David nodded slowly, then looked down at the cup of coffee in front of him. His smile was gone now. "All right," he said. "All right, I deserved that. But all of that doesn't change the way I feel about you—or the way I believe you feel about me. We can get past all this."

Susanna looked at him dumbly. "David...are you deaf? Did you hear what I just said? I don't love you. I never will. There is *nothing* between us except for an in-law relationship that will deteriorate very quickly if you can't accept the way things are."

The *smile* was crawling back onto his face again. And to make matters worse, Kate Quinn had just walked into the pub, looked at Susanna oddly and gone to the nearly empty bar for a cup of coffee. "I know, I know," David said. "I heard everything you said, but I've been in business for years, Susanna. I know when people are bluffing and when they're telling the truth. I came all the way over here from the states because I finally knew what was really important in my life—you. And like it or not, I won't go back without you."

She was dumbfounded. The gall of the man was monumental. "You won't go back *without* me? Do you know that I have a *job* here? Do you know that I have a career? That's why I'm here! This isn't a vacation I ran off on, David. This is my life, the life I've chosen." She noticed Kate watching her, and dropped her voice. "There is *nothing* between us, David. Now if you want, I'll tell you how to get in touch with Rachel, and you can maybe see some sights together, or you can go home right now."

"Stop it, Susanna," David said with soft intensity, shaking his head. His eyes were starting to look angry. "Why do you keep pretending? Why are you denying this?"

"No more discussion. I'm leaving," she said, and stood up.

"No." David grabbed her wrist. It didn't hurt, but it was tight enough that she would have to jerk it away, and she didn't want to resort to that, especially not in front of Kate Quinn, who was watching the action closely. Susanna could make David release her with her words.

"Let go of me. Right now."

"The hell I will."

Susanna was about to say more, when she heard Michael's voice. "All right, that's *it*."

Suddenly he was at her side. With one swift move he snatched David's arm away from her and then grabbed the lapels of David's topcoat, yanked him out of his chair, and tossed him to the floor like a sack of laundry, chairs clattering on the wooden floor.

"Get the hell out of here!" he said to David. "You don't lay hands on a woman in this pub! Now *move!*"

David seemed incapable of motion. He only lay there on his side, his expression one of utter fear. Michael started to kneel, ostensibly to make David obey his command, but Susanna grabbed his shoulder. "What are you *doing?*" she asked Michael. "This is *not* necessary. I can handle this."

"It looked like you needed help."

"Well, I don't, thank you. Everything is *fine.*" It wasn't the truth, but it was something Susanna needed to believe. The question was what to do now, and it seemed that acting civilized was the tack to take. "I'm sorry, David," she said, helping a still stunned David Oliver to his feet. She was certain that it wasn't every day that he got tossed around a barroom, and he was still looking at Michael with fear, though it was tempered by indignation. Michael was starting to look shamefaced.

Susanna went to him and put her arm through his, so that David would get the picture clearly. "David, this is Michael Lynch," Susanna said quietly, so that Kate couldn't hear at the bar. "Michael, this is David Oliver, my brother-in-law. He... came over here looking for Rachel. His daughter?"

"Oh...oh, I see," Michael said. Susanna pitied his confusion, but the entire truth wasn't something she could just blurt out.

She made herself smile. "We had a little family squabble, but everything's fine now." She glared at David. "Isn't it, David?"

He looked as though he wanted to tackle Michael, which would have been a great mistake. "Yeah," he said. "Fine, just fine. Look, I gotta be going. It was...interesting meeting you," he said to Michael.

"Right...well, sorry about all this," Michael said.

"No apology necessary," David said. "Sometimes our...

family squabbles get a little rough." He looked at Susanna, and his expression was no softer than with Michael. "I'd better go. I'm at the Great Southern if you need to reach me. I'm not sure how long I'll be there." He didn't wait for a reply, but turned and walked quickly out the door, humiliation trailing him.

"Jesus, I'm sorry," Michael said quietly. "I came in and I saw he had ahold of you. I didn't know who he was, I thought he was just some tourist bothering you."

"And what if he was?" Susanna asked too loudly, and looked up quickly to see if Kate Quinn was still listening, but Kate was heading out the back door. Susanna was surprised she didn't stay to relish the disagreement between her and Michael. "What if he was?" she repeated more softly. "I don't need you barging in and settling things with your fists. It's not like it was in a dark alley or something. I was in *no* danger, and there wasn't any need for violence."

"I said I was sorry, what else can I do?"

"You *could* have done something different—you didn't have to grab him like that."

"He grabbed you."

"But he didn't throw me out of my chair, Michael." She sighed. "All right, maybe I'm overreacting, but I've tried my whole life to approach things nonviolently, and to see you lose your head like that...it was just upsetting. Have you done things like that before?"

"Like...what?"

"Like throw people physically out of the pub."

Michael gave a frustrated laugh and shrugged. "It's a pub, sometimes people drink too much and they get abusive. If I'm here and that happens, I try to reason with them first, and if that doesn't work, then yes, I throw them out. But it's not like I beat them up or anything. I just use enough force to eject them from the premises."

"And what if they don't want to be ejected?"

"Then I use a bit *more* force. Just enough and no more."

"Like you did with David?"

"Look, what's up with this guy? If he just came over here to see his daughter, what were you two fighting about?"

More people were starting to drift into the pub, and several were eyeing Susanna and Michael and trying to overhear without being obvious. "It's a long story, and one I need to tell you, but we're getting too much of an audience here. Can we go somewhere else?"

"Sure. I was thinking of taking you out to the old cottage at Roscam Point today, if you're still willing to go with me."

"Cottage?"

He nodded. "Old Tim's maternal grandfather built it back in the 1880s. He and his sons were fishermen. They stored nets and gear there, slept in it now and again. It's beautiful and desolate for being so close to town. I thought you might like it."

It was difficult to stay mad at him for long, and Susanna smiled. "I would, I'm sure. And then I'll tell you all about...my distant relative."

Susanna might have lost her smile had she known that, as she and Michael made their plans for the afternoon, Kate Quinn had just accosted David as he was striding back toward his hotel. When Kate had seen which way the wind was blowing, she'd gone out the back door and then around to the front of the building to waylay the American who had caused this rift between Michael and Susanna or Julia or whatever her name really was. After all, a temporary rift could become permanent, given enough care and feeding.

Kate Quinn had wanted Michael Lynch even before her husband died five years earlier. She was aware, as was everyone else, that the relationship between Michael and Siobhan was no relationship at all. It was a shame, for Michael Lynch was a handsome and rugged man, unlike her Eamon, who bent like a straw in the wind at the hint of a breeze. The sole benefit for Kate was that he had been an easy husband to handle.

When Kate began playing in sessions with Michael ten years earlier, she was friendly but never seductive. Michael, she saw immediately, was a man who took his own sweet time with things, and besides, she would never actually cheat on her husband while he was alive. He had, however, already been diagnosed with the ALS that she and he and everyone else knew would eventually kill him, so, Kate thought practically, there was no harm in scouting around for prospects who might prove worthwhile when the inevitable occurred.

Michael, unfortunately, was no such prospect, being married and faithful to a woman he had no love for. Kate knew the story of his marrying Siobhan in prison to make their child legitimate, and knew, too, that he'd come back to Galway with no love in his heart for her, but had lived with her nonetheless.

A few women of free and easy morals fancied him an easy target for some secretive loving, but soon found otherwise. Every attempt to draw him into a bed or a car or an alley met not only with rejection but with contempt. Among a certain type of young woman Michael Lynch was referred to as *The Priest*.

So, Kate Quinn bided her time. She took care of her husband in his illness, worked eight hours a day at her job, saw her three children off as they left the nest (two to England, one to Scotland), and she escaped into the music at The Lilting Banshee and other sessions about Galway, playing the fiddle the way her father had taught her. She became a friend to Michael Lynch, but never to the point where he opened up to her over the way he truly felt about important things or matters of the heart.

In her own heart, Kate knew that Eamon dying wouldn't be enough to bring her and Michael together. As long as Siobhan lived, Michael Lynch would always be a one-woman man, or rather a *no*-woman man. But there was something about Michael that made every other prospect pale in comparison. He was kind and he was funny, with a dry wit that often had her in stitches with a single word. And when he played and sang, the feeling he expressed reached out to her and wrung her heart like a handkerchief full of tears.

She fell in love with him long before Eamon died. When her husband finally passed, her pain at his leaving was dwarfed by the pain that Michael Lynch still could not be hers.

The next four years went by wearily. Kate lived for Friday nights when she could sit next to Michael and play music with him. She had taken to going into the Banshee when she knew he would be behind the bar. She'd sit and have a glass of stout or a cup of tea and chat with him or with Mrs. Sullivan, who she suspected was aware of how Kate felt about her son, but had the grace never to reveal her knowledge.

Then Siobhan Lynch was killed in that accident, and Kate's joy was so great over it that she had to admit her feelings in the confessional. She knew it was a sin to feel that way, but she couldn't help it, and after saying all the Hail Marys and Our Fathers she tried in further penance to recall all the times that Siobhan had been kind to her. She couldn't remember Michael's late wife doing anything that had ever displeased or angered her in any way. Siobhan had been as inoffensive as a mouse, and her greatest boon to Kate had been her death.

Even then, Kate decided to play her cards close to her vest and not entice Michael in any way. Rather she would be a comforting friend to him in his grief, and let matters grow from there. What made that strategy more difficult, however, was that Michael seemed to feel not so much grief, which was no surprise, as guilt over his wife's death, as though he could have stopped it had he tried harder.

It was foolish. Kate had heard the circumstances from those who were there, and she thought Michael no more responsible for Siobhan's death than she was for Eamon's disease. Sometimes things just happened, and we were silly to question God's will in them. Kate had long felt guided by the conjoined forces of God and destiny, and had determined that the deaths of Siobhan and Eamon, regrettable as they were, had a positive side as well. God had determined that now she and Michael would at long last be able to come together, and that each would find in the other the love that had been denied them with their previous mates, a love that was God's will.

The more she tried to comfort Michael, however, the more she felt him drifting away from her, until even their previous warm friendship was in danger of being undermined. Though he still seemed responsive at the sessions, he didn't speak to her as much when she came into the pub for a drink, and when she tried to convey her sympathy to him, he responded politely but coldly. As a result, she avoided mentioning his loss.

That summer following Siobhan's death, Michael started to become his old self again. There was still an aura of sadness

about him, but he joked more than before, and the patrons of
the pub were finding him more approachable. Kate thought he
seemed warmer toward her as well, and as the summer weeks
passed she made it a habit to sit closer to him at the sessions
and now and then lay a hand on his knee or shoulder in what
might be interpreted as comradely, or something more were he
so inclined to see it.

She thought that he was. He smiled more freely at her, and
at times he would return her gesture, patting her hand on his
knee, at which point she would take it away, albeit unwillingly.
It was courtship of the old school, using the subtlest of signs and
gestures, but, with them being widow and widower, unmistak-
able in its intimations.

Following a session one Friday in August, Kate stayed for
a final glass and Michael joined her. It was after midnight, and
a heavy, unexpected rain had come up that showed no signs of
lessening. "I should be going," Kate said, looking out the window at the pelting drops, "but I left my umbrella at home."

"I could loan you one," Michael said.

"You could, but if you were a true gentleman, you'd walk
me to my car with one and save me the trouble of returning
it." Kate realized that she had had a bit more to drink than she
should have, but she might not have made the suggestion if she
hadn't.

"Think I should do that then, do you?" Michael said, and his
smile told her he didn't find the prospect unappealing.

"I think it would be a very polite thing to do, and a grand
way to reward a faithful long-time patron of your wee pub."

"Well, far be it from me to offend my faithful long-time
patrons. And what kind of umbrella is it you'd be wanting?"

"I suppose I could make do with the basic black."

Michael got an umbrella from behind the bar, then came
back to her and picked up her fiddle case. Molly Sullivan, who
was putting away glasses, glanced at them as they left together,
and Kate thought she detected a smile on her face.

Outside, Kate took Michael's arm and they began the walk
of several blocks. This was the first time she had ever had such
close physical contact with him, and she could feel her heart

beating faster. Neither spoke. With the raindrops pattering on the umbrella and with Michael's body against hers, the walk was everything for which she'd been waiting for years. When they arrived at the car, she didn't want it to end.

"Michael," she said, "come sit with me a minute."

He paused for a moment, then nodded and said, "All right." He opened the car door for her, then went around to the other side and sat in the passenger seat. He seemed tentative, but Kate thought she could relax him easily enough. "What is it?" he asked.

When she looked at him in the dim gleam of the street lights, it was as though she was seeing him through the waters of a running stream. Though his face was still, the shadows of the rain on the windscreen created constant movement upon it. She had never seen anything that she wanted so much.

She put out her hand and touched his cheek, wet with rain, and moved her fingers up into his wet hair. Then she leaned toward him and he toward her, and they kissed, and she tasted the salt and the sweetness of his mouth. A surge of need shuddered through her, and her arms went around him, and her tongue sought his, and he responded, and then she pressed her hand upon his thigh and moved it upward, desperate to feel this man's need for her in return.

But when her fingers touched him, he changed. His entire body tensed, and for a moment she felt a sense of triumph that her touch alone had brought him to completion. In another instant she knew that she was dreadfully wrong.

He drew back from her, and his hand moved hers away. 'Hold on now," he said. "Just hold on. This isn't…" He couldn't put it into words, and just shook his head instead and opened the car door. He fumbled with the umbrella, stuck it out into the rain and climbed out, closing the door behind him.

Kate quickly got out, but Michael was already half a block away, walking through the rain and making no attempt to raise the umbrella. "Michael?" Kate called after him, but she couldn't tell if the sound of the rain drowned out her voice or if he was ignoring her. "*Michael!*" she cried again, and this time he heard but didn't turn. He only raised a hand and waved it, and vanished around the corner into the night.

She stood there, the heavy rain drenching her hair and her clothes, still feeling through the warm wetness her need for him, now made greater by his rejection of her. What had been wrong? His desire was real, she had felt it as clearly as if he had spoken it. Yet he had drawn away.

It made no sense. She knew that he was attracted to her, and there was nothing standing in their way now that both Eamon and Siobhan were gone, so what had made him stop?

When she got home, there was a phone message from Michael. He said, "Kate, listen, I'm sorry about tonight. I've, uh, been confused about a lot of things lately, and I think...well, I just believe I need to take things slow right now. Again, I'm really sorry, and, uh, I hope I'll see you at the pub and at sessions, okay? Well, uh, okay...g'night then..."

She shook her head and smiled. Yes, he was an idiot like all other men after all. All right then, if he wanted to take it slow, she'd take it slow. *He* would have to make the next move. She'd be his friend like she'd been before, and if he wanted what she knew damned well he wanted he'd have to take it himself.

Her mistake had been in being too bold, in making a grab at a man who probably hadn't even had a woman in true passion for thirty years. No wonder the poor lad got spooked by the attentions of a woman as lusty and busty as her fine self. Siobhan had been skinny and flat as a plank, so to have a woman so delightfully fleshy (but not fat, oh no) offered to him was like being given apple cake after a diet of cold potatoes. Probably the poor lad scarce knew what to do with it.

Others would have, sure enough. Kate had had her share of attention from men of all kinds, divorced, single, widowed, and married alike. She'd learned early on how to deal with them, and even though she was getting no younger, those attentions kept coming, increasing greatly after Eamon's passing. The advances made before his death had been mostly in jest, as men realized that a good Catholic woman wouldn't be sharing herself while she had a husband to whom she was still wed in God's eyes. But once death parted her from Eamon, the propositions became more serious.

Still, it was Michael Lynch she'd always had her eye on, and no one else would do. Give him time and he'd come around again and see what was right in front of him for the taking.

So, she went and she drank her tea and her stout, and she talked to Michael and played with him at sessions, and never spoke of that night to him, and never invited him to walk her to her car again. They remained friends, and it got to the point where he chatted and laughed with her again without being self-conscious, and she thought that surely any day now he would ask her to walk her to her car himself, or ask her out to tea or a movie or dinner or *something*.

And then Miss Julia or Susanna or Whatever-She-Was-Calling-Herself-Today Cassidy came along, and everything was over, just like that. A woman out of his past had shown up—or at least he had *thought* she was out of his past—and Kate Quinn's hopes were smashed. Kate had even gone to the extent of finding out about "Julia" Cassidy, but when she'd come in with her news, it had been *old* news, and she'd been made a laughing-stock. She got the full story from Fiona later, on the phone.

Other women might have called it a day at that point, but Kate decided that no lying American was going to just waltz in and take her man as easily as that. As good a pretender as Susanna Cassidy was, Kate had grown used to pretending herself. For years she had pretended that Michael Lynch was nothing more than a friend, and she could go on doing it. Only that way could she see what was happening between the two of them, if Michael was showing any signs of getting tired of Susanna, or if there was a chink in Susanna's armor that Kate might be able to widen surreptitiously.

She had gone back to the pub with the intent purpose of initiating her ruse, apologizing for the way she'd acted, and being all smiles with both of them, and her tactic had already proven fruitful. The chink in the armor had come in the guise of this good-looking and well-dressed American, whose intimacy with Susanna couldn't be denied. Try as she might, Kate had hardly been able to hear a word of their discussion, except for when they raised their voices. She figured there might once have been something between them, and that might make Michael Lynch so jealous that he'd have second thoughts. She'd just seen how jealous he could be when confronted with what he might have thought a rival, so maybe that was the button to push.

At any rate, the thing to do was to stop this American lad before he left the picture entirely, and now Kate was catching up to him. "Hold on there," she called. The man looked over his shoulder, and Kate saw that he recognized her from the pub. "You know that one then," she said cryptically, and when his face grew puzzled, she added, "Susanna Cassidy, if that's her real name."

"That's her name all right," the man said. "And yeah, I know her."

"Old girlfriend?" Kate hazarded. "Or ex-wife or something like?"

"*Real* old girlfriend, if it's any of your business."

"Ah, trying to start things back up again, were you?"

"Look, is there any purpose to this conversation?" the man asked.

"Might be for you. My name's Kate Quinn." She held out her hand for him to shake. "And you're...?"

"David Oliver." He took her hand and, after he shook it, held it just long enough for her to see that she had made an impression on him.

"So, Davey—"

He snorted what might have been a laugh. "No one's called me that in years."

"So, *Davey*, do you have any idea what's going on between those two?"

"What, her and the big guy?" Kate nodded knowingly. "Apparently something, huh? I should've known, the way he jumped me when I touched her. When the hell did all this start? They know each other before?"

"No, it was her *sister* he knew. He and she had a wee fling years ago. This one came over to look him up after the sister dies and talk about old times. Seems they're doing more than talking."

The American's face narrowed. "Wait a minute, you say that Susanna's *sister* and this guy...what's his name?"

"Michael Lynch."

"And this Michael Lynch, they…" He shook his head and spread his hands wide as though trying to find the words. "They had a, a *thing?*"

"From what I've heard. Can't say myself, didn't know Michael back then."

"Like when was all this? That this Irishman and this American girl had a…an affair?"

"Oh, years ago, thirty years if it was a day. So long ago that this dead woman's daughter and Michael Lynch's son are now sweethearts, and they're far from children. Probably thirty or so themselves…" An odd and unpleasant thought struck Kate, but she let it go, reminding herself to consider it later. "So, you're an American," Kate said, trying to steer the conversation back to this man's intentions and his past with Susanna Cassidy. "Did you come over here to see Susanna, then?"

"I, uh…" David Oliver seemed suddenly distracted, and looked around him as though seeking a way to end the conversation. "Look, I'm sorry, Kate, it was nice meeting you, and, and maybe I'll see you again sometime, but, uh, I really gotta go." And with that he turned and walked briskly away from her, his head hunched down between his shoulders, even though it was far from cold.

Well, Kate thought, that didn't go too well. She wasn't even sure what she had set out to accomplish, short of finding out who David Oliver was and his relationship to Susanna, which she hadn't done to her satisfaction. She might have made him a bit more jealous, though she didn't know what that might do either. It was obvious that Susanna wanted nothing to do with David, at least not when Michael was still available.

Kate sighed. It had not been a particularly productive day so far, though the American was good to look at and, if his clothes were any indication, had money to spare.

The day had proven far more unproductive for David Oliver. As he trod toward his hotel, his head was whirling with several different emotions, all of them negative. There was his humiliation at Susanna's rejection of him, his anger at having been attacked by that big dumb Irishman, and now total chaos when he thought about how Julia had played him for a sucker all those years ago.

Jesus, when he had been worried to death about her because she was supposedly sick in a foreign country, she'd actually been screwing around with some young Irishman. When the image struck him of Julia in bed with the guy who had just yanked him out of his seat, his first thought was that he only wished he had cheated on her more.

True, David had had sex with Julia shortly after she came home, but Rachel was born in November of that year. November, for crissake, which meant that Rachel might not even be his kid, but the daughter of this Irish bastard, the man who had taken his first woman and now had taken another.

"Son of a *bitch*," David growled, loudly enough to cause a few heads to turn in Shop Street. Embarrassed, he cleared his throat roughly and walked on until he passed a small dark pub and decided that if there was ever a time that called for strong drink it was now.

He went inside, bought a double shot of Jameson's at the bar, and buried himself in a small corner booth to down it. Sitting in the snug, the dark wood around him darkened further by years of peat and tobacco smoke, he felt at his lowest ever, as though he were in a coffin of his own design.

Memories that had previously been neutral now seemed bitter as they started coming back to him, like those first few weeks after Rachel's birth, when David was caring for a child who might not have been his own. He thought, too, about Julia's lifelong love of Ireland, her desire to vacation there, her playing Celtic music while they ate dinner, the charges to the credit cards when QVC ran their St. Patrick's Day sales on TV.

Ireland, Ireland, Ireland. The hell with Ireland. It had taken Julia, it had taken Susanna, and now it was taking Rachel as well. The last thing he wanted was for her to suspect that he might not be her father. They were already estranged enough. Besides, whether he had fathered her or not, she was still his daughter. He had raised her as best as he knew how, and he still owed her whatever he could provide to keep her out of trouble.

To David, other troubles seemed miniscule compared to the prospect of Rachel's having a relationship with her half-brother. At the thought, the Jameson's grew sour in his mouth. He had come to Ireland under the pretense of caring about his daughter, but with the true purpose of claiming Susanna. Now that his initial goal seemed beyond achieving, he would ironically have to make his pretended goal the real one. He would keep Rachel from making what might very well be an incestuous and disastrous match. For once in his life, he would be a good father and save his daughter.

He kept his fatherly altruism before him like a banner, and did not, could not admit to himself that in the relationship between Rachel and Michael Lynch's son he heard, ringing down the years, the echo of Julia's love for Michael Lynch, a sound he was determined to stop forever.

CHAPTER 17

The wind was blowing hard off Roscam Point when Susanna and Michael arrived there at three o'clock. They drove out as far as they could, then left the car and went on foot.

Michael showed her a handsome round tower and the ruins of a church, and then they walked east along the shore of the bay until they saw the cottage, set back a hundred yards from the shoreline. It was quite small and made of gray stone. There were no windows, and the wooden door faced away from the bay.

"Helped keep the wind and rain out," Michael explained as he opened the door with an old iron key and pushed it inwards. "We keep it locked, otherwise you'd have kids coming out here to drink and smoke pot and whatever else they do these days. It's pretty much vandal-proof, being just stone and a heavy old door."

They stepped into the dark room, and Susanna could make out a plain wooden table, a single chair, and a pallet on the earth floor. "Fairly minimal accommodations," she said with a smile.

"True, but they stayed here only when they had to, like when a storm wouldn't let them get back to town. It's not much to look at, but it always meant a lot to old Tim. We'd often come out and picnic here when I was little, and I'd play in here." Michael set his palm upon the interior stone wall. "Sometimes Tim would just touch these stones, and his face would get all dreamy, like he was turning back the years."

Susanna put a hand on his shoulder, and he turned and took her into his arms and they kissed. "I like seeing these things," she told him, "your past..."

"And Ireland's past," he said. "Don't know how long this cottage will last. They're building out further and further. Maybe someday this land'll be a housing development."

"Do you...or your mother own the land?"

"No. But we know the man who does, and he's content to have the cottage here until he sells it or does something else with it. I think he knows what it means to the family, what's left of us anyway. Gerry comes out here sometimes in nice weather. Once I found him here writing at that table."

"That must have given you a nice feeling."

"Aye, it did. It was grand to see him there like that, sitting where his great-grandfather must have sat with the storms howling outside. Or *step*-great-grandfather, that is. Of course, he wasn't any too happy that I found him here." He sighed. "Wish I'd been a better father to him."

"You still can. It's never too late."

"What would I do? You can't just go and undo twenty years of acting like strangers."

"You can start. In fact..."

"What are you thinking about?"

"I was just thinking," she said slowly, "that since I'm dating *you* and my niece is dating your *son*, we might double date one evening."

"Double date?"

"Go out together, the four of us."

"Oh, now look, I don't know—"

"It would *not* be uncomfortable. Have you ever heard Rachel and me talking? We'll monopolize the whole evening. All you have to do is answer our questions and smile and nod and eat. And after a good meal and a few drinks we'll be like one big happy family. What do you say?"

Michael walked her outside into the sunlight. "I'd feel funny asking him," he said.

"Let me take care of that. I'll talk to Rachel, explain the situation, though I'm sure she's aware of it, and she can ease into it with Gerry. I know that girl, and I promise you he won't say no to her."

"You make it sound like peace talks at Stormont."

"Not all that bad," Susanna smiled. "All right?"

"And how can I say no to you?" He kissed her quickly. "I admit I'd like to be closer to him. He's my son, and I do love him. Proud of him, too. He's a bright lad."

"Takes after his father," she said.

Michael locked the cottage and they walked along the shore arm in arm. For a long time they didn't speak, only listened to the sounds of the wind and the waters of the bay rising and falling onto the stones, and retreating again. Then finally Susanna said, "I'm sorry I got angry at you today."

"I deserved it. I was out of line. I don't like to make you angry or sad or disappoint you, and I did all of those today. I wasn't thinking."

"You *were* thinking. You were thinking of me, of keeping me safe and free from harm." She chuckled. "Actually, I should have let you kick his ass…no, no, no, I didn't really say that."

"So even the non-violent get a hankering for giving an arse-kicking now and again, do you?"

"It's just that David is so different from you—from all decent men, really. Or maybe it's just that you decent men are few and far between."

"Don't think too much of me," Michael said, so seriously that it almost frightened her. "I'm far from perfect."

"You're just right for me," she said, cuddling close to him. "I do love you, Michael."

"And I you. More than you can know."

"I wonder where we're going," she said.

She felt him tense a bit as they walked. "Just down the shore a ways. We'll go back when you like."

"I meant you and me. What happens now."

"I don't know. I've never had a gift like this before. I'm not sure I know quite what to do with it. And everything's happened so fast. It's confusing."

"Confusing? How?"

He stopped and turned to face her. "I don't know what it's like to be happy, Susanna, not like this. I guess maybe I'm afraid I don't deserve it, that it'll be taken away from me because of that."

"The only people who can take away what we have are you and me." She touched the softness of his cheek with her hand. "And I won't take anything away if you won't."

He nodded. "Sounds like a fair deal all around then."

They walked on smiling, but Susanna kept thinking that her question hadn't been answered. Where *did* they go from here? She knew that she loved Michael enough to spend the rest of her life with him, and if that meant marrying him she would, and gladly.

Of course, there were things to be worked out. If they lived together, one of them would have to become an expatriate, and which one would do that would be a major question.

There was also the matter of religion, and while Michael often joked about his Catholicism, Susanna knew that some roots went very deep indeed. She didn't think that she would want to become a Roman Catholic, as she preferred greater simplicity in her faith, and some of the dogma of Rome struck her as not only bizarre but wrong-headed.

Still, if allying herself with the Church was the price she had to pay for Michael Lynch, she thought that she might try and tailor Catholicism to her own beliefs, an attempt that would probably be anathema in itself. Better perhaps to each retain their previous faiths. People had been doing that more and more recently, and there would be no children to be concerned about.

Slow down, girl, she thought. Michael hadn't asked her to marry him, hadn't even mentioned the possibility. Maybe, after his first disastrous marriage, he wanted no second one. Maybe he was content to leave it the way it was, and make it a long-distance romance after Susanna returned to the states. Maybe...

Enough maybes. She was with the man she loved and who loved her, and that was enough for now. She gave a small sigh of contentment and concentrated on the warmth of his arm through hers. The future would take care of itself.

Two hours later, after he had taken Susanna back to her flat, Michael Lynch sat at his mother's kitchen table, talking to her of the future. "Yes, all right," he admitted to Molly Sullivan. "I do love her. But I don't know what I can do about it."

"Do you want to marry her?" Molly asked gently.

"I'd like nothing better."

"What's stopping you then?"

"I don't know how I can ask her. She's a university professor, she loves her job in the states. What am I going to do, ask her to leave that behind to be with the owner of a little pub in Ireland?"

"Do you know what she's looking for?" Molly asked gently. "Do you think maybe she'd *like* being the wife of a pub owner, if that pub owner was you? I've seen how she looks at you, Michael. Like someone who's had a cooling drink of water after a very long time in the sun. But it's not relief, like. A woman who looks like that could have had her pick of many men over the years. She's a handsome woman."

"But suppose she wants to go back to the states? How could I leave Ireland?"

"Get on a plane."

"You know what I mean. I couldn't leave you to run the pub yourself."

"Don't be stupid. Danny may not be the sharpest nail in the wall, but he's bright enough to do what needs to be done around here, and we've got a good staff now. You're not indispensable."

Michael sat for a long time, looking down at his hands on the tabletop. "I may not be indispensable to Ireland," he said, "but Ireland's still indispensable to me."

"Oh, all *that*," Molly said.

"Yes, all that. There's still a lot to be done here. Still things I can do."

Molly shook her head slowly. "God preserve me, but I've raised a fool for a son."

"I'm not a fool."

"Fools don't *learn* from their past mistakes," Molly said.

"Oh, I've learned, believe me. I've not had a brush with the law for twenty years, as long as I've been free, and I don't intend to."

"Aye, you don't give your blood now, you give your money instead. And don't look at me like you're surprised. Did you think I was a fool, too, not to see it? I know you've been giving that cousin of yours money for years, and I know where it's going. But I've said nothing because I've known 'twould only make you want to give more. Besides, money's just money. I can pretend it goes to orphans' and widows' relief rather than something worse. Like I tell meself my tax money's going to the schools, and then I don't feel so bad paying it. Amazing what we do to make ourselves feel better, isn't it, Michael?"

"I feel good about it no matter what. And it comes out of my pocket, not out of the pub."

"It's still blood money, son. It goes to spill blood."

"You don't know that, and neither do I. It's for *support*."

"And *support* never means arms, does it?"

"Malachy says it doesn't."

"Oh, *Malachy*. Malachy's as big a bullshitter as his father was."

"Ma..."

Molly sat back and folded her arms across her breast. "I know, you don't like hearing your mother use that kind of language. Well, I don't very often, but sometimes my son just drives me to it." She relaxed then, and leaned across the table and patted Michael on the shoulder. "Maybe this peaceable woman will be a good influence on you. Just let things happen, Michael. If you truly love her and she truly loves you, things will work out. Don't worry so much. Falling in love isn't the worst thing in the world that can happen to a man, y'know."

"Aye. But it does give a man a lot to think on."

David sat down in his room at seven o'clock that evening with a room service bottle of Jack Daniels and a glass, and called Susanna. He was glad to hear her usual cheery hello when she answered. "Susanna," he said, "this is David. Please don't hang up. I'm calling to apologize...you there?"

"Yes, David, I'm here."

"I acted like a total ass today. I took a lot of things for granted that, well, that just weren't so, and I'm sorry. I really am."

"Okay." Her voice was non-committal.

"I know I made you uncomfortable, put you in a terrible position, and I shouldn't have done that. I just...well, I have no excuse or explanation. I was just dumb. I'm hoping maybe we can put it behind us and forget it ever happened. Just make it a bad judgment call on my part. What do you think?"

"It's all right with me." Now she sounded tentative.

"No strings attached, you know? I mean, I'm not going to ask to see you again. I accept what you said, and I'm sorry I was such a jerk about everything. I won't ask you out, I won't pressure you in any way. I just hope we can still be friends and... and family again."

"That's fine, David. I'm sorry, too. I shouldn't have gotten so angry, and I'm sorry about what...Michael did."

"Yeah, well, I deserved it. So, you and he are, uh, friends?"

"We've been dating, yes."

"Well, that's cool..." He took a sip of the liquor. "He seems like a...a *strong* guy," he said, and laughed.

Susanna laughed, too. "He is, in a lot of ways. Look, I didn't give you Rachel's number. Do you want it?"

"Yeah, yeah, sure. In fact, that's the other reason I called. I thought I'd hang around Ireland for a week or so, go see some of the things Julia and I saw when we were over here before. She loved this place so much, you know, so I thought I'd try and find out why...see what it is about the country that she liked. Thought I'd try and spend a little time with Rachel, too, maybe do some sightseeing with her."

"That sounds nice, David." Susanna told him the name of Rachel's hostel and gave him the phone number. "She might be tricky to get hold of," Susanna said. "She's been using Galway as a home base, so she isn't in all the time, but you can leave a message."

"Sounds good. Will do. All right then, Susanna, you have a great time over here. It was good seeing you, even if it didn't quite, well, you know."

"I know, David. It's all right. I hope you have a good visit. It really is a beautiful country."

"Oh yeah, you bet. Okay then, I'll see you around."

"All right, David. Bye."

"Bye." He heard the click of her hang-up and then hung up himself. It could have been nice, he thought, and then told himself that it was probably for the best. Susanna was right. They weren't meant for each other. He'd just been trying to live out some half-assed romantic fantasy, and had mercifully been shot down before it went too far, before he actually got married to her and found out that she was a hard-nosed bitch. He'd always known Susanna was a tough cookie, but the way she had treated him in that pub had cured him for good.

Besides, what that Irish woman—Kate, was it?—had told him when he left the pub had tossed all romantic ideas out of his head. What he thought of as Julia's infidelity to him, and the fact that his daughter (if Rachel *was* his daughter) could be carrying on an incestuous affair with the son of the man who had seduced and maybe impregnated her mother all those years ago, rankled even worse than did his rejection by Susanna.

The thing to do now was to end once and for all whatever was going on between Rachel and this Irish kid. He could come right out and tell her the kid might be her half-brother, but he wanted to avoid that. As screwed up as Rachel was, knowing that she'd been sleeping with her half-brother could make her even more so, not to mention what it would do to their own relationship, with David suddenly reduced to the status of stepfather.

David dialed the number of the hostel and asked for Rachel's room, and, to his surprise, she answered. "Hey," he said. "Guess who."

"Hi, Dad," she said, as though speaking to him was a burden. "You found me, huh? How are things in the states?"

"Wouldn't know. I'm in Galway." He tried to sound happy about it.

There was silence for a moment, and then she said, "You're kidding," as though the burden had just tripled in weight.

"Nope, I'm at the Great Southern. That's pretty close to you, isn't it?"

"Uh, *yeah*. Like just across the square. If you went to your window, I could probably see you wave. What are you *doing* here?"

"Hey, I got lonely, I wanted to see my daughter. And I wanted to see Ireland. Kinda got nostalgic for it. You know how much your mom loved it. We had some good times here."

"So, you just, what, flew over on a *whim?*"

"Pretty much."

"Dad, you never do anything on a whim."

"Well, I've gone through some changes lately, you know? I just really wanted to come over. I missed you, if you can believe that."

Again, she was silent for a moment. "So, what are you going to *do* here? Like, take a tour?"

"No, I'll just buzz around on my own a little. I would like to see my daughter, though. And maybe her young gentleman friend, too."

"Oh God, what did Aunt Sue tell you?"

"Just that you were dating some handsome Irish guy. It's no secret, is it?"

"Not anymore."

"Well, let me take you two out to dinner. Somewhere really nice, it'll be fun." When she didn't answer right away, he added, "I hear that the Park Room in the Park House Hotel is really good. Right on Eyre Square too. What do you say? Tomorrow night?"

"Well, maybe...okay, I guess, if Gerry's free."

"Gerry. That's his name, huh? Gerry what?"

"Gerry Lynch."

"Okay, great. Well, find out if Gerry's available tomorrow night. Say, dinner at eight? If you can't get me, leave a message. I'll be doing the tourist thing tomorrow. But I'd really like to see you, you know?"

"Sure, Dad. I'll call you."

"Okay, baby. I love you. Bye."

That was done, David thought as he hung up. Now the only thing he had to do was figure out how the hell he was going to break up Rachel and her Irishman.

The next day Susanna spent most of her time in the library at the university. She was speaking on Wednesday to a student seminar at Limerick, and on Friday to a small group at UCG, so had decided to ensconce herself in the halls of academe for the next two days in order to prepare.

She had tried to call Rachel the night before to let her know that David was in the country, but had received no answer. He probably would have contacted her by now, and there was no rush to make arrangements for the double date at which she was hoping to reunite Michael and Gerry. With her work starting to enter full time mode, she wouldn't be able to handle it until the weekend. Even her evenings were going to be tight.

Michael had been a dear when she explained why her time would be limited in the coming week. "That's fine," he said. "Just call me if you've got a minute or so. Sometimes work has to come first."

In bed at his town house, they tried to make up for their forthcoming separation by uniting as closely as possible, and did so again when morning came. This time she was the first to leave, right after breakfast, and she promised to call him as soon as she had some down time.

Susanna was sorry that she hadn't been able to warn Rachel her father was looking for her, but she knew that her niece would be able to take care of herself. She just hoped David wouldn't do anything else stupid.

She tried to shake David and Rachel and Michael and everything else from her mind, and turned back to her work.

It was the first time since coming to Ireland that Rachel felt underdressed. She had known the restaurant would be fancy, but she hadn't realized she would feel so shabby in the sweater and skirt that were the most formal garments she had packed. Even Gerry looked out of place with his corduroy jacket, brown slacks, blue shirt, and knit tie. Every other man in the room, her father included, was wearing a dark suit with a white shirt, looking as though they'd just stepped out of a Fortune 500 company's annual meeting.

Her father had seemed friendly enough when he met them in the hotel lobby, and gave her a hug and shook Gerry's hand heartily, smiling all the while. He was still smiling now that they were seated, but it was that shark-smile she'd seen him use before, when he wanted her to do something she didn't want to do.

"So, Gerry," he said, "you live in Galway all your life?"

"Yes sir, except when I went to university at Dublin."

"Then you must have eaten here before. How's the food?"

"I don't really know. This is the first I've been here. It's supposed to be quite good, though."

"Yeah, won a lot of awards. So how come you never ate here before?"

Gerry smiled. "It's rumored to be a bit pricey."

"Ah, I get you. What is it you do?"

"I'm a teacher here in Galway."

"At the university?"

"No, at a boy's school. I teach literature. I also do some writing."

"Uh-huh," David said. "Got anything published?"

"A number of poems and some short stories."

"Poems, eh?" Rachel could hear the trace of contempt in her father's voice. "No books or anything, then?" Gerry shook his head. "So, where do you get these poems and stories published? Have I read any?"

"Not too likely. Mostly in small literary magazines."

"Not the kind I'd find on the airport newsstands, huh?"

"I'm afraid not. Not even Aer Lingus."

The self-deprecation was lost on her father, who merely looked at Gerry oddly. The waiter brought menus, they ordered drinks, and the inquisition resumed. Though David stopped short of asking Gerry his salary, he pried into every other part of his life. Gerry didn't seem to mind, however, and answered with skill and good grace.

To her father's credit, he was never aggressive with the questions, but seemed truly interested in what life in Ireland was like for a teacher and struggling writer. Though Gerry was fooled and perhaps flattered at times by David's seeming fascination with his life, Rachel could see all too clearly what her father was trying to do. He was trying to take Gerry apart piece by piece and make him look like a poor, simple, out-of-place fool in this fancy restaurant.

What he had not counted on was Gerry's easy ways. Though it was obvious that he was not to the manor born, Gerry seemed at ease drinking the hundred-dollars-a-bottle wine and eating the pâtè and the ostrich fillet as though he feasted on such treats every day, neither overly praising nor disparaging what was set before him, but accepting it as his due, appreciative if unimpressed.

Rachel thought it a neat trick. She always felt self-conscious around the wealthy people who were her parents' friends, but she thought with delight that you could plop Gerry down in the middle of the House of Lords and he wouldn't turn a hair.

Soon, however, he turned the tables, and began asking David about his work and life in the United States. David, surprised at first, answered dismissively, but as Gerry's questions deepened Rachel's father began to open up, telling him about his company, the real estate market in the states, and even the p̈eople who worked for him. Between the two of them, they talked nonstop through the two hours it took to eat dinner.

Afterwards Gerry thanked David for being such a good host and for treating them to such a grand dinner, and David's response was equally polite. "I'd ask you one favor, though, Gerry," David said as they walked out of the hotel into the chill night. "I haven't had a chance to talk to my daughter alone since I got here. I was wondering if you'd mind me seeing her back to her place, that is if you two didn't have any plans." David slipped an arm around Rachel, and she forced a smile.

"Sure, that's fine," Gerry said. "I'll give you a call, Rachel. Thank you again for dinner, Mr. Oliver, and your company, both very enjoyable."

"It was good to meet you, Gerry. I hope I'll see you again."

Rachel moved from her father's side and gave Gerry a kiss, holding it long enough for her father to get the picture, if he hadn't already. When she finished, Gerry just looked as though the kiss was also his due, said goodnight to both of them, and walked away.

"Nice kid," David said, with the emphasis on the latter word.

"Glad you like him," Rachel said.

"I always like dreamers. Interesting to see what makes them tick."

"And is that why you were asking him question after

question, to see what makes him tick?"

"Sort of. Trying to figure out what it is you see in these guys."

"What do you mean, 'these guys?'"

"I mean it's kind of obvious that he and Tyler are cut from the same cloth."

She felt her mouth drop open. "Gerry Lynch is *nothing* like Tyler."

"Oh, come on...are you kidding, Rachel?" She turned and started walking in the direction of her hostel, and David followed, quickly catching up. "Look, no offense, but sometimes you get too close to see things clearly. Now Gerry's a charming guy. He's nice and polite, and I'm sure he treats you well. He's a real gentleman."

Rachel stopped walking and turned to her father. "Yes, he is, and the fact that he didn't tell you to mind your own damn business when you were grilling him proves it. So, what's your point? That all gentlemen turn into wife abusers and druggies?"

David laughed and held up his hands as if in surrender. "Look, I don't want to fight with you. Why don't we find a place where we can have a cup of coffee or a nightcap or something?"

"I don't want any coffee and I don't want another drink. I just want to hear why you think Gerry is a shit."

"I *don't* think he's a shit. I like the guy, really, but I see all the signs..." He let it trail away.

"Like *what?*"

"Like he isn't what he wants to be. He's a teacher, and he wants to be a writer, that's obvious. Tyler was, what, a laborer who wanted to be a rock star. When you can't make a living the way you want to, sometimes you get frustrated, and sometimes, well, people start taking out their frustrations in ways that aren't so good."

"Okay, first of all," Rachel said, "Gerry *likes* teaching. He teaches literature, and that's his field. And second, he doesn't want to *be* a writer, he already *is* one, and he's a really good one. He's not a *commercial* writer, and he doesn't want to be."

"You saying he doesn't want to make money? He doesn't want to be successful?"

"I'm *saying* that that part doesn't matter to him. He writes wonderful poetry and he writes beautiful lyrics, and if something would catch on and he'd get lucky, great, and if not, it's no big deal."

"And you believe that." David gave a sarcastic sniff, but smiled to soften it. "You know, honey, I just don't want to see you hurt again. I remember you saying the same things about Tyler, and if you're honest with yourself you'll know I'm right."

"Look, Dad, I didn't say I was gonna marry this guy, did I? For God's sake, I've only known him about a *week*. Now I like him a lot, but that doesn't mean it's anything permanent. I'm here for another week, that's all, and if we decide that this is something we want to keep going, it's going to be hard enough as it is across an ocean, okay? So, I think your worries are a little premature, okay?"

"Okay, okay, okay," David said, parroting her. "It's just that I know you pretty well, and once you set your mind on something..."

"I don't have my mind set on anything. I just want to see Ireland, and I found a great guy to show it to me, so can we just please leave it at that?"

"Sure, baby, whatever you say." They stopped in front of the hostel. "This where you're staying?"

She heard the tone of disapproval in his voice. "Yes, why?"

"Well, I just thought maybe you'd like to move in to the Great Southern. Your own room, of course, on me."

"No thanks, Dad, I'm fine here. Thanks for dinner." She gave him a peremptory kiss.

"I gonna see you again?"

"Maybe. You have my number and I have yours, let's leave it at that."

He shook his head. "The women in this family are far from welcoming." At Rachel's curious look, he shrugged and added, "Your Aunt Susanna wasn't too happy to see me either. Seems she went and found herself a boyfriend, too."

"I know. It's Gerry's dad."

David made a sound through his nose that might have been a laugh. "You Cassidy women do have your secret lovers, don't you?" A second later he blanched, as though he was sorry for what he'd said.

Rachel narrowed her eyes. "What do you mean, *secret?*"

"Nothing. Forget it. Look, call me, okay? Maybe we could do a little sightseeing together. Think about it?"

"Sure. Goodnight." She turned and walked toward the door.

"'Night,'" she heard him say as she went inside.

Damn him, Rachel thought as she walked to her room. He was so demanding and yet somehow so needy at the same time. She felt as though he'd been baiting Gerry all evening, and once they were alone, he'd made her certain of it.

Gerry was an alien entity to David. They literally were from two different worlds. Her father had never been able to comprehend people doing things for reasons other than money, and to him all creative artists were alike. Ergo, Gerry equaled Tyler. But Rachel knew that he didn't, not at all.

She'd been too young when she was seduced by Tyler's rough charm. At that age she was unable to tell bullshit from sincerity, and Tyler definitely evinced a vast amount of the former. He had a lot of chutzpah, but no real talent, and guts alone wasn't enough to take him where he wanted to go. So, when he didn't get there, he reacted as her father said, with frustration and anger that he took out on whoever happened to be closest to him, and that was his wife.

Gerry was different, and she loved him for being that way. With Tyler there had always been an edge, a tension in their relationship, in which there were brief moments of fire between periods of utter cold. But being with Gerry was like slipping on a warm old sweater on a chilly night. It was a constant that made her feel safe and comfortable, a feeling she thought she would never grow tired of.

So, of course, her father would try to sabotage it. It was as though, having never been emotionally happy himself, he couldn't bear for anyone else around him to be that way either. Why the hell had he come to Ireland in the first place? She didn't buy that story about his wanting to renew some emotional link with her mother.

Was it to see Aunt Sue? Ever since Rachel was old enough

to read the signs, she'd known that her father always had a soft spot for Susanna, and she knew they dated before her dad got together with her mom. It was also obvious to her that Aunt Sue didn't *like* her dad very much. Still, Rachel knew he always thought himself irresistible to women. But would he have had the incredibly bad judgment to fly across the ocean right after his wife died to try and woo his sister-in-law?

If he had, his comment about Aunt Sue not being glad to see him showed that it hadn't worked. But what was that other crack supposed to mean, about Cassidy women having their secret lovers? Had Aunt Sue tried to keep Michael Lynch a secret from him, or was there something else?

In her room she tried to call Gerry, but there was no answer. He had probably walked back to his flat and hadn't yet arrived. Then she dialed Susanna's number and got an answer. "Did I wake you?" she asked.

"God, no. I've got another hour of work before bedtime."

"I saw Dad," Rachel said. "He took Gerry and me to dinner."

"I saw him yesterday. I wanted to warn you he was here, but I couldn't get you on the phone. How did it go?"

"It was horrible. Of course." She told Susanna about David's baiting of Gerry and the conversation they'd had afterwards. "I mean, why the hell did he come, Aunt Sue? And why does he want to screw things up between me and Gerry? I just don't get it."

There was silence on the line for several seconds. "Your dad's always been very protective of you, Rachel," Susanna finally said. "I'm sure he's just concerned with your welfare."

"What was the bit about secret lovers then?"

"I...think he was surprised to find me with Michael."

"Is that why he really came over here? To see you?"

"I think it was to see both of us."

"Then he—"

"Honey, your dad and I dated before he met your mom, you know that. But there hasn't been anything between us since, and there won't be."

"Then you weren't like *his* secret lover or anything?"

The laugh that Rachel heard was sincere. "Oh, *God*, no. No, no, no. Put your mind at rest, child. Never happened, never will. Now you just forget about your dad and enjoy your time in Ireland, and enjoy Gerry, too. If you want to show your father some of the sights when Gerry's teaching during the day, he'd probably appreciate it. If you don't feel like it, don't. There is one thing, though, that I wanted to talk to you about…"

Rachel listened as Susanna proposed a double date with the four of them, Gerry and Rachel, Susanna and Michael, for the following Saturday night. "I think Michael would like to get closer to Gerry than they've been in the past, so if you could talk him into it, it would mean a lot to Michael."

"Okay. I don't know why he'd say no. I mean, sure, he's distant from his dad, but I haven't sensed any real animosity or anything. I'll talk to him tomorrow and let you know."

"Great, thanks. And don't worry about your dad. He's going through a tough time right now."

"No, he's not."

"What do you mean?"

"He hardly mentioned Mom. I think he let her go a long time ago. I've never seen anybody who was grieving less. Whatever the reason he came over here, it didn't have anything to do with her."

"Oh, Rachel…" Rachel thought Aunt Sue's tone was supposed to be admonitory, but it rang false. She was certain her aunt agreed with her, though she wouldn't admit it. "Can't you give your dad the benefit of the doubt?"

"Doubtful." Rachel heard her aunt sigh. "I'll call you about Saturday."

CHAPTER 18

For Susanna, the week was delightfully busy. Her lecture in Limerick on Wednesday was well-received, and the discussion afterward proved lively, the students obviously well-informed and opinionated. They were even more so at the discussion at UCG on Friday, when the principles of nonviolence nearly took a shellacking when several of the students got into a shouting match that she was fortunately able to quell.

That week she was able to fit Michael into her schedule twice. She went to his flat on Wednesday after returning from Limerick, and he made her a late supper of fresh salmon, small potatoes and vegetables, after which she spent the night with him. Friday night she was able to join him and the other musicians at the session. Kate Quinn arrived late, but seemed friendly enough. She nodded and smiled at both Susanna and Michael as though she had accepted the way things were.

Halfway through the evening, Rachel and Gerry came in and sat near the back. Several minutes later Susanna was surprised to see David Oliver enter the pub. He gave her a wave and smiled and nodded at Michael, and went back to join Rachel and Gerry. From what Susanna could see, neither of them looked happy to see him, though Gerry put on the better front. At least David didn't speak too loudly during the session, and listened quietly and respectfully when Molly sang her *Sean-Nos*.

When Molly finished, the musicians played for another hour. Susanna noticed that David, who was on one side of Rachel with Gerry on the other, was constantly speaking into his daughter's ear. His expression had turned snide, and Rachel looked more and more dismayed.

The musicians finished playing and packed up their instruments. David wandered over to them and shook Michael's hand. "Sorry about that mix-up in here the other day," Michael said.

"Is that what it was?" David said with a grin. "I apologize, too. I wasn't being very gentlemanly. Hey, I like your music. Real peppy. I liked that older lady's singing, too."

"That's Michael's mother," Susanna said.

"Oh yeah? Well, she's very good. Guess that's kind of an ancient style, huh?"

"*Sean-Nos*," Michael said.

"Gesundheit. Just kidding."

"So, what have you been up to this week?" Susanna asked him.

"Oh, a lot of touring. I got Rachel to come with me most days. Been up and down the coast. Saw Connemara National Park, that big abbey, what is it..."

"Kylemore?" Michael said.

"That's the one. The Cliffs of Moher, the Burren, toured Bunratty Castle one day. It's been fun."

"So, you've spent a lot of time with Rachel then," Susanna observed.

"Oh yeah, we've been getting along like champs. Evenings I usually give up early, but when I found out about this, and that you guys were playing and all, thought I'd make an exception."

"Well, we're glad you did," Michael said.

"Me, too. Better head back to the hotel, though. I'll just say goodnight to Rachel first—maybe have a quick one for the road. Good seeing you, Michael, especially when you're not trying to pound me." Though David grinned, Susanna could sense his hostility as he turned away.

Just as he did, Kate Quinn came walking past on her way to the bar and lightly bumped into him. David stopped, then seemed to recognize her, and said, "Oh, hey, it's, uh, *Kate*, right? How you doing?" and walked toward the bar with her. Kate glanced guiltily back at Susanna, then started talking quietly to David.

Now what was *that* all about, Susanna wondered, and looked at Michael, who was putting his guitar in its case and didn't seem to have noticed. When he looked up, she gave him a long-suffering look referencing David, and he smiled in sympathy.

In another minute, Gerry and Rachel made their way to Susanna through the thinning crowd. Gerry looked his usual imperturbable self, but Rachel looked pale and upset. At least, Susanna thought, David's attention was off his daughter. He seemed quite content chatting up Kate at the bar.

"Hi, you two," Susanna said. "Still ready for our dinner tomorrow night?"

Rachel smiled thinly and nodded, and Gerry said, "Sure," with a sidelong glance at his dad.

"Hope so," Michael said. "I'm planning to cook all day."

"So, Gerry," Susanna said, "have you seen your father's place yet?"

"No, not really."

"Well, it'll be a bit of a housewarming then." Her attempt at cheeriness fell flat, if the lack of response was any indication. "Rachel, your dad tells me you and he have been spending a lot of time together."

Her expression was less than enthusiastic. "Yeah. In fact," she said, dropping her voice, "I'd like to talk to you about that. Soon."

"What about tomorrow? I'll take you to breakfast."

"Sounds good." They arranged to meet, and Gerry and Rachel left. When Susanna looked over at the bar, she saw that Kate and David were no longer there, and wondered if they had left together. Now there, she thought, would be a pair.

"Finn and Kevin'll finish up," Michael said. "Nightcap at my place?"

"That would be *lovely*," she answered. "Let me say goodbye to your mother first."

Molly was wiping pint glasses dry behind the bar, and smiled when she saw Susanna. "Evenin', dear," she said. "You played nicely tonight. I think this place is rubbing off on you."

"It must be the fiddle," Susanna said.

"Certainly doesn't hurt."

"I loved your singing. As usual. You just...transport me."

"Well, that's grand. I don't think I've ever transported

anyone before. Be careful not to go too far away, though. I think Michael would miss you. Speaking of which, he looks anxious to be going. You two going to find another night spot, are you?"

'Um, maybe..." Susanna could feel the blood in her cheeks as she blushed.

"Well, don't let him get away with anything," Molly said, with a little smile that made Susanna laugh in spite of herself. Michael joined them, kissed his mother goodnight, swept his arm around Susanna, and they went out into the night.

"I'm not sure," Susanna said, "but I think I have your mother's blessing."

"What?"

"Never mind." She laughed as they headed toward The Long Walk and Michael's town house.

Susanna didn't feel as carefree in the dark after making love. She and Michael lay together on their sides like spoons, and Michael's sleeping breath puffed gently on her neck. Now, with everything quiet, was the first chance she had had to consider what the familiarity between David and Kate Quinn might have meant.

They had met before, that much was certain, and Kate's guilty glance at Susanna suggested that something might have transpired between them to Susanna's detriment. Could Kate have told David about her hoax as Julia? If so, that might mean that David had learned, or might have figured out by himself, about Julia's long-ago affair with Michael.

Susanna gave a sigh so loud that Michael awoke with a little start, then tightened his arm around her. "Anything wrong?"

"No, I'm fine. Bad dream."

"Ah, we can't be having those, not after such sweetness," he said, kissing her hair. "Sleep warm and well, my love." She pressed closer to him, deciding to save her concerns for the daylight.

The next morning Susanna met Rachel at a coffee shop on Middle Street. Her niece looked pale and tired, as though she hadn't been sleeping well, and Susanna talked her into having a full Irish breakfast. "I won't touch that black pudding stuff, though," Rachel said. "I hate the thought of eating blood in the morning."

"So, what's up?" Susanna asked, once they both had steaming mugs of coffee in front of them.

"It's Dad. God, I thought he was bad when I was a kid, but he's worse than ever now."

"Bad about what?"

"He's been in my face like you wouldn't believe this past week. Every day he asks me to come touring with him—I have to see this, and I have to see that, and you can't visit Ireland and not see the other, and since Gerry teaches during the day, I really don't have a good excuse not to go with him. But that's not the worst of it."

"What then?"

Rachel took a tentative sip of her coffee, then sipped some more and rubbed her eyes. "I think he hates Gerry, and I don't have any idea why. I mean, here's the sweetest and most sensitive guy I've ever met, the first guy I think that maybe I'm actually in love with since that asshole Tyler, and Dad can't seem to come up with bad enough stuff to say about him."

"How does Gerry get along with your dad?" Susanna asked.

"*Fine.* I don't think he particularly *likes* him, I mean who would, but he treats him really well, answers his nosy questions…we've gone out to eat with Dad in the evenings maybe three times total, and Gerry's even taken turns picking up the tab, not, my God, when we ate at that Park Hotel place, but the second time, and then Dad got it next, so now it's Gerry's turn again. But he's a perfect *gentleman* around Dad, and he has a good job, and I just don't *get* it."

Breakfast came, and Rachel looked with dismay at the assortment of eggs, sausages, tomato, breads, and puddings on the plate before her. "Oh God, I can't eat all this."

"Eat what you want," Susanna said. "So, there hasn't been any rift to speak of between your dad and Gerry? They haven't had any arguments or anything?"

"No, nothing. I'm telling you, Gerry bends over backwards *not* to disagree with him. I mean he's like the *Anti*-Tyler."

"So, what does your dad say about him when you two are alone?"

"Just...*crap*. Like Gerry's so quiet because he's holding in so much rage, and he's frustrated because he's not a 'successful' writer, and how he doesn't have any joy, and he's moody, and blah blah blah. Oh yeah, and how I'm probably not the first American girl he's fooled with his sensitive Irishman thing. I just don't know why he *despises* Gerry so much."

Rachel dipped a piece of bread into the egg yolk and munched on it. Susanna thought for a moment in the silence between them, thought about Kate Quinn and her guilty look, and then said, "I don't think he does despise Gerry. But I do think he wants to break the two of you up. And I think he wants to do it for what he believes is your own good."

"What? *Why?*"

Susanna pushed back her untouched plate and took another swallow of coffee, wishing it were something stronger. "When I told you about your mother being over here and falling in love with Michael Lynch...well, I didn't tell you everything. But I guess I'd better, because I believe your father found out about it. Rachel, your mother and Michael were lovers."

Rachel looked at Susanna as though she'd just told her they were having breakfast. Though she didn't say, *Well, duh,* Susanna saw it in her face. "I'd just kind of assumed that," Rachel said. "So, what's the big deal?"

"The deal, big or not, lies in the timing. When David heard—or figured out—that your mother had a lover over here, he counted months. Now look, I don't want you to get upset about this. There's probably nothing to it. But your mom was over here the last week in January, and you were born early the following November. Now, I know your mom and dad were intimate before they were married, so it's not likely that..."

She paused when she saw the look on Rachel's face. It was one of slow shock, as though she was counting months herself and didn't like the way they added up. "I knew," she said slowly, "that they had to get married because of me, but...oh my God... what you're saying is that I, I could be Gerry's *sister?*" The last word was a whisper.

"I think," said Susanna, parsing every word, "that's what your *father* might think. And I believe that's why he might be trying to break you and Gerry up."

"Oh no," Rachel said with more certainty than Susanna thought she felt. "Oh no, no, no, no, no, this isn't right. It *can't* be. That would be...just...*awful*. It'd be like...if *Luke and Leia* had slept together before they found out they were related." She laughed, and Susanna did, too, unable to hold it back. "Maybe that's why Darth Vader was trying to break the two of them up," Rachel added, and they both started laughing even harder, loudly enough so that the waitress and the other customers looked at them.

When they stopped, both of them had tears on their cheeks. "I think I'm approaching hysteria," Rachel said. She sniffed hard and took a deep breath, then blew it out. "But I've worked up an appetite," she said, and cut a bite from the sausage and ate it, washing it down with coffee. "You know," she said after she swallowed, "he probably isn't my father—Michael, I mean—and even if...if he were..." She shrugged. "You know, what's the big deal? Who knows? It's not like Gerry and I are *married...*" Her voice cracked on the word and she cleared her throat and repeated it more softly. "...married or anything."

"Look," Susanna said, leaning across the table and taking her hand. "I'm sure there's nothing to it either, but I thought you should know, since it explains your dad's behavior."

She snorted a laugh. "He always thinks the worst when it comes to stuff like this. He always thinks the worst in *general*. Look, I'm not going to be concerned about this. I mean, what's done is done, and if it would get to the point where Gerry and I were really serious about making a ... *commitment*, then...then I don't know what. But I'm not going to worry about it now." She looked at Susanna. "Does Michael know?"

"No. He doesn't know when you were born, and I haven't said anything."

"Good. Don't. Gerry hasn't put anything together, either, and I'm not going to bring it up." A quizzical expression came over her. "But if Dad is that concerned, why hasn't he said anything to me? Or made a big announcement about my...possible parentage to both me and Gerry and end it that way?"

"I'm not sure. Maybe because he believes it might pull you even further away from him if you think he's not your father. He does love you, Rachel. And he wants the best for you. It's just on how you get it that you two differ."

"Do we ever. God, Aunt Sue, I'm thirty years old and he's still trying to run my life. But you know what? He's not going to do it. I am not going to let all this crap—these suspicions and theories—upset me. I'm going to have a great day with Gerry, and we're going to have a really fun time tonight with you and Michael, and if Dad doesn't like it, he can stuff it. But first..." Once more she picked up her knife and fork. "...I'm going to eat every bite of this delicious breakfast. Except for the blood part."

Rachel tore into the Irish fry as though she hadn't eaten in a week, and Susanna started on her own breakfast as well. The girl was true to her word, and only the black pudding was left on the plate when the waitress picked it up. "I hope you're not going to be sick after all that," Susanna said.

"I'm *fine*. Never better." She glanced at her watch. "I'm meeting Gerry at eleven-thirty, so I hate to eat and run, but..."

"No problem. I hope you weren't planning an early lunch."

"Oh no. I may skip it entirely so I can enjoy Michael's dinner tonight. What's he making?"

"I don't know, it's a surprise. At least until I help him with it this afternoon. Look, you run along. I've got the check."

"Thanks, Aunt Sue, and thanks for...for telling me about all this."

"Maybe I should have kept my mouth shut."

"Oh no. Now I know what I'm fighting against with Dad, and 'knowing is half the battle.'" They both laughed at the trademark line from the *G. I. Joe* cartoons that Susanna had let Rachel watch when she babysat her years before. Then they stood and hugged, and Rachel left, while Susanna sat back down to finish her coffee.

She hoped her niece would be all right. Years of dealing with her parents had made Rachel tough-skinned, but the suggestion that she might be involved in an incestuous relationship was a lot to take. Still, Susanna felt Rachel had a right to know why her father was so hostile toward Gerry. She just hoped the girl would be able to handle what was, after all, only a possibility.

To Rachel, who was walking down Middle Street as though it was a long dark tunnel, the possibility was a certainty. Though she had delighted in shocking her parents by breaking taboos, this particular taboo was beyond the pale. The thought of Gerry being her brother made her physically ill, and it had taken every bit of willpower she had to eat the breakfast and prove, both to herself and Aunt Sue, that this particular *thou shalt not* meant no more to her than any of the others.

But this time it did, and there was no getting around it. If this nearly unspeakable prospect had intruded into her relationship with anyone else, she would have shrugged and walked away, but she *loved* Gerry Lynch. She loved him and *had* loved him, and the sex had been an extension of those feelings. There had been nothing casual or "recreational" about it for either of them, not even the first time. They had loved soul to soul, and the thought that the sense of their souls being so similar was because they might share the same blood struck her like a hammer blow.

What made it worse was that she was not prepared to give Gerry up for any reason, and the thought that they might be split apart over this unfair trick of fate hit her harder than did the concept of having been intimate with her own half-brother. If she knew for certain that they were siblings, she would not, could not change how she felt about him, and that self-knowledge was even more upsetting than the possible truth of her heritage.

She decided that she would ignore it all, forget about what her aunt had told her. She would go on with her life and love whoever she wanted to love, love the man she had no choice but to love.

As for Susanna, she spent the afternoon with the man *she* loved, her hands coated with flour and smelling of chopped scallions. When she arrived at his town house at one o'clock, Michael had the kitchen filled with the raw materials he had bought that

morning. Susanna saw parsnips, apples, onions, scallions, potatoes, mushrooms, carrots and broccoli, as well as an assortment
of spices and condiments.

"The sausages are in the fridge," he told her. "Just stuffed
this morning, so O'Reilly claims."

"Michael, there are only four of us, you know."

"And plenty to eat for all, don't you worry. Well, I think first
we'll mash the tatties for the champ."

"Are you speaking Gaelic?"

"*Champ*. Mashed potatoes mixed with scallions, milk and
butter. A very simple dish to go with the sausage and mushroom pie. First, we'll cook the potatoes and the sausages both.
We make the pie in advance then bake it this evening, but the
champ we'll do just before. We can make the soup early, too."

"Mmm, I love soup. What kind?"

"Parsnip and apple."

"You're kidding."

"Go ahead and laugh, but wait till you taste it. Ambrosia.
My ma's recipe, and Gerry loves it. See, I've got the sturdy food
as the main course—the sausage pie, the champ, and broccoli
and carrots. And the bookends are the soup and a sweet cream
drink to end it."

"Instead of dessert?"

"It *is* dessert, my darlin'. Now come on, there's work to be
done."

They peeled potatoes, chopped the scallions and parsnips
and onions, washed and sliced mushrooms and carrots, and
peeled, cored and sliced apples. Then, while the potatoes were
boiling and the sausages cooking, Susanna helped Michael
make the pastry for the pie.

"I can't believe you're doing this all from scratch," Susanna
said as she rolled out the pastry. "I didn't see you as the cooking
type."

"Full of surprises, aren't I?"

"So, who taught you, your mother?"

"She taught me a few things. A lot I learned from Malachy."

"Your cousin? He seems even less the cooking type."

"No, he's a brilliant cook. Traditional Irish, of course. Now you wouldn't think all that much could be done with potatoes, cabbage, onions, milk, and butter, but I've seen grown men get a tear in the eye when tasting Malachy's colcannon. His ma's a far better cook than mine—don't ever tell her I said that—so he must have gotten it from her."

"And he taught you?" said Susanna, pressing down hard on the rolling pin.

"Aye. In the old days." Michael's expression seemed far away, then cleared. "And recently, too. Last Christmas when he and Aunt Brigid came to visit, he stayed here with me. Showed me how to make the pie then."

"You two are very close, aren't you?" Susanna said, pretending to concentrate on the dough.

"Do anything for him...ah, looks like the stock's on the boil..."

Through the afternoon they took numerous breaks while this or that cooked, and at five o'clock they put the sausages into the pie crust, poured the sauce in on top of them, and covered it all with a top crust. "Now," Michael said, "I think if you help me set the table, you can return to your own digs and primp for the evening to come."

"You sure you can handle everything else?"

"My darlin', as a pubman many's the time I've been called upon to whip up a raft of differing toasties in as many minutes. If I can keep the cheese and ham separate from the cheese, tomato and onion, surely I can finish preparing this humble repast. The table linen's in the cupboard over there."

Susanna opened the door, took out the linen, and laid down the tablecloth with Michael's help. "Michael, this is exquisite," she said as she examined the pattern. There were Celtic symbols in circles around the drape, as well as representations of castles below it. On the top were a series of designs using Celtic knots. The heavy density of the threads made it feel like brocade beneath her fingers.

"Don't credit me. It's the lad's I'm subletting from, as is the china." He moved to the glass-fronted cabinet and began to take out white china with shamrocks around the edges. Susanna quickly identified it as a Belleek pattern that her grandmother had owned. "He told me to feel free to use anything here, and would you believe I haven't chipped a single plate?" He tossed one into the air but caught it easily before Susanna could even gasp. "That's only because I've not used them yet," he said with a devilish grin.

Susanna strode over to him and took the plate from his hands. "Suppose you let me handle this before you..." She trailed off as she looked at the underside of the plate. "Oh my God..."

"What? Did I chip it after all?"

"No, and good thing. These are black mark."

"Well, maybe we should wash them first then."

"No, black mark—see the black Belleek stamp? That means these are old—mid-forties or before. We shouldn't even use them."

"Of course, we will," he said, snatching it away. "I was concerned at first—I thought they might be *new.*"

"Michael..."

He laughed, and she had to smile. "I was told to use what was here and to enjoy it, and I intend to do just that. Now, are you going to help me or not?"

Reluctantly she helped Michael set the table, and they finished the job by placing the linen napkins and the fiddle and thread style silver flatware. Susanna was certain that it was antique, but didn't have the courage to check the hallmark.

"There," Michael said. "Everything looks grand. Now be off with you while I attend to myself and the meal. I'll see you back here at eight, yes?"

"You will indeed. I'll just close my eyes and let my nose guide me."

"And a pretty one it is." He kissed her on the nose, helped her on with her coat, and walked her to the door. "Don't be late tonight," he said. "Good cooking is all in the timing."

Susanna went back to her rooms and napped for an hour. It had been a long week, and she wanted to be fresh for the evening. Afterward she took a shower, had a cup of tea, and put on a simple, form fitting dress that she was certain would not make Rachel feel underdressed. Then she drove back to Michael's.

Rachel and Gerry were just coming up the street as she pulled into a parking spot, and she greeted them as she got out of her car. "Glorious evening," she said, and it was, with a hint of springtime warmth in the February air.

"How are you?" said Gerry, holding Rachel's hand. She looked wan, but was smiling.

"Hungry," Susanna said. "I was helping this afternoon, so I got a sneak preview, though not a sneak tasting. Your father's a great cook, at least from the visual evidence."

"Right, well, I'll believe it when I taste it," he said with a smile. "Shall we?"

They walked up to the door. Susanna nearly opened it, but thought it might be imprudent to suggest such intimacy with Michael's son there, so rang the bell instead. She heard quick footsteps inside, and Michael opened the door. He smiled when he saw her and gave her a quick kiss on the cheek, doing the same to Rachel. Then, still smiling, he shook Gerry's hand and patted him on the shoulder.

"Grand to see you all," he said. "Come in, come in, hang your coats on the hall tree—I've got to see to a pot in the kitchen and I'll be right out."

They'd no sooner hung up their coats than Michael was back. "Now, drinks?" Michael seemed at his best. Susanna had been afraid that he might be uneasy with his son there, but he showed no signs of it, although he treated Gerry like an honored guest rather than a son. There was none of the playfulness or joking that Susanna had seen between parents and their adult children, but both Michael and Gerry seemed pleasant toward each other. Perhaps the presence of their women made them civil.

Susanna was more concerned about Rachel. There was little of her usual bubbling vivacity and humor. She could be cynical, but when she was even her putdowns were funny. Tonight, however, she was reticent and uncommunicative, responding when spoken to, but seldom going beyond that.

Susanna suspected that Rachel, despite her claims to the contrary, was deeply affected by the possibility that Michael Lynch could be her father. Being in such close proximity to both

Michael and Gerry only made such speculation all the more inescapable. Unfortunately, there was never a moment in which to speak to her privately, as Michael continued playing the perfect host, serving them drinks and a tray of appetizers.

At length he suggested they all come to the table, and brought out the parsnips and apple soup. It was, to her surprise, a cream base, rich with butter, and though she had expected to find pieces of apple and parsnip floating in it, Michael had strained it so that only the flavors remained, enhanced by what she recognized as cumin, coriander, and curry.

"You made this?" Gerry asked his father in disbelief.

"I did. Why, what's wrong with it?"

"Nothing. It's brilliant. As good as Gram's."

"Better not let her hear you say that—it's her recipe," Michael said gruffly, but Susanna could tell he was pleased.

She helped him clear the soup dishes and then he carried in the sausage pie while Susanna followed with the bowl of steaming white champ. The pie was just as good as the soup, and the small nuggets of sausage nearly melted in Susanna's mouth. The champ made an ideal accompaniment, the gentle flavor of the potatoes heightened by the tang of the scallions.

Though Susanna had been worried that the conversation might flag during dinner, it did so only when everyone was simultaneously chewing. Otherwise she kept the conversation going throughout, asking Gerry about his teaching and his writing, and Michael often asked a follow-up question. Susanna had the sense that he was learning a lot about his son, and what he was finding out was both interesting him and making him proud. When he learned that Gerry and Rachel had been writing songs together, he suggested that they come to the Banshee and perform them there.

"They're really not traditional," Gerry said. "More contemporary, y'know?"

"Doesn't matter," Michael said. "We need a bit of change now and again. Fiona does her own new songs occasionally and people seem to like them. What about it, Rachel?" he asked, turning toward her. "Would you be willing to sing some of your new songs for us old folk?"

Rachel smiled, but it seemed forced to Susanna. "Sure."

"Would, uh, you like something else?" Michael asked tentatively, looking at Rachel's nearly untouched plate.

"No, no, it's really delicious," she said. "I'm sorry, I'm just not very hungry." She smiled in apology and took another bite of the pie. Susanna was certain her niece was upset by what they had talked about that morning, but there was no way to calm or reassure her short of a supportive smile.

Rachel seemed to rally, and ate well over half her portion of pie and champ. When they were finished, Susanna helped Michael clear once again. "Now for the *pièce de résistance*," Michael said. "Susanna, go sit down, I can bring it out."

In another minute he came into the living room bearing a silver tray with four tall glasses. They appeared to hold ice cream parfaits with pale flecks, but the contents seemed lighter and frothier than ice cream. "Irish cream delight," Michael announced. "With whiskey, of course. You may either use the long spoons or try and drink it, but I warn you, you'll have white moustaches before you're through."

"What's *in* this?" Susanna asked.

"Toasted raw oatmeal and sliced almonds, whipped cream, honey, whiskey, and just a touch of lemon juice. *Voilà*. Here's to us all," he finished, raising the concoction. They all sipped and laughed to see each other with dollops of whipped cream beneath their noses.

"This really is wonderful," Rachel said, and Susanna was glad to hear the delight in her voice. "Like the top of a really great sundae with a kick."

"Makes you feel like a kid again, doesn't it?" Michael asked.

Rachel's smile faded a bit, but she continued to drink. They all did, until the glasses held nothing but a film of white.

"I put coffee on, if anyone would like any," Michael said.

"I don't want to kill the taste of that drink just yet," Gerry said. "My God, Dad, but that was a grand meal. Didn't know you had it in you."

Michael opened his mouth to say something, then apparently thought better of it and merely smiled and nodded his thanks.

"It really was, Mr. Lynch," Rachel said.

"Please, make it Michael."

"It was wonderful...Michael."

"I'm glad you enjoyed it, Rachel," he said, and looked genuinely grateful for her compliment, but she quickly looked away. "Well, shall we adjourn to the front room?"

It was as unanticipated as it was shocking. They all got to their feet, and suddenly Rachel wavered. Her eyes rolled up as though she was looking at the ceiling, her head lolled, and she fell so quickly that none of them could even try to catch her. Her shoulder hit the edge of the table, and then her head bounced against it as she sank to the floor.

CHAPTER 19

Rachel opened her eyes seconds later, and saw Gerry, Michael, and Susanna all leaning over her. Gerry had a hand on her head, and it hurt where he was touching her.

"Are you all right?" she heard him say. "Rachel? *Rachel?*"

She thought she said that she was okay, but he didn't seem to hear her. *Rachel?* he kept saying and looking at her, but she was looking right back at him, wasn't she? And wasn't she saying that she was okay? She would get up and prove it to him, but when she tried her arms and legs wouldn't obey her. They wouldn't move at all, so she closed her eyes again, and Gerry's *Rachel?* sounded far away.

When she opened her eyes again, Gerry was still there, and so were Susanna and Michael, and they were both looking down at her with concern and, yes, with love, and why *shouldn't* they, because wasn't she their flesh and blood, their little girl, Aunt Sue's niece and her father's daughter?

Her father, she thought, of course her father would be worried about her, fainting like that and falling and hitting her head, and she knew she had because it hurt so much, but Daddy would make it better, Daddy and Mommy and was Aunt Sue Mommy now because she loved Daddy? Or was she still Aunt Sue, and wasn't this nice man Daddy at all? She hoped he was because he was so nice, but she hoped he *wasn't*, because then Gerry would be her brother, and she loved him too much to love him as a brother, and if he was, then they had been bad, done things that brothers and sisters shouldn't do, but she didn't really know who was who anymore, and she thought that maybe her mother could explain it all to her when she woke up.

It was all too confusing and too scary, and she wanted to go back to sleep again and not wake up so she wouldn't have to think about it anymore the way she'd been doing ever since Aunt Sue or Mommy had talked to her that morning, and she'd just go back to sleep if her *head* didn't hurt so much.

"Hey...*Rachel?*" she heard Gerry say again, and then she felt something wet and cold. Somebody was putting water on her face, and she didn't like that at all, because it would keep her awake.

"Stop it..." she said, and this time she heard herself. "*Stop it...*"

She heard Gerry sigh then, as though he was relieved that she had said something, and if that made him happy, she thought she'd talk some more.

"My hea..." The word didn't come out, so she tried again. "My *head*...hurts."

"Can you open your eyes again?" she heard Aunt Sue say, and she decided she would try. She liked her Aunt Sue. She managed to open them, and she saw the three people looking down at her, but she didn't see her mother, and that was all right, because all these people looked worried enough for a whole bunch of mothers.

"That's my girl," Aunt Sue said. "Can you move? Move your hands for us?"

"Uh-huh." Rachel thought she could do that too, and when she tried her hands moved just fine, though a little slowly.

"All right, sweetie," Aunt Sue said, and Rachel liked that she called her sweetie. "We're going to go to the hospital now, because—"

"Aw, *nooo*..." Rachel moaned. She didn't like hospitals.

"...because you could have a concussion, and we don't know what made you pass out in the first place, okay? And we have to find that out. Now do you think you can stand up."

"If I can stand up," she said, slowly choosing each word, "do I have to go the hospital?"

"Oh yes. Not going is no option. Now let's try and stand up."

Gerry got on one side of her and her new father got on the

other, while Aunt Sue stood in front, holding onto Rachel's hands, and it was like she was learning to walk again as she slowly got to her feet. But as she stood upright a wave of nausea passed over her, her skin grew cold and clammy, and her knees buckled. "I'm gonna..."

She didn't finish the sentence, but vomited that wonderful dinner and that really good drink all over. Aunt Sue stepped back just in time, and everything went right onto the table, all over that pretty linen tablecloth that she had thought was so cool. The two men held her up while she finished, and she thought that was really nice of them.

"Oh, I'm so sorry," she said when she was finished. "Aw, that nice tablecloth...I'm not drunk or anything, really..."

"'Course you're not," said that nice man who was maybe her father. "You're sick, that's all, and we're going to take care of you now."

Aunt Sue cleaned the nasty stuff off of her chin and the front of her dress. "Aw, I got it on my dress too...did I get any on the rug? I hope I didn't get any on the rug..."

"No, the rug's fine," said that nice Michael. "Now we're going to get your coat and then we'll go to the hospital, don't you worry about a thing."

"What about the tablecloth?" Rachel said. "We should clean the tablecloth..."

"It's just a tablecloth," Michael said. "That's all."

They bundled her into her coat and walked her outside and got in a car. It was a good thing they were holding on to her, or she would have fallen. She sat in the back with Gerry, her head on his lap, and she liked that, but she didn't like the way the car shook on the bumpy streets. It made her head hurt more. She fell asleep in spite of it.

Gerry woke her soon after, and she knew from the way he called her name that he was afraid she had fainted again, or whatever it was that she had done. At least she didn't feel sick to her stomach anymore. They helped her out of the car, and there were bright lights all around, and some people she didn't know helped her lie down on a cart, and they pushed her inside.

She felt Gerry squeeze her hand and Aunt Sue pat her

shoulder before the doctors or nurses or whoever they were wheeled her down the hall. Rachel waved to let Gerry and Aunt Sue and Michael know that she was all right, and that she would see them soon. She hoped she would anyway.

A few minutes after Rachel was wheeled out of sight, a nurse came out and asked what their relationship was to the patient. Susanna told her that she was Rachel's aunt, and the woman asked her to come back to an office to fill out some admission forms, and she did, leaving Michael and Gerry in the waiting area, a small room separated from the hall by high partitions.

It was the first that Michael had been alone with his son for a long time, and he felt ill at ease. Though the dinner had gone well, Susanna had provided the lion's share of conversation. Now it was up to him.

"Quite a fall she took," he said. "Hope she doesn't have a concussion."

"Yeah. Me, too."

They were silent for a moment. "This girl...she means a lot to you, doesn't she?"

"Yeah. She does. She's pretty special. Never met anybody quite like her before."

Michael nodded. "Know the feeling."

"You mean Susanna?" Gerry asked, and Michael nodded uncomfortably. "I've nothing against her. She seems like a very good woman, and Rachel adores her."

"That's good, that's good." Michael nodded again. "Rachel seems like a very good person herself. Not too talkative, though, is she?"

"Usually more than she was tonight. She's been kind of funny today."

"She was a bit funny there afterwards. Didn't think there was all that much whiskey in those drinks."

"I think she was just a little...confused when she hit her head." Gerry's tone changed then, as though he was speaking of one thing but thinking about another. "Though sometimes it doesn't take much. Rachel's not very big, and she's thin. Women like that...well, it *doesn't* take much to get them to the point where they shouldn't..." Gerry let it trail off, but Michael knew what he meant, and finished it for him.

"Shouldn't drive," he said. "I know, I know what you're getting at, and that's fine. We never talked of it, and we should have. So maybe we should now. Your mother. Your mother was like that, thin and small."

"Yeah."

"Gerry..." Michael hunched over in his chair, letting his head hang, looking between his knees at the carpeted floor. "I am so sorry for what happened. If I could go back, I'd stop her. I've thought of it a thousand times, of what I should've done. But I was...just so angry, and proud."

"You're better off the way it is."

"I didn't *want* it this way, not to happen like that, you have to believe me."

"Why should I, Dad? You didn't love her. Did you?"

Michael tried to relax the clenching of his jaw. "You want the truth then? No. No, I didn't. I might've thought I did once, a long time ago before I knew what love was. But I didn't. Not then, and not when I got out of prison. But I stayed with her, and I tried to be good to her, to at least lead a civil life with her, and tried to make a good life for you."

"Why?"

"Why?"

"Yeah, why? If you didn't love her, if you didn't love my ma, why did you care about me then?"

Michael saw the tears in his son's eyes, and felt some enter his own, both in sympathy for his boy and in pity for himself. "I *loved* you. You were my *son*. You still are and always will be my boy. Even though I haven't always told you, I'm proud of what you've done and proud of who you are. You're your own man, no one else's. No one has claim on you without your say-so. I wasn't able to lead my own life like that, but you were.

"I'm so sorry for all I've done and haven't done. I tried to love your mother, Gerry, but I couldn't. It wasn't in me. And I *hated* myself for not being able to. But all that time, I never looked at another woman or let myself think about it. She was my wife, and if I couldn't love her...I could at least honor her."

He looked at his son with pleading in his eyes. "That was as good as I could do."

Gerry looked back at him, his lips in a firm line, but his face was red, and tears were running down both cheeks. For a long time he said nothing, then finally spoke.

"She loved you, though." His voice was harsh.

"I don't know, son. I don't know if she really did…"

"She *did*. When I was little, we'd go to see you every month, and she'd start getting excited a week before. And the day we went, she'd do up her makeup and her hair, and spend a long time deciding what to wear. And we'd go up with Gram and Old Tim, and we'd go in and get our hug and kiss, and I'd show you a drawing or a poem I'd done at school that I'd brought you, and then we'd just sit there and look at each other. Maybe talk a little about what happened in Galway that month, or what I was doing in school, but the silences were so much longer than the words, and I'd look at Ma and I'd look at you, and I'd see *nothing*. Nothing between you, except for the hope in her eyes that this time would be different, this time you'd tell her how beautiful she looked or how much you missed her or *something*, something that would let her know that you gave a damn about her, that's all. Just a little something to get her through."

Gerry stopped and took several deep breaths, lowering his head and rubbing the tears from his face. "But it never came, Dad. It never came. And when you finally came home, well, that was the worst of all. Because she couldn't lie to herself anymore. She couldn't pretend that far away she had a man who loved her. Being *civil* to her wasn't enough. Not for her, not for me."

They sat, not looking at each other. "I don't know what to say," Michael finally said. He thought his voice had never sounded so small. "I could say I didn't know, but I suppose I did. I…I just don't know."

They were seated, facing away from each other, when Susanna returned. Michael looked up at her and smiled, but her face creased with concern when she saw the pair of them. They looked like two boys who'd been caught fighting by the teacher.

"How's Rachel?" Gerry said as both he and Michael stood up.

"Don't know yet," Susanna answered. "She's with the doctors. I just took care of the paperwork and called David at his hotel. He wasn't there, but I left a message. Look…is something wrong? I mean, other than what happened to Rachel?"

They spoke simultaneously, Michael saying "No…well…" while Gerry said "Well…no…"

Susanna laughed, but there was no humor in it. "Like father, like son, eh? What's the problem?"

"It's…kind of personal," Gerry said.

"Well, I didn't think it had anything to do with the state of the Euro," Susanna said. Michael looked sheepish, while Gerry appeared equally embarrassed but angry. "Is there any way I can help?"

"I doubt it," Gerry said. He looked at his father. "It's been a long time coming."

"I, uh…" Michael cleared his throat. "I think it's something we just need to talk out."

"Yeah, right. Like that'll help," Gerry said.

"It often does," Susanna said. "Listen, I don't pretend to know all about the problems between the two of you, but I think if you're able just to hear what the other one is saying, it would be good."

Gerry shook his head. "We've heard already."

"Not enough, it seems," Susanna said.

"Look, what do you care?"

"I care because I care about both of you, Gerry. I have…an emotional investment in your family. I like peace in general, and I'd like nothing better than to see peace between the two of you. Things seemed to be going well tonight—"

"That," Gerry said, "was a polite façade. The same kind that I've had with this man my whole life. It was a fine example of…" He searched for the word, and smiled coldly at Michael when he found it. "*Civility*. That's what's important, isn't it? Civility, if you can't come up with anything more."

"Then for the love of God let's *start* with that," Michael said. "Let's start with civility, Gerry, and talk civilly. But let's just *talk*."

Gerry turned away and sat down again. "I don't know that this is the time for that."

"You've nothing *but* time," Susanna said. "They're going to be testing Rachel for quite a while. And since we're all determined to stay, you two can either talk or read old magazines. But I can't think of anything that would please Rachel more than to know that you two were trying to bring peace between yourselves. Now I can go down—"

"Miss Cassidy?" The nurse who had spoken to Susanna appeared from around a partition. "Sorry, but would you mind coming back into the office again? There's just a bit more information we need."

She turned and disappeared. Susanna looked at the two men, Gerry sitting, arms dangling between his legs, and Michael standing, looking at his son. "Don't wait for me," she said, and followed the nurse.

It took Susanna only a minute to answer the woman's questions, and when she was finished, she asked if there was another waiting area. The nurse looked at her curiously, but showed her to a small lounge at the opposite end of the building. "I'll be either here or in the other waiting area if you need me," Susanna told her.

Perhaps the best thing was to just leave Michael and Gerry alone. In the short time that Susanna had previously been with the nurse, it was obvious that the issues between the two men had come to the surface. Was it too much to hope that they would continue to talk in her absence?

The two of them probably hadn't been alone in years. Well, now they were, and instead of sitting there ignoring each other, she hoped that their separate demons would continue to reveal themselves.

Susanna sat alone for an hour. She thought often of Rachel, but since she knew that her niece was getting the best possible care, she thought more about the two men. It was impossible not to, since she already loved one and was starting to love, in a different way, the other. Despite Gerry's placid exterior, he was so sensitive and in so much pain that it was all Susanna could do not to mother him.

At last, she got up to buy coffee from a machine. When she finished it, she walked down the hall toward the waiting area where she had left Michael and Gerry. As she got closer, she heard their voices, and she stopped in the hall and listened.

They were speaking softly, first one, then the other, and though she couldn't hear what they said to one another, they didn't sound angry. Susanna remained in the hall, unwilling to interrupt or to eavesdrop, but unable to turn around and leave. So, she stood in an attitude of casual waiting that she hoped would convince any staff passersby.

None came, and she perched for another ten minutes before she heard a sound other than quiet talking. It was harsh at first, as though one of the men was choking. Then she realized that it was sobbing.

She moved closer, and now she could hear that both were crying. Words came intermittently between the sobs, and when she finally looked around the partition, she saw that Michael and Gerry were sitting side by side, weeping. Michael's arm was around his son, and Gerry's head was against his father's shoulder.

It seemed to Susanna, as she felt tears pool in her own eyes, that they wept not for themselves, but for each other, as though each drew forgiveness from his own tears and applied it like a balm to the other. Susanna felt certain that it was the first time these two had held each other in many years. Though the act would not miraculously make everything right between them, it was a start. Everything had to have a start.

She walked down the hall, giving them privacy for a few more minutes, and time to let the tears dry. After all, men were still men.

In another ten minutes she wandered back into the waiting area. They were still talking quietly, but she saw no tears in their eyes, and they both smiled guardedly when she came in. "Where've you been?" Michael asked.

"Around. I went for a little walk through the halls to keep awake." She looked from one to the other. "You two all right?"

"Getting along," Michael said.

"Talking anyway," Gerry added.

Susanna nodded but said nothing. They hadn't needed her. All they'd needed was some time alone together. An hour's talk wasn't going to remedy decades of separation, but they had at least spoken together and cried together, and they would speak again.

"Shouldn't we have heard something by now?" Gerry asked.

"They're putting her though a lot of tests," Susanna said, "and that takes time. I'm sure she's fine."

"Don't worry," Michael told Gerry. "They'll look after her."

A short time later a white-coated man came into the waiting area. "Miss Cassidy?" he said.

"How is she?" asked Gerry, standing up.

"She's going to be fine," the doctor said. "How about if I take Miss Cassidy back and talk to her, her being next of kin, and then she can fill you in." It was a statement, not a suggestion, and Susanna followed the doctor as he turned with his clipboard and walked down the hall. She gave an apologetic look to the two men and followed.

"I'm Doctor Dunn, Miss Cassidy," said the man as she caught up to him. He led her to a small office and offered her a seat. "Well, the long and short of it is," he said, "that she's got a slight concussion from when she fell. Nothing that won't right itself with a bit of rest. We've run a series of tests on her to see why she passed out. So far—I say so far, mind—there doesn't seem to be any physiological cause. Has she been very upset about anything lately?"

"Actually, yes. Some big emotional ups and downs."

"Ah. Well, that could account for it, I suppose. I got the impression that she's been short of sleep and running on raw energy as well. I want to keep her a day for observation. By then we can get a full medical history from her doctor in the states, and all the test results will be back. I really don't see anything suspicious, though there are some things we can't rule out quite yet." He spread his hands and shrugged. "Questions?"

Susanna thought for a moment. "Just one thing. When you drew her blood, did you type her? I'm just thinking, in case it would be something more serious, maybe I and the others could donate for her."

"Well," said Doctor Dunn, checking his clipboard, "she's AB positive, which is—"

"Universal recipient, yes, that's good."

"I wouldn't worry about that, though. I can't foresee a situation in which she'd need a transfusion. Anything else?"

"No. Thank you. Could we see her?"

"She's sleeping now. It'd probably be best to let her rest. I understand her father's in town?"

"Yes, I called his hotel, but he's out. They have the message, so I expect him shortly."

When she rejoined Michael and Gerry, she told them what the doctor had said, then added, "Just on the long chance that Rachel would need a transfusion, would either of you be willing to donate blood?"

Gerry nodded. "In a minute. Don't know what type I am, though."

"Type O, same as me," Michael said, and smiled. "You had a blood test in school one time, and I remembered. So, we can give any other type our blood, and that includes Rachel, whatever she is."

"Absolutely right," Susanna said. "Thanks."

She sat down and let out a deep sigh. God, but she felt better. Even the sight of David Oliver entering the waiting lounge like a freight train didn't upset her.

"Where *is* she?" David said, barreling up to Susanna. "What *happened?*"

"Everything's okay," Susanna said as she stood up. "She's sleeping now and she's fine. She passed out after dinner and fell and hit her head."

"*What?*"

"She's got a slight concussion, but no permanent damage. They want to keep her a day for observation."

"Well, why the hell did she pass out? What's with *that?*" David made Michael and Gerry part of his inquisition as well, and when he turned his attention to them, Susanna looked at Michael and jerked her head toward the door.

Michael spoke. "Uh, I think Gerry and I'll go outside for a minute, for a, a..." She could see him thinking, *for a smoke? For a drink?* "For a minute," he finished lamely, and retreated with his son.

"What's going on?" David asked her. "*Why* did she *faint?*"

"The doctor thinks she was emotionally upset."

"Jesus, Rachel's *always* emotionally upset about something or other, and she never fainted that I knew about."

"Well, this was something special. Something that *you* knew about, too. It was the reason I think you've been trying to break up Rachel and Gerry."

His eyes narrowed. "Now look, I—"

"How did you find out?" Susanna said in a tone that told David she wasn't playing games. "Did Kate Quinn tell you about it?"

David's eyes flicked away for a second, then came back to Susanna. "Yeah. She told me enough that I was able to figure it out."

"And then you started figuring months, didn't you?"

"You know I did."

"And what did you figure?"

"I figured that there was a definite possibility Rachel wasn't my daughter. And if she wasn't, then she was…"

"She was dating her half-brother."

David let out a long breath. "Yeah. Dating. That's one way to put it."

"I *thought* that you knew, and I thought that was why you were trying to break them up. I told Rachel about it—I figured she ought to know—but I guess I shouldn't have. Still, if I hadn't, I wouldn't know now that Michael is definitely not her father."

"What?"

"I just learned from the doctor that Rachel's blood type is AB. Then I sneakily learned that Michael's is O. Now I know Julia's type was B, because mine is too, and I donated directly to her when she was sick. I don't know how much you know about blood types, but O plus B doesn't equal AB. What type are you?"

"I…don't know…wait, I have a card in my wallet from when I gave some blood for an employee a few years back." He pulled out his wallet almost frantically, tugging cards from their various pockets.

"It's A," Susanna said calmly. "When you *find* it, it'll be A."

"Wait, I know it's here..." His thumb riffled through still another short stack of cards, and finally he stopped at one with a hospital symbol on it. There, typed on the front, was the letter A.

"Oh, Jesus..." David said quietly. "Oh Jesus, I don't believe it."

"A plus B equals AB. That simple." She put her hand on his shoulder. "Nothing to worry about. She's fine, David, and so are you. Everything is just fine."

To Susanna's surprise, David was trembling, and she realized he was crying, his head down, his eyes closed. She didn't know if it was out of relief that Rachel was all right, or out of relief that she was his daughter after all, but when Susanna saw his tears, she wanted to make it easier for him, and she lied.

"David, listen. I don't think that Julia even slept with him. All she told me was that a long time ago, before she was married, she was with a boy in Ireland for a very short time, and she was never able to forget those days, when she was so young. She never tried to contact him again. And she married you."

"I know," he said, his voice low and cracked. He straightened up and cleared his throat, and refused to acknowledge his tears by wiping them away. "I'll come and see Rachel in the morning," he said. "And then I'll fly back home. Whatever she needs as far as money goes—for the hospital and all—I'll take care of tomorrow." He smiled. "Gotta look after my little girl." David stood up and adjusted his topcoat. "Goodnight, Susanna. And thanks."

He straightened his shoulders and walked out the door without looking back. Susanna watched him go, and thought about how this had been everyone's night to cry but hers, and then wondered why the hell should she be any different. So, she sat and cried from relief and happiness and love and the foolish coincidences and tosses of fate, that canny but benign juggler who can hurl us down and then lift us back up again, higher than before.

CHAPTER 20

Susanna, Michael, and Gerry all stayed at the hospital through the night. At eight o'clock a nurse told them that Rachel was awake and wanted to see them. They found her propped up in bed, wearing a hospital gown, and looking pale and small. Susanna kissed Rachel's cheek and squeezed her hand.

Rachel said she was feeling better, and apologized for the wreck she had made of the evening, but both Michael and Gerry blew it away. "What's important is that you're feeling better," Michael said, and Rachel nodded as if in agreement. There was still, however, desperation in the girl's face, and Susanna knew she had to do something about it immediately.

"Would you two gentlemen mind leaving us alone for a moment?" she asked, and, although the men looked at her curiously, they shuffled toward the door as though uneasy in the presence of woman talk. When the door closed, Susanna drew a chair up next to Rachel, sat down, and took her hand.

"What?" Rachel said. "Did they find anything? Anything bad?"

"Actually, something good. The thing you've been worrying about?" She lowered her voice. "You can stop worrying. David is your father."

Rachel's face was a mixture of confusion and hope. "But... how? Are you sure?"

Susanna told her how she found out, and that there wasn't a chance that Michael Lynch was her sire. Rachel leaned back and closed her eyes, and Susanna saw tears of relief coming from them. "Your turn," Susanna said.

"What?"

"To cry. You were really upset yesterday, weren't you?"

"I couldn't think of anything else," Rachel said, each word coming out as a little sob. "I thought I was going crazy."

"Do you think that's why you passed out?"

"Oh, Aunt Sue, I worked myself up into such a state..." She shook her head and covered her eyes with her hands.

"You know, honey...you're like me. For all our tough hides, we're romantics, even when it comes to tragedy. Whatever happens, we imagine that it's the worst or the best, nothing in between. And sometimes that makes us worry when we don't have to, and other times it makes us happier than we should have the sense to be. But that's the way we are, and there's no getting around it. I guess there are worse ways we could be."

Rachel's arms went out the way they did when she was a little girl, and Susanna knew what she wanted, and hugged her, letting the girl bury her face into her chest. "Oh, Aunt Sue..."

"Yes...yes, I know..."

After a while, Susanna went into the hall and told Gerry he could go back in. "Time to call it a night then," Michael said when they were alone. "I'll get you back to your flat, and if I hurry, I can still make Mass."

"Oh, but don't you want me to come back and clean up your place? All that food that was left out, and the tablecloth..."

"You know my policy on that."

"It's just a tablecloth, right?"

"Absolutely. Besides, no more harm's going to come to it now."

"I should've put it in cold water before we left."

Michael laughed. "Ah, you women. Tell you what—your car's at my place, so I'll take you back there, and if you want to mess about, fine and dandy, but I've got to shave and shower and dress and go to Mass."

"For fear of your immortal soul?"

"For fear of gettin' me arse kicked by me ma. Now let's go."

Back at Michael's, he got himself cleaned up while Susanna first filled the sink with cold water and dunked the tablecloth in it, then made a pot of coffee. After she'd taken a cup into

Michael's room and had a few sips of her own, she put on an apron and started cleaning up.

The remnants of the dinner had not weathered the night well, and the first thing she did was to get rid of it all, wrapping it in plastic bags and throwing it in the dust bin. She had put the dishes into the sink to soak when Michael came out freshly dressed and shaven, not looking at all as though he'd stayed awake the night before.

"I can do this when I get back, y'know," he said.

"You run along," she said, giving him a kiss, "and everything will be all tidy when you return. Except the tablecloth."

Her words proved all too true. The tablecloth was ruined, but she left it in cold water to soak, hoping for a miracle. When the dishes were washed and put away, Susanna decided to take a brief nap before going back to her place to change, and lay on the bed and closed her eyes.

She was awakened by Michael's arm around her. "Oh my God, what time is it?" she said, sitting up.

"About twelve-thirty. Have a nice nap?"

"Too long. Here you are all nice and clean and I'm still wearing my flop-sweat dress from last night."

"Go grab a shower then," he said, reaching around and unzipping her dress.

"I don't have anything else to wear."

"All the better."

When she came out of the bathroom after her shower, Michael had undressed and crawled under the bedcovers. She thought he was sleeping, but when she got in next to him, she found that he was anything but tired.

They made love slowly, sweetly, and lazily, then lay in each other's arms. "*Now*," Michael said, "I think I could go for a little nap."

They slept for an hour, and when they awoke mid-afternoon Susanna told Michael about the little drama that had occurred the night before, and how Susanna, Rachel, and David's concern about Rachel's parentage had been put to rest.

"You know," Michael said when she finished, "the thought crossed my mind, but I didn't know how old Rachel was and to tell the truth I was afraid to ask. I'm thankful she's not mine... not that I don't think she's a lovely girl and all."

Susanna laughed. "I understand. I'm sure Gerry would be relieved, too, not that he ever has to know about last night's trauma. And speaking of trauma," she added, "I have to head North next Thursday."

"North?" he said, and his tone changed.

She nodded. "I'll be speaking and participating in some seminars at Magee in Derry. And doing interviews of the Republican ex-prisoner community. One of the Coiste groups arranged it for me."

"What are you going to talk to *them* about?"

"Well, I want to survey their attitudes about the peace process."

"And how do you plan to do that?" Michael sounded intent, but she wondered if there wasn't also a trace of hostility, or perhaps defensiveness.

"Interview a number of them and find out what they think, first of all. I don't want to make the mistake of stereotyping them, assuming they all feel a certain way because of their experience. Then see what effect they've had on their neighbors, their colleagues, and how that in turn affects the community at large."

"You've never talked to *me* about it," he said, looking at the ceiling.

"I guess I've...I've never thought of you as a *subject*. And I always thought if you wanted to talk about it, I'd let you bring it up. If you'd like me to interview you, I'd be glad to."

"No, probably best not. You have to keep that distance, don't you? Your objectivity?"

"I...*am* somewhat closer to you than I'll be to my other interviewees."

"And let's keep it that way," he said, smiling and putting a hand on her bare hip so that she nestled into him.

"You know," she said, "I won't be able to get down to Galway next weekend, and probably not the one after that either. I was wondering if maybe you'd like to come up to Derry on one of those weekends. I'd ask you for both, but I don't know if I could be that lucky."

"To Derry…" He lay there, not speaking. Her back was to him, so she couldn't see his face. "Maybe. I'll have to see. How busy the pub is and all."

"You have family up there, don't you?"

"Just my Aunt Brigid. She's still in Derry."

"Mmm. Well, I'll be in a flat up there that belongs to a prof on sabbatical, so your staying would be no problem. If you can get away, of course."

"Right. Right…"

Susanna was disappointed. She had expected more of a positive response, and wondered if his lack of enthusiasm was for her or for the North. "I'll still be here a few more days," she said. "Let's enjoy them while we can."

She pressed closer against him, and he put an arm around her. His hand was warm in hers, and she put his fingers against her lips, wanting to hold on to them forever, but suddenly afraid. It was as though something had slipped between the two of them, and she wasn't sure exactly what it was, but feared that it might be the past encroaching on the present.

Let's enjoy them while we can.

Michael thought that Susanna's words had an air of finality about them. Throughout their time together, he had been thinking long and hard about the future of his relationship with this wonderful woman, and the doubts and concerns that he had recently expressed to his mother were starting to come to the fore.

Eventually, Susanna was going to return to the United States. Michael couldn't imagine a scenario in which she would stay in Ireland, no matter how much she loved him. The odds were long of her getting a teaching position at one of the universities. As she had told him, the colleges both in the North and the South were welcoming enough to guests, but seldom to the extent of accepting them as full colleagues. If Susanna couldn't teach, what would she do? Wait on tables at the Banshee? Get a job in a bank or a shop?

There was no way he could ask her to give up her career. He knew what it meant to her, and she had struggled too hard and too long to abandon it. But at the same time, he couldn't imagine himself leaving his home and going with her to America. Things deeper than family bound him to Ireland, and the thought of leaving it behind seemed impossible, even for the woman he loved.

That he did love her he had no doubt. He had never felt this way about anyone before. In his youth, he had been too foolish to love, during his long stay in prison he had not had the opportunity, and through his even longer marriage he had not had the permission, neither from God nor from his own sense of loyalty to the woman whose son he had fathered.

Michael had feared he had forgotten *how* to love, and when Susanna appeared in his life, he had taken it as a miracle. To have these feelings about another person was the greatest gift God had given him, even if it had come late in his life. Now he feared it would be wrenched away, and he had almost come to the point where he thought it necessary to prepare himself for the inevitable break.

Perhaps her sojourn in the North would make things easier. Michael had not gone back to Derry since he had been freed from prison twenty years before. He had no intention of doing so now, nor would he until the day the six remaining counties of the North banded together with the rest of the island and became a nation once again, as the old song had it.

That was the only way his poor land would ever know peace. That was why he couldn't leave, not yet, perhaps not ever. That was why, even as he held in his arms the only woman he had ever loved, he would have to deny the love he felt for her, the love that now made him clasp her tightly and bury his face in her hair, drowning in it as in a glorious dream from which he prayed he would never awaken, aware all the while that it was a dream and that it must end, like all dreams do.

CHAPTER 21

After she left Michael, Susanna went home and changed her clothes, then called the hospital. Rachel was still in her room, with Gerry in attendance, and was feeling much better.

"They're going to let me go tomorrow morning," she told Susanna, "after all the test results come back. I feel terrific, though. Ate a huge lunch, and it all stayed down. God, I'm so sorry about last night."

"It's all right, no apologies necessary. Michael was far more concerned about you than anything else. Was your dad there today?"

"Yeah. I couldn't believe it, he was like a different guy. He arranged to have all the medical bills taken care of, and he told me to stay in Ireland as long as I want. As soon as he gets back, he's doing a wire transfer to me. He didn't say how much, but he implied it would be plenty."

"When's he going back to the states?" Susanna asked.

"He's *gone*. I had a ticket back today and I was gonna just blow it off, try and change it to a later date? But we got it transferred to him instead. I don't know how he managed it with all the security stuff that's going on, but you know my dad."

"So, he's okay with Gerry?"

"Um, well..." Susanna could tell that Rachel was reluctant to be specific with Gerry in the room. "Actually, yeah. He said that whatever I wanted was fine with him, and he, uh, seemed to approve...of, like, whatever, you know?"

"I get the idea. So, will you be staying at the hostel indefinitely?"

"Um, no, actually I'm moving in with a friend." Susanna nearly laughed at the lightness in her niece's voice.

"Ah, the one in the room there, no doubt."

"No doubt."

"Well, it sounds to me like you're in good hands, so I'll just wish you a happy and peaceful evening. Have a good sleep."

"I will, and Aunt Sue? Thanks for everything. Really. I love you."

"I love you, too, sweetie. I'll see you tomorrow."

Susanna was relieved as she hung up, both because of the happy outcome of the previous night's crisis, and because David had returned to the states. She thought that he was probably relieved to be returning, too, and relieved that his adolescent quest for her had been futile. Now he was a free man, and his roving eye could lead him wherever he liked without guilt.

His happiness was obvious from the way he had treated his daughter, and it was about time, too. Rachel had seldom asked for anything from her parents, and about all that she had gotten from them was grief. She deserved a little bonus.

Susanna sat back in her chair and sighed. Both David and Rachel were on their way to happy endings, and that fact made her wonder about her own situation with Michael. She was concerned about the distance she had sensed in him that afternoon. His reticence to discuss his past and his feelings about the situation in Ireland didn't surprise her. Many ex-prisoners she had talked to showed the same reluctance. Still, she had hoped that Michael would trust her enough to open up more. After all, he claimed to love her.

So then why hadn't he been anxious to join her in Derry? Had his experience there been so crushing that he couldn't bear to return? It was certainly a possibility, and if it was true, it gave Michael a vulnerability that she hadn't seen in him before. She would simply have to accept it, and perhaps work subtly to change it.

It would be difficult to break away from Derry in the busy weeks to come, but she would try for the sake of their relationship. It was too precious to her to risk losing, and even the thought of it brought a metallic dryness to her mouth and a sickness to her stomach. Now that she had found her man, she would not let distance, either geographical or emotional, pull them apart.

During the next few days, Susanna divided her time between Michael and preparation for her time in Derry. Her days were spent in the university library, and her evenings with Michael. He seemed much the same as ever, but whenever she brought up the subject of her Derry sojourn, he grew quiet or changed the subject.

Wednesday night, the evening before she left, they had dinner at the restaurant where they had first eaten together. She had told him the day before that she wouldn't be able to spend the night with him, since she had to get an early start for the North, and he had been understanding about her decision. Still, as the dinner drew to an end, he seemed sad.

Susanna reached across the table and took his hand. "You know," she said, "even if you can't break away to come up and see me, I'll be back on Friday the 28th. That's only a little over two weeks away. We can make beautiful music at the session and more at your flat, wink wink, nudge nudge."

The little joke made him smile. "I know. I've just gotten used to having you around. I'll miss you."

"And I'll miss you. But it won't be long. And you can call me, and I certainly expect to call you, so get ready to have your ear talked off."

He smiled again and nodded.

When he drove her back to the guest house, she invited him up. No sooner had the door closed than he had taken her in his arms, kissing her hungrily and more savagely than ever before. His intensity frightened her, but she made herself respond, and in another moment, she didn't have to pretend. She needed him as deeply as he did her, and they pulled and tugged at each other's clothing until they stood together naked and trembling.

They staggered to the bed and fell upon it, and his hands and mouth searched and worshipped her until he joined with her, and they moved and shuddered together at the strength they shared. Then, their frenzy tamed, they stayed as they were, hips and arms and legs entangled and bound, each the willing

captive of the other. Susanna felt as though they were one creature, held together by love and the passion it created.

Michael's gentle breathing warmed the hollow of her throat,
and her hand rested on the smoothness of his hip. She felt as
though she could have remained that way forever, but, just as
she almost fell asleep, she felt him withdraw from her and she
gave a quick gasp at the sensation.

"I'm sorry," he said, and kissed her lips gently. "I must go
now and let you sleep. You've got a big day ahead of you."

"You can stay. I'd like you to stay. I can still get up early, and
you can sleep as late as you like."

"No. It's best if I go." He dressed in the dim light from the
doorway alcove, and when he was finished, he leaned over the
bed and kissed her again, then held her for a long time. "I'll see
you soon," he said, then walked toward the door.

"Michael..." she said, getting out of the bed and running
naked to him. She took his face between her hands and held it
so that he looked directly down into her eyes. "I love you. I do."

Though he smiled, she was shocked to see the pain in it. "I
love you, too, Susanna. Goodbye, my love." He took her hands
away, kissed her again, and walked out, closing the door softly
behind him.

She stood there, starting to feel cold, thinking that something was wrong, but not knowing what it was. She would see
him in two weeks. Did the prospect of that brief a separation
bring him so much pain, or was it something else?

Susanna determined to call him frequently. She would
write him letters as well, taking her time to say what needed to
be said, giving him something that he could hold in his hand
and read and reread, physical proof of the way she felt toward
him. And if she could get back to Galway earlier, she would try
and do so, though it seemed doubtful.

Whatever she could do to show this man how much she
loved him, she would.

She arrived at Magee College late the following afternoon and
was greeted by several faculty members and students who
treated her as an honored and welcome guest. Irish hospitality

was always first rank, and the academic version was even more so, so long as one stayed within certain bounds. Irish academics did not relish an outsider telling them how to run their country, no matter how august and respected that outsider might be. It was a lesson Susanna learned early on, and had always remembered.

After a small dinner held in her honor at a pub, one of the faculty members took her to the flat where she'd be staying. It was far nicer than she expected, and as she settled down on the living room sofa, she had to confess to herself that, despite Michael's absence, she was looking forward to the next few weeks of research, discussion, and debate concerning the ongoing peace process on this side of the border. Her days would be busy with classes, seminars, and working with the students generously assigned to her as her survey assistants. Her evenings and the next two weekends would be spent interviewing ex-prisoners and those in their neighborhoods.

Perhaps the busyness of the time would keep her from constantly missing Michael. She hoped so. The thought of him made her lonely, and she dialed his number on her cell phone.

The answering machine picked up after four rings, but she hung up without leaving a message. She didn't want him to hear a taped voice. He was probably at the pub, but Susanna didn't want to disturb him there. She needed to hear him when he could speak without others listening, so she got a shower and climbed into bed with a book and her phone, planning to call him later. However, the long drive and the socializing had worn her out, and she fell asleep reading. She woke up at two in the morning, far too late, she told herself, to call and awaken Michael. She would talk to him tomorrow.

At two in the morning, Michael was lying awake in his bedroom, the small television on without sound, just to keep him company. He had been working in the pub, but had gone home at eleven. There was no message on the answering machine, and he had hesitated to call Susanna, afraid that he might wake her after her long day of travel.

Sleep had come hard, and by 1:30 he had given up. He

wished she would have called, but there was nothing for it now. He finally drifted off to sleep shortly after three, the television still on, silently throwing shadows and light across his gaunt face.

Susanna talked to Michael the next morning. She called him at eight-thirty, a half hour before her first formal meeting with faculty members. He sounded drowsy, but insisted that she hadn't awakened him. The conversation was one-sided, with Susanna telling him about her drive up, the events of the night before, and the warmth with which she'd been greeted.

"The flat I'm in is really nice," she told him. "There'd be plenty of room if you're able to come up."

"It doesn't look too good," he said. "Finn and Kev are both off this weekend for one thing and the other, so we're shorthanded."

"Oh. Well, maybe the weekend after?"

"Maybe. We'll see."

Michael didn't sound enthusiastic, so Susanna didn't push it. She felt certain now that it wasn't her company he was declining, but a trip to the North. Maybe he just wasn't ready to return to Derry. Maybe he never would be.

"Well, I'll see you the evening of the 28th if not before," Susanna said when she'd told him all her news.

"Right. I'll look forward to it. Really...I miss you."

"I miss you, too. But we'll be together soon."

"Take care of yourself." He sounded as though he meant it.

"I will. Of course, I will. I love you, Michael."

"I love you. Goodbye, Susanna."

The day flew by, as Susanna tried to commit to memory the names of all the faculty members and students she was meeting. She fell into bed exhausted Friday night, and the next morning at 9:00 she met her contact in Derry at the office of one of the Coiste groups whose function was to aid Republican ex-prisoners.

The Coiste representative, a woman in her mid-sixties named Margaret Dolan, gave Susanna a list of names and addresses of ex-prisoners willing to be interviewed. Mrs. Dolan was kind enough to accompany Susanna on her visits that day, easing the way with introductions, but leaving Susanna alone with the ex-prisoners.

Susanna had requested a wide variety of people to speak to, and that was what Mrs. Dolan had prepared, even though Susanna only interviewed three people that day, and four the next. The lengthy list included some who had been free for as long as thirty years, and some who had been released only a few years before as a result of the Good Friday Agreement. Most were of the lower classes, though a few lived in solidly middle-class neighborhoods. There was even one woman on the list.

Their opinions were far from being in lockstep. Some felt that the current negotiations between the disagreeing parties were headed in the right direction, while others thought it was all talk, and that other tactics needed to be used. There were a few who said they wouldn't be content until Ireland was united again, and that violent resistance was still the only way to achieve that end.

Susanna neither agreed nor disagreed. She merely listened and recorded, and used her skills and training to ask further questions to clarify and further define her subjects' views.

Her student assistants joined her the following week, during both the interviews and the follow-up work of categorizing the opinions and placing them in a geographical context within the various neighborhoods of the city. A wider canvass of others within those neighborhoods would follow to determine the characteristics and quality of the sample.

This regimen, along with the numerous classes and seminars in which Susanna participated, gave her little leisure time. Though she could have spread out the interviews over a longer period, she felt a sense of urgency, partly because of her separation from Michael, and partly because of her own nature.

Susanna was, as her mother had told her many times, a workaholic, and when there was something to do, she did it with as much energy and speed as possible. This research would take months, she knew, and creating a presentable paper from it would take just as long again. Her time in Ireland was limited, and she admitted to herself that it could be that as much as her desire to be with Michael again that was pressing her onward. Still, no matter how quickly she worked, her schedule was set, and there was no way that she was going to be able to return to Galway until the very end of the month.

She called Michael daily, and wrote him every other day. Her letters were filled with expressions of love and with her memories of the days they had spent together, things they had done, places they had gone.

When I think of you, she wrote, *and I think of you constantly, I love to remember you as you stood smiling on that ledge at the Cliffs of Moher, the sun shining in your hair, and you holding out your hand and urging me to step across that gap to you, and how easy it was when I decided to do it, and how you were there for me just like I knew you would be. When I stepped over to you, I felt as though I was flying, and that nothing could pull me down as long as you were there with me.*

Michael wrote to her as well. His letters were not as openly affectionate as hers, though he told her that he loved her and missed her. *I miss you <u>bitterly,</u>* he had written in his first letter, and she thought the underlined word was a strange one to use. Was he bitter about her leaving, or about his inability to join her, or something else entirely?

It was a delicate line Susanna had to walk in her calls and letters. She wanted to assure Michael that she loved him deeply, yet wanted to avoid pressuring him into any decision about the future of their relationship. She could scarcely believe that they had been together only three weeks before she had left for Derry. She felt as though she had known him forever, or at least for those thirty missing years. Even though she couldn't imagine a life without him, she felt that this brief separation was of greater significance to Michael than it was to her. She found herself hoping that it was because he had never really known love before, and the separation from it was unaccustomedly painful to him.

But what concerned her more was that she might be wrong, that his bitterness and pain were caused by something else, something lodged in a secret part of him that Susanna had not yet seen. Three weeks, after all, was not that much time in which to get to know a person, and she had to admit to herself that her sense of having known him longer might be nothing more than a romantic illusion.

Still, she hoped that his current black mood was only the result of their separation. If so, she could dispel it easily enough when she saw him again.

CHAPTER 22

This is what it will be like without her. This is what I have to look forward to.

There were times when Michael Lynch felt that such thoughts were stupid. They were cowardly and unmanly and full of self-pity. But there were other times when he thought that they were only practical, that he had to buttress himself against the circumstances that would eventually separate him from Susanna Cassidy.

He could not conceive of happy endings. Such things had been alien to him. From the death of his father to his own imprisonment, first in Long Kesh and then in his loveless marriage, life had been something to endure, leavened with the infrequent rounds of music or fellowship with friends. The fact that he had finally found someone he loved and who seemed to love him in return seemed so improbable as to make him doubt the truth of it.

At least he now had the beginnings of a friendship with his son, and that would make it easier to bear when what he thought of as inevitable happened. But he wondered if even his relationship with Gerry would continue to grow.

God, was there any way he could be *more* pessimistic? Well, at least with pessimism, when the worst happened, he wouldn't be taken by surprise.

He concentrated on the music he was playing, and tried to banish his sour thoughts. This, after all, was one of those good moments, of companionship and making music, even if Susanna had not yet arrived. He hoped that when he saw her tonight all of his fatalistic fancies would vanish, and he could look ahead to a day when he could be with her always.

The tune ended, and the others set down their instruments, ready for a break for stout and conversation. Kate Quinn, he was glad to see, was once again the way she had been when he was married to Siobhan, friendly but not overly attentive. She seemed to have accepted the fact that he and Susanna were together for good. Now if only *he* could accept it—and believe it—as easily.

Michael went behind the bar and drew himself a Guinness, then went over to old Dermot Rooney, who was gesturing to him from his usual place along the wall. "Where's that pretty woman of yours?" Rooney asked him. "Thought she was going to come play tonight."

"She'll be here. Called just a bit ago to say she'd be late."

"Up in Derry, is she?"

"Aye. At the university."

"Bright woman. *Fearful* bright. And beautiful...and plays like an angel. So, what are your intentions with that one then?"

"Intentions?"

"Aye. Gonna marry her, are you? Be a fool not to, in my opinion."

"Don't recall asking for it."

"You got it, nonetheless. Why, what's stopping you?"

Michael paused a moment, then thought what the hell. "That'd be fine, wouldn't it? A university professor and a bar-man. Y'think she'll stop her teaching to wipe your beer spills?"

"Who says she's got to stop? Go back with her to America."

"Oh, and what would I do in America?"

"Pick potatoes or pick your nose, what's it to me?" Rooney said. "They don't have pubs in America? That's not what I hear from my cousin Joe. America's full o' pubs."

"I don't know any. Besides, I've never been to America."

"Well, a change of scene'd do you good. That's the trouble with people—they get settled in and they're goddamned *afraid* to go anywhere else, take a chance, make a change. Or they're too lazy."

"And where've you lived all your life, Dermot?" Michael asked.

"Galway, but only because I was too lazy. Not afraid like you."

Michael frowned at the old man. "What the hell do you mean, afraid?"

"Don't ask me. You know yourself, Michael Lynch."

Michael had just opened his mouth to argue with the man, though unsure of what he was going to say, when he heard his name called from the bar. When he turned, Kevin was holding up the telephone. "I'll deal with you later," Michael told Dermot, who responded by rudely blowing air between his lips to make a horse-like whinny.

Michael stepped behind the bar, took the phone, and put a finger in his free ear to drown the voices of the pub. "Hello?"

"It's me." Michael instantly recognized the voice of his cousin Malachy. "Got to see you."

"Where are you?"

"Here in Galway. I want you to pick me up. Meet me out on the Dublin Road in the parking lot of the sports ground, the big one right across from the Institute of Technology. Will you come?"

"What's this all about?"

"Tell you when you get here. I'll be parked in the back, away from the lights. One more thing—can you get the key to the cottage? That old one?"

"Old Tim's cottage? Yeah, I've got a key for it on my ring. But what do—"

"Look, just come, all right? And hurry?"

"Well…yeah, sure."

There was a click, and the line went dead.

"Got to go out," Michael told Kevin as he hung up the receiver. From the other end of the bar, Molly looked at him curiously, but he said nothing to her, only grabbed his coat and headed out the back door.

He jog-trotted through the streets until he reached his car parked in front of his townhouse, then drove up the Lough Atalia Road with the lake on his right and headed east on the Dublin Road until he reached the car park. A small car, its lights off, sat far in the back, and Michael pulled up next to it.

Malachy was sitting inside, but got out as soon as Michael opened his door. "Stay in," Malachy said. "We're going now." He locked his car doors and climbed in next to Michael, setting an athletic bag on the floor in front of him. "What you waitin' for, let's go."

"Where to?"

"Told you, I want to go to the cottage. Drive close as we can. I'll walk the rest of the way."

Michael headed down the road and turned right onto the Old Dublin Road for a short way, until the narrow lane appeared that led to Roscam and the ruins which he had shown Susanna several weeks earlier. He drove down the lane.

When they reached the end, he stopped the car and pulled the brake. "Turn it off," Malachy said, "and the lights."

"All right," Michael said when he'd done so, "what's all this about?"

"Michael, I didn't want to involve you," Malachy said. In the darkness Michael couldn't see his face. "But there's nowhere else for me to go right now. Jesus, things are all bollixed..."

"What *happened*, Malachy?"

"My house...the shop...and what's underneath is all *gone*. Along with two lads who were working there."

"Jesus..." Michael whispered.

"An explosion. I knew there was always a chance. I thought I'd been lucky all these years, and I probably had. But bad luck caught up with me. Or just maybe one of those stupid bastards' hands slipped or they wired up something wrong, and bang, nearly twenty years of working for the cause is over like that, in one big flash. At least I wasn't in the goddam place when it went up. Damn near, though. I'd just started driving down the lane. I'd gone out for milk and the papers and was coming back when it happened. Actually shook the car. So, I turned right around and drove away."

"Do you...do you think they'll know what happened?"

"Christ, Michael, how dumb *are* you? It's not like it was a gas explosion. This was the real goods. There's bound to be tons of residue, not to mention body parts, all over the neighborhood. All they gotta do is start sifting and they'll find plenty to hang me with."

"Well...why did you come *here*?"

"You weren't my first choice, lad, believe me. I went to what was *supposed* to be a safe house in Ballybofey, and they sent me packing. Same thing with one in Donegal. The news had preceded my arrival, y'see, and it seems they all agreed that the explosion would make me the most sought-after man on the whole island today. Not safe enough for a safe house, can you believe it? Things are a hell of a lot different now than in our fathers' time, that's for certain."

"So, what do you need? You can count on me, Malachy. You know that."

"I know, but I don't want to get you in trouble. You've been a good lad all these years, and there's no point gettin' you involved. But I need a place to lie low for tonight so I can make a few more calls..." He patted a pocket that Michael assumed had a mobile phone in it. "...and some people can get back to me. I don't think they'll let me down—Jesus, I've done too much for them over the years. Through all the stinkin' 'decommissioning' of IRA weapons, I've been a feckin' *armory*. But the news has to work its way to the top, to the lads who can do for me. Maybe they'll get me out of the country, I don't know. But with the eye and the limp, anyone who sees me will remember me." He gave a hollow laugh. "Jaysus knows I'm decommissioned for good."

"And you want to stay in the cottage?" Michael asked. "Why not come back to town? I'll put you in a room at my house."

"And where's the first place they'll look for me? Among family, that's where, and you know one of the first people they question will be the cousin with whom I went to prison for bomb making. No, that's no good."

"But the cottage is a death trap, Malachy. They get you there, there's no escape."

Malachy waved a hand. "Ah, I won't be there long enough for them to find me. I'll be out tomorrow, wait till dark and walk back to the car. Nobody'll give it a second look where it is. Then I'll go wherever I have to go."

"I could come drive you back to your car, or even take you where you need to be."

"No. Not safe. By tomorrow they might be watching you. I just need a place I can have a quick lie-down and make some calls."

"Isn't there anything I can do for you? Do you have any food?"

"Tell you what—maybe you could get me some groceries, things I could eat without cooking? Bread, biscuits, fruit, some bottled water, oh yeah, a bog-roll for emergencies. May not be able to make a toilet stop."

"Shall I bring the stuff back here?"

"No, put it in my car. Take out any bill of sale or bags that might show where it was bought, all right? Just in case. Here's the car key. Lock it again and slip the key under the right rear tire on the inside. Can you do that for me?"

"Sure, sure."

"Grand. Thank you. Now, you got the key to the cottage?"

"Here..." Michael took it off his key ring and gave it to Malachy.

"Where shall I leave it?"

"There's a big stone to the left of the door. Just put it under that." Michael felt tears start to come to his eyes. "Christ, Malachy, where are you gonna go then?"

"Don't know. I'll contact you if I can."

"At least let me know you got out of here all right. Call me from a pay phone tomorrow when you're away."

"Your phone might be tapped by then."

"Then just pretend you got a wrong number. Ask for...for Will, all right?"

"All right, that'll do." Malachy nodded. "I may not see you again, Michael. Not ever. Depending on what happens or where I go."

"Oh God..."

"Now, now, whist...don't fret yourself, little cousin." Malachy put an arm around Michael's shoulder. "We do what has to be done, don't we? Our das taught us that well enough. Just know that I won't be out of the game. I'll still do my all. And

I know you'll do...whatever you can."

"You did so much for me," Michael said, struggling not to blubber. "I owe you more than I can ever pay back."

"Pay me back by fightin' the fight, however you can. I know you won't take up arms again, and that's all right, that's your choice and I respect it. But do what you can." Malachy patted his cheek. "I love you, Michael. Always will. *Slan abhaile*, my brother."

In another second Malachy was out of the car, closing the door quickly so that the dome light blinked off and Michael was in darkness again. Through the window he could see Malachy going swiftly down the road, his limp making his figure rise and fall like waves on a choppy sea.

At the thought that he might never see his cousin again, Michael felt hollow inside, as though something had been scooped from directly under his heart. He sat until Malachy disappeared into the darkness, then started the car and turned it around, driving down the lane without lights until he was well away.

Michael drove north to Ballybaan, an area of the city he hardly ever frequented, and found an open grocery store. It was small, but had everything Malachy had asked for. Michael bought a few more items he thought his cousin might like, including the Cadbury chocolate bars they had shared as boys on the rare occasion when they had money for sweets. He threw away the receipt as he left the store.

Michael drove back to the car park at the institute and, looking carefully to make certain that no one was watching the car, unlocked the boot and put the groceries inside, first taking them from the store's plastic bags, which he balled up and stuffed in his pockets. Then he closed the boot, being careful not to let his fingers touch the smooth metal, rubbed the key on his shirt, and put it where Malachy had told him. Then he headed back toward his town house.

As anxious as he had been to see Susanna, the appearance of Malachy had nearly driven her from Michael's mind. He looked at the dashboard clock and saw that it was nearly eleven-thirty. Surely, she must be at the pub by now, probably wondering where the hell he was. He hated to admit it, but there was no way he could see her now. She would read him like a book, and he couldn't allow her to be involved in this in any way.

He took his mobile phone from his pocket and called Susanna's number. Her "Hello" was curious and expectant.

"It's me," he said. "How are you?"

"Oh, Michael, I'm so sorry I'm late. I got a late start, and there was an accident on 61 that stopped traffic. I just got in a few minutes ago."

"Glad you're safe and sound. I'm sorry I wasn't there to meet you, but I had to go out. Talk about accidents, mate of mine was drinking and had a little crack-up. He called me at the pub, so I went out to help him. Trying to get everything taken care of and get him home, but he's not cooperating. Look, I really don't think I'll be able to make it back tonight. He's going to take a lot of looking after, I'm afraid."

There was silence for a moment, and then she said, "Oh... sure, all right, if you have to."

"Good, I'm really sorry, but he's a mess. I'll call you tomorrow, yes?"

"That'll be fine, Michael. I can't wait to see you. I've really missed you."

"I've missed you, too, love, but I'll see you tomorrow. Goodbye."

Susanna put the cell phone back in her purse and looked up at Molly Sullivan with a smile. "Where is he then?" Molly asked from behind the bar.

Susanna rearranged herself on the stool. "He said a friend had an accident and he's helping him out."

"Did he say who?"

"No."

"Is he coming back?"

Susanna shook her head. "Not tonight."

Molly made a sound in her throat that Susanna thought was an expression of disgust for her son's behavior. "Nice of him to leave you like this," she said.

"Oh, it's all right," said Susanna, trying to keep tears from her eyes. All day she had been looking forward to being with Michael again, to feeling his arms around her and his cheek against hers. She just wanted to be held, and now it would not happen.

"You must be exhausted," Molly said, patting her hand.

Susanna nodded her head. "It's been a long day."

"All right, then. There's no point in traipsing across town to your lonely old room. Why don't you go upstairs, make yourself a cup of tea, and spend the night here."

"Oh no, I couldn't impose like that..."

"No imposition, I've got two extra bedrooms and they've both got clean sheets, so you can take your pick. Try the second on the left. It'll be warmer than the others."

Molly's tone suggested that it was a done deal, leaving Susanna no room for rebuttal. She thanked Molly, got her bag from the car, and Molly took her upstairs. The pub was still crowded, even though the musicians had stopped playing, and Susanna was surprised to find how quiet it was just a single story above the din. Molly showed her where the makings for tea were, then went back downstairs, leaving Susanna alone in the flat.

She made herself tea and sipped it slowly, sitting in an over-stuffed chair in the sitting room, thinking about her disappointment in not seeing Michael and about his mother's kindness in inviting her to spend the night. At least later there would be another person nearby as she slept. She would have hated to go back to her room alone, and she thought that Molly had sensed that.

When she finished her tea, Susanna took her bag and walked down the hall to the room that Molly had suggested she take. It was cozy and clean, and had a mix of framed religious paintings and old family photographs on the walls, much like the rest of the flat. The bed was slightly larger than a single, and had a plain headboard of dark wood. A chest of drawers and a small desk and chair completed the furnishings. Susanna wondered if it had been Michael's room when he was a boy.

She walked down the hall and looked in through the open doors of the other rooms, thinking that it was an invasion of

Molly's privacy, but unable not to explore the place where the man she loved had grown up. Besides, all the doors were open.

The room across the hall from Susanna's had to be Molly's, bursting as it was with the sense of occupancy, and Susanna took only a cursory glance and walked on. Near the end of the hall was a narrow staircase leading up, and she knew that it led to the flat Michael and Siobhan had shared.

She stood at the foot of the stairs for some time, and finally started up them gingerly. From talking to Michael, she knew that no one lived there now, and she couldn't pass up the opportunity to see where he and Siobhan had lived.

There was a door at the top of the stairs, but when she turned the knob, she found it was unlocked, and she pushed it open, stepping into a hallway. She didn't dare to turn on the lights, but the illumination coming into the rooms from the street lamps outside made it fairly easy to see, even in the darker hall. There was a room directly across from the stairway, and she looked inside.

It was so small that the furniture nearly filled it. There was a narrow bed, a chest of drawers, and a desk and chair placed strategically so that you could make your way to the closet at the side. The door was ajar, and Susanna opened it far enough to look inside. Men's clothing hung from the crossbar, and she knew instantly that they were Michael's old things. They had both his scent and his spirit. She frowned at the thought of him spending so many years in such a small room, like a monk's cell.

Or a prison cell, she thought with a shock of surprise. She ran her hand across the coverlet of the bed, then went back into the hall.

The bedroom at the end of the hall was the largest, and had a full double bed, along with a vanity, a writing table, a chest of drawers, and a bedside table. This then was the room in which Michael and Siobhan had slept until he moved into the smaller bedroom, leaving her there alone.

Though Susanna didn't believe in ghosts, she felt the presence of something other than herself in that dark room, an ineffable sadness, a sense of loss that made it seem as though the entire room ached. She stood on the threshold for some time, unable to go in, until she felt she could bear no more. It was as though all the sorrows of a sorrowful land had accumulated in that single chamber, and she turned away, afraid to stay longer, to look into that bleeding heart of a room.

She had no wish to explore the rest of the flat, and quickly went back down the stairs, closing the door behind her, and sat in Molly's well-lit sitting room until the mood had passed. It had surprised her, for she was not given to spells of imagination. Perhaps it had partly been the result of two weeks spent talking to ex-prisoners, some of whom indeed thought of Ireland as a heart torn in two, so that the body would not thrive until the parts were rejoined.

It made a grimly apt metaphor. Only by tearing a heart in two could so much blood have flowed over the years.

She shook the dreadful thought from her mind and prepared for sleep. The bed was comfortable, and in spite of her dark fancies she fell asleep quickly.

The light woke her in the morning, and when she looked at her watch, she saw that it was nearly nine. The comforting sound of clinking and rattling in the kitchen came to her ears, and for a moment she could believe she was a girl again, and the sound was that of her mother making a big breakfast for them all on a Saturday morning.

Susanna got up quickly and put on fresh clothes, then walked out to the kitchen. Molly Sullivan, an apron covering her thin frame, greeted her. "Good morning, sleep well? How would eggs, bacon, and potato cakes be for breakfast?"

"Sounds wonderful. And I slept marvelously, thank you."

"Grilled tomato?"

"If you like, but don't make it special for me."

Molly nodded and turned back to the stove. "Coffee's ready—help yourself. By the way, did you try and call Michael again last night?"

"No," she said as she poured coffee from the carafe.

"Well, I did. He wasn't there, but I left a message and told him you'd be staying the night here, and that he should come over in the morning. I wonder if he ever made it back to his place." Molly broke several eggs into a pan. "This friend...did he say who he was?"

"No, just a friend. Why?"

"Just wondering. Michael has a great many acquaintances, but not many friends who'd call him out of the pub, and fewer still he'd go for." Then Molly concentrated on the breakfast for a few minutes, and finally set two hot plates of food down on the kitchen table and sat across from Susanna.

"It looks delicious," Susanna said.

"It will be. Now tell me, Susanna, you love my boy, don't you?"

Susanna's fork stopped half way to her mouth, and she lowered it back down to her plate.

"Oh, go ahead, eat, eat," Molly said, taking a bite herself. "We can talk and eat at the same time, people have been doing it for ages."

Nevertheless, Susanna swallowed before she answered. "Yes. I do love Michael, Mrs. Sullivan. I think he's the first man I've ever really loved."

"And do you know he loves you, too?"

"I believe he does."

"Aye, but do you know how strong he loves you?"

"I...I hope he does."

"And do you know how scared he is of it?"

"...Scared?"

"I think when it comes to you, Michael's a little boy," Molly said. "He has a little boy's joy in what he feels for you, but at the same time he's scared like a little boy. He's never known love before, and he's known nothing but Ireland. Now he's not only found love, but...now how shall I put this?" She set down her fork, ignoring her own advice to eat and talk simultaneously. "He's found something he doesn't know how to control. Something that may, in the long run, take him away from what he's known."

"I don't understand."

"All right, I won't beat about the bush then. Do you think you'd like to spend your life with Michael? And by that I mean marrying him, or living with him if you're not the marrying kind, and God knows I hope you are."

Susanna didn't have to think, but she did have to pause. "I believe ... I'd like nothing better."

"Well, he feels the same. I know that much, after all, I'm his mother. But I also know that, like most little boys, he's unsure of himself and insecure and he's scared of change. And having someone he loved in his life would be the greatest change of all, especially if he had to leave Ireland to be with her."

"But...I don't think we're at that...that—"

"I know, I know, you're not there yet. But what I'm saying is that you may never get there with him thinking like a child. He's scared, Susanna," Molly added in a softer tone. "And to make him act like a man, you've got to take that fear away, and make him love you so much that he forgets to be afraid." Then she sat back, folded her arms, and looked more sternly at Susanna. "But I hope you don't think I'm prying."

For not the first time in the presence of Molly Sullivan, Susanna was at a loss for words. She was still searching for a response when the phone rang.

"Maybe that's him then," Molly said, and stood up to answer it. "Hello?" Her frown and the quick shake of her head told Susanna that it was not Michael. "...Yes? ... Oh, morning to ye...What kind of...No, he's not...Not that I know...All right... All right then, Brigid, I will...Of course...Yes...Yes...Goodbye." She hung up. The entire call took only a minute. "My sister-in-law," Molly said. Worry and concern weighed on her face.

"Is everything all right?" Susanna asked.

"I'm afraid not, but I don't quite know what's wrong. I'm thinking maybe I should..." And she turned on a small television set that sat on the kitchen counter and switched the channels, but apparently didn't find what she was looking for, and turned it off.

Just then came a knock on the door of the flat. "That's *Michael*," Molly said as though she'd just cursed, and walked to the door and opened it. "And there you are," she said. "Well, go see your lady."

Michael walked past his mother into the flat, and Susanna couldn't help but smile. He looked tired and distracted, but he went to her as quickly as she came to him, and they kissed, then held each other for a time while Molly pretended to be concerned with something in the hallway. "God, I missed you," he said.

"We've got a lot of catching up to do," Susanna replied, not wanting to let him go.

"Did you have coffee this morning?" Molly asked, coming up behind them. "If not, there's fresh, and then you can sit down and tell us all about this friend of yours last night. Anyone I know?" When Michael hesitated, Molly went on, "Might be he's got a game leg and only one eye, is that the one?"

Michael looked at her oddly, then went to the counter and poured some coffee. "What do you mean?" he said far too casually.

"I mean your Aunt Brigid called me not five minutes ago and asked if Malachy had shown up on our doorstep. Seems he had a bit of an accident at his place yesterday."

"Accident? What happened?"

"I was thinking you might tell us that, seeing as how you met him last night. And don't think I'm so stupid as to buy that *What cousin Malachy? What accident?* rubbish. Been a long time since the butter wouldn't melt in your mouth, me lad. Now what happened last night?"

Michael fixed his mother with a hard stare, but the old woman didn't back down an inch. Susanna felt as though she was balanced on a wire between the two of them. Something was happening, and if it had to do with Malachy, Susanna was afraid that the past was about to reassert itself in Michael's life, and in hers.

"Or do I have to tell you?" Molly said. "Seeing you get a call and go out that door with that look on your face—it was just like the old days, when your da would get word that he was *needed*, and off he'd go into the night. Now what happened, Michael?"

"Malachy called me," Michael said. "He needed a place to stay the night, so I gave him the key to the fisherman's cottage."

"He couldn't stay with us?" Molly asked.

"No. He was…on the run."

"And why was he on the run?"

"Because his house and the shop blew up, that's why." Michael's words were flat, and he looked away as he said them, as though he couldn't bear for the women to see his face.

"*God*," Molly said in a rough bark. "The stupid fool. Not bad enough he loses twelve years and an eye to such…such *shite*. All right now, suppose you tell us what I think I already know, but which Susanna here may not and should." She sat down at the kitchen table and gestured to the others to do the same. They did.

Michael's face was grim and angry, but when he looked up at Susanna his expression softened. "Malachy," he said, "continued with the paramilitaries after we got out. He never told me with what specific groups and I never asked. His bookshop was real, but it was also a front for money laundering for the Republican cause. After a while, when he felt safer, he expanded his basement and turned it into a safe house. There's…there *was* an earthen wall with a cabinet against it, but the cabinet had a false back. There was another room in there below the shop, big enough to sleep four men. There were arms stored there, too."

"That would be smuggled into the North," Molly said.

"Yes."

"And bombs," Molly said. "Or did his cooker explode?"

Michael gave her a sour look. "He told me last night they were making them down there."

"And that was news to you?" his mother asked as though she didn't believe it.

"I didn't know for sure. I never asked."

"Then when we were there," Susanna said, remembering her visit to Malachy's shop. "That sound in the basement. It wasn't a cat."

"Probably not," Michael said.

"You knew he had people down there then."

"I…assumed so," he said, averting his gaze from her again. "Anyway, he called last night and needed my help. He'll be off today, I don't know where."

"D'you know what you've done?" Molly asked him, not unkindly. "You've harbored a fugitive, Michael. Knowingly so."

"I helped a brother, that's what I did."

"As though you hadn't helped him enough over the years."

"I owe him my life. Money was nothing compared to that."

Susanna held up her hands feebly. "Slow down. I don't understand. Do you mean you gave him money? For arms? To support the paramilitaries?"

"Of course he did," Molly said. "Thousands and thousands over the past twenty years. Every time he visited his cousin and every time that Malachy came down here, Michael would make a donation to the *cause*. The cause of guns and bombs. But I could never talk him out of it."

"Michael, is this true?" Susanna's stomach felt as though she had just plunged down the steep slope of a roller coaster.

"Yes. I swore I'd not take up arms myself, but I had to do what I could."

"So, you funneled your money into that foul cause," Molly said. "And if that wasn't enough, now you're sheltering a terrorist."

"There's a difference between terrorists and freedom fighters," Michael said.

"Well, in this case I'm damned if I know what it is." Molly stood up. "I'm going out for a walk to clear my head. And I'm sure that you two might have a few words to exchange, so you'll be excusing me, Susanna." She gave Michael a look that would have withered a general, and swept out the door.

Susanna didn't know what to say. She could only look at Michael, waiting for an explanation that she wasn't certain she would understand. Finally, he spoke.

"I know you're disappointed in me, Susanna, and I'm sorry for that, but I can't confess to being sorry for anything I've done. I hope you can understand."

She thought for a moment before answering. "I might be able to understand, but I don't see how I can condone. Michael..." She spoke slowly, carefully choosing her words, knowing that each one might be a brick in a wall being built between them. "I've lived my whole life trying to work for peace. It's what I do. It's how I think. The use of violence and terror in order to settle political questions, that's...*hateful* to me. And to learn that you've been supporting these things..." She shook her head. "That's very hard for me."

"What you don't understand," he said, "is that it's more than just political. These people in the six counties, the ones we're against, the ones we're fighting, their hearts haven't changed in fifty years, in a *hundred* years, and they won't change now. They're the same ones who killed my father and my uncle. They're the ones who blinded and crippled Malachy. Even today they shout filth to little Catholic children walking to school, and they still shoot people for no reason, and they put bombs where children and old folk go."

"And because they do those things," Susanna said, "those things should be done back to them?"

He shook his head, frustrated by her lack of understanding. "It's the only way to get through. To show that their actions will bring a response."

"And all that response does is escalate matters and make things worse. So, they have to push harder the next time around. They have to kill more, and then your side does the same, and it never stops."

"It will stop when Ireland is one country again."

"But there are *other* ways to make that happen—peaceful and legal ways. They take more time, they take more care, but they're there." Susanna leaned her elbows on the table, held her head in her hands, and gave a deep sigh. Then she looked back up at him.

"Michael, I understand your anger. I empathize with you. The loss of your father started this, and I can't even imagine what that must have been like. You chose your path, and you've been on it a long time. But you told me once that you'd never fall willingly into the deep if you could fall *away* from it. That's all I'm asking—fall away from it. Because I won't let you pull me down with you." She didn't feel at all like crying. Her soul was too vacant for tears, her determination too implacable to allow them.

"What are you saying?" Michael asked.

"That if you continue in your support of the paramilitary in any way, I can't be with you."

"Susanna, don't you understand, this is who I am, who I—"

But his words were interrupted by footsteps in the hallway

and the opening of the door. Molly came in first. Behind her was a uniformed Garda Sergeant and another man, gray-haired and dressed in a dark suit. "Conor wants to talk to us," Molly said, nodding toward the Garda, "and so does this gentleman."

"Morning, Conor," Michael said as he stood to shake hands with the Sergeant, a man in his forties.

"Morning, Michael. Sorry for the interruption. This is Superintendent Malone down from County Donegal." The Sergeant looked curiously at Susanna.

"This is Susanna Cassidy," Molly said. "She's a good friend. Now what's this about, Conor?"

"Well, I've got some bad news for you, Mrs. Sullivan. I believe there's a Malachy Lynch who's your nephew?"

"That's right."

"I'm sorry to tell you...he's, uh...been killed."

"*What?*" Michael said, suddenly going pale.

"Why...why, I only..." Molly shook her head as though puzzled. "How? What happened?"

"I don't know if you've heard about it yet," the Sergeant said, "but his house in Letterkenny exploded yesterday. There's reason to believe that he was harboring fugitives, and that, well..."

"There was a bomb-making operation going on in his home," said Superintendent Malone. "Your nephew..." He turned toward Michael. "...and your *cousin* fled Donegal. We had the pieces put together by yesterday evening, and sent out a bulletin with Malachy Lynch's description and his automobile information to Garda stations around the country and in the North, asking them to be on the lookout. As luck would have it, someone called the Galway station late last night, reporting suspicious activity on Roscam Point."

"Aye," the Sergeant said. "We've had kids of late going out and smoking pot on the point. One of our lads went out there and saw a light through the cracks in the door of that fishing cottage, figured kids must've broken in."

"That cottage, I believe, is your family's, Mrs. Sullivan?" Malone asked.

"Aye, it was," said Molly. Susanna thought she sounded shaken, while Michael still looked dazed.

"When the Garda attempted to enter," the Superintendent went on, "the door was blocked, and when he looked through the crack, he saw a man answering Malachy Lynch's description taking a pistol out of a bag. He withdrew and radioed in, asking for armed backup. By then Lynch's car had been found a few miles from the cottage, so a team came in and I was called down.

"The detectives used a bullhorn to tell him to give himself up, but he shouted back that he had a gun and would shoot anyone who tried to enter. We waited for dawn, and then we battered down the door and shot in tear gas. He came out right away, and he was firing his weapon. The men had no choice." Superintendent Malone made a sharp little twist of his head that might have been intended to show regret. "I'm sorry for your loss."

"That's...terrible," said Molly. "A terrible thing."

"It is," the Superintendent said. "Unfortunately, it appears that someone in your family gave Malachy Lynch some assistance last night." Molly's face was noncommittal, but Michael's had the look of a man about to be condemned. "He had a key to the cottage. It was found inside."

"Of course," Molly said. "I gave it to him."

All eyes went to her, including Michael's, in whose face confusion was mixed with hope and panic.

"You gave him the key, Mrs. Sullivan?" the Superintendent said slowly.

"Why, yes. I went out back last night at the pub, just for a breath of air, and when I do, I see Malachy coming up the street. He says Aunt Molly, I need your help, some lads are after me, I need a place to stay. So I say go right upstairs then, but he says he doesn't want to get me involved, and asks me for the key to the cottage, that these hard men won't find him there, so I give it to him and he thanks me, but before he goes I say what've you got yourself mixed up in now, and he just smiles and says oh, Aunt Molly, don't ever get yourself involved with a married woman when the husband's murderous and has murderous friends..."

During Molly's monologue, Susanna sneaked a glance

at Michael. She could clearly read what was in his face. If he admitted that he was the one who had aided Malachy, his past history would make that aid look like conspiracy. But if the Superintendent could be persuaded that Molly had unwittingly helped Malachy, perhaps they could all walk away.

"And did anyone else besides yourself see Malachy Lynch here last night?" Superintendent Malone asked.

"I...believe I might have," Susanna heard herself saying.

"You, Miss?"

"I came in fairly late, down from Derry—I'm in Ireland doing peace studies work—and I saw a man walking away just as Mrs. Sullivan went back into the pub."

"And was it Malachy Lynch?" asked the Superintendent.

"I don't know. I only saw him from behind. But I do remember that he had red hair—I saw that in the street light—and he walked with a limp."

"Sounds like him," said the Sergeant.

"Did *you* see him at all, Mr. Lynch?" the Superintendent asked Michael.

"No...no, I didn't. I'm sorry, I'm just upset. Malachy was...he was very close to me."

"I'm sure he was," said the Superintendent, fully intending the subtext of his remark. "Where were you last night, Mr. Lynch?"

"At the pub. I left a bit early and went home."

"So, you wouldn't have been there when your cousin arrived."

"No."

"And is there anyone who might have *seen* you at home? Alone?"

Susanna cleared her throat and tried to look embarrassed. "Me."

"You, miss?"

"I, um..." She glanced at Molly as though expecting the wrath of Cuchulain, then looked down at the floor. "I spent the night with Mr. Lynch. I went over to his place as soon as I found out he wasn't here. And I can swear that he had no other visitors."

"Ah, well..." Even the Superintendent seemed discomfited by the fire in Molly Sullivan's eyes. She was, Susanna thought, good enough to be on the stage of the Abbey Theatre. Superintendent Malone cleared his throat. "We may want to speak to you again, Mrs. Sullivan. No matter what Malachy Lynch told you, you were aiding a fugitive."

"If you want to speak to me, you know where to find me, Superintendent. I won't be going anywhere."

"Thank you for your cooperation, and again I'm sorry for your loss." Superintendent Malone turned and walked out the door, and the Sergeant followed after a tip of his hat to the two women and another shaking of Michael's hand. Molly closed the door behind them.

As soon as she did, Michael's body shuddered with the tears he'd been holding back. He collapsed onto a kitchen chair and wept silently, while his mother put a hand on his shoulder and patted him. "There now, there now..." she said, over and over again.

After a minute Michael took a deep breath and straightened up. His eyes were red. "Why'd you do that?" he asked Molly in a choked voice, then looked at Susanna. "And you? Why'd you lie?"

"It's a poor mother who wouldn't sacrifice herself for her boy," Molly said, "especially when there's so little risk. That Superintendent would've taken you away in a minute, but they won't be arresting me, and if they did, they'd never convict me. As for Susanna, she's got Irish blood, son. She knows how to tell a story, too."

"Thank you," Michael said, and he sounded so like a little boy that Susanna's heart would have broken if it hadn't already. Then something else seemed to take him over, and he stood, shoulders back, head up, and looked into the middle distance, as though turning something over in his mind. "I've got to go..." he said.

"What?" said Molly. "Go where?"

"North. To Derry. I have to see Aunt Brigid, have to tell her what happened."

"*Why?*" Molly's voice was tense with anger.

"Because she deserves to know. And…and I have to be there. Malachy would want me to."

"But why now?" Molly asked. "Why not wait for the wake and we'll go up together."

"No! I have to go *now!* I don't know how to tell you, but… Malachy's calling for me. My *father* and my uncle are calling for me. Hell, maybe Ireland's calling for me, too."

"Maybe hell's calling for you, boy," Molly said, and her words were sad and bitter.

"Maybe it is. But I've got to go and look it in the face. I've not been to Derry since I left prison. I've got to go back."

"For what?" Susanna said. "For the same reason you did thirty years ago? My God, Michael, didn't that teach you?"

Molly made an angry sound in her throat. "Maybe you can talk some sense into him," she said, walking to the door. "I give up." She slammed it behind her, leaving them alone.

"Well, Michael? Didn't you learn from that?"

"I'm not going back for that," Michael said. "Believe me."

"I'd like to," she said. "But I don't know if I can."

"I *will* come back. And it won't be thirty years either. I'll be back *soon*. I swear it."

"And who will you be then? Will you be the man I've loved? The man I've seen be kind and gentle? Or will you be Malachy? Or your father?"

Michael bridled. "My father was a good man."

"Yes, but he's gone. He's been gone for nearly half a century. Forget about how he died, forget about his killers."

"I have. They're dead now, or old, old men. But I can't forget how he died, because his death was all about how he *lived*, and what he lived *for*."

"For Ireland," she said, and felt exhausted.

"Yes. Ireland. A united Ireland. An Ireland forever at peace."

"Peace." The word made her smile. "At the point of a gun."

"Maybe so," he said sadly. "Maybe not."

"Do you think," Susanna said, "that going North will help you decide? About which is the better way?"

"I think it will."

"Then go. But, Michael, I can't change. When it comes to this, I will never change."

She walked out the door without touching him or looking at him again.

CHAPTER 23

Michael left Galway at noon and drove straight through the day, crossing the border at seven in the evening. To his surprise, there were no checkpoints. He saw no soldiers and no military vehicles. Still, when he was across, he felt an odd and disquieting dichotomy, of having come home to a place he had never been.

Derry looked far different now. It seemed less slum-like and more modern, and when he drove past the street where he had lived as a boy, he saw that the houses had long been torn down and replaced by a small park and playground. There were swings and slides where his father and his father's friends had plotted and hidden.

Aunt Brigid's home was where it had always been, one in a file of dully identical row houses lined up like weary soldiers. When he knocked at the door, he was greeted by some of her friends, a small claque of women whose claim to local fame was that they were the widows or mothers of martyrs who had died for Ireland in combat, while in prison, or by mischance while serving the cause.

Aunt Brigid cried when she saw him, then insisted that he sit and eat from the vast hoard of food the women had brought. Michael had a slice of cold beef and a cup of tea, while Aunt Brigid and her friends, a grim and joyless lot, hovered around him like a flock of harpies.

"You don't have to say nothin'," Brigid told Michael. "But I know how you helped my boy. Just bad luck, that's all. He was born with bad luck. You did what you could."

Michael only nodded. There was no point in confessing to

anything with all these women about. When he finished eating, one of the women said, "You'll probably want to go out for a pint now," the way she'd have said, *I suppose you want to get drunk and fornicate now.*

The resentful suggestion came as a welcome relief, not so much for the drink as for the chance to leave the company of these women. "Mary," said Brigid to one of the others, "why don't you call Brian and Paddy and have them come round for Michael."

The woman nodded glumly and made the call, and in another fifteen minutes the two young men, who Michael assumed were Mary's grandsons, were at the door. Introductions were made, and they headed for the local pub, one which Michael dimly remembered from his youth.

"So, you've got a history, you have," said Brian, the broader of the two, once they were sitting in a booth with pints in front of them.

"A history?"

"Aye. Old Brigid...uh, Mrs. Lynch...tells stories about you and Malachy, how you built bombs in the old days, and went to Long Kesh."

"And the strikes," said Paddy, a thin young man with flaming red hair. "The hunger strikes—didja know Bobby Sands then?"

"Aye, I met him. Didn't know him well."

Paddy looked disappointed, but shook it off. "And what about them Dirty Protests—that must've pissed them off, you all smearing your shite on the walls."

"It got their attention," said Michael, and the two young men laughed. "But we were the ones who had to live with the smell."

That stopped their laughter. They seemed nice enough lads. Michael had spent evenings with far worse, but hoped the subject would change. He knew the type all too well, boys fed on the glorious tales of their fathers' and grandfathers' prods and pokes against the Orangemen and the English, the same way he had heard the stories about his own grandfather's sallies against the Black and Tans.

So, he tried to get the boys to talk about themselves, where they had gone to school, what they were working at, whether or not they had sweethearts, and anything else he could think of. It never surprised him how much people loved to talk about themselves given a chance.

Eventually, however, they steered the subject back to Michael's experiences. "Come on now," Brian said, "won't you tell about your adventures?"

"*Adventures?*" Michael repeated, and almost laughed. "We never thought of them as adventures. We did what we were told and then we got caught. We lived in cellars and then we lived in prison."

"Yeah," said Paddy, "but you brought 'em to their knees, had 'em shakin' in their boots. They weren't safe anywhere."

"Didn't drive them out, though," Michael said, looking down into the darkness of his pint.

"Well, no, but it changed things."

"Did it now?" Michael asked, looking up intently. "Do you think the bombs and the shootings changed things?"

"Well, like you said," Brian said, "it got their attention, didn't it?"

"Yeah, it did. And it got reprisals, too. It got still more killed."

"They never woulda started talkin'," Paddy said, "if it hadn't been for all of youse."

"Maybe not. Maybe you're right. But they started."

"Yeah." Brian shook his head. "And they're *still* talkin'. They'll be talkin' till doomsday."

"Maybe they will," said Michael. "But if they're talking, they're not shooting, are they?"

"Oh, not now," Paddy said, "but it'll start up again. It always does. And when it comes, we'll be ready."

Michael didn't reply. He suddenly felt weary, as though he wanted to sleep for a long time without dreams.

The two men started talking about football then, and Michael occasionally joined in the conversation, relieved that it had passed from the areas of politics, religion, and violence. He looked around the pub, and thought it seemed much like those in the South. People were laughing and drinking and eating, and the women seemed happy, not at all like the dour bunch back at his Aunt Brigid's.

Michael's mood slowly lightened, and he had a second pint, even though the two brothers had already started on their fourth each. "You don't drink much," Brian said.

"When you own a pub," Michael replied, "you learn not to drain away the inventory. The habit dies hard." Brian and Paddy chuckled, and Michael was glad he'd at least been able to amuse them, since he hadn't thrilled them with rousing tales of his brief paramilitary career.

They drank and chatted a bit more, until Brian said, "Well, we'd best be gettin' you back. Don't want my gram mad at me for keepin' you out too late."

Michael insisted on paying the bill, and the two men didn't put up a fight. When they stepped outside, the night was warm with the advent of spring, and they set off toward the block in which Brigid lived.

They had just started out when Paddy suddenly stopped and grabbed Brian's shoulder. "*Look!*" he said sharply but softly. "See him?" Michael caught a glimpse of a man disappearing around a corner forty meters away.

"Who was it?" Brian asked. Paddy had started walking swiftly toward the corner, and the others matched his pace.

"Norm Hawthorne, I'm sure of it."

"Hell, what would he be doing here?" Brian said disbelievingly.

"Don't know, but it was him all right."

"Who is he?" Michael asked.

"Son o' John Hawthorne, one of the biggest Orange bastards in Derry. He had wee Norm marchin' in Orange parades when he was four. Come on, let's get him…"

Brian and Paddy increased the pace, and Michael had to push hard to follow. When they turned the corner, he saw the man they were chasing, about twenty meters away. "Hey, Norm, ya wee shite!" Paddy called.

The man took a quick look back and started running, but in his panic tripped and went hard to one knee. Michael heard him groan and saw him get to his feet, but his injured leg nearly collapsed under him, and he limped a few more steps before Paddy and Brian caught up with him.

Paddy pushed Norman Hawthorne over, and he fell, crying out again as he landed on his injured knee. "Aw," Paddy said, "looks like baby boy fell down. Isn't daddy gonna be sorry then!"

"Leave him be," Michael said, coming up behind the two brothers.

"Leave him be, me arse," said Brian, and aimed a kick at Norman Hawthorne's kidneys. It didn't land. Michael shoved Brian's shoulder as he brought his foot forward, and he lost his balance, falling onto the pavement. Brian scuttled up and half-crouched, looking at Michael with feral rage. "What the hell you do *that* for?"

"I told you to leave him be."

"You takin' his side?" said Paddy in a near scream, as furious as his brother.

"It's not about sides. Now back off, both of you."

"The hell. He's gettin' a beatin', you like it or not," Brian said, and ran toward Michael. Though Michael drew his head back, Brian's punch caught him on the cheek, and Michael felt the sharp pain of a bone cracking in his face. He grabbed Brian around the waist, lifted him and, ignoring the flailing fists pounding the back of his neck, hurled him to the pavement. The impact pushed the air out of the boy's lungs, and Michael quickly knelt and gave him a short, sharp one to the side of the head.

Then he felt Paddy leap onto his back and snake his forearm around Michael's throat as he wrapped his legs around his thighs. It was an old trick that never worked. Choking out took far more time than it took for Michael to throw himself onto his back. Paddy cushioned Michael's fall onto the hard pavement, and his head slammed into Paddy's face, driving the back of the boy's head even harder against the street. Michael felt the body go limp beneath him and rolled off.

Norman Hawthorne was just watching from where he lay, but Brian was getting groggily to his feet. Michael pushed him back down onto the pavement so that he straddled Brian's back, then put a choke hold on him. There was no defense the big man could offer. "Get out of here," Michael told Norman Hawthorne. "Go on, *go!*"

Hawthorne got to his feet and ran limping toward the more populous streets. Michael waited until he was out of sight, and the sound of his stuttering footsteps, so much like Malachy's, had long faded away before he released Brian and quickly stood up.

Brian continued to lie on his stomach, gasping for air. Then he vomited violently, pushing himself away from the mess as he did so. While he continued to cough, Michael went over to check Paddy.

He was still out, but breathing evenly, and a small trickle of blood had come from the back of his head where the scalp had been torn by the rough pavement. Michael patted his cheeks, gently at first, then harder until Paddy stirred and his eyes fluttered open. "You'll be wanting to see a doctor," Michael told him. "You might have a concussion. And that's a damned stupid way to jump a man bigger than you. Can you stand up?"

Michael helped him get slowly to his feet, and when he let him go, he stood swaying but didn't fall. "What the...*hell* did you do that for, you goddam gobshite?" Paddy asked weakly, rubbing the back of his head.

Michael stood there for a moment, then said, "What you were doing...you shouldn't have done. You get that lad tonight, tomorrow his da or his da's bully boys get two or three of you, and maybe somebody dies again. And we keep on and keep on, and it never stops."

"But that bastard's da is the—"

"*So feckin' what?*" Michael came right up to Paddy and snarled in his face. "So, who *cares* who the hell he is? You see the bastard, *walk away!* Just *stop* all this...just...stop it," he finished weakly. Then he nodded toward Brian, who was still coughing but getting painfully to his feet. "Go help your brother," Michael told Paddy, then turned and walked back toward his aunt's house.

There was nothing for him here. He didn't know what he had expected, but what he found was only more stupidity and anger and mindlessness, and he couldn't stand it. The thought of going back into that overheated flat that smelled of old women and old hatreds was unbearable.

He had left nothing in his aunt's flat, and if he had he would have left it behind. He walked straight to his car, got in, and started driving out of Derry, out of the North, back to the South.

It was midnight when Michael crossed the border, and he drove another two hours before he felt his head nodding and his eyes closing. He snapped his head up and knew that he had to rest. He had scarcely slept the night before, and if he continued driving now, he might never make Galway. So, he started looking for a place he could pull off and sleep, and at last he found one.

When he saw the tall tower of a church looming in the darkness, he thought there could be no safer spot than its car park, and pulled in, turning off the engine and lights with relief. He reclined the seat and closed his eyes, hoping that the dead who slept only a short distance away in the churchyard wouldn't resent having a slumber-mate for a few hours.

If not, the only thing Michael had to worry about was a Garda checking on a strange car at the church in the dead of night. He thought that there must be hundreds of men throughout Ireland who slept it off in their cars on Saturday nights, and the police would be forgiving, considering the alternative of having that many more drunk drivers on the roads.

Michael intended to sleep for just a few hours and awaken near dawn, but when he opened his eyes again, it was in response to a tapping on the window. The first thing he noticed was that it was daylight, and the second was that the tapping had come from the knuckles of a priest about his own age, who, when he saw that Michael was awake, made a cranking motion with his hand. Michael obediently rolled down the window.

"Are you coming in to Mass then?" the priest asked him. "Starts in twenty minutes."

Michael cleared his throat. "I'll be there, Father. Thank you."

The priest smiled as though they shared a secret, and walked into the church. Michael looked at his watch and saw that it was eight-forty. He supposed he might as well go to Mass here as anywhere. He couldn't reach Galway in time, and he owed the priest and his church for overnight lodging.

Michael found the men's toilet in the basement, where he splashed water in his face, rinsed his mouth, and patted his hair into place. He was glad to see only a small bruise where he'd been hit the night before, and the pain had subsided.

Then he went into the sanctuary, sitting near the back so as not to distress the more well-groomed parishioners who had at least been able to brush their teeth that morning. The interior was small, but filled with sunlight that shone in through the stained glass windows. The furnishings were simple, and the colors were delicate, muted, and soft. The place gave a sense of welcome and comfort, no little thing in this age, in this day.

The priest's homily was based on the passage from *Corinthians 1* that speaks of love. "The King James Version," he said, "has the word 'charity' instead of love, which may come as a surprise to those young men and women who wish to have this passage read at their weddings. But in truth, the original word has more to do with the Latin *caritas* and the Greek *agape* than with romantic love. This love, this *charity*, is the love of one's fellow, the love of mankind in general.

"So, it's not only to your spouse or the people for whom you feel affection that you should act this way, but to everyone, and at all times. It isn't an easy thing to do. At times it seems impossible, since this great love for our fellow creatures here on earth, this great charity, must be so strong that 'it bears all things, believes all things, hopes all things, endures all things.'

"But though it seems impossible to live like this, we must try. We must hope and believe and bear and endure, look for the good in others and disregard the bad, and forgive them and hope for them and believe in them and go on. We must *love*. If we have all other things, and have not love, then we have nothing. Nothing." The priest shook his head sadly.

"Nothing."

Michael put a fifty-Euro note into the collection plate, and remained several minutes after the end of the Mass, continuing to pray. Then he stood up to see the priest in the aisle by his side.

"Is there anything you need, my son?" he asked.

"No, Father, thank you. You've given me quite enough."

Michael stopped for a large breakfast at a tea shop, ate it with gusto, and drove the rest of the way to Galway without stopping.

CHAPTER 24

After she walked out the door on Saturday, leaving Michael alone, Susanna found Molly Sullivan at the bottom of the stairs, just inside the front of the pub. Molly took Susanna to a back booth and told Danny Clarke to bring them tea.

"You have to let him go," Molly said, when the steaming cups were in front of them. "You can never stop them from doing what they think they have to do, but you can be there when they come back."

"Do you think he will? Come back, I mean."

Molly took a sip. "I think he'll find Derry, even changed as it is, a cold place. He'll find no love there. And now that he's known it, I don't believe he'll be able to live without it. Susanna, you've had a greater influence on him than he imagines. I've seen him change in the few weeks you've been in his life. I think he'll come back, and he'll come back soon. He might still have those feelings about what he should be doing, but whether he'll act on them or not, well, that may be up to you." She chuckled. "Men think they control their own lives, but their women have a great effect on them, a great effect."

"I hope you're right."

"So, you'll be staying here in Galway the next few days?"

"Yes. I'll be going back North on Wednesday."

"Tell me, I know you're not Catholic, but would you go to Mass with me tomorrow, and then perhaps join me and my friends for luncheon? If you recall, you said you would sometime."

Susanna also recalled what Michael had told her about the inquisition she could expect to receive from Molly's friends, but she needed the older woman's company now. They both felt the same loss and the same pain, and Molly's presence was calming and reassuring. "I'd like that," she said.

They made arrangements to meet the next day, and Susanna drove to the university library, thinking that work would be the best thing to take her mind off of Michael. She hoped that Molly was right, and that he would return soon. She hoped even more that he would do nothing foolish in Derry. From her conversations within the ex-prisoner community, she knew there was still great bitterness among some of the Northern Republicans, and that bitterness could easily spill over into violence.

Perhaps Michael wanted only to see his aunt, extend his sympathies, and see the changes in the place where he had been a little boy. Then, his duty done and his curiosity assuaged, he could come home to Galway, and come back to her.

Susanna went to The Lilting Banshee that evening, and Molly got down Tim Sullivan's fiddle for her to play, but the session seemed joyless without Michael there. It broke up earlier than usual, and Susanna went back to her room, where she slept fitfully and got up early. She spent a lot of time choosing just the right outfit with which to go to Mass, and settled on an ankle-length black silk with a subtle dragonfly pattern, and a long silk scarf.

She met Molly at a quarter of eleven at the mouth of Buttermilk Lane in front of the church, and the woman greeted her with a kiss on the cheek. "The girls are already inside," she told Susanna. "They're great for praying, they are."

The "girls" turned out to be four other ladies, all around Molly's age. They smiled when Molly and Susanna joined them in their pew, though Susanna had the distinct impression that she was being carefully examined.

Though she was afraid that the Mass might be a bit awkward, the ladies seemed to take little notice of her, involved as they were in their rites. When they went to the front to take the Sacrament, they all left on the side opposite Susanna and returned the same way, so there was none of the squeezing past each other that she feared might occur.

When the Mass was over, they shuffled outside, happily

greeting the priest, to whom Molly introduced Susanna. "Oh yes," said the father, a beaming, middle-aged man with red cheeks, "I've heard a lot about you. Welcome."

The remark made Susanna uneasy at first, but she realized that such gossip was only natural, particularly among little old ladies. She supposed that she should feel flattered to be so worthy of remark.

Once they were on the street, Molly introduced Susanna to the ladies, all of whom she found to be as delightfully spunky as Molly. Three were widows, one's husband lived in a nursing facility, and the other's was in good health but hadn't gone to Mass in fifteen years. "I hate the thought of him burnin' in hell while I'm up in heaven," Mrs. Sheehan said, "but there's no talkin' to him. He likes his Sunday telly too much."

Luncheon was great fun. Susanna barely had to speak, with the five ladies swiftly trading quips, anecdotes, and gossip back and forth. They were like hummingbirds of conversation, constantly on the move and never landing permanently on any one subject.

At last, the meal over, they rose and parted, with many kind and complimentary words to Susanna about how lovely it had been to meet her, and how they certainly hoped they would see her again at Mass. When all the goodbyes were said, Susanna walked with Molly back to the pub. It was the first day of March, and a strong breeze was blowing, but the air had more than a trace of warmth.

"Would you like to come up and sit?" asked Molly. "Maybe you could tell me something about your work. I'd truly like to know."

After the chatter of the luncheon, a restful and placid talk with Molly seemed appealing, and it was far better than being alone and thinking about Michael. Susanna agreed and soon found herself in Molly's sitting room, talking in low tones and explaining her work. Molly seemed sincerely interested, and would not be satisfied until Susanna had recapped her entire career in promoting peace, and talked about what she was planning in her teaching and writing when she returned to the states.

A soft knock on the door interrupted Susanna in mid-sentence, and both women looked up in surprise. Then Molly looked at Susanna and said, "Would you get that, my dear?" as though she knew who had knocked.

Susanna was filled with hope as she walked quickly to the door and opened it, and her hope was not misplaced. Michael, his face unshaven, stood in the doorway, wearing the same clothes in which he had left the day before. "I'm back," he said with a shy smile. "Back for good."

She held him, pressing her cheek against his chest, and he slowly put his arms around her, as though expecting her to push him away in spite of her initial embrace.

"You weren't gone long," said Molly, still sitting and not even looking at her son, as though his return were the most natural thing she could imagine. "Did you give your regards to your Aunt Brigid?"

"I did."

"Sit down and tell us about it then," Molly said.

Michael and Susanna sat together, and she kept tight hold of his hand, fearing that he would go away again. He told them about seeing his Aunt Brigid, and about the women who had surrounded and supported her. He told them about Brian and Paddy, and about how they had tried to beat the other young man, and how he had not let them.

"I'm not proud to say it," Michael said, "but I beat them pretty badly. I'm afraid I don't have your diplomatic skills, Susanna. I'd rather not have hurt them, but there wasn't any other way I could see at the time." He gave a helpless shrug. "Nor even now, in retrospect. Words wouldn't have done it, and if I'd lain down over the lad, as I saw you do that day, they'd have just kicked my ribs in as well. So, I did what I did. It was in a good cause, I hope, but I'm not sure."

"What do you mean?" Susanna asked.

"I mean that even though I saved that boy, he'll go tell his da that two Catholic lads tried to kill him and that another crazy one stopped them. And then this Hawthorne will send some boys out tomorrow to smack down a couple Republican lads. Maybe my stopping Brian and Paddy didn't do a damned thing."

"But it did," Susanna said. "Maybe this man will send out someone for revenge, but maybe his son will remember that mercy was shown to him, and that might make a difference, not tomorrow, but a month or a year from now."

"Or maybe he'll think that I was just another daft or drunken Catholic. And right now those boys—and their grandmother and her friends, and maybe even Aunt Brigid—think that I'm a traitor. If I'd stayed up there, they'd have been after me next."

"Well, you're not up there," Molly said. "You're here in the South, and you won't be going up North again. And you won't be supporting them either, not with your fists nor your money."

"They're still my people," Michael said, and his words pounded in Susanna's heart. "And I still feel..." He paused, searching.

"You feel anger. And you feel guilt," Susanna said.

"Guilt?"

"Yes, for not doing enough. You felt guilt over Malachy's losing an eye and his bad leg, because you came out of Long Kesh unscathed, at least physically."

Michael took his hand away from hers. "Malachy was crippled because of me. He took the blame for something I did, and they *beat* him. They beat him until he was a cripple. I owed him for that, but I could never pay it back, not with all the money in the world."

"And you don't have to, not anymore," Susanna said. "Malachy's gone. You can let your guilt go, Michael. When he needed you at the end, you helped him. At the risk of your own freedom, you did everything you could for him. He knew that when he died. So let it go. Just let it go."

"Aye...I suppose I can. But the anger you mentioned, Susanna—that doesn't go as easily."

"And *what*," said Molly, looking somewhere over Michael's head, "are you so...God...Damned...angry about?" The profanity fell on their ears like chimes.

"What I've *always* been angry about," Michael returned with as much intensity as his mother had shown. "My *father*. My father who was *murdered* when I was a little boy. He taught me to love Ireland and to respect her, and they took him out and they killed him, and no one ever paid for his life, and they never will. The only thing, Mother...the *only* thing that could put my mind at ease would be if somehow I could avenge his death. And *that* is the *only* thing that could give me peace, once and for all."

They sat there in silence for what seemed like hours, until finally Molly Sullivan spoke, so softly that Susanna could just make out the words. "So, do you think you're Hamlet then? Do you think your life is such a tragedy because you lost your father at an early age? Do you want to avenge him? If you do, then it's me you'd better be killing, boy."

"What?" Michael said.

Molly turned slowly and looked at him. "Did you ever think that maybe other people's lives were just as tragic as your own, maybe even more so? Did you ever imagine that your mother could be feeling some pain as well? All right then, as long as we're in the Hamlet mood, I'll tell you a tale that—what was it his father's ghost said?—that will harrow up your soul and freeze your young blood. But it finally has to be told. After a few years short of half a century, I think it's time."

"What are you talking about, Ma?" Michael asked.

"I'm talking about how your father really died. And about the man he really was...and the woman, God help me, that I was." She looked at Susanna. "I'm sorry you have to hear this, Susanna, but it's for the best. You should know." She settled back in her chair.

After the black Protestants ruined your father (Molly began), damaged him so that he could never have children again, he lost all interest in the act. I don't know if he was capable of it, but whether or no, he had no desire for it. That was no great loss to me, and, even if it had been, I was the wife. I did as my husband wished.

But he changed in other ways too. He became cold and cruel toward me, like I was a constant reminder of what he couldn't do any more, and he hated to even look at me. Try and think back and remember him ever holding me or kissing me, and I think you'll not be able to.

Before his injury we'd loved each other in a quiet way, I overlooking his foibles and foolishness. But afterward he loved me not at all. Never showed a sign of affection. And he loved his son only enough to fill him with the hatred of those he hated. I was lonely, not so much for the touch of a man as just for one's company, for someone to tell me something funny and make me laugh, or to look at me in a way that told me I mattered. To do something that was for me and not only for himself, something he did not because he felt he should, but because he valued me.

I won't tell you the name of the man. You might remember him, you might not, it doesn't matter now anyway. He was a young man and he was kind to me. I was twenty-five years old and you were a lad of seven. Patrick was never home. He spent many nights with the lads, doing whatever it was he did, and often wouldn't appear until mid-morning. He gave me plenty of opportunities to become this man's lover.

At first, I thought it was grand, but I told no one, and insisted that he stay quiet, too. If there was even a hint that anyone knew, I told him I wouldn't see him again. When I saw him in public, I treated him like any other man, no more nor no less friendly, and he behaved just as normally toward me. We were a fine pair of actors, we were.

But then I started to feel badly about it. Once the bloom wore off, once the freshness and the novelty of being cared for began to fade, I realized I had sinned greatly, and that it had to stop. About that same time, he had decided that he wanted me to leave Patrick and be with him. That wasn't possible. It was an affront to God, and I told him so. I'd sworn to be with Patrick till death parted us, and I'd be true to that vow at least, even though I betrayed both him and God in another way.

I told the young man I'd not see him again, but he said that this wasn't the end of what was between us, but the beginning. I didn't know what he meant, and I thought he was just talking.

But two weeks later Patrick was found dead, shot in the back of the head. We all, including myself at first, thought the Orangemen had done it. Your father talked a bigger game than he played. He was always on the outskirts of the IRA, wanting to do more than he really did, and no one took him particularly serious, so most people were surprised when the Orangemen thought him important enough to kill. It seemed that in death he finally managed to get the importance he'd never had in life.

A few days after his burial, my young man came to my home late at night and told me that now I was a widow we could be married. There was something about the way he talked and acted, a pride in him, that whispered the truth to me, and I asked him flat out *Did you do it? Did you do it for me?* And I made it seem as though I was as wicked as he, and that the thought of it gave me pleasure, and that was enough for him. He said he had, and it worked just the way he thought it would, that the Orangemen were blamed and no one would ever know the difference.

I knew, though.

I told him we'd have to wait a few months for decency's sake. I wouldn't even let him come in. I said we couldn't be seen together, that it was too dangerous for him. If we were together too soon after Patrick's death, people might talk and even start to suspect what really happened.

That night, after he went away, I started thinking about how to kill him. It was far easier than I thought it would be. I just put a few bees in the right people's bonnets, made the suggestion that this young man might not be so strong a Republican as he seemed, told a few things that I'd overheard him say, not maliciously, mind you, but just as conversation, just something to talk about and pass the time.

Two weeks after I began, I actually heard a rumor that he was an informer, that he had betrayed Patrick to the Orangemen to save his own skin. I had started the stories, and that was how they'd grown by the time they came back to me. Two days after I heard that, my young man was found dead down by the river, just a few yards from where they found Patrick. He'd been shot in the back of the head.

I never knew who did it. No one ever even spoke of it to me, to tell me that Patrick's death had been avenged. They'd avenged it more directly than they knew.

Still, when I heard of it, it made me sick. I loved him, and I loved Patrick at the start, so I took my son to Galway where I had some family, to get him away from the violence of the North. I confessed it all to a priest in a strange parish, and received my absolution. As part of my penance, I decided that I'd never feel passion for a man again, and that was why I married Tim Sullivan. He was kind to you, and he was fifteen years older than I, and I never felt a thing stir inside me for him, though I came to love him for being a good husband.

So, it wasn't the Orangemen who killed your father. It was another Catholic, a Republican, and the reason he did it was because of me. You can't kill him, for long ago I set the wheels in motion that did just that. So, if you want your father fully avenged, then you'll have to take my life as well, and if that'll give you peace, you're welcome to it.

Molly Sullivan put her head back against the chair and closed her eyes. Susanna could see tears seeping out from under the paper-thin eyelids. Michael had gone pale and slouched, his mouth partly open, his arms leaning on his thighs, as though he was too weary to sit up straight. He looked at his mother with an expression Susanna couldn't read.

"So," Molly said, her voice breaking, "will you hate me now? Will you hate me until you die?"

Michael gave a deep sigh, and looked down at the floor. "No. No, Ma, I could never hate you." He stood up slowly and went to her, knelt by her side and put a hand on her shoulder. She grasped it and her thin body shook with sobbing. "I'm sorry, Ma. I'm sorry. I never…I'm so sorry…"

They held each other then, mother and son, and Susanna felt tears come to her own eyes. The embrace lasted for a long time, and finally Molly straightened, and she patted Michael on the shoulder and kissed his cheek.

"You'd better be leaving me alone for a while," she said, her voice still shaking. "You go and take your girl for a nice walk down by the bay. It's a beautiful day. You can feel spring coming."

"All right," Michael said. "All right, Ma, I will…. Can I get you anything first?"

"No, you just go. I'll be fine." Molly waved him away, and

Susanna wiped her eyes as Michael got her coat and held it for her. After she put it on, he returned to his mother's side and kissed her cheek, then walked to the door.

Just before Susanna followed him, Molly looked at her and gave her a small smile. It was a knowing and almost conspiratorial look, but Susanna had no time to respond to it. Michael turned back to see if she was coming, and she smiled at Molly and said goodbye, then followed him out the door.

They didn't speak until they were on the street. "Let's go walk by the river," Michael said. His voice was soft, and Susanna knew that his mind was still on what Molly had told him about what happened so long ago. They held hands as they walked, but he said nothing more until they reached the Corrib and began to stroll down the walk by its bank. It was as though the rushing river freed his voice.

"Susanna, I've carried so much hate around for so many years," he said. "I don't know how easy it'll be to let it go."

"I can help."

"I know you can. You've helped already. But this poor wounded and beautiful country is in my blood and my bones. I sat in jail ten years for it, and then I tried to help it with money, with Malachy as my go-between. But he's gone, and I don't know how to help it now. The thing that sticks in my craw is that this war—and it *is* a war—isn't going to end. Neither side will let it, not the Loyalists, and not the Republicans."

"But it *can* end. For you. It ends when you want it to, Michael. It ends when you choose to stop fighting."

"That's a hard choice for me to make."

At least, she thought, he was no longer argumentative. He spoke quietly, as though he was thinking things through, turning them over, looking for a way. They walked on hand in hand until they came to the place they had met. Susanna stepped away from him, into the small recess that overlooked the river just before it swept under the bridge.

"It's just a step," she said. "Do you remember that day at the cliffs, when you held out your hand to me and I was scared to cross that gap? To you it was just something to step over, but to me it was an abyss. I never could have gotten across it alone. But you were there, and you held out your hand, and I took it and I stepped across. The reason I was able to do it was that I wasn't stepping across an abyss—I was just stepping over to *you*."

She held out her hand. "That's all I'm asking you to do, Michael. I came across an ocean to find you. Now all I want you to do is take my hand and step over to me."

He looked into her face, and then down at her outstretched hand. At first she was afraid that he wasn't going to take it, but after a moment he stepped toward her and grasped her hand in his, and then he was next to her, and she felt his body against hers, and his arms went around her, and she knew it would be all right.

A half hour later they were sitting on one of the wide concrete curbs that ran the length of The Long Walk, watching the birds over the quay. His arm was around her, and she was nestling against him, at peace.

"I love you, Susanna. I spent too many years without you, but I want to spend what's left with you."

"I feel the same way."

"I don't know what to do about it, though."

"Most people who feel this way get married."

"I want to marry you, I do, but I don't know what comes next."

"Happiness. Ever after, if we're lucky."

"But I can't ask you to stay here in Galway, be a pubman's wife. That wouldn't be fair. You've worked too hard, and your work means too much to you to give it up."

"Then it's simple. Come back with me to America."

"And do what then?"

"Just what you do here. Over there pubs are opening and closing and changing hands every time you turn around. It takes money to get started, but I have money."

"I don't need your money, love. Except for what I gave to Malachy, I saved mine over the years. And the Banshee is mine and Ma's, free and clear. Danny would be happy to buy out my half."

"You say that as though you're not sure."

"Oh, he would, and my ma loves him like a son, but it's a lot to think about, leaving Ireland, starting somewhere new."

"I'll make a deal with you. Come to America with me, give it a try, and if you don't like it, we'll come back here."

"You couldn't do that."

"I could do anything for you, Michael."

"And I for you. I've never been to America, but what better way to see it than with the woman I love? What better way than with my wife?"

That night Susanna lay in Michael's arms. Just before she drifted off to sleep, she remembered the look on Molly Sullivan's face, and thought about what it might mean.

Then she had it. It came to her as such a shock that she nearly gasped and sat up in bed. She remembered how, when the two Gardai had come to Molly's flat, she had been such a cool liar that Susanna had thought she would have been a great actress. She remembered, too, how Molly, just that day, had said of the young man with whom she had had the affair, *we were a fine pair of actors, we were.*

Acting. Was that look she had given Susanna a signal? Was Molly telling her that what she had just witnessed was a performance, a story that had been cut from whole cloth? Had she taken the risk of changing in her son's eyes from Madonna to whore in order to extinguish his last spark of hatred? Then she recalled something else Molly had said.

It's a poor mother who wouldn't sacrifice herself for her boy, especially when there's so little risk.

Maybe that final risk wasn't as great as it seemed. Molly knew her son well. A man with less empathy and sensitivity might have stalked from her home and never spoken to her again, thinking only of her unfaithfulness to his father. But Michael had seen beyond that to her own pain, her own loneliness, and forgiven Molly's words as soon as they were spoken.

The tale, Susanna had to admit, might well have been true. It had the ring of sincerity and the sense of random and awkward reality, and Molly's tears had been real.

But true or false or somewhere in-between, Molly Sullivan's

confession had had its desired effect. Susanna lay there quietly with the man she would marry, a man of peace who had left his war behind.

CHAPTER 25

It was just the kind of June wedding Kate Quinn would have wished on herself. The weather was grand, with sunlight streaming in through the gloriously-colored stained glass window at the front of St. Augustine's Church. The pews were filled, both the bride's and the groom's side, and Kate was surprised, things having gone the way they had, to find herself on the side of the bride.

Still, that was where Davey was sitting, so that was where she sat. There was something she liked about this Yank, and it wasn't just his money, though that was nothing to sneeze at. He was good-looking, dressed well, and she liked his way of taking what he wanted, which had included her, though to be honest she hadn't played all that hard to get. What he'd gotten he'd surely liked, and words had been spoken that she'd taken to heart and would make sure he remembered, too.

It didn't seem that would be necessary. If the past few days were any indication, and if Kate was any judge of men, Davey Oliver was pretty well smitten with her. True, she'd been wrong about Michael, but God almighty he was an odd case, preferring that skinny schoolteacher over a real woman. Still, she wished him well. He'd surely had enough suffering through his sad life, and deserved a bit of happiness.

Kate lightly slapped Davey's hand that had worked its way over against her thigh, muttered, "You're in *church*, m'boy," and looked around the pews. Susanna's family was represented by only one row of people, two if you counted Davey. Her mother was sitting in front of them with Rachel and Gerry, who, it was obvious, would be taking their own vows before too long. They had written a whole batch of songs together and were singing them at different clubs in Galway. Two nights before, Kate had gone with Davey to hear them, and she thought they were damned good. So did the rest of the audience, who showed it with loud applause.

They didn't play the Banshee, though. Apparently old Molly Sullivan didn't think them suitable, in spite of Michael's urging. Kate guessed, however, that Molly realized all too well that the disapproval of elders was a major element in the creativity of youth.

Along with the small array of family, there were a number of Susanna's friends and colleagues from her university who had flown over. Davey had even paid to bring over a friend of Rachel's, a nice Vietnamese-American girl who had arrived with Susanna's cat. Davey was a sweetheart, no two ways about it.

Still, there was no denying that Michael Lynch was a beautiful man. He looked as good as Kate had ever seen him as he walked in from the side with Danny Clarke, his best man. No man looked bad in formal wear, but Michael looked brilliant. Kate was certain, however, that Susanna would have her hands full with him. Far better, she thought, to have a man like Davey, who liked to *think* he was his own man, but who you could steer like a little car if you knew how to do it. Kate had no doubt that Davey had an eye for the ladies, but she'd cure him of that right enough.

Finally, the organ started to play the processional, and they all looked back to see the bride. Kate had to admit that Susanna looked lovely. Her dress was white, straight, simple, and elegant, with the train falling from her shoulders like a long cape, and her head was uncovered, displaying that bright mass of red-blonde hair that shimmered like gold in the light.

She towered over Dermot Rooney, through whose arm she had her own. From where Kate sat, she could see that Dermot's eyes were bright with tears, even though he was beaming at having been chosen to give the bride away. Then the two of them started to walk slowly down the aisle. Susanna looked happy, and Kate wished her well.

As the faces turned to watch her, Susanna felt a rush of panic. She kept the smile on her face, but couldn't help thinking of all those years on her own. Now she was giving up her independence to be with someone she'd known for only several months. Her heart tripped, and her mouth went dry at the thought of the finality of this walk, and for one mad second she actually considered turning and running back up the aisle.

But then she saw Michael, and all her fear left her. She wasn't marrying a stranger, she was marrying *Michael*. Her own dear Michael.

He came around the golden rail and went down the step toward her, as though he couldn't wait for her to come to him. She put her arm through his, but he didn't take her up to the altar. Instead he looked up at the priest, who smiled and nodded and addressed the congregation. "Before the ceremony begins, Michael has something to say to his bride."

Surprised, Susanna looked at Michael, who seemed bashful but determined. "Susanna," he began, "the Church has certain rules as to what may be spoken during the actual marriage ceremony. So, if I'm to say this, it has to be beforehand. There's a poem by Yeats that says what you mean to me, and also what you've done for me." He took her hands in his and looked full into her face, and spoke.

> *"If Michael, leader of God's host*
> *When Heaven and Hell are met,*
> *Looked down on you from Heaven's door-post*
> *He would his deeds forget.*
> *Brooding no more upon God's wars*
> *In his divine homestead,*
> *He would go weave out of the stars*
> *A chaplet for your head.*
> *And all folk seeing him bow down,*
> *And white stars tell your praise,*
> *Would come at last to God's great town,*
> *Led on by gentle ways;*
> *And God would bid His warfare cease,*

Saying all things were well;
And softly make a rosy peace,
A peace of Heaven with Hell."

"Thank you," he said so softly that only she could hear. "Thank you for giving me peace."

Then they took one step upward, and faced the priest and the altar, and she knew that was how it would be from now on.

For the rest of their journey, they would walk together.

ABOUT THE AUTHORS

Though Laurie and Chet Williamson have been married for pver half a century, they'd never before collaborated on a book. When Laurie retired from her teaching career, she and Chet wrote both *Murder Old & New* and this novel, *A Step Across*.

Edgar Nominee Chet Williamson has written mystery and suspense for 40 years. Among his novels are *Second Chance, Hunters, Defenders of the Faith, Ash Wednesday,* and *Psycho: Sanitarium*. His short stories have appeared in *The New Yorker, Playboy, Alfred Hitchcock's Mystery Magazine,* and many other magazines and anthologies. He has won the International Horror Guild Award, and has been shortlisted for the Edgar Award, the World Fantasy Award, and the HWA's Stoker Award. He has recorded over 50 audiobooks, both of his own work and that of many other writers. Follow him on Twitter (@chetwill) or at www.chetwilliamson.com.

Laurie Williamson has been a lifelong teacher and musician, playing first violin in the Hershey Symphony Orchestra for decades. After her retirement from teaching, she has continued her musical activities and become an avid and award-winning quilter. This is her second work of fiction.

Laurie and Chet's son Colin makes video games in Kyoto, Japan.